I0576531

Robert Michael Ballantyne

**The Red Eric**

Or, the whaler's last cruise

Robert Michael Ballantyne

**The Red Eric**
*Or, the whaler's last cruise*

ISBN/EAN: 9783337324841

Printed in Europe, USA, Canada, Australia, Japan

Cover: Foto ©Andreas Hilbeck / pixelio.de

More available books at **www.hansebooks.com**

# THE

# RED ERIC

OR

# THE WHALER'S LAST CRUISE.

## BY R. M. BALLANTYNE,

AUTHOR OF "THE WILD MAN OF THE WEST;" "FREAKS ON THE FELLS;" "THE YOUNG
TRAWLER;" "DUSTY DIAMONDS;" "THE BATTERY AND THE BOILER;" "THE
GIANT OF THE NORTH;" "POST HASTE, A TALE OF HER MAJESTY'S MAILS;"
"IN THE TRACK OF THE TROOPS;" "THE SETTLER AND THE SAVAGE;"
"UNDER THE WAVES;" "RIVERS OF ICE;" "BLACK IVORY;" "THE
PIRATE CITY;" "THE NORSEMEN IN THE WEST;" "THE IRON
HORSE;" "THE FLOATING LIGHT OF THE GOODWIN SANDS;"
"ERLING THE BOLD;" "FIGHTING THE FLAMES;"
"SHIFTING, WINDS;" "DEEP DOWN;" "THE
LIGHTHOUSE;" "GASCOYNE;" "THE LIFEBOAT;"
"THE GOLDEN DREAM," "THE LONELY
ISLAND;" ETC. ETC.

**With Illustrations.**

## LONDON:
### JAMES NISBET & CO., 21 BERNERS STREET.

*[All rights reserved.]*

# CONTENTS.

## CHAPTER I.

## CHAPTER VI.

## CHAPTER VII.

## CHAPTER VIII.

## CHAPTER IX.

## CHAPTER X.

## CHAPTER XI.

## CHAPTER XII.

## CHAPTER XIII.

# CONTENTS.

## CHAPTER XXI.

## CHAPTER XXII.

## CHAPTER XXIII.

## CHAPTER XXIV.

## CHAPTER XXV.

## CHAPTER XXVI.

## CHAPTER XXVII.

## CHAPTER XXVIII.

# LIST OF ILLUSTRATIONS.

# THE RED ERIC.

## CHAPTER I.

CAPTAIN DUNNING stood with his back to the fire-place in the back-parlour of a temperance coffee-house in a certain town on the eastern sea-board of America.

The name of that town is unimportant, and, for reasons with which the reader has nothing to do, we do not mean to disclose it.

Captain Dunning, besides being the owner and commander of a South-sea whale-ship, was the owner of a large burly body, a pair of broad shoulders, a pair of immense red whiskers that met under his chin, a short, red little nose, a large firm mouth, and a pair of light-blue eyes, which, according to their owner's mood, could flash like those of a tiger or twinkle sweetly like the eyes of a laughing child. But his eyes seldom flashed; they more frequently twinkled, for the captain was

B

the very soul of kindliness and good-humour.   Yet he was abrupt and sharp in his manner, so that superficial observers sometimes said he was hasty.

Captain Dunning was, so to speak, a sample of three primary colours—red, blue, and yellow—a walking fragment, as it were, of the rainbow.  His hair and face, especially the nose, were red; his eyes, coat, and pantaloons were blue, and his waistcoat was yellow.

At the time we introduce him to the reader, he was standing, as we have said, with his back to the fireplace, although there was no fire, the weather being mild, and with his hands in his breeches' pockets.  Having worked with the said hands for many long years before the mast, until he had at last worked himself *behind* the mast, in other words, on to the quarter-deck and into possession of his own ship, the worthy captain conceived that he had earned the right to give his hands a long rest; accordingly he stowed them away in his pockets and kept them there at all times, save when necessity compelled him to draw them forth.

" Very odd," remarked Captain Dunning, looking at his black straw hat which lay on the table before him, as if the remark were addressed to it— " very odd if, having swallowed the cow, I should now be compelled to worry at the tail."

As the black straw hat made no reply, the Captain looked up at the ceiling, but not meeting with any response from that quarter, he looked out at the window and encountered the gaze of a seaman flattening his nose on a pane of glass, and looking in.

The captain smiled. " Ah ! here's a tail at last," he said, as the seaman disappeared, and in another moment reappeared at the door with his hat in his hand.

It may be necessary, perhaps, to explain that Captain Dunning had just succeeded in engaging a first-rate crew for his next whaling voyage (which was the "cow" he professed to have swallowed), with the exception of a cook (which was the " tail," at which he feared he might be compelled to worry).

" You're a cook, are you ?" he asked, as the man entered and nodded.

" Yes, sir," answered the " tail," pulling his fore-lock.

" And an uncommonly ill-favoured rascally looking cook you are," thought the captain ; but he did not say so, for he was not utterly regardless of men's feelings. He merely said, " Ah !" and then followed it up with the abrupt question—

" Do you drink ?"

" Yes, sir, and smoke too," replied the " tail," in some surprise.

" Very good ; then you can go," said the captain, shortly.

" Eh !" exclaimed the man

"You can go," repeated the captain. "You wont suit. My ship is a temperance ship, and all the hands are teetotallers. I have found from experience that men work better, and speak better, and in every way act better, on tea and coffee than on spirits. I don't object to their smoking; but I don't allow drinkin' aboard my ship; so you wont do, my man. Good morning."

The tail gazed at the captain in mute amazement.

"Ah! you may look," observed the captain, replying to the gaze; "but you may also mark my words, if you will. I've not sailed the ocean for thirty years for nothin'. I've seen men in hot seas and in cold—on grog, and on tea—and *I* know that coffee and tea carry men through the hardest work better than grog. I also know that there's a set o' men in this world who look upon teetotallers as very soft chaps—old wives, in fact. Very good (here the captain waxed emphatic, and struck his fist on the table). Now look here, young man, *I'm* an old wife, and my ship's manned by similar old ladies; so you wont suit."

To this the seaman made no reply, but feeling doubtless, as he regarded the masculine specimen before him, that he would be quite out of his element among such a crew of females, he thrust a quid of tobacco into his cheek, put on his hat, turned on his heel and left the room, shutting the door after him with a bang.

He had scarcely left when a tap at the door announced a second visitor.

"Hum! Another "tail," I suppose.  Come in."

If the new comer *was* a "tail," he was decidedly a long one, being six feet three in his stockings at the very least.

"You wants a cook, I b'lieve?" said the man, pulling off his hat."

"I do.  Are you one?"

"Yes, I jist guess I am.  Bin a cook for fifteen year."

"Been to sea as a cook?" inquired the captain.

"I jist have.  Once to the South Seas, twice to the North, an' once round the world.  Cook all the time.  I've roasted, and stewed, and grilled, and fried, and biled, right round the 'arth, I have."

Being apparently satisfied with the man's account of himself, Captain Dunning put to him the question—"Do you drink?"

"Ay, like a fish; for I drinks nothin' but water, I don't.  Bin born and raised in the State of Maine, d'ye see, an' never tasted a drop all my life."

"Very good," said the captain, who plumed himself on being a clever physiognomist, and had already formed a good opinion of the man.  "Do you ever swear?"

"Never, but when I can't help it."

"And when's that?"

"When I'm fit to bu'st."

"Then," replied the Captain, "you must learn to bu'st without swearin', 'cause I don't allow it aboard my ship."

The man evidently regarded his questioner as a very extraordinary and eccentric individual; but he merely replied, "I'll try;" and after a little further conversation, an agreement was come to; the man was sent away with orders to repair on board immediately, as everything was in readiness to "up anchor and away next morning."

Having thus satisfactorily and effectually disposed of the "tail," Captain Dunning put on his hat very much on the back of his head, knit his brows, and pursed his lips firmly, as if he had still some important duty to perform; then, quitting the hotel, he traversed the streets of the town with rapid strides.

## CHAPTER II.

IMPORTANT PERSONAGES ARE INTRODUCED TO THE READER
—THE CAPTAIN MAKES INSANE RESOLUTIONS, FIGHTS
A BATTLE, AND CONQUERS.

IN the centre of the town whose name we have declined to communicate, there stood a house—a small house—so small that it might have been more appropriately, perhaps, styled a cottage. This house had a yellow-painted face, with a green

door in the middle, which might have been regarded as its nose, and a window on each side
thereof, which might have been considered its eyes.
Its nose was, as we have said, painted green, and
its eyes had green Venetian eyelids, which were
half shut at the moment Captain Dunning walked
up to it, as if it were calmly contemplating that
seaman's general appearance.

There was a small garden in front of the house,
surrounded on three sides by a low fence. Captain
Dunning pushed open the little gate, walked up to
the nose of the house, and hit it several severe
blows with his knuckles. The result was that the
nose opened, and a servant girl appeared in the
gap.

"Is your mistress at home?" inquired the
captain.

"Guess she is—both of 'em!" replied the
girl.

"Tell both of 'em I'm here, then," said the
captain, stepping into the little parlour without
further ceremony; "and is my little girl in?"

"Yes, she's in."

"Then send her here, too, an' look alive, lass."
So saying, Captain Dunning sat down on the sofa,
and began to beat the floor with his right foot
somewhat impatiently.

In another second a merry little voice was heard
in the passage, the door burst open, a fair-haired
girl of about ten years of age sprang into the

room, and immediately commenced to strangle her
father in a series of violent embraces.

"Why, Ailie, my darling, one would think you
had not seen me for fifty years, at least," said the
captain, holding his daughter at arm's length, in
order the more satisfactorily to survey her.

"It's a whole week, papa, since you last came
to see me," replied the little one, striving to get at
her father's neck again, "and I'm sure it seems to
me like a hundred years at least."

As the child said this she threw her little arms
round her father, and kissed his large weather-
beaten visage all over—eyes, mouth, nose, chin,
whiskers, and, in fact, every attainable spot. She
did it so vigorously, too, that an observer would
have been justified in expecting that her soft delicate cheeks would be lacerated by the rough
contact ; but they were not. The result was a
heightening of the colour, nothing more. Having
concluded his operation, she laid her cheek on the
captain's, and endeavoured to clasp her hands at
the back of his neck, but this was no easy matter.
The captain's neck was a remarkably thick one,
and the garments about that region were voluminous ; however, by dint of determination, she
got the small fingers intertwined, and then gave
him a squeeze that ought to have choked him,
but it didn't : many a strong man had tried that
in his day, and had failed signally.

"You'll stay a long time with me before you go

away to sea again, wont you, dear papa?" asked
the child, earnestly, after she had given up the
futile effort to strangle him.

"How like!" murmured the captain, as if to
himself, and totally unmindful of the question,
while he parted the fair curls and kissed Ailie's
forehead.

"Like what, papa?

"Like your mother — your beloved mother,"
replied the captain, in a low sad voice.

The child became instantly grave, and she looked
up in her father's face with an expression of awe,
while he dropped his eyes on the floor.

Poor Alice had never known a mother's love.
Her mother died when she was a few weeks old,
and she had been confided to the care of two
maiden aunts—excellent ladies, both of them;
good beyond expression; correct almost to a fault;
but prim, starched, and extremely self-possessed
and judicious, so much so that they were injudicious
enough to repress some of the best impulses of their
natures, under the impression that a certain amount
of dignified formality was essential to good breed-
ing and good morals in every relation of life.

Dear, good, starched Misses Dunning! if they
had had their way, boys would have played cricket
and football with polite urbanity, and girls would
have kissed their playmates with gentle solemnity.
They did their best to subdue little Alice, but
that was impossible. The child *would* rush about

the house at all unexpected and often inopportune seasons, like a furiously insane kitten, and she *would* disarrange their collars too violently every evening when she bade them good-night.

Alice was intensely sympathetic. It was quite enough for her to see any one in tears, to cause her to open-up the flood-gates of her eyes and weep—she knew not and she cared not why. She threw her arms round her father's neck again, and hugged him, while bright tears trickled like diamonds from her eyes. No diamonds are half so precious or so difficult to obtain as tears of genuine sympathy !

"How would you like to go with me to the whale-fishery ?" inquired Captain Dunning, somewhat abruptly, as he disengaged the child's arms and set her on his knee.

The tears stopped in an instant, as Alice leaped, with the happy facility of childhood, totally out of one idea and thoroughly into another.

"Oh, I should like it *so* much !"

"And how much is 'so' much, Ailie ?" inquired the captain.

Ailie pursed her mouth, and looked at her father earnestly, while she seemed to struggle to give utterance to some fleeting idea.

"Think," she said, quickly, " think something good *as much as ever you can*. Have you thought ?"

"Yes," answered the captain, smiling.

"Then," continued Ailie, " it's twenty thousand

million times as much as that, and a great deal
more !"

The laugh with which Captain Dunning received
this curious explanation of how much his little
daughter wished to go with him to the whale-
fishery, was interrupted by the entrance of his
sisters, whose sense of propriety induced them to
keep all visitors waiting at least a quarter of an
hour before they appeared, lest they should be
charged with unbecoming precipitancy.

"Here you are, lassies; how are ye?" cried the
captain, as he rose and kissed each lady on the
cheek, heartily.

The sisters did not remonstrate. They knew
that their brother was past hope in this respect,
and they loved him, so they suffered it meekly.

Having admitted that they were well—as well,
at least, as could be expected, considering the
cataract of "trials" that perpetually descended
upon their devoted heads — they sat down as
primly as if their visitor were a perfect stranger,
and entered into a somewhat lengthened conversation as to the intended voyage, commencing, of
course, with the weather.

"And now," said the captain, rubbing the crown
of his straw hat in a circular manner, as if it were
a beaver, "I'm coming to the point."

Both ladies exclaimed, "What point, George?"
simultaneously, and regarded the captain with a
look of anxious surprise.

"*The* point," replied the captain, "about which I've come here to-day. It ain't a point o' the compass; nevertheless, I've been steerin' it in my mind's eye for a considerable time past. The fact is (here the captain hesitated), I—I've made up my mind to take my little Alice along with me this voyage."

The Misses Dunning wore unusually tall caps, and their countenances were by nature uncommonly long, but the length to which they grew on hearing this announcement was something preternaturally awful.

"Take Ailie to sea!" exclaimed Miss Martha Dunning, in horror.

"To fish for whales!" added Miss Jane Dunning, in consternation.

"Brother, you're mad!" they exclaimed together, after a breathless pause; "and you'll do nothing of the kind," they added, firmly.

Now, the manner in which the Misses Dunning received this intelligence greatly relieved their eccentric brother. He had fully anticipated, and very much dreaded, that they would at once burst into tears, and being a tender-hearted man he knew that he could not resist that without a hard struggle. A flood of woman's tears, he was wont to say, was the only sort of salt-water storm he hadn't the heart to face. But abrupt opposition was a species of challenge which the captain always accepted at once—off-hand. No human power could force him to any course of action.

In this latter quality Captain Dunning was neither eccentric nor singular.

"I'm sorry you don't like my proposal, my dear sisters," said he; "but I'm resolved."

"You wont!" said Martha.

"You sha'n't!" cried Jane.

"I *will !*" replied the captain.

There was a pause here of considerable length, during which the captain observed that Martha's nostrils began to twitch nervously. Jane, observing the fact, became similarly affected. To the captain's practised eye these symptoms were as good as a barometer. He knew that the storm was coming, and took in all sail at once (mentally) to be ready for it.

It came! Martha and Jane Dunning were for once driven from the shelter of their wonted propriety—they burst simultaneously into tears, and buried their respective faces in their respective pocket-handkerchiefs, which were immaculately clean and had to be hastily unfolded for the purpose.

"Now, now, my dear girls," cried the captain, starting up and patting their shoulders, while poor little Ailie clasped her hands, sat down on a footstool, looked up in their faces—or, rather, at the backs of the hands which covered their faces—and wept quietly.

"It's very cruel, George—indeed it is," sobbed Martha; "you know how we love her."

"Very true," remarked the obdurate captain;

" but you *don't* know how *I* love her, and how sad
it makes me to see so little of her, and to think
that she may be learning to forget me—or, at least,"
added the captain, correcting himself as Ailie
looked at him reproachfully through her tears—
" at least, to do without me. I can't bear the
thought. She's all I have left to me, and——"

" Brother," interrupted Martha, looking hastily
up, " did you ever before hear of such a thing as
taking a little girl on a voyage to the whale-fish-
ing ?"

" No, never," replied the captain ; " what has
that got to do with it ?"

Both ladies held up their hands and looked
aghast. The idea of any man venturing to do what
no one ever thought of doing before was so utterly
subversive of all their ideas of propriety—such a
desperate piece of profane originality—that they
remained speechless.

" George," said Martha, drying her eyes, and
speaking in tones of deep solemnity, " did you ever
read ' Robinson Crusoe' ?"

" Yes I did, when I was a boy ; an' that wasn't
yesterday."

" And did you," continued the lady in the same
sepulchral tone, " did you note how that man—
that beacon, if I may use the expression, set up as
a warning to deter all wilful boys and men from
reckless, and wicked, and wandering, and obstreperous courses—did you note, I say, how that man,

that beacon, was shipwrecked, and spent a dreary
existence on an uninhabited and dreadful island,
in company with a low, dissolute, black, unclothed
companion called Friday.

"Yes," answered the captain, seeing that she
paused for a reply.

"And all," continued Martha, "in consequence
of his resolutely, and obstinately and wilfully, and
wickedly going to sea?"

"Well, it couldn't have happened if he hadn't
gone to sea, no doubt."

"Then," argued Martha, "will you, can you,
George, contemplate the possibility of your only
daughter coming to the same dreadful end?"

George, not exactly seeing the connexion, rubbed
his nose with his fore-finger, and replied—"Certainly not."

"Then you are bound," continued Martha, in
triumph, "by all that is upright and honourable,
by all the laws of humanity and *propriety*, to give
up this wild intention—and you *must!*"

"There," cried Miss Jane, emphatically, as if
the argument were unanswerable—as indeed it
was, being incomprehensible.

The last words were unfortunate. They merely
riveted the captain's determination.

"You talk a great deal of nonsense, Martha,"
he said, rising to depart. "I've fixed to take her,
so the sooner you make up your minds to it the
better."

The sisters knew their brother's character too well to waste more time in vain efforts ; but Martha took him by the arm, and said, earnestly—" Will you promise me, my dear George, that when she comes back from this voyage, you will never take her on another ?"

" Yes, dear sister," replied the captain, some-what melted, " I promise that."

Without another word Martha sat down and held out her arms to Ailie, who incontinently rushed into them.  Propriety fled for the nonce, discomfited.  Miss Martha's curls were disarranged beyond repair, and Miss Martha's collar was crushed to such an extent that the very laundress who had washed and starched and ironed it would have utterly failed to recognise it.  Miss Jane looked on at these improprieties in perfect indifference— nay, when, after her sister had had enough, the child was handed over to her, she submitted to the same violent treatment without a murmur.  For once Nature was allowed to have her way, and all three had a good hearty satisfactory cry ; in the midst of which Captain Dunning left them, and proceeding on board his ship, hastened the pre-parations for his voyage to the Southern Seas.

# CHAPTER III.

### THE TEA-PARTY—ACCIDENTS AND INCIDENTS OF A MINOR KIND—GLYNN PROCTOR GETS INTO TROUBLE.

ON the evening of the day in which the foregoing scenes were enacted, the Misses Dunning prepared a repast for their brother and one or two of his officers, who were to spend their last evening in port there, and discuss various important and un-important matters in a sort of semi-convivio-busi-ness way.

An event of this kind was always of the deepest interest and productive of the most intense anxiety to the amiable though starched sisters; first, because it was of rare occurrence; and second, because they were never quite certain that it would pass without some unhappy accident, such as the upsetting of a tea-cup or a kettle, or the scalding of the cat, not to mention visitors' legs. They seemed to regard a tea-party in the light of a fire-arm—a species of blunderbuss—a thing which, it was to be hoped, would "go off well;" and certainly, if loading the table until it groaned had anything to do with the manner of its "going off," there was every prospect of its doing so with pre-eminent success upon that occasion.

But besides the anxieties inseparable from the details of the pending festivities, the Misses Dun-

c

ning were overwhelmed and weighed down with
additional duties consequent upon their brother's
sudden and unexpected determination.    Little
Ailie had to be got ready for sea by the following morning!  It was absolute and utter insanity!
No one save a madman or a sea-captain could
have conceived such a thing, much less have carried it into effect tyrannically.

The Misses Dunning could not attempt any
piece of duty or work separately.   They always
acted together, when possible ; and might, in fact,
without much inconvenience, have been born
Siamese twins.   Whatever Martha did, Jane attempted to do or to mend ; wherever Jane went,
Martha followed.   Not, by any means, that one
thought she could improve upon the work of the
other ; their conduct was simply the result of a
desire to assist each other mutually.   When
Martha spoke, Jane echoed or corroborated ; and
when Jane spoke, Martha repeated her sentences
word for word in a scarcely audible whisper—not
after the other had finished, but during the course
of the remarks.

With such dispositions and propensities, it is
not a matter to be wondered at that the good
ladies, while arranging the tea-table, should suddenly remember some forgotten article of Ailie's
wardrobe, and rush simultaneously into the child's
bedroom to rectify the omission ; or, when thus
engaged, be filled with horror at the thought of

having left the buttered toast too near the fire in the parlour.

"It is really quite perplexing," said Martha, sitting down with a sigh, and regarding the tea-table with a critical gaze; "quite perplexing. I'm sure I don't know how I shall bear it. It is too bad of George—darling Ailie—(dear me, Jane, how crookedly you have placed the urn)—it is really too bad."

"Too bad, indeed; yes, isn't it?" echoed Jane, in reference to the captain's conduct, while she assisted Martha, who had risen to readjust the urn.

"Oh!" exclaimed Martha, with a look of horror.

"What?" cried Jane, who looked and felt equally horrified, although she knew not yet the cause.

"The eggs!"

"The eggs?"

"Yes, the eggs. You know every one of the last dozen we got was bad, and we've forgot to send for more," said Martha.

"For more; so we have!" cried Jane; and both ladies rushed into the kitchen, gave simultaneous and hurried orders to the servant-girl, and sent her out of the house impressed with an undefined feeling that life or death depended on the instant procuring of two dozen fresh eggs.

It may be as well to remark here, that the Misses Dunning, although stiff and starched, and formal, had the power of speeding nimbly from room to room, when alone and when occasion required, without in the least degree losing any of their stiffness or formality, so that we do not use the terms "rush," "rushed," or "rushing," inappropriately. Nevertheless, it may also be remarked that they never acted in a rapid or impulsive way in *company*, however small in numbers or unceremonious in character the company might be—always excepting the servant-girl and the cat, to whose company, from long habit, they had become used, and therefore indifferent.

The sisters were on their knees, stuffing various articles into a large trunk, and Ailie was looking on, by way of helping, with very red and swollen eyes, and the girl was still absent in quest of eggs, when a succession of sounding blows were administered to the green door, and a number of gruff voices were heard conversing without.

" *There !*" cried Martha and Jane, with bitter emphasis, looking in each other's faces as if to say, " We knew it. Before that girl was sent away for these eggs, we each separately and privately prophesied that they would arrive, and that we should have to open the door. And you see, so it has happened, and we are not ready !"

But there was no time for remark. The case was desperate. Both sisters felt it to be so, and acted accordingly, while Ailie, having been forbidden to open the door, sat down on her trunk.

and looked on in surprise. They sprang up, washed their hands simultaneously in the same basin, with the same piece of soap broken in two; dried them with the same towel, darted to the mirror, put on two identically similar clean tall caps, leaped down stairs, opened the door with slow dignity of demeanour, and received their visitors in the hall with a calmness and urbanity of manner that contrasted rather strangely with their flushed countenances and heaving bosoms.

"Hallo! Ailie!" exclaimed the captain, as his daughter pulled down his head to be kissed. "Why, you take a fellow all aback, like a white squall. Are you ready, my pet? Kit stowed and anchor tripped? Come this way, and let us talk about it. Dear me, Martha, you and Jane look as if you had been running a race, eh? Here are my messmates come to talk a bit with you. My sisters Martha and Jane—Dr. Hopley." (Dr. Hopley bowed politely.) "My first mate, Mr. Millons." (Mr. Millons also bowed, somewhat loosely); "and Rokens—Tim Rokens, my chief harpooneer." (Mr. Rokens pulled his forelock, and threw back his left leg, apparently to counterbalance the bend in his body). "He didn't want to come; said he warn't accustomed to ladies' society; but I told him you warn't ladies—a—I don't mean that—not ladies o' the high-flyin' fashionable sort, that give themselves airs, you know. Come along, Ailie.'

While the captain ran on in this strain, hung

up his hat, kissed Ailie, and ran his fingers through his shaggy locks, the Misses Dunning performed a mingled bow and curtsey to each guest as his name was mentioned, and shook hands with him, after which the whole party entered the parlour, where the cat was discovered enjoying a preliminary meal of its own at one of the pats of butter. A united shriek from Martha and Jane, a nautical howl from the guests, and a rolled-up pocket-handkerchief from Rokens, sent that animal from the table as if it had received a galvanic shock.

"I ax yer parding, ladies," said Mr. Rokens, whose aim had been so perfect that his handkerchief not only accelerated the flight of the cat, but carried away the violated pat of butter along with it. "I ax yer parding, but them brutes is such thieves—I could roast 'em alive, so I could."

The harpooneer unrolled his handkerchief, and picking the pat of butter from its folds with his fingers, threw it into the fire. Thereafter he smoothed down his hair, and seated himself on the extreme edge of a chair, as near the door as possible. Not that he had any intention whatever of taking to flight, but he deemed that position to be more suited to his condition than any other.

In a few minutes the servant-girl returned with the eggs. While she is engaged in boiling them, we shall introduce Captain Dunning's friends and messmates to the reader.

Dr. Hopley was a surgeon, and a particular friend

of the captain's. He was an American by birth, but had travelled so much about the world that he had ceased to "guess" and "calculate," and to speak through his nose. He was a man about forty, tall, big-boned, and muscular, though not fat; and besides being a gentlemanly man, was a good-natured, quiet creature, and a clever enough fellow besides, but he preferred to laugh at and enjoy the jokes and witticisms of others rather than to perpetrate any himself. Dr. Hopley was intensely fond of travelling, and being possessed of a small independence, he indulged his passion to the utmost. He had agreed to go with Captain Dunning as the ship's doctor, simply for the sake of seeing the whale-fishery of the South Seas, having already, in a similar capacity, encountered the dangers of the North.

Dr. Hopley had few weaknesses. His chief one was an extravagant belief in phrenology. We would not be understood to imply that phrenology is extravagant; but we assert that the doctor's belief in it was extravagant, assigning, as he did, to every real and ideal faculty of the human mind 'a local habitation and a name' in the cranium, with a corresponding depression or elevation of the surface to mark its whereabouts. In other respects he was a commonplace sort of man.

Mr. Millons, the first mate, was a short, hale, thick-set man, without any particularly strong points of character. He was about thirty-five, and

possessed a superabundance of fair hair and
whiskers, with a large, broad chin, a firm mouth,
rather fierce-looking eyes, and a hasty, but by no
means a bad temper. He was a trustworthy,
matter-of-fact seaman, and a good officer, but
not bright intellectually. Like most men of his
class, his look implied that he did not under-
estimate his own importance, and his tones were
those of a man accustomed to command.

Tim Rokens was an old salt; a bluff, strong,
cast-iron man, of about forty-five years of age, who
had been at sea since he was a little boy, and
would not have consented to live on dry land,
though he had been " offered command of a sea-
port town all to himself," as he was wont to affirm
emphatically. His visage was scarred and knotty,
as if it had been long used to being pelted by
storms—as indeed it had. There was a scar over
his left eye and down his cheek, which had been
caused by a slash from the cutlass of a pirate in
the China Seas; but although it added to the
rugged effect of his countenance, it did not detract
from the frank, kindly expression that invariably
rested there. Tim Rokens had never been caught
out of temper in his life. Men were wont to say
he had no temper to lose. Whether this was true
or no, we cannot presume to say, but certainly he
never lost it. He was the best and boldest harpooneer in Captain Dunning's ship, and a sententious deliverer of his private opinion on all occasions

whatsoever. When we say that he wore a rough blue pilot-cloth suit, and had a large black beard, with a sprinkling of silvery hairs in it, we have completed his portrait.

"What's come of Glynn?" inquired Captain Dunning, as he accepted a large cup of smoking tea with one hand, and with the other handed a plate of buttered toast to Dr. Hopley, who sat next him.

"I really cannot imagine," replied Miss Martha.

"No, cannot imagine," whispered Miss Jane.

"He promised to come, and to be punctual," continued Miss Martha ('Punctual,' whispered Miss J.); "but something seems to have detained him. Perhaps——"

Here Miss Martha was brought to an abrupt pause by observing that Mr. Rokens was about to commence to eat his egg with a teaspoon.

"Allow me, Mr. Rokens," she said, handing that individual an ivory egg-spoon.

"Oh, cer'nly, ma'am. By all means," replied Rokens, taking the spoon and handing it to Miss Jane, under the impression that it was intended for her.

"I beg pardon, it is for yourself, Mr. Rokens," said Martha and Jane together.

"Thank'ee, ma'am," replied Rokens, growing red, as he began to perceive he was a little "off his course" somehow. "I've no occasion for *two*, an' this one suits me oncommon."

"Ah! you prefer big spoons to little ones, my man, don't you ?" said Captain Dunning, coming to the rescue. "Let him alone, Martha, he's used to take care of himself. Doctor, can you tell me now, which is easiest of digestion—a hard egg or a soft one ?"

Thus appealed to, Dr. Hopley paused a moment and frowned at the teapot, as though he were about to tax his brain to the uttermost in the solution of an abstruse question in medical science.

"Well now," he replied, stirring his tea gently, and speaking with much deliberation, "that depends very much upon circumstances. Some digestions can manage a hard egg best, others find a soft one more tractable. And then the state of the stomach at the time of eating has to be taken into account. I should say now, that my little friend Ailie here, to judge from the rosy colour of her cheeks, could manage hard or soft eggs equally well; couldn't you, eh ?"

Ailie laughed, as she replied, "I'm sure I don't know, Doctor Hopley ; but I *like* soft ones best."

To this, Captain Dunning said, "Of course you do, my sensible little pet ;" although it would be difficult to show wherein lay the sensibility of the preference, and then added—"There's Rokens, now; wouldn't you, Doctor—judging from his rosy, not to say purple cheeks—conclude that he wasn't able to manage even two eggs of any kind ?"

"Wot, *me !*" exclaimed Mr. Rokens, looking up

in surprise, as indeed he well might, having just concluded his fourth, and being about to commence his fifth egg, to the no small anxiety of Martha and Jane, into whose limited and innocent minds the possibility of such a feat had never entered. "Wot, me! Wur, Capting, if they was biled as hard as the head of a marline-spike——"

The expanding grin on the captain's face, and a sudden laugh from the mate, apprised the bold harpooneer at this point of his reply that the captain was jesting, so he felt a little confused, and sought relief by devoting himself assiduously to egg No. 5.

It fared ill with Tim Rokens that evening that he had rashly entered into ladies' society, for he was a nervous man in refined company, though cool and firm as a grounded iceberg when in the society of his messmates, or when towing with the speed of a steamboat in the wake of a sperm-whale.

Egg No. 5 proved to be a bad one. Worse than that, egg No. 5 happened to belong to that peculiar class of bad eggs which "go off" with a little crack when hit with a spoon, and sputter their unsavoury contents around them. Thus it happened, that when Mr. Rokens, feeling confused, and seeking relief in attention to the business then in hand, hit egg No. 5 a smart blow on the top, a large portion of its contents spurted over the fair white table-cloth, a small portion fell on Mr. Rokens's vest, and a minute yellow globule thereof alighted on the fair Martha's hand, eliciting from that lady a scream, and as a matter of course, an echo from Jane in the shape of a screamlet.

Mr. Rokens flushed a deep Indian-red, and his nose assumed a warm blue colour instantly.

"Oh ! ma'am, I ax yer parding."

"Pray don't mention it—a mere accident. I'm so sorry you have got a bad—— Oh !"

The little scream with which Miss Martha interrupted her remark, was caused by Mr. Rokens (who had just observed the little yellow globule above referred to), seizing her hand, and wiping away the speck with the identical handkerchief that had floored the cat and swept away the pat of butter. Immediately thereafter, feeling heated, he wiped the perspiration from his forehead, and unwittingly transferred the spot thereto in the form of a yellow streak, whereat Ailie and the first mate burst into an uncontrollable fit of laughter. Even Miss Martha smiled, although she rather objected to jesting, as being a dangerous amusement, and never laughed at the weaknesses or misfortunes of others, however ludicrous they might be, when she could help it.

"How can you, brother?" she said, reproachfully, shaking her head at the captain, who was winking at the doctor with one eye in a most obstreperous manner. "Do try another egg, Mr. Rokens; the others, I am sure, are fresh. I cannot imagine how a bad one came to be amongst them."

" Ah, try another, my lad," echoed the captain.
" Pass 'em up this way, Mr. Millons."

" By no manner o' means; I'll eat this 'un !" replied the harpooneer, commencing to eat the bad egg
with apparent relish. " I like 'em this way—better
than nothin', anyhow. Bless ye, marm, ye've no
notion wot sort o' things I've lived on aboard ship—"

Rokens came to an abrupt pause in consequence
of the servant girl, at a sign from her mistresses (for
she always received duplicate orders), seizing his
plate and carrying it off bodily. It. was immediately replaced by a clean one and a fresh egg.
While Rokens somewhat nervously tapped the
head of No. 6, Miss Martha, in order to divert at·
tention from him, asked Mr. Millons if sea-fare was
always salt junk and hard biscuit?

" Oh, no, madam," answered the first mate.
" We've sometimes salt pork, and vegetables now
and agin ; and pea-soup, and plum-duff——"

" Plum-duff, Ailie," interrupted the captain, in
order to explain, " is just a puddin' with few plums
and fewer spices in it. Something like a white-
painted cannon-shot, with brown spots on it here
and there."

" Is it good ?" inquired Ailie.

" Oh, ain't it !" remarked Mr. Rokens, who had
just concluded No. 6, and felt his self-possession
somewhat restored. " Yes, miss, it is ; but it ain't
equal to whale's-brain fritters, it ain't ; them's first
chop."

" Have whales got brains?" inquired Miss Martha, in surprise.

" Brains !" echoed Miss Jane, in amazement.

" Yes, madam, they 'ave," answered the first mate, who had hitherto maintained silence, but having finished tea was now ready for any amount of talk ; " and what's more remarkable still, they've got several barrels of oil in their skulls besides."

" Dear me !" exclaimed the sisters.

" Yes, ladies, capital oil it is, too ; fetches a 'igher price hin the markit than the other sort."

" By the bye, Millons, didn't you once fall into a whale's skull, and get nearly drowned in oil?" inquired the doctor.

" I did," answered the first mate, with the air of a man who regarded such an event as a mere trifle, that, upon consideration, might almost be con-sidered as rather a pleasant incident than other-wise in one's history.

" Nearly drowned in oil !" exclaimed the sisters, while Ailie opened her eyes in amazement, and Mr. Rokens became alarmingly purple in the face with suppressed chuckling.

" It's true," remarked Rokens, in a hoarse whisper to Miss Martha, putting his hand up to his mouth, the better to convey the sound to her ears; " I seed him tumble in, and helped to haul him out."

" Let's have the story, Millons," cried the captain, pushing forward his cup to be replenished : " it's so long since I heard it, that I've almost forgotten it. Another cup o' tea, Martha, my dear — not quite so strong as the last, and three times as sweet. I'll drink 'Success to the cup that cheers, but don't inebriate.' Go ahead, Millons."

Nothing rejoiced the heart of Mr. Millons more than being asked to tell a story. Like most men who are excessively addicted to the habit, his stories were usually very long and very dry; but he had a bluff good-natured way of telling them, that rendered his yarns endurable on shore, and positively desirable at sea. Fortunately for the reader, the story he was now requested to relate was not a long one.

"It ain't quite a *story*," he began—and in beginning he cleared his throat with emphasis, thrust his thumbs into the arm-holes of his vest, and tilted his chair on its hind legs—" it ain't quite a story; it's a hanecdote, a sort of hincident, so to speak, and this is 'ow it 'appened :—

"Many years ago, w'en I was a very young man, or a big boy, I was on a voyage to the South Seas after whales. Tim Rokens was my messmate then, and has bin so almost ever since, off and on. (Mr. Rokens nodded assent to this statement.) Well, we came up with a big whale, and fixed an iron cleverly in him at the first throw——"

"An iron?" inquired Miss Martha, to whose mind flat and Italian-irons naturally occurred.

"Yes, madam, an iron; we call the 'arpoons irons. Well, away went the fish, like all alive.

not down, but straight for'ard, takin' out the line at a rate that nearly set the boat on fire, and away we went along with it. It *was* a chase, that. For six hours, off and on, we stuck to that whale, and pitched into 'im with 'arpoons and lances ; but he seemed to have the lives of a cat—nothin' would kill 'im. At last the 'arpooneer gave him a thrust in the life, an' up went the blood and water, and the fish went into the flurries, and came nigh capsizin' the boat with its tail as it lashed the water into foam. At last it gave in, and we had a four hours' pull after that, to tow the carcase to the ship, for there wasn't a cat's-paw of wind on the water.

"W'en we came alongside, we got out the tackles, and before beginnin' to flense (that means, ma'am, to strip off the blubber), we cut a hole in the top o' the skull to get out the oil that was there ; for you must know that the sperm-whale has got a sort of 'ollow or big cavern in its 'ead, w'ich is full o' the best oil, quite pure, that don't need to be cleared, but is all ready to be baled out and stowed away in casks. Well, w'en the 'ole was cut in its skull I went down on my knees on the edge of it to peep in, when my knees they slipped on the blubber, and in I went 'ead foremost, souse into the whale's skull, and began to swim for life in the oil.

"Of course I began to roar for 'elp like a bull, and Rokens there, w'o 'appened to be near, 'e let down the hend of a rope, but my 'ands was so slippy with oil I couldn't ketch 'old of it; so 'e 'auls it up again, and let's down a rope with a 'ook at the hend, and I got 'old of this and stuck it into the waist-band o' my trousers, and gave the word, ' 'Eave away, my 'earties;' and sure enough so they did, and pulled me out in a trice. And that's 'ow it was; and I lost a suit o' clo's, for nothing on 'arth would take the oil out, and I didn't need to use pomatum for six months after."

"No more you did," cried Rokens, who had listened to the narrative with suppressed delight; "no more you did. I never see sich a glazed rat as you wos when you comed out o' that hole, in all my life; an' he wos jist like a' eel; it wos all we could do to keep 'old on 'im, marm, he was so slippery."

While the captain was laughing at the incident, and Rokens was narrating some of the minute details in the half-unwilling yet half-willing ears of the sisters, the door opened, and a young man entered hastily and apologized for being late.

"The fact is, Miss Dunning, had I not promised faithfully to come, I should not have made my appearance at all to-night."

"Why, Glynn, what has kept you, lad?" interrupted the captain. "I thought you were a man of your word."

"Ay, that's the question, Capting, said Rokens, who evidently regarded the new arrival with no favourable feelings; "it's always the way with

them *gentlemen* sailors till they're got into blue
water and brought to their bearin's."

Mr. Rokens had wisdom enough to give forth
the last part of his speech in a muttered tone, for
the youth was evidently a favourite with the
captain, as was shown by the hearty manner in
which he shook him by the hand.

"Messmates, this is Glynn Proctor, a friend o'
mine," said Captain Dunning, in explanation : " he
is going with us this voyage *before* the mast, so
you'll have to make the most of him as an equal
to-night, for I intend to keep him in his proper
place when afloat. He chooses to go as an ordinary
seaman, against my advice, the scamp; so I'll make
him keep his head as low as the rest when aboard.
You'll have to keep your time better, too, than you
have done to-night, lad," continued the captain,
giving his young friend a slap on the shoulder.
" What has detained you, eh ?"

" Necessity, Captain," replied the youth, with a
smile, as he sat down to table with an off-hand
easy air that savoured of recklessness ; " and I am
prepared to state, upon oath if need be, that necessity is not 'the mother of invention.' If she had
been, she would have enabled me to invent a way
of escape from my persecutors in time to keep my
promise to Miss Dunning."

" Persecutors, Glynn !" exclaimed Martha ; " to
whom do you refer ?"

"To the police of this good city."

" Police !" echoed the captain, regarding his young friend seriously, while the doctor and the first mate and Tim Rokens listened in some surprise.

" Why, the fact is," said Glynn, " that I have just escaped from the hands of the police, and if it had not been that I was obliged to make a very wide détour, in order to reach this house without being observed, I should have been here long ago."

" Boy, boy, your hasty disposition will bring you into serious trouble one of these days," said the captain, shaking his head.  " What mischief have you been about ?"

" Ay, there you go—it's my usual fate," cried Glynn, laughing.  " If I chance to get into a scrape, you never think of inquiring whether it was my fault or my misfortune.  This time, however, it *was* my misfortune, and if Miss Dunning will oblige me with a cup of tea, I'll explain how it happened.

" Little more than two hours ago I left the ship to come here to tea, as I had promised to do. Nikel Sling, the long-legged cook you engaged this morning, went ashore with me.  As we walked up the street together, I observed a big porter passing along with a heavy deal plank on his shoulder. The street was somewhat narrow and crowded at that part, and Sling had turned to look in at a shop-window just as the big fellow came up.  The man shouted to my shipmate to get out o' the way, but the noise in the street prevented him from hearing.  Before I could turn to touch the cook's arm, the fellow uttered an oath and ran the end of the plank against his head. Poor Sling was down in an instant. Before I well knew what I was about, I hit the porter between the eyes and down he went with a clatter, and the plank above him. In a moment three policemen had me by the collar. I tried to explain, but they wouldn't listen. As I was being hurried away to the lock-up, it flashed across me that I should not only lose my tea and your pleasant society this evening, but be prevented from sailing to-morrow, so I gave a sudden twist, tripped up the man on my left, over-turned the one on my right, and bolted.

"They ran well, the rascals, and shouted like maniacs, but I got the start of 'em, dived down one street, up another, into a by-lane, over a back-garden wall, in at the back-door of a house and out at the front, took a round of two or three miles, and came in here from the west ; and, whatever other objections there may be to the whole proceeding, I cannot say that it has spoiled my appe-tite."

"And so, sir," said Captain Dunning, "you call this your ' misfortune' ?"

"Surely, Captain," said Glynn, putting down his cup and looking up in some surprise—" surely, you cannot blame me for punishing the rascal who behaved so brutally, without the slightest provoca-tion, to my shipmate !"

"Hear, hear !" cried Rokens, involuntarily.

"I do blame you, lad," replied the captain, seriously. "In the first place, you have no right to take the law into your own hands. In the second place, your knocking down the man did no good whatever to your shipmate; and in the third place, you've got yourself and me and the ship into a very unsatisfactory scrape."

Rokens' face, which had hitherto expressed approval of Glynn's conduct, began to elongate as the captain went on in this strain; and the youth's recklessness of manner altogether disappeared as he inquired, "How so, Captain? I have escaped, as you see; and poor Sling, of course, was not to blame, so he'll be all safe aboard, and well, I hope, by this time."

"There you're mistaken, boy. They will have secured Sling and made him tell the name of his ship, and also the name of his pugnacious comrade."

"And do you think he'd be so mean as to tell?" asked Glynn, indignantly.

"You forget that the *first* act in this nice little melodrama was the knocking down of Sling, so that he could not know what happened after, and the police would not be so soft as to tell him *why* they wanted such information until after they had got it."

Poor Glynn looked aghast, and Rokens was overwhelmed.

"It seems to me, I'd better go and see about this," said Millons, rising and buttoning his coat with the air of a man who had business to transact and meant to transact it.

"Right, Millons," answered the captain. "I'm sorry to break up our evening so soon, but we must get this man aboard by hook or crook as speedily as possible. You had better go too, doctor. Rokens and I will take care of this young scamp, who must be made a nigger of in order to be got on board, for his face, once seen by these sharp limbs of justice, is not likely soon to be forgotten."

Glynn Proctor was indeed a youth whose personal appearance was calculated to make a lasting impression on most people. He was about eighteen years of age, but a strong, well-developed muscular frame, a firm mouth, a large chin, and an eagle eye, gave him the appearance of being much older. He was above the middle height, but not tall, and the great breath of his shoulders and depth of his chest made him appear shorter than he really was. His hair was of that beautiful hue called nut-brown, and curled close round his well-shaped head. He was a model of strength and activity.

Glynn Proctor had many faults. He was hasty and reckless. He was unsteady, too, and preferred a roving idle life to a busy one ; but he had redeeming qualities. He was bold and generous. Above all, he was unselfish, and therefore speedily became a favourite with all who knew him. Glynn's history is briefly told. He was an Englishman. His father and mother had died when he was a child, and left him in charge of an uncle, who emigrated to America shortly after his brother's death. The uncle was a good man, after a fashion, but he was austere and unloveable. Glynn didn't like him; so when he attained the age of thirteen, he quietly told him that he meant to bid him good bye, and go seek his fortune in the world. The uncle as quietly told Glynn that he was quite right, and the sooner he went the better. So Glynn went, and never saw his uncle again, for the old man died while he was abroad.

Glynn travelled far and encountered many vicissitudes of fortune in his early wanderings; but he was never long without occupation, because men liked his looks, and took him on trial without much persuasion. To say truth, Glynn never took the trouble to persuade them. When his services were declined, he was wont to turn on his heel and walk away without a word of reply; and not unfrequently, he was called back and employed. He could turn his hand to almost anything, but when he tired of it he threw it up and sought other work elsewhere.

In the course of his peregrinations, he came to reside in the city in which our story finds him. Here he had become a compositor in the office of a daily newspaper, and, happening to be introduced to the Misses Dunning, soon became a favourite with them, and a constant visitor at their house. Thus he became acquainted with their brother. Becoming disgusted with the constant work and late hours of the printing-office, he resolved to join Captain Dunning's ship, and take a voyage to southern seas as an ordinary seaman. Glynn and little Alice Dunning were great friends, and it was a matter of extreme delight to both of them that they were to sail together on this their first voyage.

Having been made a nigger of,—that is, having had his face and hands blackened in order to avoid detection—Glynn sallied forth with the captain and Rokens to return to their ship, the Red Eric—which lay in the harbour, not ten minutes' walk from the house.

They passed the police on the wharf without creating suspicion, and reached the vessel.

---

## CHAPTER IV.

### THE ESCAPE.

"WELL, Millons, what news?" inquired the captain, as he stepped on deck.

"Bad news, sir, I fear," replied the first mate. "I found, on coming aboard, that no one knew anything about Sling, so I went ashore at once and 'urried up to the hospital, w'ere, sure enough, I found 'im lyin' with his 'ead bandaged, and lookin' as if 'e were about gone. They asked me if I knew what ship 'e belonged to, as the police wanted to know. So I told 'em I knew well enough, but I wasn't going to tell if it would get the poor fellow into a scrape."

" 'Why don't you ask himself ?' says I.

"They told me 'e was past speakin', so I tried to make 'im understand, but 'e only mumbled in reply. W'en I was about to go 'e seemed to mumble very 'ard, so I put down my ear to listen, and 'e w'ispered quite distinct tho' very low— ' All right, my 'eartie. I'm too cute for 'em by a long way ; go aboard an' say nothin'. So I came away, and I've scarce been five minutes aboard before you arrived. My own opinion is, that 'e's crazed, and don't know what 'e's sayin'."

" Oh !" ejaculated Captain Dunning. " He said *that*, did he ? Then *my* opinion is, that he's not so crazed as you think. Tell the watch, Mr. Millons, to keep a sharp look-out."

So saying, Captain Dunning descended to the cabin, and Rokens to the forecastle (in sea phraseology the ' fok-sail'), while Glynn Proctor procured a basin and a piece of soap, and proceeded to rub the coat of charcoal off his face and hands.

Half an hour had not elapsed when the watch on deck heard a loud splash near the wharf, as if some one had fallen into the water. Immediately after, a confused sound of voices and rapid foot-steps was heard in the street that opened out upon the quay, and in a few seconds the end of the wharf was crowded with men who shouted to each

other, and were seen in the dim starlight to move
rapidly about as if in search of something.

"Wot can it be?" said Tim Rokens, in a low
voice, to a seaman who leaned on the ship's bulwarks close to him.

"Deserter, mayhap," suggested the man.

While Rokens pondered the suggestion, a light
plash was heard close to the ship's side, and a voice
said, in a hoarse whisper, "Heave us a rope, will
ye. Look alive now. Guess I'll go under in two
minits if ye don't."

"Oho!" exclaimed Rokens, in a low impressive
voice, as he threw over the end of a rope, and, with
the aid of the other members of the watch, hauled
Nikel Sling up the side, and landed him dripping
and panting on the deck.

"W'y—Sling! what on airth —— ?" exclaimed
one of the men.

"It's lucky—I am—on airth—" panted the tall
cook, seating himself on the breech of one of the
main-deck carronades, and wringing the water
from his garments. "An' it's well I'm not at the
bottom o' this 'ere 'arbour."

"But where did ye come from, an' why are they
arter ye, lad?" inquired Rokens.

"W'y? cause they don't want to part with me,
and I've gi'n them the slip, I guess."

When Nikel Sling had recovered himself so as
to talk connectedly, he explained to his wondering
shipmates how that, after being floored in the

street, he had been carried up to the hospital, and on recovering his senses, found Mr. Millons standing by the bed-side, conversing with the young surgeons. The first words of their conversation showed him that something was wrong, so, with remarkable self-possession, he resolved to counterfeit partial delirium, by which means he contrived to give the first mate a hint that all was right, and declined, without creating suspicion, to give any intelligible answers as to who he was or where he had come from.

The blow on his head caused him considerable pain, but his mind was relieved by one of the young surgeons, who remarked to another, in going round the wards, that the "skull of that long chap wasn't fractured after all, and he had no doubt he would be dismissed cured in a day or two." So the cook lay quiet until it was dark.

When the house-surgeon had paid his last visit, and the nurses had gone their rounds in the accident-ward, and no sound disturbed the quiet of the dimly-lighted apartment save the heavy fitful breathing and occasional moans and restless motions of the sufferers, Nikel Sling raised himself on his elbow, and glanced stealthily round on the rows of pain-worn and haggard countenances around him. It was a solemn sight to look upon, especially at that silent hour of the night. There were men there with almost every species of painful wound and fracture. Some had been long there, wasting away from day to day, and now lay quiet, though suffering, from sheer exhaustion. Others there were who had been carried in that day, and fidgeted impatiently in their unreduced strength, yet nervously in their agony ; or, in some cases, where the fear of death was on them, clasped their hands and prayed in whispers for mercy to Him whose name perhaps they had almost never used before except for the purpose of taking it in vain.

But such sights had little or no effect on the cook, who had rubbed hard against the world's roughest sides too long to be easily affected by the sight of human suffering, especially when exhibited in men. He paused long enough to note that the nurses were out of the way or dozing, and then slipping out of bed, he stalked across the room like a ghost, and made for the outer gateway of the hospital. He knew the way, having once before been a temporary inmate of the place. He reached the gate undiscovered, tripped up the porter's heels, opened the wicket, and fled towards the harbour, followed by the porter and a knot of chance passers-by. The pursuers swelled into a crowd as he neared the harbour.

Besides being long limbed, Nikel Sling was nimble. He distanced his pursuers easily, and, as we have seen, swam off and reached his ship almost as soon as they gained the end of the wharf.

The above narration was made much more abruptly and shortly than we have presented it, for oars were soon heard in the water, and it behoved the poor hunted cook to secrete himself in case they should take a fancy to search the vessel. Just as the boat came within a few yards of the ship he hastily went below.

"Boat a-hoy!" shouted Tim Rokens; "wot boat's that?"

The men lay on their oars.

"Have you a madman on board your ship?" inquired the gatekeeper of the hospital, whose wrath at the unceremonious treatment he had received had not yet cooled down.

"No," answered Rokens, laying his arms on the bulwarks, and looking down at his questioner with a sly leer; "no, we ha'n't, but you've got a madman aboord that boat."

"Who's that?" inquired the warder, who did not at first understand the sarcasm.

"Why, yourself, to be sure," replied Rokens, an' the sooner you takes yourself off, an' comes to an anchor in a loo-natick asylum, the better for all parties consarned."

"No, but I'm in earnest, my man——"

"As far as that goes," interrupted the imperturbable Rokens, "so am I."

"The man," continued the gatekeeper, "has run out of the hospital with a smashed head, I calc'late, stark starin' mad, and gone off the end o' the w'arf into the water——"

"You don't mean it !" shouted Rokens, starting with affected surprise. "Now you *are* a fine fellow, ain't you, to be talkin' here an' wastin' time while a poor feller-mortal is bein' drownded, or has gone and swummed off to sea—p'r'aps without chart, compass, or rudder ?  Hallo, lads ! tumble up there ! Man overboard ! tumble up, tumble up !"

In less than three minutes half-a-dozen men sprang up the hatchway, hauled up the gig which swung astern, tumbled into it, and began to pull wildly about the harbour in search of the drowning man.  The shouts and commotion roused the crew of the nearest vessels, and ere long quite a fleet of boats joined in the search.

"Wos he a big or a little feller ?" inquired Rokens, panting from his exertions, as he swept up to the boat containing the hospital warder, round which several of the other boats began to congregate.

"A big fellow, I guess, with legs like steeples. He was sloping when they floored him.  A thief, I expect he must ha' bin."

"A thief !" echoed Rokens, in disgust; "why didn't ye say so at first ?  If he's a thief, he's born to be hanged, so he's safe and snug aboard his ship long ago, I'll-be bound.  Good night t'ye, friend, and better luck next time."

A loud laugh greeted the ears of the discomfited warder as the crews of the boats dipped their oars in the water and pulled towards their respective ships.

Next morning, about day-break, little Alice Dunning came on board her father's ship, accompanied by her two aunts, who, for once, became utterly and publicly regardless of appearances and contemptuous of all propriety, as they sobbed on the child's neck and positively refused to be comforted.

Just as the sun rose, and edged the horizon with a gleam of liquid fire, the Red Eric spread her sails and stood out to sea.

---

## CHAPTER V.

### DAY-DREAMS AND ADVENTURES AMONG THE CLOUDS— A CHASE, A BATTLE, AND A VICTORY.

EARLY morning on the ocean! There is poetry in the idea; there is music in the very sound. As there is nothing new under the sun, probably a song exists with this or a similar title; if not, we now recommend it earnestly to musicians.

Ailie Dunning sat on the bulwarks of the Red Eric, holding on tightly by the mizen-shrouds, and gazing in open-eyed, open-mouthed, inexpressible delight upon the bright calm sea. She was far, far out upon the bosom of the Atlantic now. Sea-sickness—which, during the first part of the voyage, had changed the warm pink of her pretty face into every imaginable shade of green—was gone, and the hue of health could not now be banished even by the rudest storm. In short, she

had become a thorough sailor, and took special
delight in turning her face to windward during the
wild storm, and drinking-in the howling blast as
she held on by the rigid shrouds, and laughed at
the dashing spray—for little Ailie was not easily
frightened.   Martha and Jane Dunning had made
it their first care to implant in the heart of their
charge a knowledge of our Saviour's love, and
especially of His tenderness towards, and watchful
care over, the lambs of His flock.   Besides this,
little Ailie was naturally of a trustful disposition.
She had implicit confidence in the strength and
wisdom of her father, and it never entered into her
imagination to dream that it was possible for any
evil to befall the ship which *he* commanded.

But, although Ailie delighted in the storm, she
infinitely preferred the tranquil beauty and rest of
a "great calm," especially at the hour just before
sunrise, when the freshness, brightness, and light-
ness of the young day harmonized peculiarly with
her elastic spirit.   It was at this hour that we find
her alone upon the bulwarks of the Red Eric.

There was a deep, solemn stillness around, that
irresistibly and powerfully conveyed to her mind
the idea of rest.   The long, gentle undulation of
the deep did not in the least detract from this idea.
So perfect was the calm, that several masses of
clouds in the sky, which shone with the richest
saffron light, were mirrored in all their rich details
as if in a glass.   The faintest possible idea of a line

alone indicated, in one direction, where the water terminated and the sky began. A warm golden haze suffused the whole atmosphere, and softened the intensity of the deep-blue vault above.

There was, indeed, little variety of object to gaze upon—only the water and the sky. But what a world of delight did not Ailie find in that vast sky and that pure ocean, that reminded her of the sea of glass before the great white throne, of which she had so often read in Revelation. The towering masses of clouds were so rich and thick, that she almost fancied them to be mountains and valleys, rocks and plains of golden snow. Nay, she looked so long and so ardently at the rolling mountain heights in the sky above, and their magical counterparts in the sky below, that she soon, as it were, *thought herself into* Fairyland, and began a regular journey of adventures therein.

Such a scene at such an hour is a source of gladsome, peaceful delight to the breast of man in every stage of life; but it is a source of unalloyed, bounding, exhilarating, romantic, unspeakable joy, only in the years of childhood, when the mind looks hopefully forward, and before it has begun—as, alas! it must begin, sooner or later—to gaze regretfully back.

How long Ailie would have sat in motionless delight, it is difficult to say. The man at the wheel having nothing to do, had forsaken his post, and was leaning over the stern, either lost in reverie, or n the vain effort to penetrate with his vision the

E

blue abyss to the bottom. The members of the
watch on deck were either similarly engaged or had
stowed themselves away to sleep in quiet corners
among blocks and cordage. No one seemed inclined to move or speak, and she would probably
have sat there immovable for hours to come, had
not a hand fallen gently on her shoulder, and by
the magic of its simple contact scattered the bright
dreams of Fairyland as the finger-touch destroys
the splendour of the soap-bubble.

"Oh! Glynn," exclaimed Ailie, looking round
and heaving a deep sigh; "I've been away—far,
far away—you can't believe how far."

"Away, Ailie! Where have you been?" asked
Glynn, patting the child's head as he leaned over
the gunwale beside her.

"In Fairyland! Up in the clouds yonder. Out
and in, and up and down. Oh, you've no idea.
Just look." She pointed eagerly to an immense
towering cloud that rose like a conspicuous land-
mark in the centre of the landscape of the airy
world above. "Do you see that mountain?"

"Yes, Ailie; the one in the middle, you mean,
don't you? Yes, well?"

"Well," continued the child, eagerly and hurriedly, as if she feared to lose the thread of memory
that formed the warp and woof of the delicate fabric
she had been engaged in weaving; "well, I began
there; I went in behind it, and I met a fairy—not
really, you know, but I tried to think I met one,

so I began to speak to her, and then I made her speak to me, and her voice was so small and soft and sweet. She had on silver wings, and a star— a bright star in her forehead—and she carried a wand with a star on the top of it too. So I asked her to take me to see her kingdom, and I made her say she would—and, do you know, Glynn, I really felt at last as if she didn't wait for me to tell her what to say, but just went straight on, answering my questions, and putting questions to me in return Wasn't it funny?

"Well, we went on, and on, and on—the fairy and me—up one beautiful mountain of snow and down another, talking all the time so pleasantly, until we came to a great dark cave; so I made up my mind to make a lion come out of it; but the fairy said, ' No, let it be a bear ;' and immediately a great bear came out. Wasn't it strange? It really seemed as if the fairy had become real, and could do things of her own accord."

The child paused at this point, and looking with an expression of awe into her companion's face, said—"Do you think, Glynn, that people can *think* so hard that fairies *really* come to them?"

Glynn looked perplexed.

"No, Ailie, I suspect they can't—not because we can't think hard enough, but because there are no fairies to come."

"Oh, I'm *so* sorry!" replied the child, sadly.

"Why?" inquired Glynn.

" Because I love them *so* much—of course, I mean the good ones. I don't like the bad ones—though they're very useful, because they're nice to kill, and punish, and make examples of, and all that, when the good ones catch them."

"So they are," said the youth, smiling. "I never thought of that before. But go on with your ramble in the clouds."

"Well," began Ailie; "but where was I?"

"Just going to be introduced to a bear."

"Oh yes; well—the bear walked slowly away, and then the fairy called out an elephant, and after that a 'noceros——"

"A 'noceros!" interrupted Glynn; "what's that?"

"Oh, you know very well. A beast with a thick kin hanging in folds, and a horn on its nose——"

"Ah, a *rhi*noceros—I see. Well, go on, Ailie."

"Then the fairy told a camel to appear, and after that a monkey, and then a hippopotamus, and they all came out one after another, and some of them went away, and others began to fight. But the strangest thing of all was, that every one of them was *so* like the pictures of wild beasts that are hanging in my room at home! The elephant, too, I noticed, had his trunk broken exactly the same way as my toy elephant's one was. Wasn't it odd?"

"It was rather odd," replied Glynn; "but where did you go after that?"

" Oh, then we went on, and on again, until we came to——"

" It's your turn at the wheel, lad, ain't it ?" inquired Mr. Millons, coming up at that moment, and putting an abrupt termination to the walk in Fairyland.

" It is, sir," answered Glynn, springing quickly to the wheel, and relieving the man who had been engaged in penetrating the ocean's depths.

The mate walked forward ; the released sailor went below, and Ailie was again left to her solitary meditations ; for she was enough of a sailor now, in heart, to know that she ought not to talk too much to the steersman, even though the weather should be calm and there was no call for his undivided attention to the duties of his post.

While Nature was thus, as it were, asleep, and the watch on deck were more than half in the same condition, there was one individual in the ship whose faculties were in active play, whose " steam," as he himself would have remarked, " was up." This was the worthy cook, Nikel Sling, whose duties called him to his post at the galley-fire at an early hour each day.

We have often thought that a cook's life must be one of constant self-denial and exasperation of spirit. Besides the innumerable anxieties in reference to such important matters as boiling over and over-boiling, being done to a turn, or over-done, or singed or burned, or capsized, he has the diurnal

misery of being the first human being, in his little
circle of life, to turn out of a morning, and must
therefore experience the discomfort—the peculiar
discomfort—of finding things *as they were left* the
night before. Any one who does not know what
that discomfort is, has only to rise an hour before
the servants of a household, whether at sea or on
shore, to find out. Cook, too, has generally, if not
always, to light the fire; and that, especially in
frosty weather, is not agreeable. Moreover, cook
roasts *himself* to such an extent, and at meal-
times, in nine cases out of ten, gets into such physical and mental perturbation, that he cannot possibly appreciate the luxuries he has been occupied
all the day in concocting. Add to this, that he
spends all the morning in preparing breakfast; all
the forenoon in preparing dinner; all the afternoon
in preparing tea and supper, and all the evening in
clearing up, and perhaps all the night in dreaming of the meals of the following day, and mentally
preparing breakfast, and we think that we have
clearly proved the truth of the proposition with
which we started—namely, that a cook's life must
be one of constant self-denial and exasperation of
spirit.

But this is by the way, and was merely suggested
by the fact that, while all other creatures were
enjoying either partial or complete repose, Nickel
Sling was washing out pots and pans and kettles,
and handling murderous-looking knives and two-

pronged tormentors with a demoniacal activity that was quite appalling.

Beside him, on a little stool close to the galley fire, sat Tim Rokens—not that Mr. Rokens was cold—far from it. He was, to judge from appearances, much hotter than was agreeable. But Tim had come there and sat down to light his pipe, and being rather phlegmatic when not actively employed, he preferred to be partially roasted for a few minutes to getting up again.

" We ought," remarked Tim Rokens, puffing at a little black pipe which seemed inclined to be obstinate, " we ought to be gittin' among the fish by this time. Many's the one I've seed in them 'ere seas."

" I rather guess we should," replied the cook, pausing in the midst of his toils and wiping the perspiration from his forehead with an immense bundle of greasy oakum. " But I've seed us keep dodgin' about for weeks, I have, later in the year than this, without clappin' eyes on a fin. What sort o' baccy d'ye smoke, Rokens ?"

" Dun know. Got it from a Spanish smuggler for an old clasp-knife. Why ?"

" 'Cause it smells like rotten straw, an' wont improve the victuals. Guess you'd better take yourself off, old chap."

" Wot a cross-grained crittur ye are," said Rokens, as he rose to depart.

At that moment there was heard a cry that sent

the blood tingling to the extremities of every one on board the Red Eric.

"Thar she blows! thar she blows!" shouted the man in the crow's-nest.

The crow's-nest is a sort of cask, or nest, fixed at the top of the mainmast of whale ships, in which a man is stationed all day during the time the ships are on the fishing ground, to look out for whales; and the cry, "Thar she blows," announced the fact that the look-out had observed a whale rise to the surface and blow a spout of steamy water into the air.

No conceivable event—unless perhaps the blowing-up of the ship itself—could have more effectually and instantaneously dissipated the deep tranquillity to which we have more than once referred. Had an electric shock been communicated through the ship to each individual, the crew could not have been made to leap more vigorously and simultaneously. Many days before, they had begun to expect to see whales. Every one was therefore on the *qui vive,* so that when the well-known signal rang out like a startling peal in the midst of the universal stillness, every heart in the ship leaped in unison.

Had an observant man been seated at the time in the forecastle, he would have noticed that from out of the ten or fifteen hammocks that swung from the beams, there suddenly darted ten or fifteen pairs of legs which rose to the perpendicular position in order to obtain leverage to "fetch way." Instantly thereafter the said legs descended, and where the feet had been, ten or fifteen heads appeared. Next moment the men were "tumbling up" the fore-hatch to the deck, where the watch had already sprung to the boat-tackles.

"Where away ?" sang out Captain Dunning, who was among the first on deck.

"Off the weather bow, sir, three points."

"How far ?"

"About two miles. Thar she blows !"

"Call all hands," shouted the captain.

"Starboard watch, ahoy !" roared the mate, in that curious hoarse voice peculiar to boatswains of men-of-war. "Tumble up, lads, tumble up ! Whale in sight ! Bear a hand, my hearties !"

The summons was almost unnecessary. The "starboard watch" was—with the exception of one or two uncommonly heavy sleepers—already on deck pulling on its ducks and buckling its belts.

"Thar she breaches, thar she blows !" again came from the crow's-nest in the voice of a Stentor.

"Well done, Dick Barnes, you're the first to raise the oil," remarked one of the men ; implying by the remark, that the said Dick was fortunate enough to be the first to sight a whale.

"Where away now ?" roared the captain, who was in a state of intense excitement.

"A mile an' a half to leeward, sir."

"Clear away the boats," shouted the captain.

"Masthead, ahoy ! D'ye see that whale now ?"

" Ay, ay, sir. Thar she blows !"

" Bear a hand, my hearties," cried the captain,
as the men sprang to the boats which were swinging at the davits. " Get your tubs in ! Clear your
falls ! Look alive, lads ! Stand-by to lower ! All
ready !"

" All ready, sir."

" Thar she blows !" came again from the mast-
head with redoubled energy. "Sperm-whales,
sir ; there's a school of 'em."

" A *school* of them !" whispered Ailie, who had
left her post at the mizen-shrouds, and now stood
by her father's side, looking on at the sudden hubbub
in unspeakable amazement. " Do whales go to
school ?" she said, laughing.

" Out of the road, Ailie, my pet," cried her father,
hastily. " You'll get knocked over. Lower away,
lads, lower away !"

Down went the starboard, larboard, and waist
boats as if the falls had been cut, and almost before
you could wink, the men literally tumbled over
the side into them, took their places, and seized
their oars.

" Here, Glynn, come with me, and I'll show you
a thing or two," said the captain. " Jump in,
lad ; look sharp."

Glynn instantly followed his commander into the
starboard boat, and took the aft-oar. Tim Rokens,
being the harpooneer of that boat, sat at the bow-
oar with his harpoons and lances beside him, and

the whale-line coiled in a tub in the boat's head. The captain steered.

And now commenced a race that taxed the boats' crews to the utmost ; for it is always a matter keenly contested by the different crews, who shall fix the first harpoon in the whale. The larboard boat was steered by Mr. Millons, the first mate ; the waist boat by Mr. Markham, the second mate— the latter an active man of about five-and-twenty, whose size and physical strength were herculean, and whose disposition was somewhat morose and gloomy.

" Now, lads, give way ! That's it ! that's the way. Bend your backs, now ! *do* bend your backs," cried the captain, as the three boats sprang from the ship's side and made towards the nearest whale, with the white foam curling at their bows.

Several more whales appeared in sight spouting in all directions, and the men were wild with excitement.

"That's it ! Go it, lads !" shouted Mr. Millons, as the waist boat began to creep a-head. " Lay it on ! give way ! What d'ye say, boys; shall we beat 'em?"

Captain Dunning stood in the stern-sheets of the starboard boat, almost dancing with excitement as he heard these words of encouragement.

" Give way, boys !" he cried. " They can't do it ! That whale's ours—so it is. Only bend your backs ! A steady pull ! Pull like steam-tugs ! That's it !

Bend the oars ! Double 'em up ! Smash 'em in bits, *do !*"

Without quite going the length of the captain's last piece of advice, the men did their work nobly. They bent their strong backs with a will, and strained their sinewy arms to the utmost. Glynn, in particular, to whom the work was new, and therefore peculiarly exciting and interesting, almost tore the rowlocks out of the boat in his efforts to urge it on, and had the oar not been made of the toughest ash, there is no doubt that he would have obeyed the captain's orders literally, and have smashed it in bits.

On they flew like racehorses. Now one boat gained an inch on the others, then it lost ground again as the crew of another put forth additional energy, and the three danced over the glassy sea as if the inanimate planks had been suddenly endued with life, and inspired with the spirit that stirred the men.

A large sperm-whale lay about a quarter of a mile ahead, rolling lazily in the trough of the sea. Towards this the starboard boat now pulled with incredible speed, leaving the other two gradually astern. A number of whales rose in various directions. They had got into the midst of a shoal, or school of them, as the whale-men term it; and as several of these were nearer the other boats than the first whale was, they diverged towards them.

"There go flukes," cried Rokens, as the whale

raised its huge tail in the air and "sounded"—in other words, dived. For a few minutes the men lay on their oars, uncertain in what direction the whale would come up again ; but their doubts were speedily removed by its rising within a few yards of the boat.

"Now, Rokens," cried the captain ; " now for it; give him the iron. Give way, lads ; spring, boys. Softly now, softly."

In another instant the boat's bow was on the whale's head, and Rokens buried a harpoon deep in its side.

"Stern all !" thundered the captain.

The men obeyed, and the boat was backed off the whale just in time to escape the blow of its tremendous flukes as it dived into the sea, the blue depths of which were instantly dyed red with the blood that flowed in torrents from the wound.

Down it went, carrying out the line at a rate that caused the chocks through which it passed to smoke. In a few minutes the line ceased to run out, and the whale returned to the surface. It had scarcely showed its nose, when the slack of the line was hauled in, and a second harpoon was fixed in its body.

Infuriated with pain, the mighty fish gave vent to a roar like a bull, rolled half over, and lashed the sea with his flukes, till, all round for many yards, it was churned into red slimy foam. Then he turned round, and dashed off with the speed of a locomotive engine, tearing the boat through the waves behind it, the water curling up like a white wall round the bows.

"She wont stand that long," muttered Glynn Proctor, as he rested on his oar, and looked over his shoulder at the straining line.

"That she will, boy," said the captain; "and more than that, if need be. You'll not be long of havin' a chance of greasin' your fingers, I'll warrant."

In a few minutes the speed began to slacken, and after a time they were able to haul in on the line. When the whale again came to the surface, a third harpoon was cleverly struck into it, and a spout of blood from its blow-hole showed that it was mortally wounded. In throwing the harpoon, Tim Rokens slipped his foot, and went down like a stone head-foremost into the sea. He came up again like a cork, and just as the boat flew past fortunately caught hold of Glynn Proctor's hand. It was well that the grasp was a firm one, for the strain on their two arms was awful. In another minute Tim was in his place, ready with his lance to finish off the whale at its next rise.

Up it came again, foaming, breaching, and plunging from wave to wave, flinging torrents of blood and spray into the air. At one moment he reared his blunt gigantic head high above the sea the next he buried his vast and quivering carcass deep in the gory brine, carrying down with him a perfect whirlpool of red foam. Then he rose again.

and made straight for the boat. Had he known his own power, he might have soon terminated the battle, and come off the victor, but fortunately he did not. Tim Rokens received his blunt nose on the point of his lance, and drove him back with mingled fury and terror. Another advance was made, and a successful lance-thrust delivered.

"That's into his life," cried the captain.

"So it is," replied Rokens.

And so it was. A vital part had been struck. For some minutes the huge leviathan lashed and rolled and tossed in the trembling waves in his agony, while he spouted up gallons of blood at every throe; then he rolled over on his back, and lay extended a lifeless mass upon the waters.

"Now, lads; three cheers for our first whale. Hip ! hip ! hip !——"

The cheer that followed was given with all the energy and gusto inspired by a first victory, and it was repeated again and again, and over again, before the men felt themselves sufficiently relieved to commence the somewhat severe and tedious labour of towing the carcase to the ship.

It was a hard pull, for the whale had led them a long chase, and as the calm continued, those left aboard could not approach to meet the boats. The exhausted men were cheered, however, on getting aboard late that night, to find that the other boats had been equally successful, each of them having captured a sperm-whale.

## CHAPTER VI.

DISAGREEABLE CHANGES—SAGACIOUS CONVERSATIONS,
AND A TERRIBLE ACCIDENT.

A STRIKING and by no means a pleasant change took place in the general appearance of the Red Eric immediately after the successful chase detailed in the last chapter.

Before the arrival of the whales the decks had been beautifully clean and white, for Captain Dunning was proud of his ship, and fond of cleanliness and order. A few hours after the said arrival the decks were smeared with grease, oil, and blood, and everything from stem to stern became from that day filthy and dirty.

This was a sad change to poor Ailie, who had not imagined it possible that so sudden and disagreeable an alteration could take place. But there was no help for it; the duties of the fishery in which they were engaged required that the whales should not only be caught, but cut up, boiled down to oil, and stowed away in the hold in casks.

If the scene was changed for the worse a few hours after the cutting-up operations were begun, it became infinitely more so when the *try-works* were set going, and the melting-fires were lighted, and huge volumes of smoke begrimed the masts, and sails, and rigging. It was vain to think of clearing up; had they attempted that, the men would have been over-tasked without any good being accomplished. There was only one course open to those who didn't like it, and that was—to "grin and bear it."

"Cutting out" and "trying in" are the terms used by whale-men to denote the processes of cutting off the flesh or "blubber" from the whale's carcase, and reducing it to oil.

At an early hour on the following morning the first of these operations was commenced.

Ailie went about the decks, looking on with mingled wonder, interest, and disgust. She stepped about gingerly, as if afraid of coming in contact with slimy objects, and with her nose and mouth screwed up after the fashion of those who are obliged to endure bad smells. The expression of her face under the circumstances was amusing.

As for the men, they went about their work with relish, and total indifference as to consequences.

When the largest whale had been hauled alongside, ropes were attached to its head and tail, and the former was secured near the stern of the ship, while the latter was lashed to the bow; the cutting-tackle was then attached. This consisted of an arrangement of pulleys depending from the main-top, with a large blubber-hook at the end thereof. The cutting was commenced at the neck, and the hook attached; then the men hove on the wind-lass, and, while the cutting was continued in a

F

spiral direction round the whale's body, the tackle raised the mass of flesh until it reached the fixed blocks above. This mass, when it could be hauled up no higher, was then cut off, and stowed away under the name of a " blanket-piece." It weighed upwards of a ton. The hook being lowered and again attached, the process was continued until the whole was cut off. Afterwards, the head was severed from the body and hoisted on board, in order that the oil contained in the hollow of it might be baled out.

From the head of the first whale ten barrels of oil were obtained. The blubber yielded about eighty barrels.

When the " cutting out" was completed, and the remnants of bone and flesh were left to the sharks which swarmed round the vessel, revelling in their unusually rich banquet, the process of " trying-in" commenced. Trying-in is the term applied to the melting of the fat and the stowing it away in barrels in the form of oil; and an uncommonly dirty process it is. The large "blanket-pieces" were cut into smaller portions, and put into the try-pots, which were kept in constant operation. At night the ship had all the appearance of a vessel on fire, and the scene on deck was particularly striking and unearthly.

One night several of the men were grouped on and around the windlass, chatting, singing, and "spinning yarns." Ailie Dunning stood near them,

lost in wonder and admiration; for the ears and
eyes of the child were assailed in a manner never
before experienced or dreamed of even in the most
romantic mood of cloud-wandering.

It was a very dark night, darker than usual,
and not a breath of wind ruffled the sea, which
was like a sheet of undulating glass—for, be it remembered, there is no such thing at any time as
absolute stillness in the ocean. At all times, even
in the profoundest calm, the long, slow, gentle
swell rises and sinks with unceasing regularity, like
the bosom of a man in deep slumber.

Dense clouds of black smoke and occasional lurid
sheets of flame rose from the try-works, which were
situated between the foremast and the main-hatch.
The tops of the masts were lost in the curling
smoke, and the black waves of the sea gleamed
and flashed in the red light all round the ship.
One man stood in front of the melting-pot, pitching
in pieces of blubber with a two-pronged pitchfork.
Two comrades stood by the pots, stirring up their
contents, and throwing their figures into wild
uncouth attitudes, while the fire glared in their
greasy faces, and converted the front of their entire
persons into deep vermilion.

The oil was hissing in the try-pots; the rough
weather-beaten faces of the men on the windlass
were smeared, and their dirty-white ducks saturated, with oil. The decks were blood-stained:
huge masses of flesh and blubber lay scattered

about: sparks flew upwards in splendid showers
as the men raked up the fires: the decks, bulwarks,
railing, try-works, and windlass, were covered with
oil and slime, and glistering in the red glare. It
was a terrible, murderous-looking scene, and filled
Ailie's mind with mingled feelings of wonder, disgust, and awe, as she leaned on a comparatively
clean spot near the foremast, listening to the men
and gazing at the rolling smoke and flames.

"Ain't it beautiful?" said a short, fat little seaman named Gurney, who sat swinging his legs
on the end of the windlass, and pointed, as he
spoke, with the head of his pipe, to a more than
usually brilliant burst of sparks and flame that
issued that moment from the works.

"Beautiful!" exclaimed a long-limbed, shambling fellow named Jim Scroggles, "why, that
ain't the word at all. Now, I calls it splendiferous."

Scroggles looked round at his comrades, as if to
appeal to their judgment as to the fitness of the
word, but not receiving any encouragement, he
thrust down the glowing tobacco in his pipe with
the end of his little finger, and reiterated the word
"splendiferous," with marked emphasis.

"Did ye ever see that word in Johnson?" inquired Gurney.

"Whose Johnson?" said Scroggles, contemp-
tuously.

"Wot, don't ye know who Johnson is?" cried
Gurney, in surprise.

"In course I don't; how should I?" retorted Scroggles. "There's ever so many Johnson's in the world; which on 'em all do you mean?"

"Why, I mean Johnson wot wrote the diksh'-nary—the great lexikragofer."

"Oh! it's *him* you mean, is it? In course I've knowd him ever since I wos at school."

A general laugh interrupted the speaker.

"At school!" cried Nikel Sling, who approached the group at that moment, with a carving-knife in his hand—he seldom went anywhere without an instrument of office in his hand—"At school! Wal now, that beats creation. If ye wos, I'm sartin' ye only larned to forgit all ye orter to have remembered. I'd take a bet, now, ye wosn't at school as long as I've been settin' on this here windlass."

"Yer about right, Sling, it ud be unpossible for me to be as *long* as you anywhere, cause everybody knows I'm only five fut two, whereas you're six fut four!"

"Hear, hear!" shouted Dick Barnes—a man with a huge black beard, who the reader may perhaps remember was the first to "raise the oil." "It'll be long before you make another joke like that, Gurney. Come, now, give us a song, Gurney, do; there's the cap'n's darter standin' by the foremast, a'waitin' to hear ye. Give us 'Long, long ago.'"

"Ah! that's it, give us a song," cried the men. "Come, there's a good fellow."

"Well, it's so long ago since I sung that song, shipmates," replied Gurney, "that I've bin and forgot it; but Tim Rokens knows it; where's Rokens?"

"He's in the watch below."

In sea parlance, the men whose turn it is to take rest after their long watch on deck, are somewhat facetiously said to belong to the "watch below."

"Ah! that's a pity; so we can't have that ere partikler song. But I'll give ye another, if ye don't object."

"No, no. All right; go ahead, Gurney! Is. there a *chorus* to it?"

"Ay, in course there is. Wot's a song without a *chorus*? Wot's plum-duff without the plums? Wot's a ship without a 'elm? It's my opinion, shipmates, that a song without a *chorus* is no better than it should be. It's wus snor nothin'. It puts them wot listens in the blues, an' the man wot sings into the stews—an' sarve him right. I wouldn't, no I wouldn't give the fag-end o' nothin' mixed in a bucket o' salt water for a song without a *chorus* —that's flat; so here goes."

Having delivered himself of these opinions in an extremely vigorous manner, and announced the fact that he was about to begin, Gurney cleared his throat and drew a number of violent puffs from his pipe in quick succession, in order to kindle that instrument into a glow which would last through the first verse and the commencement of the chorus. This he knew was sufficient, for the men, when once fairly started on the chorus, would infallibly go on to the end with or without his assistance, and would therefore afford him time for a few restorative whiffs.

"It hain't got no name, lads."

"Never mind, Gurney—all right—fire away."

"Oh, I once know'd a man as hadn't got a nose,
    An' this is how he come to hadn't—
One cold winter night he went and got it froze—
    By the pain he wos well-nigh madden'd.
        (*Chorus.*) Well-nigh madden'd,
           By the pain he was well-nigh madden'd

"Next day it swoll up as big as my head,
    An' it turn'd like a piece of putty;
It kivered up his mouth, oh, yes, so it did,
    So he could not smoke his cutty.
        (*Chorus.*) Smoke his cutty,
           So he could not smoke his cutty.

"Next day it grew black, and the next day blue,
    An' tough as a junk of leather;
(Oh! he yelled, so he did, fit to pierce ye through)—
    An' then it fell off altogether!
        (*Chorus.*) Fell off altogether,
           An' then it fell off altogether!

"But the morial is wot you've now got to hear,
    An' it's good—as sure as a gun;
An' you'll never forget it, my messmates dear,
    For this song it hain't got none!
        (*Chorus.*) Hain't got none,
           For this song it hain't got none!"

The applause that followed this song was most enthusiastic, and evidently gratifying to Gurney, who assumed a modest deprecatory air as he proceeded to relight his pipe, which had been allowed to go out at the third verse, the performer having become so engrossed in his subject as to have forgotten the interlude of puffs at that point.

"Well sung, Gurney. Who made it?" inquired Phil Briant, an Irishman, who, besides being a jack-of-all-trades and an able-bodied seaman, was at that time acting-assistant to the cook and steward, the latter—a half Spaniard and half negro, of Californian extraction—being unwell.

"I'm bound not to tell," replied Gurney, with a conscious air.

"Ah, then, yer right, my boy, for it's below the average entirely."

"Come, Phil, none o' yer chaff," cried Dick Barnes; "that song desarves somethin' arter it. Suppose, now, Phil, that you wos to go below and fetch the bread-kid."

"Couldn't do it," replied Phil, looking solemn, "on no account wotiver."

"Oh, nonsense, why not?"

"'Cause it's unpossible. Why, if I did, sure that surly compound o' all sorts o' human blood would pitch into me with the carvin'-knife."

"Who? Tarquin?" cried Dick Barnes, naming the steward.

"Ay, sure enough that same—Tarquin's his name, an' it's kuriously befittin' the haythen, for of all the cross-grained mixtures o' buffalo, bear, bandicoot, and crackadile I iver seed, he's out o' sight——"

"Did I hear any one mention my name," inquired the steward himself, who came aft at that moment. He was a wild Spanish-like fellow, with a handsome-enough figure, and a swart countenance that might have been good-looking but for the thickish lips and nose and the bad temper that marked it. Since getting into the tropics, the sailors had modified their costumes considerably, and as each man had in some particular allowed himself a slight play of fancy, their appearance, when grouped together, was varied and picturesque. Most of them wore no shoes, and the caps of some were, to say the least, peculiar. Tarquin wore a broad-brimmed straw hat, with a conical crown, and a red silk sash tied round his waist.

"Yes, Tarquin," replied Barnes, "we *wos* engaged in makin' free-an'-easy remarks on you ; and Phil Briant there gave us to understand that you wouldn't let us have the bread-kid up. Now, it's my opinion you ain't goin' to be so hard on us as that ; you will let us have it up to comfort our hearts on this fine night, wont you ?"

The steward, whose green visage showed that he was too ill to enter into a dispute at that time, turned on his heel and walked aft, remarking that they might eat the bottom out o' the ship, for all he cared.

"There now, you misbemannered Patlander, go

and get it, or we'll throw ye overboard," cried
Scroggles, twisting his long limbs awkwardly as
he shifted his position on the windlass.

"Now, then, shipmates, don't go for to ax it,"
said Briant, remaining immovable.   "Don't I
know wot's best for ye ?  Let me spaake to ye now.
Did any of ye iver study midsin ?"

"No !" cried several, with a laugh.

"Sure I thought not," continued Phil, with a
patronizing air, "or ye'd niver ask for the bread-
kid out o' saisin.   Now I was in the medical way
meself wance—ay, ye may laugh, but its thrue—
I wos 'prentice to a pothecary, an I've mixed up
more midsins than would pisen the whole popila-
tion of owld Ireland—barrin the praists, av coorse.
And didn't I hear the converse o' all the doctors
in the place ?   And wasn't the word always—' Be
rigglar with yer mails—don't ait, avic, more nor three
times a day, and not too much, now.   Be sparin'.'"

"Hah ! ye long-winded grampus," interrupted
Dick Barnes, impatiently.   "An' warn't the doctors right.   Three times a day for sick folk, and six
times—or more—for them wot's well."

"Hear ! hear !" cried the others, while two of
them seized Briant by the neck, and thrust him
forcibly towards the after-hatch.   "Bring up the
kid, now ; an' if ye come without it, look out for
squalls."

"Och ! worse luck," sighed the misused assistant,
as he disappeared.

In a few minutes Phil returned with the kid,

which was a species of tray filled with broken sea-biscuit, which, when afloat, goes by the name of " bread."

This was eagerly seized, for the appetites of sailors are always sharp, except immediately after meals. A quantity of the broken biscuit was put into a strainer, and fried in whale oil, and the men sat round the kid to enjoy their luxurious feast, and relate their adventures—all of which were more or less marvellous, and many of them undoubtedly true.

The more one travels in this world of ours, and the more one reads of the adventures of travellers upon whose narratives we can place implicit confidence, the more we find that men do not now require, as they did of old, to draw upon their imaginations for marvellous tales of wild romantic adventure. In days gone by, travellers were few; foreign lands were almost unknown. Not many books were written ; and of the few that were, very few were believed. In the present day men of un-doubted truthfulness have roamed far and wide over the whole world ; their books are numbered by hundreds, and much that was related by ancient travellers, but not believed, has now been fully cor-roborated. More than that, it is now known that men have everywhere received, as true, statements which modern discovery has proved to be false, and on the other hand they have often refused to be-lieve what is now ascertained to be literally true.

We would suggest, in passing, that a lesson

might be learned from this fact—namely, that w
ought to receive a statement in regard to a foreig
land, not according to the probability or the im
probability of the statement itself, but accordin
to the credibility of him who makes it. Aili
Dunning had a trustful disposition; she acted o
neither of the above principles. She believed a
she heard, poor thing, and therefore had a hea
pretty well stored with mingled fact and nonsens

While the men were engaged with their mea
Dr. Hopley came on deck and found her leanin
over the stern, looking down at the waves whic
shone with sparkling phosphorescent light. A
almost imperceptible breeze had sprung up, and th
way made by the vessel as she passed through th
water was indicated by a stream of what appeare
lambent blue flame.

"Looking at the fish, Ailie, as usual?" said th
doctor as he came up. "What are they saying t
you to-night?"

"I'm not looking at the fish," answered Ailie
"I'm looking at the fire—no, not the fire; pap
said it wasn't fire, but it's so like it, I can scarcel
call it anything else. What *is* it, doctor?"

"It is called phosphorescence," replied the doc
tor, leaning over the bulwarks, and looking down ε
the fiery serpent that seemed as if it clung to th
ship's rudder. "But I daresay you don't kno
what that means. You know what fire-flies an
glow-worms are?"

"Oh! yes; I've often caught them."

"Well, there are immense numbers of very small and very thin jelly-like creatures in the sea, so thin and so transparent that they can scarcely be observed in the water. These Medusæ, as they are called, possess the power of emitting light similar to that of the fire-fly. In short, Ailie, they are the fire-flies and glow-worms of the ocean."

The child listened with wonder, and for some minutes remained silent. Before she could again speak, there occurred one of those incidents which are generally spoken of as "most unexpected" and sudden, but which, nevertheless, are the result of natural causes, and might have been prevented by means of a little care.

The wind, as we have said, was light, so light that it did not distend the sails; the boom of the spanker-sail hung over the stern, and the spanker-braces lay slack along the seat on which Ailie and the doctor knelt. A little gust of wind came: it was not strong—a mere puff; but the man at the wheel was not attending to his duty: the puff, light as it was, caused the spanker to jibe—that is, to fly over from one side of the ship to the other— the heavy boom passed close over the steersman's head as he cried, "Look out!" The braces taughtened, and in so doing they hurled Dr. Hopley violently to the deck, and tossed Ailie Dunning over the bulwarks into the sea.

It happened at that moment that Glynn Proctor chanced to step on deck.

"Hallo! what's wrong?" cried the youth, springing forward, catching the doctor by the coat, as he was about to spring overboard, and pulling him violently back, under the impression that he was deranged.

The doctor pointed to the sea, and, with a look of horror, gasped the word "Ailie."

In an instant Glynn released his hold, plunged over the stern of the ship, and disappeared in the waves.

---

## CHAPTER VII.

### THE RESCUE—PREPARATIONS FOR A STORM.

IT is impossible to convey by means of words an adequate idea of the terrible excitement and uproar that ensued on board the Red Eric after the events narrated in the last chapter. From those on deck who witnessed the accident there arose a cry so sharp, that it brought the whole crew from below in an instant. But there was no confusion. The men were well trained. Each individual knew his post, and whalemen are accustomed to a sudden and hasty summons. The peculiarity of the present one, it is true, told every man in an instant, that something was wrong, but each mechanically sprang to his post, while one or two shouted to ascertain what had happened, or to explain.

But the moment Captain Dunning's voice was heard there was perfect silence.

"Clear away the starboard quarter-boat," he cried, in a deep firm tone.

" Ay, ay, sir."

" Stand by the falls—lower away !"

There was no occasion to urge the sailors ; they sprang to the work with the fervid celerity of men who knew that life or death depended on their speed. In less time than it takes to relate, the boat was leaping over the long ocean swell, as it had never yet done in chase of the whale, and, in a few seconds, passed out of the little circle of light caused by the fires and into the gloom that surrounded the ship.

The wind had been gradually increasing during all these proceedings, and although no time had been lost, and the vessel had been immediately brought up into the wind, Ailie and Glynn were left struggling in the dark sea a long way behind ere the quarter-boat could be lowered ; and now that it was fairly afloat, there was still the danger of its failing to hit the right direction of the objects of which it was in search.

After leaping over the stern, Glynn Proctor, the moment he rose to the surface, gave a quick glance at the ship, to make sure of her exact position, and then struck out in a straight line astern ; for he knew that wherever Ailie fell, there she would remain struggling until she sank. Glynn was a fast and powerful swimmer. He struck out with desperate energy, and in a few minutes the ship was

out of sight behind him.   Then he paused suddenly,
and letting his feet sink until he attained an upright position, trod the water and raised himself
breast-high above the surface, at the same time
listening intently, for he began to fear that he might
have overshot his mark.   No sound met his straining ear save the sighing of the breeze and the ripple
of the water as it lapped against his chest.   It was
too dark to see more than a few yards in any
direction.

Glynn knew that each moment lost rendered his
chance of saving the child terribly slight.   He
shouted "Ailie !" in a loud agonizing cry, and swam
forward again with redoubled energy, continuing
the cry from time to time, and· raising himself occasionally to look round him.   The excitement of
his mind, and the intensity with which it was bent
on the one great object, rendered him at first almost
unobservant of the flight of time.   But suddenly
the thought burst upon him that fully ten minutes
or a quarter of an hour had elapsed since Ailie fell
overboard, and that no one who could not swim
could exist for half that time in deep water.   He
shrieked with agony at the thought, and, fancying
that he must have passed the child, he turned
round and swam desperately towards the point
where he supposed the ship lay.   Then he thought,
" What if I have turned just as I was coming up
with her?"   So he turned about again, but as the
hopelessness of his efforts once more occurred to

him, he lost all presence of mind, and began to shout furiously, and to strike out wildly in all directions.

In the midst of his mad struggles his hand struck an object floating near him. Instantly he felt his arm convulsively grasped, and the next moment he was seized round the neck in a gripe so violent that it almost choked him. He sank at once, and the instinct of self-preservation restored his presence of mind. With a powerful effort he tore Ailie from her grasp, and quickly raised himself to the surface, where he swam gently with his left hand, and held the struggling child at arm's-length with his right.

The joy caused by the knowledge that she had still life to struggle infused new energy into Glynn's well-nigh exhausted frame, and he assumed as calm and cheerful a tone as was possible under the circumstances, when he exclaimed — " Ailie, Ailie, don't struggle, dear, I'll save you *if you keep quiet.*"

Ailie was quiet in a moment. She felt in the terror of her young heart an almost irresistible desire to clutch at Glynn's neck ; but the well-known voice reassured her, and her natural tendency to place blind implicit confidence in others, served her in this hour of need, for she obeyed his injunctions at once.

" Now, dear," said Glynn, with nervous rapidity, "don't grasp me, else we shall sink. Trust me, *I'll never let you go.* Will you trust me ?"

G

Ailie gazed wildly at her deliverer through her wet and tangled tresses, and with great difficulty gasped the word "Yes," while she clenched the garments on her labouring bosom with her little hands, as if to show her determination to do as she was bid.

Glynn at once drew her towards him and rested her head on his shoulder. The child gave vent to a deep, broken sigh of relief, and threw her right arm round his neck, but the single word "Ailie," uttered in a remonstrative tone, caused her to draw it quickly back and again grasp her breast.

All this time Glynn had been supporting himself by that process well known to swimmers as "treading water," and had been so intent upon his purpose of securing the child, that he failed to observe the light of a lantern gleaming in the far distance on the sea, as the boat went ploughing hither and thither, the men almost breaking the oars in their desperate haste, and the captain standing in the stern-sheets pale as death, holding the light high over his head, and gazing with a look of unutterable agony into the surrounding gloom.

Glynn now saw the distant light, and exerting his voice to the utmost, gave vent to a prolonged cry. Ailie looked up in her companion's face while he listened intently. The moving light became stationary for a moment, and a faint reply floated back to them over the waves. Again Glynn raised his voice to its utmost, and the cheer that came back told him that he had been heard.

But the very feeling of relief at the prospect of immediate deliverance had well-nigh proved fatal to them both; for Glynn experienced a sudden relaxation of his whole system, and he felt as if he could not support himself and his burden a minute longer.

"Ailie," he said, faintly but quickly, "we shall be saved if you *obey at once;* if not, we shall be drowned. Lay your two hands on my breast, and let yourself sink *down to the very lips.*"

Glynn turned on his back as he spoke, spread out his arms and legs to their full extent, let his head fall back, until it sank, leaving only his lips, nose, and chin above water, and lay as motionless as if he had been dead. And now came poor Ailie's severest trial. When she allowed herself to sink, and felt the water rising about her ears, and lipping round her mouth, terror again seized upon her, but she felt Glynn's breast heaving under her hands, so she raised her eyes to heaven and prayed silently to Him who is the only true deliverer from danger. Her self-possession was restored, and soon she observed the boat bearing down on the spot, and heard the men as they shouted to attract attention.

Ailie tried to reply, but her tiny voice was gone, and her soul was filled with horror as she saw the boat about to pass on. In her agony she began to struggle. This roused Glynn, who had rested sufficiently to have recovered a slight degree of strength. He immediately raised his head, and uttered a wild cry as he grasped Ailie again with his arm.

The rowers paused; the light of the lantern gleamed over the sea, and fell upon the spray tossed up by Glynn. Next moment the boat swept up to them—and they were saved.

The scene that followed baffles all description. Captain Dunning fell on his knees beside Ailie, who was too much exhausted to speak, and thanked God, in the name of Jesus Christ, again and again for her deliverance. A few of the men shouted; others laughed hysterically; and some wept freely as they crowded round their shipmate, who, although able to sit up, could not speak except in disjointed sentences. Glynn, however, recovered quickly, and even tried to warm himself by pulling an oar before they regained the ship, but Ailie remained in a state of partial stupor, and was finally carried on board and down into the cabin, and put between warm blankets by her father and Dr. Hopley.

Meanwhile, Glynn was hurried forward, and dragged down into the forecastle by the whole crew, who seemed unable to contain themselves for joy, and expressed their feelings in ways that would have been deemed rather absurd on ordinary occasions.

" Change yer clo's, avic, at wance," cried Phil Briant, who was the most officious and violent in his offers of assistance to Glynn. "Och ! but it's wet ye are, darlin'. Give me a howld."

This last request had reference to the right leg of Glynn's trousers, which happened to be blue cloth of a rather thin quality, and which therefore clung to his limbs with such tenacity that it was a matter of the utmost difficulty to get them off.

"That's your sort, Phil—a long pull, and a strong pull, and a pull all together," cried Dick Barnes, hurrying forward, with a bundle of garments in his arms. "Here's dry clo's for him."

"Have a care, Phil," shouted Gurney, who stood behind Glynn and held him by the shoulders ; "it'll give way."

"Niver a taste," replied the reckless Irishman. But the result proved that Gurney was right, for the words had scarce escaped his lips when the garment parted at the knee, and Phil Briant went crashing back among a heap of tin pannikins, pewter plates, blocks, and cordage. A burst of laughter followed, of course, but the men's spirits were too much roused to be satisfied with this, so they converted the laugh into a howl, and pro-longed it into a cheer, as if their comrade had suc-cessfully performed a difficult and praiseworthy deed.

"Hold on, lads," cried Glynn; "I'm used up, I can't stand it."

"Here you are," shouted Nikel Sling, pushing the men violently aside, and holding a steaming tumbler of hot brandy-and-water under Glynn's nose. "Down with it; that's the stuff to get up the steam fit to bust yer biler, I calc'late."

The men looked on for a moment in silence, while Glynn drank, as if they expected some remarkable chemical change to take place in his constitution.

"Och! ain't it swate?" inquired Phil Briant, who, having gathered himself up, now stood rubbing his shoulder with the fragment of the riven garment. "Av I wasn't a taytotaller, it's meself would like some of that same."

In a few minutes our hero was divested of his wet garments, rubbed perfectly dry by his kind messmates, and clad in dry costume; after which he felt almost as well as if nothing unusual had happened to him. The men, meanwhile, cut their jokes at him or at each other as they stood round and watched, assisted, or retarded the process. As for Tim Rokens, who had been in the boat and witnessed the rescue, he stood gazing steadfastly at Glynn without uttering a word, keeping his thumbs the while hooked in the arm-holes of his vest, and his legs very much apart. By degrees—as he thought on what had passed, and the narrow escape poor little Ailie had had, and the captain's tears, things he never saw the captain shed before and had not believed the captain to have possessed— as he pondered these things, we say, his knotty visage began to work, and his cast-iron chin began to quiver, and his shaggy brows contracted, and his nose, besides becoming purple, began to twist, as if it were an independent member of his face, and he came, in short, to that climax which is familiarly expressed by the words "bursting into tears."

But if anybody thinks the act, on the part of Tim Rokens, bore the smallest resemblance to the generally received idea of that sorrowful affection, anybody," we take leave to tell him, is very much mistaken. The bold harpooneer did it thus—he suddenly unhooked his right hand from the arm-hole of his vest, and gave his right thigh a slap which produced a crack that would have made a small pistol envious ; then he uttered a succession of ferocious roars, that might have quite well indicated pain, or grief, or madness, or a drunken cheer, and, unhooking the left hand, he doubled himself up, and thrust both knuckles into his eyes. The knuckles were wet when he pulled them out of his eyes, but he dried them on his pantaloons, bolted up the hatchway, and, rushing up to the man at the wheel, demanded, in a voice of thunder— "How's 'er head ?"

"Sou, sou-east and by east," replied the man, in some surprise.

"Sou, sou-east and by east !" repeated Mr. Rokens, in a savage growl of authority, as if he were nothing less than the admiral of the Channel fleet; "that's two points and a half off yer course, sir. Luff, luff, you—you——"

At this point Tim Rokens turned on his heel,

and began to walk up and down the deck as calmly as if nothing whatever had occurred to disturb his equanimity.

"The captain wants Glynn Proctor," said the second mate, looking down the forehatch.

"Ay, ay, sir," answered Glynn, ascending, and going aft.

"Ailie wants to see you, Glynn, my boy," said Captain Dunning, as the former entered the cabin; "and I want to speak to you myself—to thank you, Glynn. Ah, lad! you can't know what a father's heart feels when——go to her, boy." He grasped the youth's hand, and gave it a squeeze that revealed infinitely more of his feelings than could have been done by words.

Glynn returned the squeeze, and, opening the door of Ailie's private cabin, entered and sat down beside her crib.

"Oh, Glynn, I want to speak to you; I want to thank you. I love you *so* much for jumping into the sea after me," began the child, eagerly, and raising herself on one elbow while she held out her hand.

"Ailie," interrupted Glynn, taking her hand, and holding up his finger to impose silence, "you obeyed me *in* the water, and now I insist on your obedience *out* of the water. If you don't, I'll leave you. You're still too weak to toss about and speak loud in this way. Lie down, my pet."

Glynn kissed her forehead, and forced her gently back on the pillow.

" Well, I'll be good, but don't leave me yet, Glynn. I'm much better. Indeed, I feel quite strong. Oh! it was good of you——"

" There you go again."

" I love you," said Ailie.

" I've no objection to that," replied Glynn, " but don't excite yourself. But tell me, Ailie, how was it that you managed to keep afloat so long. The more I think of it the more I am filled with amazement, and, in fact, I'm half inclined to think that God worked a miracle in order to save you."

" I don't know," said Ailie, looking very grave and earnest, as she always did when our Maker's name happened to be mentioned. " Does God work miracles still?"

" Men say not," replied Glynn.

" I'm sure I don't quite understand what a miracle is," continued Ailie, although Aunt Martha and Aunt Jane have often tried to explain it to me. Is floating on your back a miracle?"

" No," said Glynn, laughing ; " it isn't."

" Well, that's the way I was saved. You know, ever since I can remember, I have bathed with Aunt Martha and Aunt Jane, and they taught me how to float—and it's *so* nice, you can't think how nice it is—and I can do it so easily now, that I never get frightened. But, oh! when I was tossed over the side of the ship into the sea I *was* frightened just. I don't think I *ever* got such a fright. And I splashed about for some time, and swallowed some water, but I got upon my back some-

how. I can't tell how it was, for I was too frightened to try to do anything. But when I found
myself floating as I used to do long ago, I felt my
fear go away a little, and I shut my eyes and
prayed, and then it went away altogether; and I
felt quite sure you would come to save me, and
you *did* come, Glynn, and I know it was God who
sent you. But I became a good deal frightened
again when I thought of the sharks, and——"

"Now, Ailie, stop!" said Glynn. "You're forgetting your promise, and exciting yourself again."

"So she is, and I must order you out, Master
Glynn," said the doctor, opening the door, and
entering at that moment.

Glynn rose, patted the child's head, and nodded
cheerfully as he left the little cabin.

The captain caught him as he passed, and began
to reiterate his thanks, when their conversation
was interrupted by the voice of Mr. Millons, who
put his head in at the skylight and said—

"Squall coming, sir, I think."

"So, so," cried the captain, running upon deck.
"I've been looking for it. Call all hands, Mr.
Millons, and take in sail—every rag except the
storm-trysails."

Glynn hurried forward, and in a few minutes
every man was at his post. The sails were furled,
and every preparation made for a severe squall;
for Captain Dunning knew that that part of the
coast of Africa, off which the Red Eric was then

sailing, was subject to sudden squalls, which, though usually of short duration, were sometimes terrific in their violence.

"Is everything snug, Mr. Millons?"

"All snug, sir."

"Then let the men stand by till it's over."

The night had grown intensely dark, but away on the starboard quarter the heavens appeared of an ebony blackness that was quite appalling. This appearance, that rose on the sky like a shroud of crape, quickly spread upwards until it reached the zenith. Then a few gleams of light seemed to illuminate it very faintly, and a distant hissing noise was heard.

A dead calm surrounded the ship, which lay like a log on the water, and the crew, knowing that nothing more could be done in the way of preparation, awaited the bursting of the storm with uneasy feelings. In a few minutes its distant roar was heard, like muttered thunder. On it came, with a steady continuous roar, as if chaos were about to be restored, and the crashing wreck of elements were being hurled in mad fury against the yet unshattered portions of creation. Another second, and the ship was on her beam-ends, and the sea and sky were white as milk as the wind tore up the waves and beat them flat, and whirled away broad sheets of driving foam.

# CHAPTER VIII.

### THE STORM, AND ITS RESULTS.

ALTHOUGH the Red Eric was thrown on her beam-
ends, or nearly so, by the excessive violence of the
squall, the preparations to meet it had been so
well made that she righted again almost immediately, and now flew before the wind under bare
poles with a velocity that was absolutely terrific.

Ailie had been nearly thrown out of her berth
when the ship lay over, and now when she listened
to the water hissing and gurgling past the little
port that lighted her cabin, and felt the staggering
of the vessel, as burst after burst of the hurricane
almost tore the masts out of her, she lay trembling
with anxiety and debating with herself whether or
not she ought to rise and go on deck.

Captain Dunning well knew that his child would
be naturally filled with fear, for this was the first
severe squall she had ever experienced, so, as he
could not quit the deck himself, he called Glynn
Proctor to him and sent him down with a message.

"Well, Ailie," said Glynn, cheerfully, as he
opened the door and peeped in ; "how d'ye get on,
dear ?   The captain has sent me to say that the
worst o' this blast is over, and you've nothing to
fear."

"I'm glad to hear that, Glynn," replied the child,
holding out her hand, while a smile lighted up her

face and smoothed out the lines of anxiety from
her brow. " Come and sit by me, Glynn, and tell
me what like it is. I wish so much that I had been
on deck. Was it grand, Glynn ?"

" It was uncommonly grand ; it was even terrible
—but I cannot sit with you more than a minute,
else my shipmates will say that I'm skulking."

" Skulking, Glynn ! What's that ?"

" Why, it's—it's shirking work, you know," said
Glynn, somewhat puzzled.

Ailie laughed. " But you forget that I don't
know what ' shirking' means. You must explain
that too."

" How terribly green you are, Ailie."

" No ! am I ?" exclaimed the child in some surprise. " What *can* have done it ? I'm not
sick."

Glynn laughed outright at this, and then proceeded to explain the meaning of the slang phraseology he had used. " Green, you must know, means
ignorant," he began.

" How funny ! I wonder why."

" Well, I don't know exactly. Perhaps it's because when a fellow's asked to answer questions he
don't understand, he's apt to turn either blue with
rage or yellow with fear—or both ; and that, you
know, would make him green. I've heard it said
that it implies a comparison of men to plants—very
young ones, you know, that are just up, just born,
as it were, and have not had much experience of

life, are green of course—but I like my own definition best."

It may perhaps be scarcely necessary to remark
that our hero was by no means singular in this
little preference of his own definition to that of any
one else !

"Well, and what does skulking mean, and shirking work ?" persisted Ailie.

"It means hiding so as to escape duty, my little
catechist ; but——"

"Hallo ! Glynn, Glynn Proctor," roared the
first mate from the deck—"where's that fellow ?
skulking, I'll be bound.   Lay aloft there and shake
out the foretopsail.   Look alive."

"Ay, ay, sir," was the ready response as the men
sprang to obey.

"There, you have it now, Ailie, explained and
illustrated," cried Glynn, starting up.   "Here I
am, at this minute in a snug dry berth chatting to
you, and in half a minute more I'll be out on the
end o' the foreyard holding on for bare life, with
the wind fit to tear off my jacket and blow my ducks
into ribbons, and the rain and spray dashing all
over me fit to blot me out altogether.   There's a
pretty little idea to turn over in your mind, Ailie,
while I'm away."

Glynn closed the door at the last word, and, as
he had prophesied, was, within half a minute, in
the unenviable position above referred to.

The force of the squall was already broken, and

the men were busy setting close-reefed topsails
but the rain that followed the squall bid fair to
"blot them out," as Glynn said, altogether. It
came down, not in drops, but in masses, which were
caught up by the fierce gale and mingled with the
spray, and hurled about and on with such violent
confusion, that it seemed as though the whole
creation were converted into wind and water, and
had engaged in a war of extermination, the central
turmoil of which was the Red Eric.

But the good ship held on nobly. Although not
a fast sailer she was an excellent sea boat, and
danced on the billows like a sea-mew. The squall,
however, was not over. Before the topsails had
been set many minutes it burst on them again with
redoubled fury, and the maintopsail was instantly
blown into ribbons. Glynn and his comrades were
once more ordered aloft to furl the remaining sails,
but before this could be done the foretopmast was
carried away, and in falling it tore away the jib-
boom also. At the same moment a tremendous
sea came rolling on astern ; in the uncertain light
it looked like a dark moving mountain that was
about to fall on them.

"Luff, luff a little—steady !" roared the captain,
who saw the summit of the wave toppling over
the stern, and who fully appreciated the danger of
being "pooped," which means having a wave
launched upon the quarter-deck.

"Steady it is," replied the steersman.

"Look out!" shouted the captain and several of the men, simultaneously.

Every one seized hold of whatever firm object chanced to be within reach; next moment the black billow fell like an avalanche on the poop, and rushing along the decks, swept the waist-boat and all the loose spars into the sea. The ship staggered under the shock, and it seemed to every one on deck that she must inevitably founder; but in a few seconds she recovered, the water gushed from the scuppers and sides in cataracts, and once more they drove swiftly before the gale.

In about twenty minutes the wind moderated, and while some of the men went aloft to clear away the wreck of the topsails and make all snug, others went below to put on dry garments.

"That was a narrow escape, Mr. Millons," remarked the captain, as he stood by the starboard-rails.

"It was, sir," replied the mate. "It's a good job, too, sir, that none o' the 'ands were washed overboard."

"It is, indeed, Mr. Millons; we've reason to be thankful for that; but I'm sorry to see that we've lost our waist-boat."

"We've lost our spare sticks, sir," said the mate, with a lugubrious face, while he wrung the brine out of his hair; "and I fear we've nothink left fit to make a noo foretopmast or a jibboom."

"True, Mr. Millons; we shall have to run to

the nearest port on the African coast to refit; luckily we are not very far from it. Meanwhile, tell Mr. Markham to try the well; it is possible that we may have sprung a leak in all this straining, and see that the wreck of the foretopmast is cleared away. I shall go below and consult the chart; if any change in the weather takes place, call me at once."

"Yes, sir," answered the mate, as he placed his hand to windward of his mouth, in order to give full force to the terrific tones in which he proceeded to issue his captain's commands.

Captain Dunning went below and, looking into Ailie's berth, nodded his wet head several times and smiled with his damp visage benignly—which acts, however well meant and kindly they might be, were, under the circumstances, quite unnecessary, seeing that the child was sound asleep. The captain then dried his head and face with a towel about as rough as the mainsail of a seventy-four, and with a violence that would have rubbed the paint off the figurehead of the Red Eric. Then he sat down to his chart, and having pondered over it for some minutes, he went to the foot of the companion-ladder and roared up—

"Lay the course nor'-nor'-east-and-by-nor'-half-nor', Mr. Millons."

To which Mr. Millons replied in an ordinary tone, "Ay, ay, sir," and then roared—"Lay her head nor'-nor'-east-and-by-nor'-half-nor'," in an unneces-

H

sarily loud and terribly fierce tone of voice to the
steersman, as if that individual were in the habit of
neglecting to obey orders, and required to be perpetually threatened in what may be called a tone
of implication.

The steersman answered in what, to a landsman,
would have sounded as a rather amiable and for-
giving tone of voice—" Nor'-nor'-east-and-by-nor'-
half-nor' it is, sir ;" and thereupon the direction of
the ship's head was changed, and the Red Eric,
according to Tim Rokens, "bowled along" with a
stiff breeze on the quarter, at the rate of ten knots.
for the west coast of Africa.

## CHAPTER IX.

### RAMBLES ON SHORE, AND STRANGE THINGS AND CEREMONIES WITNESSED THERE.

VARIETY is charming. No one laying claim to
the smallest amount of that very uncommon attribute,
common sense, will venture to question the truth
of that statement. Variety is so charming that
men and women, boys and girls, are always, all of
them, hunting after it. To speak still more emphatically on this subject, we venture to affirm
that it is an absolute necessity of animal nature.
Were any positive and short-sighted individual to
deny this position, and sit down during the remainder of his life in a chair and look straight
before him, in order to prove that he could live

without variety, he would seek it in change of position. If he did not do that, he would seek it in change of thought. If he did not do *that*, he would die !

Fully appreciating this great principle of our nature, and desiring to be charmed with a little variety, Tim Rokens and Phil Briant presented themselves before Captain Dunning one morning about a week after the storm, and asked leave to go ashore. The reader may at first think the men were mad, but he will change his opinion when we tell him that four days after the storm in question the Red Eric had anchored in the harbour formed by the mouth of one of the rivers on the African coast, where white men trade with the natives for bar wood and ivory, and where they also carry on that horrible traffic in negroes, the existence of which is a foul disgrace to humanity.

"Go ashore !" echoed Captain Dunning. "Why, if you all go on at this rate, we'll never get ready for sea. However, you may go, but don't wander too far into the interior, and look out for elephants and wild men o' the woods boys—keep about the settlements."

"Ay ay, sir, and thank'ee," replied the two men, touching their caps as they retired.

"Please sir, I want to go too," said Glynn Proctor, approaching the captain.

"What! more wanting to go ashore ?"

"Yes, and so do I," cried Ailie, running forward

and clasping her father's rough hand; " I did enjoy
myself *so* much yesterday, that I must go on shore
again to-day, and I must go with Glynn. He'll
take such famous care of me ; now *wont* you let
me, papa ?"

" Upon my word, this looks like preconcerted
mutiny. However, I don't mind if I do let you
go, but have a care, Glynn, that you don't lose
sight of her for a moment, and keep to the shore
and the settlements. I've no notion of allowing
her to be swallowed by an alligator, or trampled on
by an elephant, or run away with by a gorilla."

" Never fear, sir. You may trust me ; I'll take
good care of her."

With a shout of delight the child ran down to
the cabin to put on her bonnet, and quickly reappeared, carrying in her hand a basket which she
purposed to fill with a valuable collection of plants,
minerals, and insects. These she meant to preserve
and carry home as a surprise to aunts Martha and
Jane, both of whom were passionately fond of
mineralogy, delighted in botany, luxuriated in
entomology, doted on conchology, and raved
about geology—all of which sciences they studied
superficially, and specimens of which they collected
and labelled beautifully, and stowed away carefully
in a little cabinet, which they termed (not jocularly,
but seriously) their " Bureau of Omnology."

It was a magnificent tropical morning when the
boat left the side of the Red Eric and landed

Glynn and Ailie, Tim Rokens and Phil Briant on
the wharf that ran out from the yellow beach of
the harbour in which their vessel lay. The sun
had just risen. The air was cool (comparatively)
and motionless, so that the ocean lay spread out
like a pure mirror, and revealed its treasures and
mysteries to a depth of many fathoms. The sky
was intensely blue and the sun intensely bright,
while the atmosphere was laden with the delightful
perfume of the woods—a perfume that is sweet and
pleasant to those long used to it, how much more
enchanting to nostrils rendered delicately sensitive
by long exposure to the scentless gales of ocean?

One of the sailors who had shown symptoms of
weakness in the chest during the voyage, had
begged to be discharged and left ashore at this
place. He could ill be spared, but as he was fit
for nothing, the captain agreed to his request, and
resolved to procure a negro to act as cook's assistant in the place of Phil Briant, who was too useful
a man to remain in so subordinate a capacity. The
sick man was therefore sent on shore in charge of
Tim Rokens.

On landing they were met by a Portuguese slave-
dealer, an American trader, a dozen or two partially
clothed negroes, and a large concourse of utterly
naked little negro children, who proved to demonstration that they were of the same nature and
spirit with white children, despite the colour of
their skins, by taking intense delight in all the

amusements practised by the fair-skinned juveniles of more northern lands—namely, scampering after each other, running and yelling, indulging in mischief, spluttering in the water, rolling on the sand, staring at the strangers, making impudent remarks, and punching each other's heads.

If the youth of America ever wish to prove that they are of a distinct race from the sable sons of Africa, their only chance is to become paragons of perfection, and give up *all* their wicked ways.

"Oh!" exclaimed Ailie, half amused, half frightened, as Glynn lifted her out of the boat; "oh! how funny! Don't they look so *very* like as if they were all painted black?"

"Good day to you, gentlemen," cried the trader, as he approached the landing. "Got your foretop damaged, I see. Plenty of sticks here to mend it. Be glad to assist you in any way I can. Was away in the woods when you arrived, else I'd have come to offer sooner."

The trader, who was a tall sallow man in a blue cotton shirt, sailor's trowsers, and a broad-brimmed straw hat, addressed himself to Glynn, whose gentlemanly manner led him to believe he was in command of the party.

"Thank you," replied Glynn, "we've got a little lamage—lost a good boat, too, but we'll soon repair the mast. We have come ashore just now, however, mainly for a stroll."

"Ay," put in Phil Briant, who was amusing the

black children and greatly delighting himself by
nodding and smiling ferociously at them, with a
view to make a favourable impression on the natives
of this new country. "Ay, sir, an' sure we've
comed to land a sick shipmate who wants to see
the doctor uncommon. Have ye sich an article in
them parts?"

"No, not exactly," replied the trader, "but I
do a little in that way myself; perhaps I may
manage to cure him if he comes up to my house."

"We wants a nigger too," said Rokens, who,
while the others were talking, was extremely busy
filling his pipe.

At this remark the trader looked knowing.

"Oh!" he said, "that's your game, is it? There's
your man then; I've nothing to do with such
wares." He pointed to the Portuguese slave-dealer
as he spoke.

Seeing himself thus referred to, the slave-dealer
came forward, hat in hand, and made a polite bow.
He was a man of extremely forbidding aspect. A
long dark visage, which terminated in a black
peaked beard, and was surmounted by a tall
crowned broad-brimmed straw hat, stood on the
top of a long raw-boned, thin, sinewy, shrivelled but
powerful frame, that had battled with and defeated
all the fevers and other diseases peculiar to the
equatorial regions of Africa. He wore a short
light-coloured cotton jacket and pantaloons—the
latter much too short for his limbs, but the deficiency

was more than made up by a pair of Wellington
boots. His natural look was a scowl. His assumed
smile of politeness was so unnatural, that Tim
Rokens thought, as he gazed at him, he would have
preferred greatly to have been frowned at by him.
Even Ailie, who did not naturally think ill of any
one, shrank back as he approached and grasped
Glynn's hand more firmly than usual.

"Goot morning, gentl'm'n. You vas vish for
git nigger, I suppose."

"Well, we wos," replied Tim, with a faint touch
of sarcasm in his tone. "Can *you* get un for us?"

"Yees, sare, as many you please," replied the
slave-dealer, with a wink that an ogre might have
envied. "Have great many ob 'em stay vid me
always."

"Ah! then, they must be fond o' bad company,"
remarked Briant, in an undertone, "to live along
wid such a alligator."

"Well, then," said Tim Rokens, who had completed the filling of his pipe, and was now in the
full enjoyment of it; "let's see the feller, an' I'll
strike a bargain with him, if he seems a likely chap."

"You vill have strike de bargin vid *me*," said the
dealer. "I vill charge you ver' leetle, suppose you
take full cargo."

The whole party, who were ignorant of the man's
profession, started at this remark, and looked at
the dealer in surprise.

"Wot!" exclaimed Tim Rokens, withdrawing
his pipe from his lips; "do you *sell* niggers?"

" Yees, to be surely," replied the man, with a peculiarly saturnine smile.

" A slave-dealer?" exclaimed Briant, clenching his fists.

" Even so, sare."

At this Briant uttered a shout, and throwing forward his clenched fists in a defiant attitude, exclaimed between his set teeth,—

"Arrah ! come on !"

Most men have peculiarities. Phil Briant had many ; but his most striking peculiarity, and that which led him frequently into extremely awkward positions, was a firm belief that his special calling— in an amateur point of view—was the redressing of wrongs—not wrongs of a particular class, or wrongs of an excessively glaring and offensive nature, but *all* wrongs whatsoever. It mattered not to Phil whether the wrong had to be righted by force of argument or force of arms. He considered himself an accomplished practitioner in both lines of business—and in regard to the latter his estimate of his powers was not very much too high, for he was a broad-shouldered, deep-chested, long-armed fellow, and had acquired a scientific knowledge of boxing under a celebrated bruiser at the expense of a few hard-earned shillings, an occasional bottle of poteen, and many a severe thrashing.

Justice to Phil's amiability of character requires, however, that we should state that he never sought to terminate an argument with his fists unless he was invited to do so, and even then he invariably gave his rash challenger fair warning, and offered to let him retreat if so disposed. But when injustice met his eye, or when he happened to see cruelty practised by the strong against the weak, his blood fired at once, and he only deigned the short emphatic remark—" Come on," sometimes preceded by " Arrah !" sometimes not. Generally speaking, he accepted his own challenge, and *went* on forthwith.

Of all the iniquities that draw forth the groans of humanity on this sad earth, slavery, in the opinion of Phil Briant, was the worst. He had never come in contact with it, not having been in the Southern States of America. He knew from hearsay that the coast of Africa was its fountain, but he had forgotten the fact, and in the novelty of the scene before him, it did not at first occur to him that he was actually face to face with a " live slave-dealer."

" Let me go !" roared the Irishman, as he struggled in the iron gripe of Tim Rokens, and the not less powerful grasp of Glynn Proctor. " Och ! let me go ! *Doo*, darlints. I'll only give him wan— jist *wan !* Let me go, will ye ?"

" Not if I can help it," said Glynn, tightening his grasp.

" Wot a cross helephant it is," muttered Rokens, as he thrust his hand into his comrade's neckcloth and quietly began to choke him as he dragged him away towards the residence of the trader, who was an amused as well as surprised spectator of this unexpected ebullition of passion.

At length Phil Briant allowed himself to be forced away from the beach where the slave-dealer stood with his arms crossed on his breast, and a sarcastic smile playing on his thin lips. Had that Portuguese trafficker in human flesh known how quickly Briant could have doubled the size of his long nose and shut up both his eyes, he would probably have modified the expression of his countenance; but he didn't know it, so he looked after the party until they had entered the dwelling of the trader, and then sauntered up towards the woods, which in this place came down to within a few yards of the beach.

The settlement was a mere collection of rudely-constructed native huts, built of bamboos and roofed with a thatch of palm-leaves. In the midst of it stood a pretty white-painted cottage with green-edged windows and doors, and a verandah in front. This was the dwelling of the trader; and alongside of it, under the same roof, was the store, in which were kept the guns, beads, powder and shot, &c. &c., which he exchanged with the natives of the interior for elephants' tusks and bar-wood, from which latter a beautiful dye is obtained; also ebony, Indiarubber, and other products of the country.

Here the trader entertained Tim Rokens and Phil Briant with stories of the slave-trade · and

here we shall leave them while we follow Glynt
and Ailie, who went off together to ramble along
the shore of the calm sea.

They had not gone far when specimens of the
strange creatures that dwell in these lands presented themselves to their astonished gaze.  There
were birds innumerable on the shore, on the surface
of the ocean, and in the woods.  The air was alive
with them; many being similar to the birds they
had been familiar with from infancy, while others
were new and strange.

To her immense delight Ailie saw many living
specimens of the bird-of-paradise, the graceful
plumes of which she had frequently beheld on very
high and important festal occasions, nodding on the
heads of Aunt Martha and Aunt Jane.  But the
prettiest of all the birds she saw there was a small
creature with a breast so red and bright, that it
seemed, as it flew about, like a little ball of fire.
There were many of them flying about near a steep
bank, in holes of which they built their nests.  She
observed that they fed upon flies which they caught
while skimming through the air, and afterwards
learned that they were called bee-eaters.

" Oh ! look !" exclaimed Ailie, in that tone of
voice which indicated that a surprising discovery
had been made.  Ailie was impulsive, and the
*tones* in which she exclaimed " Oh !" were so
varied, emphatic, and distinct, that those who knew
her well could tell exactly the state of her mind on

hearing the exclamation. At present, her "Oh !" indicated surprise mingled with alarm.

"Eh ! what, where ?" cried Glynn, throwing forward his musket—for he had taken the precaution to carry one with him, not knowing what he might meet with on such a coast.

"The snake ! look—oh !"

At that moment a huge black snake, about ten feet long, showed itself in the grass. Glynn took aim at once, but the piece being an old flint-lock, missed fire. Before he could again take aim the loathsome-looking reptile had glided into the underwood, which in most places was so overgrown with the rank and gigantic vegetation of the tropics as to be quite impenetrable.

"Ha ! he's gone, Ailie !" cried Glynn, in a tone of disappointment, as he put fresh priming into the pan of his piece. "We must be careful in walking here it seems. This wretched old musket ! Lucky for us that our lives did not depend on it. I wonder if it was a poisonous serpent ?"

"Perhaps it was," said Ailie, with a look of deep solemnity, as she took her companion's left hand, and trotted along by his side. "Are not all serpents poisonous ?"

"Oh dear, no. Why, there are some kinds that are quite harmless. But as I don't know which are and which are not, we must look upon all as enemies until we become more knowing."

Presently they came to the mouth of a river—

one of those sluggish streams on the African coast, which suggest the idea of malaria and the whole family of low fevers. It glided through a mango swamp, where the trees seemed to be standing on their roots, which served the purpose of stilts to keep them out of the mud. The river was oily, and sluggish, and hot-looking, and its mud-banks were slimy and liquid, so that it was not easy to say whether the water of the river was mud, or the mud on the bank was water. It was a place that made one involuntarily think of creeping monsters, and crawling objects, and slimy things !

" Look ! oh ! oh ! such a darling pet !" exclaimed Ailie, as they stood near the banks of this river wondering what monster would first cleave the muddy waters, and raise its hideous head. She pointed to the bough of a dead tree near which they stood, and on which sat the " darling pet" referred to. It was a very small monkey with white whiskers ; a dumpy little thing, that looked at them with an expression of surprise quite equal in intensity to their own.

Seeing that it was discovered, the " darling pet" opened its little mouth, and uttered a succession of " Ohs !" that rendered Ailie's exclamations quite insignificant by comparison. They were sharp and short, and rapidly uttered, while, at the same time, two rows of most formidable teeth were bared, along with the gums that held them.

At this Ailie and her companion burst into a

ALICE DISCOVERS "SUCH A DARLING PET."—Page 110.

fit of irrepressible laughter, whereupon the "darling pet" put itself into such a passion—grinned,
and coughed, and gasped, and shook the tree, and
writhed, and glared, to such an extent, that Glynn
said he thought it would burst, and Ailie agreed
that it was very likely. Finding that this terrible
display of fury had no effect on the strangers, the
"darling pet" gave utterance to a farewell shriek
of passion, and, bounding nimbly into the woods,
disappeared.

"Oh, *what* a funny beast," said Ailie, sitting
down on a stone, and drying her eyes, which had
filled with tears, from excessive laughter.

"Indeed it was," said Glynn. "It's my opinion
that a monkey is the funniest beast in the world."

"No, Glynn; a kitten's funnier," said Ailie,
with a degree of emphasis that showed she had
considered the subject well, and had fully made up
her mind in regard to it long ago. "I think a
kitten's the *very* funniest beast in all the whole
world."

"Well, perhaps it is," said Glynn, thoughtfully.

"Did you ever see *three* kittens together?" asked
Ailie.

"No; I don't think I ever did. I doubt if I
have seen even two together. Why?"

"Oh! because they are so very, very funny. Sit
down beside me, and I'll tell you about three
kittens I once had. They were very little—at least
they were little before they got big."

Glynn laughed.

"Oh, you know what I mean. They were able to play when they were very little, you know."

"Yes, yes, I understand. Go on."

"Well, two were grey, and one was white and grey, but most of it was white; and when they went to play, one always hid itself to watch, and then the other two began, and came up to each other with little jumps, and their backs up and tails curved, and hair all on end, glaring at each other, and pretending that they were *so* angry. Do you know, Glynn, I really believe they sometimes forgot it was pretence, and actually became angry. But the fun was, that, when the two were just going to fly at each other, the third one, who had been watching, used to dart out and give them *such* a fright—a *real* fright, you know—which made them jump, oh! three times their own height up into the air, and they came down again with a *fuff* that put the third one in a fright too; so that they all scattered away from each other as if they had gone quite mad. What's that?"

"It's a fish, I think," said Glynn, rising and going towards the river to look at the object that had attracted his companion's attention. "It's a shark, I do believe."

In a few seconds the creature came so close that they could see it quite distinctly; and on a more careful inspection, they observed that the mouth of the river was full of these ravenous monsters.

Soon after they saw monsters of a still more ferocious aspect; for while they were watching the sharks, two crocodiles put up their snouts, and crawled sluggishly out of the water upon a mud-bank, where they lay down, apparently with the intention of taking a nap in the sunshine. They were too far off, however, to be well seen.

"Isn't it strange, Glynn, that there are such ugly beasts in the world," said Ailie. "I wonder why God made them?"

"So do I," said Glynn, looking at the child's thoughtful face in some surprise. "I suppose they must be of some sort of use."

"Oh! yes, *of course* they are," rejoined Ailie, quickly. "Aunt Martha and Aunt Jane used to tell me that every creature was made by God for some good purpose; and when I came to the crocodile in my book, they said it was certainly of use, too, though they did not know what. I remember it very well, because I was *so* surprised to hear that Aunt Martha and Aunt Jane did not know *everything*."

"No doubt Aunt Martha and Aunt Jane were right," said Glynn, with a smile. "I confess, however, that crocodiles seem to me to be of no other use than to kill and eat up everything that comes within the reach of their terrible jaws. But, indeed, now I think of it, the very same may be said of man, for *he* kills and eats up at least everything that he *wants* to put into his jaws."

I

"So he does," said Ailie; "isn't it funny?"

"Isn't what funny?" asked Glynn.

"That we should be no better than crocodiles—at least—I mean about eating."

"You forget, Ailie, we cook our food."

"Oh! so we do.    I did not remember to think of that.    That's a great difference, indeed."

Leaving Glynn and his little charge to philosophize on the resemblance between men and crocodiles, we shall now return to Tim Rokens and Phil Briant, whom we left in the trader's cottage.

The irate Irishman had been calmed down by reason and expostulation, and had again been roused to great indignation several times since we left him, by the account of things connected with the slave-trade given him by the trader, who, although he had no interest in it himself, did not feel very much aggrieved by the sufferings he witnessed around him.

"You don't mane to tell me, now, that *whalers* comes in here for slaves, do ye?" said Briant, placing his two fists on his two knees, and thrusting his head towards the trader, who admitted that he meant to say that; and that he meant, moreover, to add, that the thing was by no means of rare occurrence—that whaling ships occasionally ran into that very port on their way south, shipped a cargo of negroes, sold them at the nearest slave-buying port they could make on the American coast, and then proceeded on their voyage, no one being a whit the wiser.

"You don't mean it?" remarked Tim Rokens, crossing his legs and devoting himself to his pipe with the air of a man who mourned the depravity of his species, but did not feel called upon to disturb his equanimity very much because of it.

Phil Briant clenched his teeth, and glared.

"Indeed I do mean it," reiterated the trader. "Would you believe it, there was one whaler put in here, and what does he do but go and invite a lot o' free blacks aboard to have a blow-out; and no sooner did he get them down into the hold than he shut down the hatches, sailed away, and sold 'em every one."

"Ah! morther, couldn't I burst?" groaned Phil; "an' ov coorse they left a lot o' fatherless children and widders behind 'em."

"They did; but all the widows are married again, and most of the children are grown up."

Briant looked as if he did not feel quite sure whether he ought to regard this as a comforting piece of information or the reverse, and wisely remained silent.

"And now you must excuse me if I leave you to ramble about alone for some time, as I have business to transact; meanwhile I'll introduce you to a nigger who will show you about the place, and one who, if I mistake not, will gladly accompany you to sea as steward's assistant."

The trader opened a door which led to the back part of his premises, and shouted to a stout negro who was sawing wood there, and who came forward with alacrity.

" Ho ! Neepeelootambo, go take these gentlemen round about the village, and let them see all that is to be seen."

"Yes, massa."

" And they've got something to say to you about going to sea—would you like to go ?"

The negro grinned, and as his mouth was of the largest possible size, it. is not exaggeration to say that the grin extended from ear to ear, but he made no other reply.

" Well, please yourself. You're a free man—you may do as you choose."

Neepeelootambo, who was almost naked, having only a small piece of cloth wrapped round his waist and loins, grinned again, displaying a double row of teeth worthy of a shark in so doing, and led his new friends from the house.

" Now," said Tim Rokens, turning to the negro, and pointing along the shore, " we'll go along this way and jaw the matter over. Business fust, and pleasure, if ye' can get it, arterwards—them's my notions, Nip—Nip—Nippi—what's your name ?"

" Coo Tumble, I think," suggested Briant.

" Ay, Nippiloo Bumble—wot a jaw-breaker ! so git along, old boy."

The negro, who was by no means an " old boy,"

but a stalwart man in the prime of life, stepped out, and as they walked along, both Rokens and Briant did their best to persuade him to ship on board the Red Eric, but without success. They were somewhat surprised as well as chagrined, having been led to expect that the man would consent at once. But no alluring pictures of the delights of seafaring life, or the pleasures and excitements of the whale-fishery, had the least effect on their sable companion. Even sundry shrewd hints, thrown out by Phil Briant, that "the steward had always command o' the wittles, and that his assistant would only have to help himself when convanient," failed to move him.

"Well, Nippi-Boo-Tumble," cried Tim Rokens, who in his disappointment unceremoniously contracted his name, "it's my opinion—private opinion mark'ee—that you're a ass, an' you'll come for to repent of it."

"Troth, Nippi-Bumble, he's about right," added Briant, coaxingly. "Come now, avic, wot's the raisin ye wont go? Sure we ain't blackguards enough to ax ye to come for to be sold; it's all fair an' above board. Why wont ye, now?"

The negro stopped, and turning towards them, drew himself proudly up; then, as if a sudden thought had occurred to him, he advanced a step and held up his forefinger to impose silence.

"You no tell what I go to say? at least, not for one, two day."

" Niver a word, honour bright !" said Phil, in a
confidential tone, while Rokens expressed the same
sentiment by means of an emphatic wink and nod.

" You mus' know," said the negro, earnestly,
" me expec's to be made a king !"

" A wot ?" exclaimed both his companions in the
same breath, and very much in the same tone.

" A king."

" Wot!" said Rokens ; " d'ye mean a ruler of this
here country ?"

" Neepeelootambo nodded his head so violently
that it was a marvel it remained on his shoulders.

" Yis.  Ho ! ho ! ho ! 'xpec's to be a king."

" And when are ye to be crowned, Bumble ?"
inquired Briant, rather sceptically, as they resumed
their walk.

" Oh, me no say me *goin'* to be king ; me only
*'xpec's* dat."

" Werry good," returned Rokens; " but wot
makes ye for to expect it ?"

" Aha !    Me berry clebber fellow—know most
ebberyting.   Me hab doo'd good service to dis here
country.   Me can fight like one leopard, and me
hab kill great few elephant and gorilla.  Not much
mans here hab shoot de gorilla, him sich terriferick
beast ; 'bove five foot six tall, and bigger round de
breast dan you or me—dat is a great true fact.
Also, me can spok Englis'."

" An' so you expec's they're goin' to make you a
king for all that."

" Yis, dat is fat me 'xpec's, for our old king be

just dead ; but dey nebber tell who dey going to make king till dey do it. I not more sure ob it dan the nigger dat walk dare before you."

Neepeelootambo pointed as he spoke to a negro who certainly had a more kingly aspect than any native they had yet seen. He was a perfect giant, considerably above six feet high, and broad in proportion. He wore no clothing on the upper part of his person, but his legs were encased in a pair of old canvas trousers, which had been made for a man of ordinary stature, so that his huge bony ankles were largely exposed to view.

Just as Phil and Rokens stopped to take a good look at him before passing on, a terrific yell issued from the bushes, and instantly after, a negro ran towards the black giant and administered to him a severe kick on the thigh, following it up with a cuff on the side of the head, at the same time howling something in the native tongue, which our friends of course did not understand. This man was immediately followed by three other blacks, one of whom pulled the giant's hair, the other pulled his nose, and the third spat in his face !

It is needless to remark that the sailors witnessed this unprovoked assault with unutterable amazement. But the most remarkable part of it was, that the fellow, instead of knocking all his assailants down, as he might have done without much trouble, quietly submitted to the indignities heaped upon him ; nay, he even smiled upon his tormentors, who increased in numbers every minute, running out from among the bushes and surrounding the unoffending man, and uttering wild shouts as they maltreated him.

"Wot's he bin doin'?" inquired Rokens, turning to his black companion. But Rokens received no answer, for Neepeelootambo was looking on at the scene with an expression so utterly wobegone and miserable that one would imagine he was himself suffering the rough usage he witnessed.

"Arrah! ye don't appear to be chairful," said Briant, laughing, as he looked in the negro's face. "This is a quare counthrie, an' no mistake; it seems to be always blowin' a gale o' surprises. Wot's wrong wid ye, Bumble?"

The negro groaned.

"Sure that may be a civil answer, but it's not o' much use. Hallo! what air they doin' wid the poor cratur now?"

As he spoke the crowd seized the black giant by the arms and neck and hair, and dragged him away towards the village, leaving our friends in solitude.

"A very purty little scene," remarked Phil Briant, when they were out of sight; "very purty, indade, av we only knowed wot it's all about."

If the surprise of the two sailors was great at what they had just witnessed, it was increased tenfold by the subsequent behaviour of their negro companion.

That eccentric individual suddenly checked his

groans, gave vent to a long deep sigh, and assuming a resigned expression of countenance, rose up and said,

"Ho! It all ober now, massa."

"I do believe," remarked Rokens, looking gravely at his shipmate, "that the feller's had an attack o the mollygrumbles, an's got better all of a suddint.'

"No, massa, dat not it. But me willin' to go wid you now to de sea."

"Eh! willin' to go? Why, Nippi-too-cumble, wot a rum customer you are, to be sure!"

"Yis, massa," rejoined the negro. "Me not goin' to be king now, anyhow; so it ob no use stoppin' here. Me go to sea."

"Not goin' to be king? How d'ye know that?"

"'Cause dat oder nigger, him be made king in a berry short time. You mus' know, dat w'en dey make wan king in dis here place, de peeple choose de man; but dey not let him know. He may guess if him please—like me—but p'raps him guess wrong—like me! Ho! ho! Den arter dey fix on de man, dey run at him and kick him, as you hab seen dem do, and spit on him, and trow mud ober him, tellin' him all de time, 'You no king yet, you black rascal; you soon be king, and den you may put your foots on our necks and do w'at you like, but not yit: take dat, you teif!' An' so dey 'buse him for a littel time. Den dey take him straight away to de palace and crown him, an', oh! arter dat dey become very purlite to him. Him

know dat well 'nuff, and so him not be angry just
now. Ah! me did 'xpec' to hab bin kick and
spitted on dis berry day!"

Poor Neepeelootambo uttered the last words in
such a deeply touching tone, and seemed to be so
much cast down at the thought that his chance of
being "kicked and spitted upon" had passed away
for ever, that Phil Briant burst into a hearty fit of
laughter, and Tim Rokens exhibited symptoms of
internal risibility, though his outward physiognomy
remained unchanged.

"Och! Bumble, you'll be the death o' me,"
cried Briant. "An' are they a-crownin' of him now?"

"Yis, massa. Dat what dey go for to do jist
now."

"Troth, then, I'll go an' inspict the coronation.
Come along, Bumble, me darlint, and show us the
way."

In a few minutes Neepeelootamlo conducted his
new friends into a large rudely-constructed hut,
which was open on three sides and thatched with
palm-leaves. This was the palace before referred
to by him. Here they found a large concourse of
negroes, whose main object at that time seemed to
be the creation of noise; for besides yelling and
hooting, they beat a variety of native drums, some
of which consisted of bits of board, and others of
old tin and copper kettles. Forcing their way
through the noisy throng they reached the inside
of the hut, into which they found that Ailie Dun-

ning and Glynn Proctor had pushed their way
before them. Giving them a nod of recognition,
they sat down on a mat by their side to watch the
proceedings, which by this time were nearly concluded.

The new king—who was about to fill the throne
rendered vacant by the recent death of the old
king of that region—was seated on an elevated
stool looking very dignified, despite the rough
ordeal through which he had just passed. When
the noise above referred to had calmed down, an
old grey-headed negro rose and made a speech in
the language of the country, after which he advanced
and crowned the new king, who had already been
invested in a long scarlet coat covered with tarnished
gold-lace, and cut in the form peculiar to the last
century. The crown consisted of an ordinary
black-silk hat, considerably the worse for wear.
It looked familiar and common-place enough in
the eyes of their white visitors; but, being the
only specimen of the article in the district, it was regarded by the negroes with peculiar admiration, and
deemed worthy to decorate the brows of royalty.

Having had this novel crown placed on the top
of his woolly pate, which was much too large for it,
the new king hit it an emphatic blow on the top,
partly with a view to force it on, and partly, no
doubt, with the design of impressing his new subjects with the fact that he was now their rightful
sovereign, and that he meant thenceforth to exercise

all the authority, and avail himself of all the privileges that his high position conferred on him. He then rose and made a pretty long speech, which was frequently applauded, and which terminated amid a most uproarious demonstration of loyalty on he part of the people.

If you wish to gladden the heart of a black man, reader, get him into the midst of an appalling noise. The negro's delight is to shout, and laugh, and yell, and beat tin kettles with iron spoons. The greater the noise, the more he enjoys himself. Great guns and musketry, gongs and brass bands, kettledrums and smashing crockery, crashing railway-engines blending their utmost whistles with the shrieks of a thousand pigs being killed, all going at once, full blast, and as near to him as possible, is a species of Elysium to the sable son of Africa. On their occasions of rejoicing, negroes procure and produce as much noise as is possible, so that the white visitors were soon glad to seek shelter, and find relief to their ears, on board ship.

But even there the sounds of rejoicing reached them, and long after the curtain of night had enshrouded land and sea, the hideous din of royal festivities came swelling out with the soft warm breeze that fanned Ailie's cheek as she stood on the quarter-deck of the Red Eric, watching the wild antics of the naked savages as they danced round their bright fires, and holding her father's hand tightly as she related the day's adventures, and told

of the monkeys, crocodiles, and other strange
creatures she had seen in the mangrove-swamps
and on the mud-banks of the slimy river.

***

## CHAPTER X.

AN INLAND JOURNEY—SLEEPING IN THE WOODS—WILD
BEASTS EVERYWHERE—SAD FATE OF A GAZELLE.

THE damage sustained by the Red Eric during
the storm was found to be more severe than was
at first supposed. Part of her false keel had been
torn away by a sunken rock, over which the vessel
had passed, and scraped so lightly that no one on
board was aware of the fact, yet with sufficient
force to cause the damage to which we have referred. A slight leak was also discovered, and the
injury to the top of the foremast was neither so
easily nor so quickly repaired as had been anticipated.

It thus happened that the vessel was detained
on this part of the African coast for nearly a couple
of weeks, during which time Ailie had frequent
opportunities of going on shore, sometimes in charge
of Glynn, sometimes with Tim Rokens, and occasionally with her father.

During these little excursions the child lived in
a world of romance. Not only were the animals,
and plants, and objects of every kind with which
she came in contact, entirely new to her, except in
so far as she had made their acquaintance in

pictures, but she invested everything in the roseate
hue peculiar to her own romantic mind. True,
she saw many things that caused her a good deal
of pain, and she heard a few stories about the
terrible cruelty of the negroes to each other, which
made her shudder, but unpleasant thoughts did
not dwell long on her mind; she soon forgot the
little annoyances or frights she experienced, and
revelled in the enjoyment of the beautiful sights
and sweet perfumes which more than counter-
balanced the bad odours and ugly things that came
across her path.

Ailie's mind was a very inquiring one, and often
and long did she ponder the things she saw, and
wonder why God made some so very ugly and some
so very pretty, and to what use He intended them
to be put. Of course, in such speculative inquiries,
she was frequently very much puzzled, as also were
the companions to whom she propounded the
questions from time to time; but she had been
trained to *believe* that everything that was made
by God was good, whether she understood it or not;
and she noticed particularly, and made an involuntary memorandum of the fact in her own mind,
that ugly things were very few in number, while
beautiful objects were absolutely innumerable.

The trader, who rendered good assistance to
Captain Dunning in the repair of his ship,
frequently overheard Ailie wishing "so much"
that she might be allowed to go far into the wil

woods, and one day suggested to the captain that, as the ship would have to remain a week or more in port, he would be glad to take a party an excursion up the river in his canoe, and show them a little of forest life, saying at the same time that the little girl might go too, for they were not likely to encounter any danger which might not be easily guarded against.

At first the captain shook his head, remembering the stories that were afloat regarding the wild beasts of those regions. But, on second thoughts, he agreed to allow a well-armed party to accompany the trader ; the more so that he was urged thereto very strongly by Dr. Hopley, who being a naturalist, was anxious to procure specimens of the creatures and plants in the interior, and being a phrenologist, was desirous of examining what Glynn termed the " bumpological developments of the negro skull."

On still further considering the matter, Captain Dunning determined to leave the first mate in charge of the ship, head the exploring party him-self, and take Ailie along with him.

To say that Ailie was delighted, would be to understate the fact very much. She was wild with joy, and went about all the day, after her father's decision was announced, making every species of insane preparation for the canoe voyage, clasping her hands, and exclaiming, " Oh ! *what* fun !" while her bright eyes sparkled to such an extent that the sailors fairly laughed in her face when they looked at her.

Preparations were soon made. The party consisted of the captain and his little child, Glynn Proctor (of course), Dr. Hopley, Tim Rokens, Phil Briant, Jim Scroggles, the trader, and Neepeelootambo, which last had been by that time regularly domesticated on board, and was now known by the name of King Bumble, which name, being as good as his own, and more pronounceable, we shall adopt from this time forward.

The very morning after the proposal was made, the above party embarked in the trader's canoe ; and plying their paddles with the energy of men bent on what is vulgarly termed "going the whole hog," they quickly found themselves out of sight of their natural element, the ocean, and surrounded by the wild rich luxuriant vegetation of equatorial Africa.

"Now," remarked Tim Rokens, as they ceased paddling, and ran the canoe under the shade of a broad palm-tree that overhung the river, in order to take a short rest and a smoke after a steady paddle of some miles—"Now this is wot I calls glorious, so it is ! Ain't it ? Pass the 'baccy this way."

This double remark was made to King Bumble, who passed the tobacco-pouch to his friend, after helping himself, and admitted that it was "mugnifercent."

"Here have I bin a sittin' in this here canoe,"
continued Rokens, "for more nor two hours, an',
to my sartin knowledge I've seed with my two
eyes twelve sharks (for I counted 'em every one)
at the mouth of the river, and two crocodiles, and
the snout of a hopplepittimus; is that wot ye
calls it ?"

Rokens addressed his question to the captain,
but Phil Briant, who had just succeeded in getting
his pipe to draw beautifully, answered instead.

"Och! no," said he; "that's not the way to pur-
nounce it at all, at all. It's a huppi-puppi-
puttimus."

"I dun know," said Rokens, shaking his head
gravely; "it appears to me there's too many
huppi-puppies in that word."

This debate caused Ailie infinite amusement,
for she experienced considerable difficulty herself
in pronouncing that name, and had a very truthful
picture of the hippopotamus hanging at that
moment in her room at home.

"Isn't Tim Rokens very funny, papa ?" she remarked in a whisper, looking up in her father's face.

"Hush! my pet, and look yonder. There is
something funnier, if I mistake not."

He pointed, as he spoke, to a ripple in the
water on the opposite side of the river, close under
a bank which was clothed with rank, broad-leaved,
and sedgy vegetation. In a few seconds a large
crocodile put up its head, not farther off than

K

twenty yards from the canoe, which apparently it did not see, and, opening its tremendous jaws, afforded the travellers a splendid view of its teeth and throat. Briant afterwards asserted that he could see down its throat, and could *almost* tell what it had had for dinner!

"Plaze, sir, may I shot him?" cried Briant, seizing his loaded musket, and looking towards the captain for permission.

"It's of no use while in that position," remarked the trader, who regarded the hideous-looking monster with the calm unconcern of a man accustomed to such sights.

"You may try," said the captain with a grin. Almost before the words had left his lips, Phil took a rapid aim and fired. At the same identical moment the crocodile shut his jaws with a snap, as if he had an intuitive perception that something uneatable was coming. The bullet consequently hit his forehead, off which it glanced as if it had struck a plate of cast iron. The reptile gave a wabble, expressive of lazy surprise, and sank slowly back into the slimy water.

The shot startled more than one huge creature, for immediately afterwards they heard several flops in the water near them, but the tall sedges prevented their seeing what animals they were. A whole troop of monkeys, too, went shrieking away into the woods, showing that those nimble creatures had been watching all their movements

although, until that moment, they had taken good
care to keep themselves out of sight.

"Never fire at a crocodile's head," said the
trader, as the party resumed their paddles, and
continued their ascent of the stream ; "you might
as well fire at a stone wall. It's as hard as iron.
The only place that's sure to kill is just behind
the fore-leg. The niggers always spear them
there."

"What do they spear them for?" asked Dr.
Hopley.

"They eat 'em," replied the trader ; "and the
meat's not so bad after you get used to it."

"Ha!" exclaimed Glynn Proctor; "I should
fancy the great difficulty is to get used to it."

"If you ever chance to go for a week without
tasting fresh meat," replied the trader, quietly,
"you'll not find it so difficult as you think."

That night the travellers encamped in the woods,
and a wild charmingly romantic scene their night
bivouac was—so thought Ailie, and so, too, would
you have thought, reader, had you been there.
King Bumble managed to kindle three enormous
fires, for the triple purpose of keeping the party
warm—for it was cold at night—of scaring away
wild beasts, and of cooking their supper. These
fires he fed at intervals during the whole night
with huge logs, and the way in which he made the
sparks fly up in among the strange big leaves of
the tropical trees and parasitical plants overhead,

was quite equal, if not superior, to a display of regular fireworks.

Then Bumble and Glynn built a little platform of logs, on which they strewed leaves and grass, and over which they spread a curtain or canopy of broad leaves and boughs.   This was Ailie's couch. It stood in the full blaze of the centre fire, and com-manded a view of all that was going on in every part of the little camp ; and when Ailie lay down on it, after a good supper, and was covered up with a blanket, and further covered over with a sort of gauze netting to protect her from the mosquitoes, which were very numerous,—when all this was done, we say, and when, in addition to this, she lay and witnessed the jovial laughter and enjoy-ment of His Majesty King Bumble, as he sat at the big fire smoking his pipe, and the supreme happiness of Phil Briant, and the placid joy of Tim Rokens, and the exuberant delight of Glynn, and the semi-scientific enjoyment of Dr. Hopley as he examined a collection of rare plants ; and the quiet comfort of the trader, and the awkward, shambling, loose-jointed pleasure of long Jim Scroggles ; and the beaming felicity of her own dear father, who sat not far from her, and turned occasionally in the midst of the conversation to give her a nod—she felt in her heart that then and there she had fairly reached the very happiest moment in all her life.

Ailie gazed in dreamy delight until she suddenly and unaccountably saw at least six fires, and fully half a dozen Bumbles, and eight or nine Glynns, and no end of fathers, and thousands of trees, and millions of sparks, all jumbled together in one vast complicated and magnificent pyrotechnic display; and then—she fell asleep.

It is a curious fact, and one for which it is not easy to account, that however happy you may be when you go to sleep out in the wild woods, you invariably awake in the morning in possession of a very small amount of happiness indeed. Probably, it is because one in such circumstances is usually called upon to turn out before he has had enough sleep; perhaps it may be that the fires have burned low or gone out altogether, and the gloom of a forest before sunrise is not calculated to elevate the spirits. Be this as it may, it is a fact that when Ailie was awakened on the following morning about daybreak, and told to get up, she felt sulky—positively and unmistakeably sulky!

We do not say that she looked sulky or acted sulkily—far from it; but she felt sulky, and that was a very uncomfortable state of things. We dwell a little on this point because we do not wish to mislead our young readers into the belief that life in the wild woods is *all* delightful together. There are shadows as well as lights there—some of them, alas! so deep that we would not like even to refer to them while writing in a sportive vein.

But it is also a fact, that when Ailie was fairly up and once more in the canoe, and when the sun began to flood the landscape with his golden light and turn the water into liquid fire, her temporary feelings of discomfort passed away, and her sensation of intense enjoyment returned.

The scenery through which they passed on the second day was somewhat varied. They emerged early in the day upon the bosom of a large lake which looked almost like the ocean. Here there were immense flocks of waterfowl, and among them that strange ungainly bird, the pelican. Here, too, there were actually hundreds of crocodiles. The lake was full of little mud islands, and on all of them these hideous and gigantic reptiles were seen basking lazily in the sun.

Several shots were fired at them, but although the balls hit, they did not penetrate their thick hides, until at last one took effect in the soft part close behind the fore leg. The shot was fired by the trader, and it killed the animal instantly. It could not have been less than twenty feet long, but before they could secure it the carcase sank in deep water.

"What a pity!" remarked Glynn, as the eddies circled round the spot where it had gone down.

"Ah, so it is!" replied the doctor; "but he would have been rather large to preserve and carry home as a specimen."

"I ax yer parding, sir," said Tim Rokens, ad-dressing Dr. Hopley; "but I'm curious to know if crocodiles has got phrenoligy?"

"No doubt of it," replied the doctor, laughing. "Crocodiles have brains, and brains when exercised must be enlarged and developed, especially in the organs that are most used, hence corresponding development must take place in the skull."

"I should think, doctor," remarked the captain, who was somewhat sceptical, "that their bumps of combativeness must be very large."

"Probably they are," continued the doctor: "something like my friend Phil Briant here. I would venture to guess, now, that his organ of combativeness is well developed—let me see."

The doctor, who sat close beside the Irishman, caused him to pull in his paddle and submit his head for inspection.

"Ah! then, don't operate on me, doctor dear! I've a mortial fear o' operations iver since me owld grandmother's pig got its fore-leg took off at the hip-jint."

"Hold your tongue, Paddy. Now the bump lies here—just under—eh! why, you haven't got so much as—what!"

"Plaze, I think it's lost in fat, sur," remarked Briant, in a plaintive tone, as if he expected to be reprimanded for not having brought his bump of combativeness along with him.

"Well," resumed the doctor, passing his fingers through Briant's matted locks, "I suppose you're not so combative as we had fancied——"

"Thrue for ye," interrupted Phil.

"But, strange enough, I find your organ of veneration is very large, *very* large, indeed; singularly so for a man of your character; but I cannot feel it easily, you have such a quantity of hair."

"Which is it, doctor dear ?" inquired Phil.

"This one I am pressing now."

"Arrah ! don't press so hard, plaze, it's hurtin' me ye are. Shure that's the place where I run me head slap up agin the spanker-boom four days ago. Av *that's* me bump o' vineration, it wos three times as big an' twice as hard yesterday—it wos, indade."

Interruptions in this world of uncertainty are not uncommon, and in the African wilds they are peculiarly frequent. The interruption which occurred on the present occasion to Dr. Hopley's reply was, we need scarcely remark, exceedingly opportune. It came in the form of a hippopotamus, which rose so close to the boat that Ailie got a severe start, and Tim Rokens made a blow at its head with his paddle. It did not seem to notice the boat, but after blowing a quantity of water from its nostrils, and opening its horrible mouth as if it were yawning, it slowly sank again into the flood.

"Wot an 'orrible crittur !" exclaimed Jim Scroggles, in amazement at the sight.

"The howdacious willain !" remarked Rokens.

"Is that another on ahead ?" said Glynn, pointing to an object floating on the water about a hundred yards up the river ; for they had passed the

THE CONCEALED ENEMY.—Page 137.

lake, and were now ascending another stream. " D'ye see it, Ailie ?   Look !"

The object sank as he spoke, and Ailie looked round just in time to see the tail of a crocodile flop the water and follow its owner to the depths below.

"Oh ! oh !" exclaimed Ailie, with one of those peculiar intonations that told Glynn she saw something very beautiful, and that induced the re-mainder of the crew to rest on their paddles, and turn their eyes in the direction indicated.

They did not require to ask what she saw, for the child's finger directed their eyes to a spot on the bank of the river, where, under the shadow of a spreading bush with gigantic leaves, stood a lovely little gazelle.   The graceful creature had trotted down to the stream to drink, and did not observe the canoe which had been on the point of round-ing a bank that jutted out into the river where its progress was checked.   The gazelle paused a mo-ment, looked round to satisfy itself that no enemy was near, and then put its lips to the water.

Alas ! for the timid little thing !   There were enemies near it and round it in all directions. There were leopards and serpents of the largest size in the woods, and man upon the river,—al-though on this occasion it chanced that most of the men who gazed in admiration at its pretty form were friends.   But its worst enemy, a crocodile, was lurking close under the mud-bank at its feet.

Scarcely had its parched lips reached the stream

when a black snout darted from the water, and the next instant the gazelle was struggling in the crocodile's jaws. A cry of horror burst from the men in the boat, and every man seized a musket; but before an aim could be taken the struggle was over; the monster had dived with its prey, and nothing but a few streaks of red foam floated on the troubled water.

Ailie did not move. She stood with her hands tightly clasped and her eyes starting almost out of their sockets. At last her feelings found vent. She threw her arms round her father's neck, and burying her face in his bosom, burst into a passionate flood of tears.

----

## CHAPTER XI.

NATIVE DOINGS, AND A CRUEL MURDER—JIM SCROGGLES
SEES WONDERS, AND HAS A TERRIBLE ADVENTURE.

IT took two whole days and nights to restore Ailie to her wonted cheerful state of mind, after she had witnessed the death of the gazelle. But although she sang and laughed, and enjoyed herself as much as ever, she experienced the presence of a new and strange feeling, that, ever after that day, tinged her thoughts and influenced her words and actions.

The child had for the first time in her life experienced one of those rude shocks—one of those rough contacts with the stern realities of life which tend to deepen and intensify our feelings. The mind does not always grow by slow, imperceptible degrees, although it usually does so.  There are periods in the career of every one when the mind takes, as it were, a sharp run and makes a sudden and stupendous jump out of one region of thought into another in which there are things new as well as old.

The present was such an occasion to little Ailie Dunning.  She had indeed seen bloody work before, in the cutting up of a whale.  But although she had been told it often enough, she did not *realize* that whales have feelings and affections like other creatures.  Besides, she had not witnessed the actual killing of the whale; and if she had, it would probably have made little impression on her beyond that of temporary excitement—not even that, perhaps, had her father been by her side.  But she *sympathized* with the gazelle.  It was small, and beautiful, and loveable.  Her heart had swelled the moment she saw it, and she had felt a longing desire to run up to it and throw her arms round its soft neck, so that, when she saw it suddenly struggling and crushed in the tremendous jaws of the horrible crocodile, every tender feeling in her breast was lacerated; every fibre of her heart trembled with a conflicting gush of the tenderest pity and the fiercest rage.  From that day forward new thoughts began to occupy her mind, and old ideas presented themselves in different aspects.

We would not have the reader suppose, for a

moment, that Ailie became an utterly changed creature. To an unobservant eye—such as that of Jim Scroggles, for instance—she was the same in all respects a few days after as she had been a few hours before the event. But new elements had been implanted in her breast, or rather, seeds which had hitherto lain dormant were now caused to burst forth into plants by the all-wise Author of her being. She now *felt* for the first time—she could not tell why—that enjoyment was *not* the chief good in life.

Of course she did not argue or think out all this clearly and methodically to herself. Her mind, on most things, material as well as immaterial, was very much what may be termed a jumble; but undoubtedly the above processes of reasoning and feeling, or something like them, were the result to Ailie of the violent death of that little gazelle.

The very next day after this sad event the travellers came to a native village, at which they stayed a night, in order to rest and procure fresh provisions. The trader was well known at this village, but the natives, all of whom were black, of course, and nearly naked, had never seen a little white girl before, so that their interest in and wonder at Ailie were quite amusing to witness. They crowded round her, laughing and exclaiming and gesticulating in a most remarkable manner, and taking special notice of her light-brown glossy

hair, which seemed to fill them with unbounded
astonishment and admiration ; as well it might, for
they had never before seen any other hair except
the coarse curly wool on their own pates, and the
long lank hair of the trader, which happened to be
coarse and black.

The child was at first annoyed by the attentions
paid her, but at last she became interested in the
sooty little naked children that thronged round her,
and allowed them to handle her as much as they
pleased, until her father led her to the residence of
the chief or king of the tribe. Here she was well
treated, and she began quite to like the people
who were so kind to her and her friends. But she
chanced to overhear a conversation between the
doctor and Tim Rokens, which caused her afterwards to shrink from the negroes with horror.

She was sitting on a bank picking wild flowers
some hours after the arrival of her party, and teach-
ing several black children how to make necklaces
of them, when the doctor and Rokens happened to
sit down together at the other side of a bush which
concealed her from their view. Tim was evidently
excited, for the tones of his voice were loud and
emphatic.

"Yes," he said, in reply to some question put to
him by the doctor ; "yes, I seed 'em do it, not ten
minutes agone, with my own two eyes. Oh ! but
I would like to have 'em up in a row—every black
villain in the place—an' a cutlass in my hand, an'

—an' wouldn't I whip off their heads? No, I
wouldn't; oh, no, by ᴀo means wotiver."

There was something unusually fierce in Rokens'
voice that alarmed Ailie.

"I wos jist takin' a turn," continued the sailor,
"down by the creek yonder, when I heerd a great
yellin' goin' on, and saw the trader iᴀ the middle
of a crowd o' black-fellows, a-shakin' his fists; so I
made sail, of course, to lend a hand if he'd got into
trouble. He was scoldin' away in the native lingo,
as if he'd bin a born nigger.

" ' Wot's all to do?' says I.

" ' They're goin' to kill a little boy,' says he, quite
fierce like, ''cause they took it into their heads he's
betwitched.'

"An' sayin' that, he sot to agin in the other
lingo, but the king came up an' told him that the
boy had to be killed 'cause he had a devil in him,
and had gone and betwitched a number o' other
people; an' before he had done speakin', up comes
two fellers, draggin' the poor little boy between
them. The king axed him if he wos betwitched,
and the little chap—from sheer fright, I do believe
—said he wos. Of coorse I couldn't understand 'em,
but the trader explained it all arter. Well, no
sooner had he said that, than they all gave a yell,
and rushed upon the poor boy with their knives,
and cut him to pieces. It's as sure as I'm sittin'
here," cried Rokens, savagely, as his wrath rose
again at the bare recital of the terrible deed he had

witnessed. "I would ha' knocked out the king's brains there and then, but the trader caught my hand, and said, in a great fright, that if I did, it would not only cost me my life, but likely the whole party ; so that cooled me, and I come away ; an' I'm goin' to ax the captin wot we shud do."

"We can do nothing," said the doctor, sadly. "Even suppose we were strong enough to punish them, what good would it do ? We can't change their natures. They are superstitious, and are firmly persuaded they did right in killing that poor boy."

The doctor pondered for a few seconds, and then added, in a low voice, as if he were weighing the meaning of what he said. "Clergymen would tell us that nothing can deliver them from this bondage save a knowledge of the true God and of His Son Jesus Christ ; that the Bible might be the means of curing them, if Bibles were only sent, and ministers to preach the gospel."

"Then why ain't Bibles sent to 'em at once?" asked Rokens, in a tone of great indignation, supposing that the doctor was expressing his own opinion on the subject. "Is there nobody to look-arter these matters in Christian lands ?"

"Oh, yes, there are many Bible Societies, and both Bibles and missionaries have been sent to this country ; but it's a large one, and the societies tell us that their funds are limited."

"Then why don't they git more funds ?" con-

tinued Rokens, in the same indignant tone, as his
mind still dwelt upon the miseries and wickedness
that he had seen, and that *might* be prevented ;
"why don't they git more funds, and send out
heaps o' Bibles, an' no end o' missionaries ?"

"Tim Rokens," said the doctor, looking earnestly
into his companion's face, "if I were one of the
missionaries, I might ask you how much money
*you* ever gave to enable societies to send Bibles
and missionaries to foreign lands ?"

Tim Rokens was for once in his life completely
taken aback. He was by nature a stolid man, and
not easily put out. He was a shrewd man, too,
and did not often commit himself. When he did,
he was wont to laugh at himself, and so neutralize
the laugh raised against him. But here was a
question that was too serious for laughter, and yet
one which he could not answer without being self-
condemned. He looked gravely in the doctor's
face for two minutes without speaking ; then he
heaved a deep sigh, and said slowly, and with a
pause between each word :

"Doctor Hopley—I—never—gave—a rap—in
—all—my—life."

"So, then, my man," said the doctor, smiling,
"you're scarcely entitled to be indignant with
others."

"Wot you remark, doctor, is true; I—am—not."

Having thus fully and emphatically condemned
himself, and along with himself all mankind who
are in a similar category, Tim Rokens relapsed

into silence, deliberately drew forth his pipe, filled it, lit it, and began to smoke.

None of the party of travellers slept well that night, except perhaps the trader, who was accustomed to the ways of the negroes, and King Bumble, who had been born and bred in the midst of cruelty. Most of them dreamed of savage orgies, and massacres of innocent children, so that when daybreak summoned them to resume their journey, they arose and embarked with alacrity, glad to get away from the spot.

During that day and the next they saw a great number of crocodiles and hippopotami, besides strange birds and plants innumerable. The doctor filled his botanical-box to bursting. Ailie filled her flower-basket to overflowing. Glynn hit a crocodile on the back with a bullet, and received a lazy stare from the ugly creature in return, as it waddled slowly down the bank on which it had been lying, and plumped into the river. The captain assisted Ailie to pluck flowers when they landed, which they did from time to time, and helped to arrange and pack them when they returned to the canoe. Tim Rokens did nothing particularly worthy of record; but he gave utterance to an immense number of sententious and wise remarks, which were listened to by Bumble with deep respect, for that sable gentleman had taken a great fancy for the bold harpooneer, and treasured up all his sayings in his heart.

Phil Briant distinguished himself by shooting an immense serpent, which the doctor, who cut off and retained its head, pronounced to be an anaconda. It was full twenty feet long, and part of the body was cut up, roasted, and eaten by Bumble and the trader, though the others turned from it with loathing.

"It be more cleaner dan one pig, anyhow," remarked Bumble, on observing the disgust of his white friends ; "an' you no objic' to eat dat."

"Clainer than a pig, ye spalpeen !" cried Phil Briant; "that only shows yer benighted haithen ignerance. Sure I lived in the same cabin wid a pig for many a year—not to mintion a large family o' cocks and hens—an' a clainer baste than that pig didn't stop in that cabin."

"That doesn't say much for your own cleanliness, or that of your family," remarked Glynn.

"Och ! ye've bin to school, no doubt, haven't ye ?" retorted Phil.

"I have," replied Glynn.

"Shure I thought so. It's there ye must have larned to be so oncommon cliver. Don't you iver be persuaded for to go to school, Bumble, if ye iver git the chance. It's a mighty lot o' taichin' they'd give ye, but niver a taste o' edication. Tin to wan, they'd cram ye till ye turned white i' the face, an' that wouldn't suit yer complexion, ye know, King Bumble, be no manes."

As for the trader, he acted interpreter when the

party fell in with negroes, and explained everything that puzzled them, and told them anecdotes without end about the natives and the wild creatures, and the traffic of the regions through which they passed. In short, he made himself generally useful and agreeable.

But the man who distinguished himself most on that trip was Jim Scroggles. That lanky individual one day took it into his wise head to go off on a short ramble into the woods alone. He had been warned by the trader, along with the rest of the party, not to venture on such a dangerous thing; but being an absent man, the warning had not reached his intellect although it had fallen on his ear. The party were on shore cooking dinner when he went off, without arms of any kind, and without telling whither he was bound. Indeed, he had no defined intentions in his own mind. He merely felt inclined for a ramble, and so went away, intending to be back in half an hour or less.

But Jim Scroggles had long legs and loved locomotion. Moreover, the woods were exceedingly beautiful and fragrant, and comparatively cool: for it happened to be the coolest season of the year in that sultry region, else the party of Europeans could not have ventured to travel there at all.

Wandering along beneath the shade of palm-trees and large-leaved shrubs and other tropical productions, with his hands in his breeches pockets, and whistling a variety of popular airs, which must have

not a little astonished the monkeys and birds and
other creatures—such of them, at least, as had any
taste for or knowledge of music—Jim Scroggles
penetrated much farther into the wilds than he had
any intention of doing.   There is no saying how
far, in his absence of mind, he might have wandered,
had he not been caught and very uncomfortably
entangled in a mesh-work of wild vines and thorny
plants that barred his further progress.

Jim had encountered several such before in his
walk, but had forced his way through without more
serious damage than a rent or two in his shirt and
pantaloons, and several severe scratches to his hands
and face ; but Scroggles had lived a hard life from
infancy, and did not mind scratches.   Now, however,
he could not advance a step, and it was only by
much patient labour and by the free use of his
clasp-knife, that he succeeded at length in releasing
himself.   He left a large portion of one of the legs
of his trousers and several bits of skin on the
bushes, as a memorial of his visit to that spot.

Jim's mind was awoke to the perception of three
facts—namely, that he had made himself late for
dinner ; that he would be the means of detaining
his party ; and that he had lost himself.

Here was a pretty business !   Being a man of
slow thought and much deliberation, he sat down
on the trunk of a fallen tree and looking up, as
men usually do when soliloquizing, exclaimed,

"My eye, here's a go !   Wot is to be done ?"

A very small monkey, with an uncommonly wriukled and melancholy cast of visage, which chanced to be seated on a branch hard by, peering down at the lost mariner, replied,

" O ! o-o-o, O ! o—o !" as much as to say, " Ah ! my boy, that's just the question."

Jim Scroggles shook his head, partly as a rebuke to the impertinent little monkey and partly as an indication of the hopelessness of his being able to return a satisfactory answer to his own question.

At last he started up, exclaiming, " Wotever comes on it, there's no use o' sitting here," and walked straight forward at a brisk pace. Then he suddenly stopped, shook his head again, and said, " If I goes on like this, an' it shud turn out to be the wrong course arter all—wot'll come on't ?"

Being as unable to answer this question as the former, he thrust both hands into his pockets, looked at the ground, and began to whistle. When he looked up again he ceased whistling very abruptly, and turned deadly pale—perhaps we should say yellow. And no wonder, for there, straight befor him, not more than twenty yards off, stood a crea- ture which, to his ignorant eyes, appeared to be a fiend incarnate, but which was in reality a large- sized and very ancient sheego monkey.

It stood in an upright position like a man, and was above four feet high. It had a bald head, grey whiskers, and an intensely black wrinkled face, and, at the moment Jim Scroggles' eyes encountered it, that face was working itself into such a variety of remarkable and hideous contortions that no description, however graphic, could convey a correct notion of it to the reader's mind. Seen behind the bars of an iron cage it might, perhaps, have been laughable ; but witnessed as it was, in the depths of a lonely forest, it was appalling.

Jim Scroggles' knees began to shake. He was fascinated with horror. The huge ape was equally fascinated with terror. It worked its wrinkled visage more violently than ever. Jim trembled all over. In another second the sheego displayed not only all its teeth—and they were tremendous— but all its gums, and they were fearful to behold, besides being scarlet. Roused to the utmost pitch of fear, the sheego uttered a shriek that rang through the forest like a death-yell. This was the culminating point. Jim Scroggles turned and fled as fast as his long and trembling legs could carry him.

The sheego, at the same instant, was smitten with an identically similar impulse. It turned, uttered another yell and fled in the opposite direction ; and thus the two ran until they were both out of breath. What became of the monkey we cannot tell ; but Jim Scroggles ran at headlong speed straight before him, crashing through brake and bush, in the full belief that the sheego was in hot pursuit, until he came to a mangrove swamp ; here his speed was checked somewhat, for the trees grew in a curious fashion that merits special notice.

Instead of rising out of the ground, the mangroves rose out of a sea of mud, and the roots stood up in a somewhat arched form, supporting their stem, as it were, on the top of a bridge. Thus, had the ground beneath been solid, a man might have walked *under* the roots. In order to cross the swamp, Jim Scroggles had to leap from root to root—a feat which, although difficult, he would have attempted without hesitation. But Jim was agitated at that particular moment. His step was uncertain at a time when the utmost coolness was necessary. At one point the leap from one root to the next was too great for him. He turned his eye quickly to one side to seek a nearer stem; in doing so he encountered the gaze of a serpent. It was not a large one, probably about ten feet long, but he knew it to be one whose bite was deadly. In the surprise and fear of the moment, he took the long leap, came short of the root by about six inches, and alighted up to the waist in the soft mud.

Almost involuntarily he cast his eyes behind him, and saw neither sheego nor serpent. He breathed more freely, and assayed to extricate himself from his unpleasant position. Stretching out his hands to the root above his head, he found that it was beyond his reach. The sudden fear that this produced caused him to make a violent struggle, and in his next effort he succeeded in catching a twig; it supported him for a moment, then broke, and he fell back again into the mud. Each successive struggle only sank him deeper. As the

thick adhesive semi-liquid clung to his lower limbs
and rose slowly on his chest, the wretched man
uttered a loud cry of despair.   He felt that he was
brought suddenly face to face with death in its
most awful form.   The mud was soon up to his
arm-pits.   As the hopelessness of his condition
forced itself upon him, he began to shout for help
until the dark woods resounded with his cries; but
no help came, and the cold drops of sweat stood
upon his brow as he shrieked aloud in agony, and
prayed for mercy.

## CHAPTER XII.

JIM SCROGGLES RESCUED, AND GLYNN AND AILIE LOST—
A CAPTURE, UPSET, CHASE, ESCAPE, AND HAPPY RE-
TURN.

THE merciful manner in which God sends deliverance at the eleventh hour has been so often
experienced and recognised, that it has originated
the well-known proverb, "Man's extremity is God's
opportunity;" and this proverb is true not only in
reference to man's soul, but often, also, in regard
to his temporal affairs.

While the wretched sailor was uttering cries for
help, which grew feebler every moment as he sank
deeper and deeper into what now he believed should
be his grave, his comrades were hastening forward
to his rescue.

Alarmed at his prolonged absence, they had

armed themselves, and set out in search of him, headed by the trader and led by the negro, who tracked his steps with that unerring certainty which seems peculiar to all savages. The shrieks uttered by their poor comrade soon reached their ears, and after some little difficulty, owing to the cries becoming faint and at last inaudible, they discovered the swamp where he lay, and revived his hope and energy by their shouts. They found him nearly up to the neck in mud, and the little of him that still remained above ground was scarcely recognisable.

It cost them nearly an hour, with the aid of poles, and ropes extemporized out of their garments, to drag Jim from his perilous position and place him on solid ground ; and after they had accomplished this, it took more than an hour longer to clean him and get him recruited sufficiently to accompany them to the spot where they had left the canoe.

The poor man was deeply moved ; and when he fully realized the fact that he was saved, he wept like a child, and then thanked God fervently for his deliverance. As the night was approaching, and the canoe, with Ailie in it, had been left in charge only of Glynn Proctor, Jim's recovery was expedited as much as possible, and as soon as he could walk they turned to retrace their steps.

Man knows not what a day or an hour will bring forth. For many years one may be permitted to move on "the even tenour of his way," without anything of momentous import occurring to mark the passage of his little span of time as it sweeps him onward to eternity. At another period of life, events, it may be of the most startling and abidingly impressive nature, are crowded into a few months or weeks, or even days. So it was now with our travellers on the African river. When they reached the spot where they had dined, no one replied to their shouts. The canoe, Glynn, and the child, were gone.

On making this terrible discovery the whole party were filled with indescribable consternation, and ran wildly hither and thither, up and down the banks of the river, shouting the names of Glynn Proctor, and Ailie, until the woods rang again. Captain Dunning was almost mad with anxiety and horror. His imagination pictured his child in every conceivable danger. He thought of her as drowned in the river and devoured by crocodiles ; as carried away by the natives into hopeless captivity ; or, perhaps, killed by wild beasts in the forest. When several hours had elapsed, and still no sign of the missing ones could be discovered, he fell down exhausted on the river's bank, and groaned aloud in his despair.

But Ailie was not lost. The Heavenly Father in whom she trusted, still watched over and cared for her, and Glynn Proctor's stout right arm was still by her side to protect her.

About half an hour after the party had gone off in search of their lost companion a large canoe, full of negroes, came sweeping down the river. Glynn and Ailie hid themselves in the bushes, and lay perfectly still, hoping they might be passed by. But they forgot that the blue smoke of their fire curled up through the foliage and revealed their presence at once. On observing the smoke, the savages gave a shout, and, running their canoe close into the bank, leaped ashore and began to scamper through the woods like baboons.

Only a few minutes passed before they discovered the two hiders, whom they surrounded and gazed upon in the utmost possible amazement, shouting the while with delight, as if they had discovered a couple of new species of monkey. Glynn was by nature a reckless and hasty youth. He felt the power of a young giant within him, and his first impulse was to leap upon the new comers, and knock them down right and left. Fortunately, for Ailie's sake as well as his own, he had wisdom enough to know that though he had possessed the power of ten giants, he could not hope, singly, to overcome twenty negroes, all of whom were strong, active, and lithe as panthers. He therefore assumed a good-humoured free-and-easy air, and allowed himself and Ailie to be looked at and handled without ceremony.

The savages were evidently not ill-disposed towards the wanderers. They laughed a great deal, and spoke to each other rapidly in what, to Glynn, was of course an unknown tongue. One

who appeared to be the chief of the party passed
his long black fingers through Ailie's glossy curls
with evident surprise and delight. He then advanced to Glynn, and said something like—

"Holli - boobo - gaddle - bump - um - peepi - daddle
dumps."

To which Glynn replied very naturally, "I don't
understand you."

Of course he did not. And he might have
known well enough that the negro could not
understand *him*. But he deemed it wiser to make
a reply of some kind, however unintelligible, than
to stand like a post and say nothing.

Again the negro spoke, and again Glynn made
the same reply ; whereupon the black fellow turned
round to his comrades and looked at them, and
they, in reply to the look, burst again into an im-
moderate fit of laughter, and cut a variety of capers,
the very simplest of which would have made the
fortune of any merry-Andrew in the civilized world,
had he been able to execute it. This was all very
well, no doubt, and exceedingly amusing, not to
say surprising ; but it became quite a different
matter when, after satisfying their curiosity, these
dark gentlemen coolly collected the property of the
white men, stowed it away in the small canoe, and
made signs to Glynn and Ailie to enter.

Glynn showed a decided objection to obey, on
which two stout fellows seized him by the shoulders,
and pointed sternly to the canoe, as much as to

say, " Hobbi-doddle-hoogum-toly-whack," which,
being interpreted (no doubt) meant, " If you don't
go quietly, we'll force you."

Again the young sailor's spirit leaped up.     He
clenched his fists, his brow flushed crimson, and,
in another instant, whatever might have been the
consequence, the two negroes would certainly have
lain recumbent on the sward, had it not suddenly
occurred to Glynn that he might, by appearing to
submit, win the confidence of his captors, and, at
the first night-encampment, quietly make his escape
with Ailie in his arms !

Glynn was at that romantic age when young
men have a tendency to think themselves capable
of doing almost anything, with or without ordinary
facilities, and in the face of any amount of adverse
circumstance.     He therefore stepped willingly and
even cheerfully into the canoe, in which his and
his comrades' baggage had been already stowed,
and seating himself in the stern took up the
steering-paddle.     He was ordered to quit that post,
however, in favour of a powerful negro, and made
to sit in the bow and paddle there.     Ailie was
placed with great care in the centre of the canoe
among a heap of soft leopard-skins; for the
savages evidently regarded her as something
worth preserving—a rare and beautiful specimen,
perhaps, of the white monkey !

This done, they leaped into their large canoe,
and, attaching the smaller one to it by means of a

rope, paddled out from the bank, and descended the stream.

"Oh! Glynn," exclaimed Ailie, in a whisper—for she felt that things were beginning to look serious—"what *are* we to do?"

"Indeed, my pet, I don't know," replied Glynn, looking round, and encountering the gaze of the negro in the stern, at whom he frowned darkly, and received a savage grin by way of reply.

"I would like *so* much to say something to you," continued Ailie, "but I'm afraid *he* will know what I say.

"Never fear, Ailie; he's as deaf as a post to our language.    Out with it."

"Could you not," she said, in a half whisper, "cut the rope, and then paddle away back while *they* are paddling down the river!"

Glynn laughed in spite of himself at this proposal.

"And what, my pretty one," he said, "what should we do with the fellow in the stern? Besides, the rascals in front might take it into their heads to paddle after us, you know, and what then?"

"I'm sure I don't know," said Ailie, beginning to cry.

"Now, dón't cry, my darling," said Glynn, looking over his shoulder with much concern. "I'll manage to get you out of this scrape somehow—now, see if I don't."

The youth spoke so confidently, that the child

felt somewhat comforted, so drying her eyes she ay back among the leopard-skins, where, giving vent to an occasional sob, she speedily fell fast asleep.

They continued to advance thus in silence for nearly an hour, crossed a small lake, and again entered the river. After descending this some time, the attention of the whole party was attracted to a group of hippopotami, gambolling in the mud-banks and in the river a short distance ahead. At any other time Glynn would have been interested in the sight of these uncouth monsters, but he had seen so many within the last few days that he was becoming comparatively indifferent to them, and at that moment he was too much filled with anxiety to take any notice of them. The creatures themselves, however, did not seem to be so utterly indifferent to the strangers. They continued their gambols until the canoes were quite near, and then they dived. Now, hippopotami, as we have before hinted, are clumsy and stupid creatures, so much so that they occasionally run against and upset boats and canoes, quite unintentionally. Knowing this, the natives in the large canoe kept a sharp lookout in order to steer clear of them.

They had almost succeeded in passing the place, when a huge fellow, like a sugar-puncheon, rose close to the small canoe, and grazed it with his tail. Apparently he considered this an attack made upon him by the boat, for he wheeled round in a rage, and swam violently towards it. The negro and Glynn sprang to their feet on the instant, and the former raised his paddle to deal the creature a blow on the head. Before he could do so, Glynn leaped lightly over Ailie, who had just awakened, caught the savage by the ankles, and tossed him overboard. He fell with a heavy splash just in front of the cavernous jaws of the hippopotamus! In fact, he had narrowly escaped falling head first into the creature's open throat.

The nearness of the animal at the time was probably the means of saving the negro's life, for it did not observe where he had vanished to, as he sank under its chin, and was pushed by its forelegs right under its body. In its effort to lay hold of the negro, the hippopotamus made a partial dive, and thus passed the small canoe. When it again rose to the surface the large canoe met its eye. At this it rushed, drove its hammer-like skull through the light material of which it was made, and then seizing the broken ends in its strong jaws upset the canoe, and began to rend it to pieces in its fury.

Before this occurred, the crew had leaped into the water, and were now swimming madly to the shore. At the same moment Glynn cut the line that fastened the two canoes together, and seizing his paddle, urged his craft up the river as fast as possible. But his single arm could not drive it with much speed against the stream, and before he had advanced a dozen yards, one of the natives overtook him and several more followed close behind. Glynn allowed the first one to come near, and then gave him a tremendous blow on the head with the edge of the paddle.

The young sailor was not in a gentle frame of mind at that time, by any means. The blow was given with a will, and would probably have fractured the skull of a white man ; but that of a negro is proverbially thick. The fellow was only stunned, and fell back among his comrades, who judiciously considering that such treatment was not agreeable and ought not to be courted, put about, and made for the shore.

Glynn now kept his canoe well over to the left side of the stream while the savages ran along the right bank, yelling ferociously and occasionally attempting to swim towards him, but without success. He was somewhat relieved, and sent them a shout of defiance, which was returned, of course with interest. Still he felt that his chance of escape was poor. He was becoming exhausted by the constant and violent exertion that was necessary in order to make head against the stream. The savages knew this, and bided their time.

As he continued to labour slowly up, Glynn came to the mouth of a small stream which joined the river. He knew not where it might lead to but feeling that he could not hold out much longer, he turned into it, without any very definite idea as

M

*to* what he would attempt next. The stream was sluggish. He advanced more easily, and after a few strokes of the paddle doubled round a point and was hid from the eyes of the negroes, who immediately set up a yell and plunged into the river, intending to swim over ; but fortunately it was much too rapid in the middle, and they were compelled to return. We say, fortunately, because, had they succeeded in crossing, they would have found Glynn in the bushes of the point behind which he had disappeared, in a very exhausted state, though prepared to fight to the last with all the energy of despair.

As it was, he had the extreme satisfaction of seeing his enemies, after regaining the right bank, set off at a quick run down the river. He now remembered having seen a place about two miles farther down that looked like a ford, and he at once concluded his pursuers had set off to that point, and would speedily return and easily re-capture him in the narrow little stream into which he had pushed. To cross the large river was im-possible—the canoe would have been swamped in the rapid. But what was to hinder him from paddling close in along the side, and perhaps reach the lake while the negroes were looking for him up the small stream ?

He put this plan in execution at once ; and Ailie took a paddle in her small hands and did her utmost to help him. It wasn't much, poor thing :

but to hear the way in which Glynn encouraged her and spoke of her efforts, one would have supposed she had been as useful as a full-grown man ! After a couple of hours' hard work, they emerged upon the lake, and here Glynn felt that he was pretty safe, because, in the still water, no man could swim nearly as fast as he could paddle. Besides, it was now getting dark, so he pushed out towards a rocky islet on which there were only a few small bushes, resolved to take a short rest there, and then continue his flight under cover of the darkness.

While Glynn carried ashore some biscuit, which was the only thing in the boat they could eat without cooking, Ailie broke off some branches from the low bushes that covered the little rocky islet, and spread them out on a flat rock for a couch ; this done, she stood on the top of a large stone and gazed round upon the calm surface of the beautiful lake, in the dark depths of which the stars twinkled as if there were another sky down there.

" Now, Ailie," said Glynn, " come along and have supper. It's not a very tempting one, but we must content ourselves with hard fare and a hard bed to-night, as I dare not light a fire lest the negroes should observe it and catch us."

. " I'm sorry for that," replied the child ; " for a fire is so nice and cheery ; and it helps to keep off the wild beasts, too, doesn't it ?"

" Well, it does ; but there are no wild beasts on

such a small rock as this, and the sides are luckily too steep for crocodiles to crawl up."

" Shall we sleep here till morning ?" asked Ailie, munching her hard biscuit and drinking her tin panikinful of cold water with great relish, for she was very hungry.

" Oh, no !" replied Glynn. " We must be up and away in an hour at farthest. So, as I see you're about done with your luxurious supper, I propose that you lie down to rest."

Ailie was only too glad to accede to this proposal. She lay down on the branches, and after Glynn had covered her with a blanket, he stretched himself on a leopard-skin beside her, and both of them fell asleep in five minutes. The mosquitoes were very savage that night, but the sleepers were too much fatigued to mind their vicious attacks.

Glynn slept two hours, and then he wakened with a start, as most persons do when they have arranged, before going to sleep, to rise at a certain hour. He rose softly, carried the provisions back to the canoe, and in his sleepy condition almost stepped upon the head of a huge crocodile, which, ignorant of their presence, had landed its head on the islet in order to have a snooze. Then he roused Ailie, and led her, more than half asleep, down to the beach, and lifted her into the canoe, after which he pushed off, and paddled briskly over the still waters of the star-lit lake. Ailie merely yawned during all these proceedings ; said, " Dear me ! is

BRIANT IMITATES THE BIRDS.—Page 164.

it time to—yeaow! oh, I'm *so* sleepy;" mumbled
something about papa wondering what had become
of Jim Scroggles, and about her being convinced
that—"yeaow!—the ship must have lost itself
among the whales and monkeys;" and then, dropping her head on the leopard-skins with a deep sigh
of comfort, she returned to the land of Nod.

Glynn Proctor worked so well that it was still
early in the morning and quite dark when he arrived at the encampment where they had been
made prisoners. His heart beat audibly as he approached the dark landing-place, and observed no
sign of his comrades. The moment the bow of the
canoe touched the shore, he sprang over the side,
and, without disturbing the little sleeper, drew it
gently up the bank, and fastened the bow-rope to
a tree; then he hurried to the spot where they
had slept and found all the fires out except one, of
which a few dull embers still remained; but no
comrade was visible.

It is a felicitous arrangement of our organs of
sense, that where one organ fails to convey to our
inward man information regarding the outward
world, another often steps in to supply its place,
and perform the needful duty. We have said that
Glynn Proctor saw nothing of his comrades,—although he gazed earnestly all round the camp—
for the very good reason that it was almost pitch
dark; but although his eyes were useless, his ears
were uncommonly acute, and through their instru-

mentality he became cognizant of a sound. It might have been distant thunder, but was too continuous and regular for that. It might have been the distant rumbling of heavy waggons or artillery over a paved road; but there were neither waggons nor roads in those African wilds. It might have been the prolonged choking of an alligator—it might, in fact, have been *anything* in a region like that, where *everything*, almost, was curious, and new, and strange, and wild, and unaccountable; and the listener was beginning to entertain the most uncomfortable ideas of what it probably was, when a gasp and a peculiar snort apprized him that it was a human snore!—at least, if not a human snore, it was that of·some living creature which indulged to a very extravagant degree in that curious and altogether objectionable practice.

Stepping cautiously forward on tip-toe, Glynn searched among the leaves all round the fire, following the direction of the sounds, but nothing was to be found; and he experienced a slight feeling of supernatural dread creeping over him, when a peculiarly loud metallic snore sounded clear above his head. Looking up, he beheld by the dull red light of the almost extinct fire, the form of Phil Briant, half-seated, half-reclining, on the branch of a tree not ten feet from the ground, and clasping another branch tightly with both arms.

At that moment, Ailie, who had awakened, ran up, and caught Glynn by the hand.

" Hallo ! Briant !" exclaimed Glynn.

A very loud snore was the reply.

"Briant! Phil Briant, I say; hallo! Phil!" shouted Glynn.

"Arrah! howld yer noise, will ye," muttered the still sleeping man—"sno-o-o-o-re!"

"A fall! a fall!—all hands ahoy! tumble up there, tumble up!" shouted Glynn, in the nautical tones which he well knew would have their effect upon his comrade.

He was right. They had more than their usual effect on him. The instant he heard them, Phil Briant shouted—"Ay, ay, sir!" and, throwing his legs over the side of what he supposed to be his hammock, he came down bodily on what he supposed to be the deck with a whack that caused him to utter an involuntary but tremendous howl.

"Oh! och! oh! murther! oh whirra!" he cried, as he lay half stunned. "Oh, it's kilt I am entirely—dead as mutton at last, an' no mistake. Sure I might have knowd it—och! worse luck? Didn't yer poor owld mother tell ye, Phil, that ye'd come to a bad end—she did——"

"Are ye badly hurt?" said Glynn, stooping over his friend in real alarm.

At the sound of his voice Briant ceased his wails, rose into a sitting posture, shaded his eyes with his hand (a most unnecessary proceeding under the circumstances), and stared at him.

"It's me, Phil; all right, and Ailie. We've escaped, and got safe back again."

"It's jokin' ye are," said Briant, with the imbecile smile of a man who only half believes what he actually sees. "I'm draimin', that's it. Go away, avic, an' don't be botherin' me."

"It's quite true, though, I assure you, my boy. I've managed to give the niggers the slip; and here's Ailie, too, all safe, and ready to convince you of the fact."

Phil Briant looked at one and then at the other in unbounded amazement for a few seconds, after which he gave a short laugh as if of pity for his own weakness, and his face resumed a mild aspect as he said softly, "It's all a draim, av' coorse it is!" He even turned away his eyes for a moment in order to give the vision time to dissipate. But on looking round again, there it was, as palpable as ever. Faith in the fidelity of his own eyesight returned in a moment, and Phil Briant, forgetting his bodily pains, sprang to his feet with a roar of joy, seized Ailie in his arms and kissed her, embraced Glynn Proctor with a squeeze like to that of a loving bear, and then began to dance an Irish jig, quite regardless of the fact that the greater part of it was performed in the fire, the embers of which he sent flying in all directions like a display of fireworks. He cheered, too, now and then like a maniac,—

"Oh, happy day! I've found ye, have I? after all me trouble, too! Hooray! an' wan chair more, for luck. Av me sowl only don't lape clane out o' me body, it's meself 'll be thankful! But, sure— I'm forgittin'——"

Briant paused suddenly in the midst of his uproarious dance, and seized a burning stick, which he attempted to blow into a flame with intense vehemence of action. Having succeeded, he darted towards an open space a few yards off, in the centre of which lay a large pile of dry sticks. To these he applied the lighted brand, and the next instant a glare of ruddy flame leaped upwards, and sent a shower of sparks high above the forest trees into the sky. He then returned, panting a good deal, but much composed, and said—

"Now, darlints, come an' help me to gather the bits o' stick; somebody's bin scatterin' them all over the place, they have, bad luck to them! an' then ye'll sit down and talk a bit, an' tell me all about it."

"But what's the fire for?" asked Ailie.

"Ay, ye may say that," added Glynn; we don't need such a huge bonfire as that to cook our supper with."

"Och! be aisy, do. It'll do its work; small doubt o' that. The cap'n, poor man, ye know, is a'most deranged, an' they're every one o' them off at this good minute scourin' the woods lookin' for ye. O, then, it's sore hearts we've had this day! An' wan was sent wan way, an' wan another, an' the cap'n hisself he wint up the river, and, before he goes, he says to me, says he, 'Briant, you'll stop here and watch the camp, for maybe they'll come wanderin' back to it, av they've bin and lost theirselves; an' mind ye don't lave it or go to slape    An' if they do come, or ye hear any news o' them, jist you light up a great fire, an' I'll be on the look-out, an' we'll all on us come back as fast as we can. Now, that's the truth, an' the whole truth, an' nothin' but the truth, as the judge said to the witness when he swore at him."

This was a comforting piece of information to Glynn and Ailie, so, without further delay, they assisted their overjoyed comrade to collect the scattered embers of the fire and boil the kettle. In this work they were all the more energetic that the pangs of hunger were beginning to remind them of the frugal and scanty nature of their last meal.

The bonfire did its work effectually. From all parts of the forest to which they had wandered, the party came, dropping in one by one to congratulate the lost and found pair. Last of all came Captain Dunning and Tim Rokens, for the harpooneer had vowed he would "stick to the cap'n through thick and thin." Tim kept his word faithfully. Through thick tangled brakes and thin mud-swamps did he follow his wretched commander that night until he could scarcely stand for fatigue, or keep his eyes open for sleep; and when the captain rushed into the camp at last, and clasped his sobbing child to his heart, Tim Rokens rushed in along with him, halted beside him, thrust his hands into his pockets, and looked on, while his eyes blinked with irresistible drowsiness, and his mud-bespattered visage beamed with excessive joy.

# CHAPTER XIII.

PHILOSOPHICAL REMARKS ON " LIFE"—A MONKEY SHOT
AND A MONKEY FOUND—JACKO DESCRIBED.

" Such is life !" There is deep meaning in that
expression, though it is generally applied in a
bantering manner to life in all its phases, under all
its peculiar and diversified circumstances. Taking
a particular view of things in general, we may say
of life that it is composed of diverse and miscella-
neous materials :—the grave and the gay ; the sad
and the comic ; the extraordinary and the common-
place ; the flat and the piquant ; the heavy and
the light ; the religious and the profane ; the bright
and the dark ; the shadow and the sunshine. All
these, and a great deal more, similar as well as dis-
similar, enter into the composition of what we familiarly term life.

These elements, too, are not arranged according
to order, at least, order that is perceptible to our
feeble human understandings. That there does
exist both order and harmony is undeniable ; but
we cannot see it. The elements appear to be mis-
cellaneously intermingled—to be accidentally
thrown together ; yet, while in looking at them in
detail, there seems to us a good deal of unreason-
able and chaotic jumble, in regarding them as a
whole, or as a series of wholes, it becomes apparent
that there is a certain harmony of arrangement

that may be termed kaleidoscopically beautiful ;
and when, in the course of events, we are called to
the contemplation of something grand or lovely,
followed rather abruptly by something curiously
contemptible or absurd, we are tempted to give
utterance to the thoughts that are too complicated
and deep for rapid analysis, in the curt expression
" Such is life."

The physician invites his friends to a social *ré-
union*. He chats and laughs at the passing jest, or
takes part in the music—the glee, or the comic
song. A servant whispers in his ear. Ten minutes
elapse, and he is standing by the bed of death. He
watches the flickering flame ; he endeavours to
relieve the agonized frame ; he wipes the cold sweat
from the pale brow, and moistens the dry lips, or
pours words of true, earnest, tender comfort into
the ears of the bereaved. The contrast here is very
violent and sudden. We have chosen, perhaps, the
most striking instance of the kind that is afforded
in the experience of men ; yet such, in a greater
or less degree, is life, in the case of every one born
into this wonderful world of ours, and such, undoubtedly, it was intended to be. " There is a
time for all things." We were made capable of
laughing and crying ; therefore, these being sinless
indulgences in the abstract, we *ought* to laugh and
cry. And one of our great aims in life should be
to get our hearts and affections so trained that we
shall laugh and cry at the right time. It may be

well to remark, in passing, that we should avoid, if possible, doing both at once.

Now, such being life, we consider that we shall be doing no violence to the harmonies of life, if we suddenly, and without further preface, transport the reader into the middle of next day, and a considerable distance down the river up which we have for some time been travelling.

Here he (or she) will find Ailie and her father, and the whole party in fact, floating calmly and pleasantly down the stream in their canoe.

" Now, this is wot I do enjoy," said Rokens, laying down his paddle and wiping the perspiration from his brow; " it's the pleasantest sort o' thing I've known since I went to sea."

To judge from the profuse perspiration that flowed from his brow and from the excessive redness of his face, one would suppose that Rokens' experience of " pleasant sort o' things" had not hitherto been either extensive or deep. But the man meant what he said, and a well-known proverb clears up the mystery—" What's one man's meat is another's poison !" Hard work, violent physical exertion, and excessive heat were Rokens' delight, and, whatever may be the opinion of flabby-muscled, flat individuals, there can be no reasonable doubt that Rokens meant it, when he added emphatically, " It's fuss-rate ; tip top ; A 1 on Lloyd's, that's a fact."

Phil Briant on hearing this laid down his paddle,

also wiped his forehead with the sleeve of his coat, and exclaimed,—

" Ditto, says I."

Whereupon Glynn laughed, and Jim Scroggles grunted (this being *his* method of laughing), and the captain shook his head and said,—

" P'r'aps it is, my lads, a pleasant sort o' thing, but the sooner we're out of it the better. I've no notion of a country where the natives murder poor little boys in cold blood, and carry off your goods and chattels at a moment's notice."

The captain looked at Ailie as he spoke, thereby implying that she was part of the " goods and chattels" referred to.

" Shure it's a fact ; an' without sayin' by yer lave, too," added Briant, who had a happy facility of changing his opinion on the shortest notice to accommodate himself to circumstances.

" Oh, the monkey !" screamed Ailie.

Now as Ailie screamed this just as Briant ceased to speak, and, moreover, pointed, or appeared to point, straight into that individual's face, it was natural to suppose that the child was becoming somewhat personal—the more so that Briant's visage, when wrinkled up and tanned by the glare of a tropical sun, was not unlike to that of a large baboon. But every one knew that Ailie was a gentle well-behaved creature—except perhaps when she was seized with one of her gleeful fits that bordered sometimes upon mischief—so that instead of supposing that she had made a personal attack on the unoffending Irishman, the boat's crew instantly directed their eyes close past Briant's face and into the recesses of the wood beyond, where they saw a sight that filled them with surprise.

A large-leaved tree of the palm species overhung the banks of the river and formed a support to a wild vine and several bright flowering parasitical plants that drooped in graceful luxuriance from its branches and swept the stream, which at that place was dark, smooth, and deep. On the top of this tree, in among the branches, sat a monkey—at least so Ailie called it; but the term ape or baboon would have been more appropriate, for the creature was a very large one, and, if the expression of its countenance indicated in any degree the feelings of its heart, also a very fierce one—an exceedingly ferocious one indeed. This monkey's face was as black as coal, and its two deep-seated eyes were, if possible, blacker than coal. Its head was bald, but the rest of its body was plentifully covered with hair.

Now this monkey was evidently caught—taken by surprise—for instead of trying to escape as the canoe approached, it sat there chattering and exhibiting its teeth to a degree that was quite fiendish, not to say—under the circumstances—unnecessary. As the canoe dropped slowly down the river, it became obvious that this monkey had a baby, for a very small and delicate creature was seen clinging round the big one's waist with its little hands grasping tightly the long hair on the mother's sides, its arms being much too short to encircle her body. Ailie's heart leapt with an emotion of tender delight as she observed that the baby monkey's face was white and sweet-looking; yes, we might even go the length of saying that, for a monkey, it was actually pretty. But it had a sub- dued, sorrowful look that was really touching to behold. It seemed as though that infantine monkey had, in the course of its brief career, been subjected to every species of affliction, to every imaginable kind of heart-crushing sorrow, and had remained deeply meek and humble under it all. Only for one brief instant did a different expression cross its melancholy face. That was when it first caught sight of the canoe. Then it exposed its very small teeth and gums after the fashion of its mother; but repentance seemed to follow instantly, for the sad look, mixed with a dash of timidity, resumed its place, and it buried its face in its mother's bosom.

At that moment there was a loud report. A bullet whistled through the air and struck the old monkey in the breast. We are glad to say, for the credit of our sailors, that a howl of indignation immediately followed, and more than one fist was raised to smite the trader who had fired the shot. But Captain Dunning called the men to order in a peremptory voice, while every eye was turned

vards the tree to observe the effect of the shot.
for Ailie she sat breathless with horror at the
ielty of the act.

The old monkey gave vent to a loud yell, clutched
r breast with her hands, sprang wildly into the
, and fell to the ground. Her leap was so violent
it the young one was shaken off and fell at some
tance from its poor mother, which groaned once
twice and then died. The baby seemed unhurt.
thering itself nimbly up, it ran away from the
n who had now landed, but who stood still, by
: captain's orders, to watch its motions. Look-
; round, it observed its mother's form lying on
: ground, and at once ran towards it and buried
little face in her breast, at which sight Ailie
gan to cry quietly. In a few seconds the little
nkey got up and gently pawed the old one;
n, on receiving no sign of recognition, it uttered
aint wail, something like " Wee-wee-wee-wee-
!" and again hid its face in the breast of its
ad parent.

"Ah! the poor cratur," said Briant, in a tone
voice that betrayed his emotion. " O, why did
kill her ?"

"Me ketch 'im ?" said Bumble, looking inquir-
;ly at the captain.

"Oh, do!" answered Ailie, with a sob.

The negro deemed this permission sufficient, for
instantly sprang forward, and throwing a piece
net over the little monkey, secured it.

N

Now the way in which that baby monkey struggled and kicked and shrieked, when it found itself
a prisoner, was perfectly wonderful to see! It
seemed as if the strength of fifty little monkeys
had been compressed into its diminutive body, and
King Bumble had to exert all his strength in order
to hold the creature while he carried it into the
canoe. Once safely there and in the middle of the
stream, it was let loose. The first thing it did on
being set free was to give a shriek of triumph, for
monkeys, like men, when at last *allowed* to do
that which they have long struggled in vain to accomplish, usually take credit for the achievement
of their own success.

Its next impulse was to look round at the faces
of the men in search of its mother; but the poor
mother was now lying dead and covered with a
cloth in the bottom of the canoe, so the little monkey turned from one to another with disappointment in its glance and then uttered a low wail of
sorrow. Glynn Proctor affirmed positively that it
looked twice at Phil Briant and even made a motion
towards him; but we rather suspect that Glynn
was jesting. Certain it is, however, that it looked
long and earnestly at Ailie, and there is little doubt
that, young though it was, it was able to distin-
guish something in her tender gaze of affection and
pity that proved attractive. It did not, however,
accept her invitation to go to her, although given
in the most persuasive tones of her silvery voice,

and when any of the men tried to pat its head,
it displayed such a row of sharp little teeth and
made such a fierce demonstration of its intention
to bite, that they felt constrained to leave it alone.
At last Ailie held her hands towards it and said,—

"Wont it come to me, dear, sweet pet? *do* come ;
I'll be as kind to you almost as your poor mother."

The monkey looked at the child, but said nothing.

"Come, monkey, dear puggy, *do* come," repeated
Ailie, in a still more insinuating voice.

The monkey still declined to "come," but it
looked very earnestly at the child, and trembled
a good deal, and said, "Oo-oo-wee ; oo-oo-wee !"

As Ailie did not quite understand this, she said,
"Poor thing !" and again held out her hand.

"Try it with a small taste o' mate," suggested
Briant.

"Right," said the captain. "Hand me the biscuit-
bag, Glynn. There, now, Ailie, try it with that."

Ailie took the piece of biscuit offered to her by
her father, and held it out to the monkey, who advanced with nervous caution, and very slowly,
scratching its side the while. Putting out its very
small hand, it touched the biscuit, then drew back
the hand suddenly, and made a variety of sounds, accompanied by several peculiar contortions of visage,
all of which seemed to say, "Don't hurt me, now ;
*don't* deceive me, pray." Again it put forth its
hand, and took the biscuit, and ate it in a very

great hurry indeed; that is to say, it stuffed it
into the bags in its cheeks.

Ailie gave it a bit more biscuit, which it received
graciously, and devoured voraciously; whereupon
she put forth her hand, and sought to pat the little
creature on the head. The attempt was successful.
With many slight grins, as though to say, "Take
care, now, else I'll bite," the small monkey allowed
Ailie to pat its head and stroke its back.  Then it
permitted her to take hold of its hand, and draw
it towards her.  In a few minutes it showed evident symptoms of a desire to be patted again,
and at length it drew timidly towards the child,
and took hold of her hand in both of its delicate
pink paws.  Ailie felt quite tenderly towards the
creature, and stroked its head again, whereupon
it seemed suddenly to cast aside all fear.  It
leaped upon her knee, put its slender arms as far
round her neck as possible, said "Oo-oo-wee!"
several times in a very sad tone of voice, and laid
its head upon her bosom.

This was too much for poor Ailie; she thought
of the dead mother of this infant monkey, and
wept as she stroked its hairy little head and
shoulders.  From that time forward the monkey
adopted Ailie as its mother, and Ailie adopted the
monkey as her child.

Now the behaviour of that monkey during the
remainder of that voyage was wonderful.  Oh, you
know, it was altogether preposterous, to say the

very least of it. Affection, which displayed itself
in a desire to conciliate the favour of every one,
was ingrained in its bones ; while deception, which
was evinced in a constant effort to appear to be
intent upon one thing, when it was really bent
upon another, was incorporated with its marrow !

At first it was at war with every one, excepting,
of course, Ailie, its adopted mother ; but soon it
became accustomed to the men, and in the course
of a few days would go to any one who called it.
Phil Briant was a particular favourite ; so was
Rokens, with whose black beard it played in
evident delight, running its slender fingers through
it, disentangling the knots and the matted portions
which the owner of the beard had never yet been
able to disentangle in a satisfactory way for himself ; and otherwise acting the part of a barber and
hair-dresser to that bold mariner, much to his
amusement, and greatly to the delight and admiration of the whole party.

To say that that small monkey had a face,
would be to assert what was unquestionably true,
but what, also, was very far short of the whole
truth. No one ever could make up his mind
exactly as to how many faces it had. If you looked
at it at any particular time, and then shut your
eyes and opened them a moment after, that monkey, as far as expression went, had another and a
totally different face. Repeat the operation, and
it had a third face ; continue the process, and it

had a fourth face; and so on, until you lost count altogether of its multitudinous faces. Now it was grave and pensive; anon it was blazing with amazement; again it bristled with indignation; then it glared with anger, and presently it was all serene—blended love and wrinkles. Of all these varied expressions, that of commingled surprise and indignation was the most amusing, because those emotions had the effect of not only opening its eyes and its mouth to the form of three excessively round O's, but also raised a small tuft of hair just above its forehead into a bristling position, and threw its brow into an innumerable series of wrinkles. This complex expression was of frequent occurrence, for its feelings were tender and sensitive, so that it lived in the firm belief that its new friends (always excepting Ailie) constantly wished to insult it; and was afflicted with a chronic state of surprise at the cruelty, and of indignation at the injustice, of men who could wantonly injure the feelings of so young, and especially so small a monkey.

When the men called it, it used to walk up to them with calm, deliberate condescension in its air; when Ailie held out her hand, it ran on its two legs, and being eager in its affections, it held out its arms in order to be caught up. As to food, that monkey was not particular. It seemed to be omniverous. Certain it is that it never refused anything, but more than once it was observed quietly to throw away things that it did not relish.. Once, in an unguarded moment, it accepted and chewed a small piece of tobacco; after which it made a variety of entirely new faces, and became very sick indeed—so sick that its adopted mother began to fear she was about to lo‐e her child ; but after vomiting a good deal, and moaning piteously for several days, it gradually re‐overed, and from that time entertained an unquenchable hatred for to‐bacco, and for the man who had given it to him, ‐ who happened to be Jim Scroggles.

Ailie, being of a romantic temperament, named her monkey Albertino, but the sailors called him Jacko, and their name ultimately became the well‐known one of the little foundling, for Ailie was not obstinate ; so, seeing that the sailors did not or could not remember Albertino, she soon gave in, and styled her pet Jacko to the end of the chapter, with which piece of information we shall conclude *this* chapter.

---

## CHAPTER XIV.

RENCONTRE WITH SLAVE-TRADERS — ON BOARD AGAIN — A START, A MISFORTUNE, A GHOST STORY, A MISTAKE, AND AN INVITATION TO DINNER.

ON the evening of the second day after the capture of Jacko, as the canoe was descending the river and drawing near to the sea-coast, much to the delight of every one—for the heat of the interior had be-

gun to grow unbearable—a ship's boat was observed moored to the wharf near the slave-station
which they had passed on the way up. At first it
was supposed to be one of the boats of the Red
Eric, but on a nearer approach this proved to be
an erroneous opinion.

"Wot can it be a-doin' of here?" inquired Tim
Rokens, in an abstracted tone of voice, as if he
put the question to himself, and therefore did not
expect an answer.

"No doubt it's a slaver's boat," replied the trader;
"they often come up here for cargoes of niggers."

"Och! the blackguards!" exclaimed Phil Briant,
all his blood rising at the mere mention of the
horrible traffic; "couldn't we land, capting, and
give them a lickin'? I'll engage meself to put six
at laste o' the spalpeens on their beam-ends."

"No, Phil, we sha'n't land for that purpose; but
we'll land for some gunpowder an' a barrel or two
of plantains; so give way, lads."

In another moment the bow of the canoe slid
upon the mud-bank of the river close to the slaver's
boat, which was watched by a couple of the most
villanous-looking men that ever took part in that
disgraceful traffic. They were evidently Portuguese sailors, and the scowl of their bronzed faces,
when they saw the canoe approach the landing-
place, showed that they had no desire to enter into
amicable converse with the strangers.

At this moment the attention of the travellers

was drawn to a gang of slaves who approached the
wharf, chained together by the neck, and guarded
by the crew of the Portuguese boat. Ailie looked
on with a feeling of dread that induced her to
cling to her father's hand, while the men stood with
folded arms, compressed lips, and knitted brows.

On the voyage up they had landed at this station,
and had seen the slaves in their places of confine-
ment. The poor creatures were apparently happy
at that time, and seemed totally indifferent to their
sad fate; but their aspect was very different now.
They were being hurried away, they knew not
whither, by strangers whom they had been taught
to believe were monsters of cruelty besides being
cannibals, and who had purchased them for the
purpose of killing them and eating their bodies.
The wild, terrified looks of the men, and the subdued
looks and trembling gait of the women showed that
they expected no mercy at the hands of their
captors.

They hung back a little as they drew near to
the boat, whereupon one of their conductors, who
seemed to be in command of the party, uttered a
fierce exclamation in Portuguese, and struck several
of the men and women indiscriminately severe blows
with his fists. In a few minutes they were all
placed in the boat, and the crew had partly embarked, when Phil Briant, unable to restrain himself, muttered between his teeth to the Portuguese
commander as he passed,—

"Ye imp o' darkness, av I only had ye in the ring for tshwo minits—jist tshwo—ah thin wouldn't I polish ye off."

"Fat you say, sare?" cried the man, turning fiercely towards Briant, and swearing at him in bad English.

"Say, is it? Oh, then *there's* a translation for ye, that's understood in all lingos."

Phil shook his clenched fist as close as possible to the nose of the Portuguese commander without actually coming into contact with that hooked and prominent organ.

The man started back and drew his knife, at the same time calling to several of his men, who advanced with their drawn knives.

"Ho!" cried Briant, and a jovial smile overspread his rough countenance as he sprang to a clear spot of ground and rolled up both sleeves of his shirt to the shoulders, thereby displaying a pair of arms that might, at a rapid glance, have been mistaken for a pair of legs—"that's yer game, is it? wont I stave in yer planks! wont I shiver yer timbers, and knock out yer day-lights, bless yer purty faces! I didn't think ye had it in ye; come on, darlints— toothpicks and all—as many as ye like; the more the better,—wan at a time, or all at wance, it don't matter, not the laste, be no manes!"

While Briant gave utterance to these liberal invitations, he performed a species of revolving dance, and flourished his enormous fists in so ludicrous a

manner, that despite the serious nature of the
fray the two parties were likely to be speedily engaged in, his comrades could not restrain their
laughter.

"Go it, Pat!" cried one.

"True blue!" shouted another.

"Silence!" cried Captain Dunning, in a voice
that enforced obedience. "Get into the canoe,
Briant."

"Och! capting," exclaimed the wrathful Irishman, reproachfully, "sure ye wouldn't spile the fun?"

"Go to the canoe, sir."

"Ah! capting dear, jist wan round!"

"Go the canoe, I say."

"I'll do it all in four minits an' wan quarter, av
ye'll only shut yer eyes," pleaded Phil.

"Obey orders, will you?" cried the captain, in a
voice there was no mistaking.

Briant indignantly thrust his fists into his
breeches pockets, and rolled slowly down towards
the canoe, as—to use one of his own favourite expressions—sulky as a bear with a broken head.

Meanwhile the captain stepped up to the Portuguese sailors and told them to mind their own
business, and let *honest* men alone; adding, that
if they did not take his advice, he would first give
them a licking and then pitch them all into the
river.

This last remark caused Briant to prick up his
ears and withdraw his fists from their inglorious

retirement, in the fond hope that there might still
be work for them to do ; but on observing that
the Portuguese, acting on the principle that discre-
tion is the better part of valour, had taken the
advice and were returning to their own boat, he
relapsed into the sulks, and seated himself doggedly
in his place in the canoe.

During all this little scene, which was enacted
much more rapidly than it has been described,
master Jacko, having escaped from the canoe, had
been seated near the edge of the wharf, looking on,
apparently, with deep interest.  Just as the Portuguese turned away to embark in their boat, Ailie's
eye alighted on her pet ; at the same moment the
foot of the Portuguese commander alighted on her
pet's tail.  Now the tails of all animals seem to
be peculiarly sensitive.  Jacko's certainly was so,
for he instantly uttered a shriek of agony, which
was as quickly responded to by its adopted mother
in a scream of alarm as she sprang forward to the
rescue.  When one unintentionally treads on the
tail of any animal and thereby evokes a yell, he is
apt to start and trip—in nine cases out of ten he
does trip.  The Portuguese commander tripped
upon this occasion.  In staggering out of the
monkey's way he well-nigh tumbled over Ailie,
and in seeking to avoid her, he tumbled over the
edge of the wharf into the river.

The difference between the appearance of this
redoubtable slave-buying hero before and after his

mvoluntary imr^          ^so remarkable and great
that his most ir          id would have failed to
recognise him. 'i▁ ▁     wn into the slimy liquid
an ill-favoured Portuguese, clad in white duck ; he
came up a worse-favoured monstrosity, clothed in
mud ! Even his own rascally comrades grinned at
him for a moment, but their grins changed into a
scowl of anger when they heard the peals of laughter
that burst from the throats of their enemies. As for
Briant, he absolutely hugged himself with delight.

"Och ! ye've got it, ye have," he exclaimed, at
intervals. "Happy day ! who'd ha' thought it? to
see him tumbled in the mud after all by purty little
Ailie and Jacko. Come here to me, Jacko, owld
coon. Oh, ye swate cratur !"

Briant seized the monkey, and squeezed it to his
breast, and kissed it—yes, he actually kissed its
nose in the height of his glee, and continued to
utter incoherent exclamations, and to perpetrate
incongruous absurdities, until long after they had
descended the river and left the muddy Portuguese
and his comrades far behind them.

Towards evening the party were once more safe
and sound on board the Red Eric, where they
found everything repaired, and the ship in a fit
state to proceed to sea immediately.

His Majesty King Bumble was introduced to the
steward, then to the cook, and then to the caboose.
Master Jacko was introduced to the ship's crew
and to his quarters, which consisted of a small box

filled with straw, and was lashed near the foot of
the mizzen-mast.   These introductions having been
made, the men who had accompanied their commander on his late excursion into the interior, went
forward and regaled their messmates for hours with
anecdotes of their travels in the wilds of Africa.

It is well known, and generally acknowledged,
that all sublunary things, pleasant as well as unpleasant, must come to an end.   In the course of
two days more the sojourn of the crew of the Red
Eric on the coast of Africa came to a termination.
Having taken in supplies of fresh provisions,
the anchor was weighed, and the ship stood out to
sea with the first of the ebb tide.   It was near sunset when the sails were hoisted and filled by a
gentle land breeze, and the captain had just promised Ailie that he would show her blue water
again by breakfast-time next morning, when a slight
tremor passed through the vessel's hull, causing
the captain to shout, with a degree of vigour that
startled every one on board, "All hands ahoy!
lower away the boats, Mr. Millons, we're hard and
fast aground on a mud-bank!"

The boats were lowered away with all speed, and
the sails clewed up instantly, but the Red Eric remained as immovable as the bank on which she
had run aground ; there was, therefore, no recourse
but to wait patiently for the rising tide to float her
off again.   Fortunately the bank was soft and the
wind light, else it might have gone ill with the
good ship.

There is scarcely any conceivable condition so favourable to quiet confidential conversation and story-telling as the one in which the men of the whale-ship now found themselves. The night was calm and dark, but beautiful, for a host of stars sparkled in the sable sky, and twinkled up from the depths of the dark ocean. The land-breeze had fallen, and there was scarcely any sound to break the surrounding stillness except the lipping water as it kissed the black hull of the ship. A dim, scarce perceptible light rendered every object on board mysterious and unaccountably large.

"Wot a night for a ghost story," observed Jim Scroggles, who stood with a group of the men, who were seated on and around the windlass.

"I don't b'lieve in ghosts," said Dick Barnes, stoutly, in a tone of voice that rendered the veracity of his assertion, to say the least of it, doubtful.

"Nother do I," remarked Nikel Sling, who had just concluded his culinary operations for the day, and sought to employ his brief interval of relaxation in social intercourse with his fellows. Being engaged in ministering to the animal wants of his comrades all day, he felt himself entitled to enjoy a little of the "feast of reason and the flow of soul" at night.

"No more duv I," added Phil Briant, firmly, at the same time hitting his thigh a slap with his open hand that caused all around him to start.

"You don't, don't you?" said Tim Rokens, addressing the company generally, and looking round, gravely, while he pushed the glowing tobacco into his pipe with the point of a marline-spike.

To this there was a chorus of " Noes," but a close observer would have noticed that nearly the whole conversation was carried on in low tones, and that many a glance was cast behind, as if these bold sceptics more than half expected all the ghosts that did happen to exist to seize them then and there and carry them off as a punishment for their un-belief.

Tim Rokens drew a few whiffs of his pipe, and looked round gravely before he again spoke; then he put the following momentous question, with the air of a man who knew he could overturn his adversary whatever his reply should be :—

" An' why don't ye b'lieve in 'em ?"

We cannot say positively that Tim Rokens put the question to Jim Scroggles, but it is certain that Jim Scroggles accepted the question as addressed to him, and answered in reply—.

" 'Cause why? I never seed a ghost, an' nobody never seed a ghost, an' I don't b'lieve in what I can't see."

Jim said this as if he thought the position in-contestable. Tim regarded him with a prolonged stare, but for some time said nothing. At last he emitted several strong puffs of smoke, and said—

" Young man, did you ever *see* your own mind ?"

" No, in course not ?"

" Did anybody else ever see it ?"

" Cer'nly not."

"Then of course you don't believe in it!" added Rokens, while a slight smile curled his upper lip.

The men chuckled a good deal at Jim's confusion, while he in vain attempted to explain that the two ideas were not parallel by any means. At this juncture, Phil Briant came to the rescue.

"Ah now, git out," said he. "I agree with Jim, intirely; an' Tim Rokens isn't quite so cliver as he thinks. Now look here, lads, here's how it stands, 'xactly. Jim says he niver seed his own mind— very good; and he says as how nobody else niver seed it, nother; well, and wot then? Don't you observe it's 'cause he ha'n't got none at' all to see? He ha'n't got even the ghost of one, so how could ye expect anybody to see it?"

"Oh, hold yer noise, Paddy," exclaimed Dick Barnes, "an' let's have a ghost story from Tim Rokens. He b'lieves in ghosts, anyhow, an' could give us a yarn about 'em, I knows, if he likes. Come along now, Tim, like a good fellow."

"Ay, that's it," cried Briant; "give us a stiff 'un now. Don't be afeard to skear us, old boy."

"Oh, I can give ye a yarn about ghosts, cer'nly," said Tim Rokens, looking into the bowl of his pipe in order to make sure that it was sufficiently charged to last out the story. "I'll tell ye of a ghost I once seed and knocked down."

"Knocked down!" cried Nikel Sling, in surprise; "why, I allers thought as how ghosts was spirits, an' couldn't be knocked down or cotched neither."

" Not at all," replied Rokens ; " ghosts is made
of all sorts o' things—brass, and iron, and linen,
and buntin', and timber ; it wos a brass ghost the
feller that I'm goin' to tell ye about——"

"I say, Sling," interrupted Briant, " av ghost
wos spirits, as you thought they wos, would they
be allowed into the State of Maine ?"

" Oh, Phil, shut up, do !  Now then, Tim, fire
away."

"Well then," began Rokens, with great deliberation, " it was on a Vednesday night as it happened.
I had bin out at supper with a friend that night,
and we'd had a glass or two o' grog; for ye see, lads,
it was some years ago, afore I tuk to temp'rance.
I had a long way to go over a great dark moor
a'fore I could git to the place where I lodged, so
I clapped on all sail to git over the moor, seein' the
moon would go down soon ; but it wouldn't do : the
moon set when I wos in the very middle of the
moor, and as the road wasn't over good, I wos in a
state o' confumble lest I should lose it altogether.
I looks round in all directions, but I couldn't see
nothin—cause why? there wasn't nothin' to be seen.
It wos 'orrid dark, I can tell ye.  Jist one or two
stars a shinin', like half a dozen farden dips in a
great church ; they only made darkness wisible.
I began to feel all over a cur'ous sort o' peculiar
unaccountableness, which it ain't easy to explain,
but is most oncommon disagreeable to feel. It wos
very still, too—desperate still.  The beatin' o' my

own heart sounded quite loud, and I heer'd the tickin' o' my watch goin' like the click of a church clock. O, it was awful!"

At this point in the story the men crept closer together, and listened with intense earnestness.

"Suddenly," continued Rokens—"for things in sich circumstances always comes suddenly—suddently I seed somethin' black jump up right ahead o' me."

Here Rokens paused.

"Wot was it?" inquired Gurney, in a solemn whisper.

"It was," resumed Rokens, slowly, "the stump of a old tree."

"Oh, I thought it had been the ghost," said Gurney, somewhat relieved, for that fat little Jacktar fully believed in apparitions, and always listened to a ghost story in fear and trembling.

"No, it wasn't the ghost; it wos the stump of a tree. Well, I set sail again, an' presently I sees a great white thing risin' up right ahead o' me—"

"Hah! *that* was it," whispered Gurney.

"No, that wasn't it," retorted Rokens; "that was a hinn, a white painted hinn, as stood by the roadside, and right glad wos I to see it, I can tell ye, shipmates, for I wos gittin' tired as well as frightened. I soon roused the landlord by kickin' at the door till it nearly comed off its hinges; and arter gittin' another glass o' grog, I axed the landlord to show me my bunk, as I wanted to turn in.

It was a queer old house that hinn wos. A great ramblin' place, with no end o' staircases and passages. A dreadful gloomy sort o' place. No one lived in it except the landlord, a dark-faced surly fellow as one would like to kick out of his own door, and his wife, who wos little better than hisself. They also had a hostler, but he slept with the cattle in a hout-house.

" 'Ye wont be fear'd,' says the landlord, as he hove ahead through the long passages holdin' the candle high above his head to show the way, ' to sleep in the far-eud o' the house. It's the old bit; the new bit's undergoin' repairs. You'll find it comfortable enough, though it's raither gusty, bein' old, ye see ; but the weather ain't cold, so ye wont mind it.'

" ' Oh ! niver a bit,' says I, quite bold like ; ' I don't care a rap for nothin'. There ain't no ghosts, is there ?'

" Well, I'm not sure; many travellers wot has stayed here has said to me they've seed 'em, particklerly in the old part o' the buildin', but they seems to be quite harmless, and never hurts any one as lets 'em alone. I never seed 'em myself, an' there's cer'nly not more nor half-a-dozen on 'em—hallo !——'

" At that moment, shipmates, a strong gust o' cold air came rushin' down the passage we was in, and blow'd out the candle. ' Ah ! it's gone out,' said the landlord ; ' just wait here a moment, and

I'll light it;' and with that he shuffled off, and
left me in the blackest and most thickest darkness
I ever wos in in all my life. I didn't dare to move,
for I didn't know the channels, d'ye see, and might
ha' run myself aground or again' the rocks in no
time. The wind came moanin' down the passage
as if all the six ghosts the landlord mentioned, and
a dozen or two o' their friends besides, was a-dyin'
of stummick-complaint. I'm not easy frightened,
lads, but my knees did feel as if the bones in 'em
had turned to water, and my hair began to git up
on end, for I felt it risin'. Suddently I saw somethin' comin' along the passage towards me——"

"That's the ghost *now*," interrupted Gurney, in
a tremulous whisper.

Rokens paused, and regarded his fat shipmate
with a look of contemptuous pity; then turning
to the others, he said—"It wos *the landlord*,
a-comin' back with the candle. He begged pardon
for leavin' me in the dark so long, and led the way
to a room at the far end o' the passage. It was a
big, old-fashioned room, with a tree-mendius high
ceiling, and no furniture, 'cept one chair, one
small table, and a low camp-bed in a corner.
'Here's your room,' says the landlord; 'it's well-
aired. I may as well mention that the latch of
the door ain't just the thing. It sometimes blows
open with a bang, but when you know it may
happen, you can be on the look-out for it, you
know, and so you'll not be taken by surprise.

Good night.' With that the fellow set the candle down on the small table at the bed-side, and left me to my cogitations. I heerd his footsteps echoin' as he went clankin' along the passages; then they died away, an' I was alone.

Now, I tell ye wot it is, shipmates; I've bin in many a fix, but I niver wos in sich a fix as that. The room was empty and big; so big that the candle could only light up about a quarter of it, leavin' the rest in gloom. There wos one or two old picturs on the walls; one on 'em a portrait of a old admiral, with a blue coat and brass buttons and white veskit. It hung just opposite the fut o' my bunk, an' I could hardly make it out, but I saw that the admiral kep his eye on me whereiver I turned or moved about the room, an twice or thrice, if not more, I saw him wink with his weather eye. Yes, he winked as plain as I do myself. Says I to myself, says I, ' Tim Rokens, you're a British tar, an' a whaler, an' a harpooneer; so Tim, my boy, don't you go for to be a babby.'

"With that I smoked a pipe, and took off my clo's, and tumbled in, and feeling a little bolder by this time, I blew out the candle. In gittin' into bed I knocked over the snuffers, w'ich fell with an awful clatter, and my heart lep' into my mouth as I lep' under the blankets, and kivered up my head. Howsever, I was uncommon tired, so before my head was well on the pillow, I went off to sleep.

" How long I slep' I can't go for to say, but w'en
I wakened it wos pitch dark. I could only just
make out the winder by the pale starlight that
shone through it, but the moment I set my two
eyes on it, wot does I see? I seed a sight that
made the hair on my head stand on end, and my
flesh creep up like a muffin. It was a ——"

" A ghost !" whispered Gurney, while his eyes
almost started out of his head.

Before Tim Rokens could reply, something fell
with a heavy flop from the yard over their heads
right in among the men, and vanished with a
shriek. It was Jacko, who, in his nocturnal
rambles in the rigging, had been shaken off the
yard on which he was perched, by a sudden lurch
of the vessel as the tide began to move her about.
At any time such an event would have been startling, but at such a time as this it was horrifying.
The men recoiled with sharp cries of terror, and
then burst into laughter as they observed what it
was that had fallen amongst them. But the
laughter was subdued, and by no means hearty.

" I'll be the death o' that brute yet," said
Gurney, wiping the perspiration from his forehead ;
" but go on, Rokens ; what was it you saw ?"

" It *was* the ghost," replied Rokens, as the men
gathered round him again—" a long, thin ghost,
standin' at my bedside. The light was so dim that
I couldn't well make it out, but I saw that it was
white, or pale-like, and that it had on a pointed

cap, like the cap o' an old witch. I thought I should ha' died outright, and I lay for full five minits tremblin' like a leaf and starin' full in its face. At last I started up in despair, not knowin' well wot to do ; and the moment I did so the ghost disappeared.

"I thought this was very odd, but you may be sure I didn't find fault with it ; so after lookin' all round very careful to make quite sure that it was gone, I lay down again on my back. Well, would ye b'lieve it, shipmates, at that same moment up starts the ghost again as bold as iver ? And up starts I in a fright ; but the moment I was up the ghost was gone. 'Now, Tim Rokens,' says I to myself, always keepin' my eye on the spot where I'd last seed the ghost; 'this *is* queer ; this is quite re-markable. You're dreamin', my lad, an' the sooner ye put a stop to that ere sort o' dreamin' the better.'

"Havin' said this, I tried to feel reckless, and lay down again, and up started the ghost again with its long thin white body, an' the pointed cap on its head. I noticed, too, that it wore its cap a little on one side quite jaunty like. So, wheniver I sot up that 'ere ghost disappeared, and wheniver I lay down it bolted up again close beside me. At last I lost my temper, and I shouts out quite loud, 'Shiver my timbers,' says I, 'ghost or no ghost, I'll knock in your daylights if ye carry on like that any longer ;' and with that I up fist and let drive straight out at the spot where its bread-basket should ha' bin. Down it went, that ghost did, with a clatter that made the old room echo like an empty church. I guv it a rap, I did, sich as it hadn't had since it was born—if ghosts be born at all—an' my knuckles paid for it, too, for they was skinned all up; then I lay down tremblin', and then, I dun know how it was, I went to sleep.

"Next mornin' I got up to look for the ghost, and, sure enough, I found his *remains!* His pale body lay in a far corner o' the room doubled up and smashed to bits, and his pointed cap lay in another corner almost flat. That ghost," concluded Rokens, with slow emphasis—"that ghost was the *candle*, it wos!"

"The candle!" exclaimed several of the men in surprise.

"Yes, the candle, and brass candlestick with the stinguisher a-top o't. Ye see, lads, the candle stood close to the side o' my bed on the table, an' when I woke up and I saw it there, it seemed to me like a big thing in the middle o' the room, instead o' a little thing close to my nose; an' when I sot up in my bed of coorse I looked right over the top of it and saw nothin'; an' when I lay down of coorse it rose up in the very same place. An', let me tell you, shipmates," added Tim, in conclusion, with the air of a philosopher, "*all* ghosts is o' the same sort. They're most of 'em made o' wood or brass, or some sich stuff, as I've good cause to re-

mimber, for I had to pay the price o' that 'ere
ghost before I left that there hinn on the lonesome
moor, and for the washin' of the blankets too, as
wos all kivered with blood nixt mornin' from my
smashed knuckles.   There's a morial contained in
most things, lads, if ye only try for to find it out;
an' the morial of my story is this,—don't you go
for to b'lieve that everythin' ye don't 'xactly understand is a ghost until ye've got to know more
about it."

While Tim Rokens was thus recounting his,
ghostly experiences, and moralizing thereon, for the
benefit of his comrades, the silent tide was stealthily
creeping up the sides of the Red Eric, and placing
her gradually on an even keel.   At the same time
a British man-of-war was creeping down upon that
innocent vessel with the murderous intention of
blowing her out of the water, if possible."

In order to explain this latter fact, we must remind the reader of the boat and crew of the Portuguese slaver which was encountered by the party
of excursionists on their trip down the river.   The
vessel to which that boat belonged had been for
several weeks previous creeping about off the coast,
watching her opportunity to ship a cargo of slaves,
and at the same time to avoid falling into the hands
of a British cruiser which was stationed on the
African coast to prevent the villanous traffic.   The
Portuguese ship, which was very similar in size and
shape to the Red Eric, had hitherto managed to

elude the cruiser, and had succeeded in taking a number of slaves on board ere she was discovered. The cruiser gave chase so her on the same after-noon as that on which the Red Eric grounded on the mud-bank off the mouth of the river. Dark-ness, however, favoured the slaver, and when the land-breeze failed, she was lost sight of in the in-tricacies of the navigation at that part of the coast.

Towards morning, while it was yet dark, the Red Eric floated, and Captain Dunning, who had paced the deck all night with a somewhat impatient tread, called to the mate,—

"Now, Mr. Millons, man the boats, and let some of the hands stand by to trim the sails to the first puff of wind."

"Ay, ay, sir," answered the mate, as he sprang to obey.

Now it is a curious fact, that at that identical moment the captain of the cruiser addressed his first lieutenant in precisely the same words, for he had caught a glimpse of the whaler's topmasts against the dark sky, and mistook them, very naturally, for those of the slaver. In a few seconds the man-of-war was in full pursuit.

"I say, Dr. Hopley," remarked Captain Dun-ning, as he gazed intently into the gloom astern, "did you not hear voices? and, as I live, there's a large ship bearing right down on us!"

"It must be a slaver," replied the doctor; "probably the one that owned the boat we saw up the river."

"Ship on the larboard bow !" shouted the look-out on the forecastle.

"Hallo ! ships ahead and astern !" remarked the captain, in surprise. "There seems to be a ' school' of 'em in these waters."

At this moment the oars of the boats belonging to the ship astern were heard distinctly, and a light puff of wind at the same time bulged out the sails of the Red Eric, which instantly forged ahead.

"Ship, ahoy !" shouted a voice from the boats astern in a tone of authority ; "heave-to, you rascal, or I'll sink you !"

Captain Dunning turned to the doctor with a look of intense surprise.

"Why, doctor, that's the usual hail of a pirate, or something like it. What it can be doing here is past my comprehension. I would as soon expect to find a whale in a wash-tub as a black flag in these waters ! Port, port a little (turning to the steersman)—steady—so. We must run for it, any-how, for we're in no fightin' trim. The best answer to give to such a hail is silence."

Contrary to expectation the boats did not again hail, but in a few minutes the dark hull of the British cruiser became indistinctly visible as it slipped swiftly through the water before the freshen-ing breeze, and neared the comparatively slow-going whaler rapidly. Soon it came within easy range, and while Captain Dunning looked over the taffrail with a troubled countenance, trying to make her out, the same voice came hoarsely down on the night breeze issuing the same peremptory command.

"Turn up the hands, Mr. Millons, and serve out pistols and cutlasses. Get the carronades on the forecastle and quarter-deck loaded, Mr. Markham, and look alive ; we must show the enemy a bold front, whoever he is."

As the captain issued these orders, the darkness was for an instant illuminated by a bright flash ; the roar of a cannon reverberated over the sea ; a round-shot whistled through the rigging of the Red Eric, and the next instant the foretopsail-yard came rattling down upon the deck.

Immediately after, the cruiser ranged up alongside, and the order to heave-to was repeated with a threat that was calculated to cause the hair of a man of peace stand on end. The effect on Captain Dunning was to induce him to give the order—

"Point the guns there lads, and aim high; I don't like to draw first blood—even of a pirate."

"Ship ahoy ! Who are you, and where from ?" inquired Captain Dunning, through the speaking-trumpet.

"Her British Majesty's frigate Firebrand. If you don't heave-to, sir, instantly, I'll give you a broadside. Who are you, and where bound ?"

"Whew !" whistled Captain Dunning, to vent

his feelings of surprise ere he replied, " The Red Eric, South Sea whaler, outward bound."

Having given this piece of information, he ordered the topsails to be backed and the ship was hove-to. Meanwhile a boat was lowered from the cruiser, and the captain thereof speedily leaped upon the whaler's quarter-deck.

The explanation that followed was not by any means calculated to allay the irritation of the British captain. He had made quite sure that the Red Eric was the slaver of which he was in search, and the discovery of his mistake induced him to make several rather severe remarks in reference to the crew of the Red Eric generally and her commander in particular.

" Why didn't you heave-to when I ordered you," he said, " and so save all this trouble and worry ?"

"Because," replied Captain Dunning, drily, " I'm not in the habit of obeying orders until I know that he who gives 'em has a right to do so. But 'tis a pity to waste time talking about such trifles when the craft you are in search of is not very far away at this moment."

" What mean you, sir ?" inquired the captain of the cruiser, quickly.

" I mean that yonder vessel, scarcely visible now on the lee bow, is the slaver, in all likelihood."

The captain gave but one hasty glance in the direction pointed to by Captain Dunning, and next moment he was over the side of the ship, and the boat was flying swiftly towards his vessel. The rapid orders given on board the cruiser soon after, showed that her commander was eagerly in pursuit of the strange vessel ahead, and the flash and report of a couple of guns proved that he was again giving orders in his somewhat peremptory style.

When daylight appeared, Captain Dunning was still on deck, and Glynn Proctor stood by the wheel. The post of the latter, however, was a sinecure, as the wind had again fallen. When the sun rose it revealed the three vessels lying becalmed within a short distance of each other and several miles off shore.

"So, so," exclaimed the captain, taking the glass and examining the other vessels. "I see it's all up with the slaver. Serves him right; don't it, Glynn?"

"It does," replied Glynn, emphatically. "I hope they will all be hanged. Isn't that the usual way of serving these fellows out?"

"Well, not exactly, lad. They don't go quite that length—more's the pity; if they did, there would be less slave-trading; but the rascals will lose both ship and cargo."

"I wonder," said Glynn, "how they can afford to carry on the trade when they lose so many ships as I am told they do every year."

"You wouldn't wonder, boy, if you knew the enormous prices got for slaves. Why, the profits on one cargo, safely delivered, will more than cover the loss of several vessels and cargoes. You may

depend on't they would not carry it on if it did
not pay."

"Humph!" ejaculated Glynn, giving the wheel
a savage turn, as if to express his thorough disap-
probation of the slave-trade, and his extreme disgust at not being able, by the strength of his own
right arm, at once to repress it. "And who's to
pay for our foretopsail-yard?" he inquired, abruptly,
as if desirous of changing the subject.

"Ourselves, I fear," replied the captain. "We
must take it philosophically, and comfort ourselves
with the fact that it *is* the foretopsail-yard, and not
the bowsprit or the mainmast, that was carried
away. It's not likely the captain of the cruiser
will pay for it, at any rate."

Captain Dunning was wrong. That same morning he received a polite note from the commander
of the said cruiser, requesting the pleasure of his
company to dinner, in the event of the calm continuing, and assuring him that the carpenter and
sailmaker of the man-of-war should be sent on
board his ship after breakfast to repair damages.
Captain Dunning, therefore, like an honest straight-
forward man as he was, admitted that he had been
hasty in his judgment, and stated to Glynn Proctor,
emphatically, that the commander of the Firebrand
was "a trump."

## CHAPTER XV.

NEW SCENES — A FIGHT PREVENTED BY A WHALE — A
STORM—BLOWN OFF THE YARDARM—WRECK OF "THE
RED ERIC."

FIVE weeks passed away, and really, when one
comes to consider the matter, it is surprising what
a variety of events may be compressed into five
weeks; what an amount of space may be passed
over, what an immense change of scene and circumstance may be experienced in that comparatively short period of time.

Men and women who remain quietly at home do
not, perhaps, fully realize this fact. Five weeks to
them does not usually seem either very long or
very short. But let those quiet ones travel; let
them rush away headlong, by the aid of wind and
steam, to the distant and wonderful parts of this
wonderful world of ours, and, ten to one, they will
afterwards tell you that the most wonderful dis
covery they have made during their travels, is the
fact that a miniature lifetime (apparently) can be
compressed into five weeks.

Five weeks passed away, and in the course of
that time the foretopsail-yard of the Red Eric had
been repaired; the Red Eric herself had passed
from equatorial into southern seas; Alice Dunning
had become very sea-sick, which caused her to look
uncommonly green in the face, and had got well

P

again, which caused her to become fresh and rosy
as the early morning; Jacko had thoroughly established his reputation as the most arrant and accomplished thief that ever went to sea; King
Bumble had been maligned and abused again and
again, and over again, despite his protestations of
innocence, by grim-faced Tarquin, the steward, for
having done the deeds which were afterwards discovered to have been committed by Jacko; fat
little Gurney had sung innumerable songs of his
own composing, in which he was ably supported by
Glynn Proctor; Dr. Hopley had examined, phre-
nologically, all the heads on board, with the exception of that of Tarquin, who would not submit to
the operation on any account, and had shot, and
skinned, and stuffed a variety of curious sea-birds,
and caught a number of remarkable sea-fish, and
had microscopically examined—to the immense
interest of Ailie, and consequently of the captain—
a great many surprising animalcules, called *Medusæ*, which possessed the most watery and the
thinnest possible bodies, yet which had the power
of emitting a beautiful phosphoric light at night,
so as to cause the whole ocean sometimes to glow
as if with liquid fire; Phil Briant had cracked more
jokes, good, bad, and indifferent, than would serve
to fill a whole volume of closely-printed pages, and
had told more stories than would be believed by
most people; Tim Rokens and the other har-
pooners had, with the assistance of the various

boats' crews, slain and captured several large whales, and Nikel Sling had prepared, and assisted to consume, as many breakfasts, dinners, and suppers, as there are days in the period of time above referred to ;—in short, those five weeks, which we thus dismiss in five minutes, might, if enlarged upon, be expanded into material to fill five volumes such as this, which would probably take about five years to write—another reason for cutting this matter short. All this shows how much may be compressed into little space, how much may be done and seen in little time, and, therefore, how much value men ought to attach to little things.

Five weeks passed away, as we have already remarked, and at the end of that time the Red Eric found herself, one beautiful sunny afternoon, becalmed on the breast of the wide ocean with a strange vessel, also a whaler, a few miles distant from her, and a couple of sperm-whales sporting playfully about midway between the two ships. Jim Scroggles on that particular afternoon found himself in the crow's-nest at the mast-head, roaring "Thar she blows!" with a degree of energy so appalling that one was almost tempted to believe that that long-legged individual had made up his mind to compress his life into one grand but brief minute, and totally exhaust his powers of soul and body in the reiterated vociferation of that one faculty of the sperm-whale. Allowance must be made for Jim, seeing that this was the first time he had been fortunate enough to "raise the oil" since he became a whaler.

The usual scene of bustle and excitement immediately ensued. The men sprang to their appointed places in a moment; the tubs, harpoons, &c., were got ready, and in a few minutes the three boats were leaping over the smooth swell towards the fish.

While this was taking place on board the Red Eric, a precisely similar scene occurred on board the other whale-ship, and a race now ensued between the boats of the two ships, for each knew well that the first boat that harpooned either of the whales claimed it.

"Give way, my lads," whispered Captain Dunning, eagerly, as he watched the other boats, "we shall be first—we shall be first; only bend your backs."

The men needed not to be urged; they were quite as anxious as their commander to win the race, and bent their backs, as he expressed it, until the oars seemed about to break. Glynn sat on the after thwart, and did good service on this occasion.

It soon became evident that the affair would be decided by the boats of the two captains, both of which took the lead of the others, but as they were advancing in opposite directions it was difficult to tell which was the fleeter of the two. When the excitement of the race was at its height the whales went down, and the men lay on their oars to wait until they should rise again. They lay in anxious suspense for about a minute, when the crew of Captain Dunning's boat were startled by the sudden apparition of a waterspout close to them, by which they were completely drenched. It was immediately followed by the appearance of the huge blunt head of one of the whales, which rose like an enormous rock out of the sea close to the starboard-quarter.

The sight was received with a loud shout, and Tim Rokens leaped up and grasped a harpoon, but the whale sheered off. A spare harpoon lay on the stern-sheets close to Glynn, who dropped his oar and seized it. Almost without knowing what he was about, he hurled it with tremendous force at the monster's neck, into which it penetrated deeply. The harpoon fortunately happened to be attached to a large buoy, called by whalers a drog, which was jerked out of the boat like a cannon-shot as the whale went down, carrying harpoon and drog along with it.

"Well done, lad," cried the captain, in great delight, "you've made a noble beginning! Now, lads, pull gently ahead, she wont go far with such an ornament as that dangling at her neck. A capital dart! couldn't have done it half so well myself, even in my young days!"

Glynn felt somewhat elated at this unexpected piece of success; to do him justice, however, he

took it modestly. In a few minutes the whale rose,
but it had changed its course while under water,
and now appeared close to the leading boat of the
other ship.

By the laws of the whale fishery, no boat of one
vessel has a right to touch a whale that has been
struck by the boat of another vessel, so long as the
harpoon holds fast and the rope remains unbroken,
or so long as the float to which the harpoon is connected remains attached. Nevertheless, in defiance
of this well-known law, the boat belonging to the
captain of the strange ship gave chase, and succeeded in making fast to the whale.

To describe the indignation of Captain Dunning
and his men on witnessing this act is impossible.
The former roared rather than shouted, "Give
way, lads!" and the latter bent their backs as if
they meant to pull the boat bodily out of the
water, and up into the atmosphere. Meanwhile
all the other boats were in hot pursuit of the
second whale, which had led them a considerable
distance away from the first.

"What do you mean by striking that fish?"
shouted Captain Dunning, when, after a hard pull,
he came up with the boat, the crew of which had
just succeeded in thrusting a lance deep into a
mortal part of the huge animal, which soon after
rolled over, and lay extended on the waves.

"What right have you to ask?" replied the captain of the strange ship, an ill-favoured, powerful

man, whose countenance was sufficient to condemn him in any society, save that of ruffians. "Don't you see your drog has broke loose ?"

"I see nothing of the sort. It's fast at this moment; so you'll be good enough to cut loose and take yourself off as fast as you please."

To this the other made no reply, but, turning to his men, said : "Make fast there, lads; signal the other boats, and pull away for the ship ; look sharp, you lubbers."

"Och ! captain, dear," muttered Phil Briant, baring both arms up to the shoulders, "only give the word ; *do*, now !"

Captain Dunning, who was already boiling with rage, needed no encouragement to make an immediate attack on the stranger, neither did his men require an order ; they plunged their oars into the water, ran right into the other boat, sprang to their feet, seized lances, harpoons, and knives, and in another moment would have been engaged in a deadly struggle had not an unforeseen event occurred to prevent the fray. This was the partial recovery of the whale, which, apparently resolved to make one final struggle for life, turned over and over, lashed the sea into foam, and churned it up with the blood which spouted in thick streams from its numerous wounds.

Both boats were in imminent danger, and the men sprang to their oars in order to pull out of the range of the monster's dying struggles. In this effort the strange boat was successful, but that of Captain Dunning fared ill. A heavy blow from the whale's tail broke it in two, and hurled it into the air, whence the crew descended, amid a mass of harpoons, lances, oars, and cordage, into the blood-stained water.

The fish sheered away for some distance, dragging the other boat along with it, and then rolled over quite dead. Fortunately not one of the crew of the capsized boat was hurt. All of them succeeded in reaching and clinging to the shattered hull of their boat; but there they were destined to remain a considerable time, as the boat of the stranger, having secured the dead fish, proceeded leisurely to tow it towards their ship, without paying the slightest attention to the shouts of their late enemies.

A change had now come over the face of the sky. Clouds began to gather on the horizon, and a few light puffs of air swept over the sea, which enabled the strange vessel to bear down on her boat, and take the whale in tow. It also enabled the Red Eric to beat up, but more slowly, towards the spot where their disabled boat lay, and rescue their comrades from their awkward position. It was some time before the boats were all gathered together. When this was accomplished the night had set in and the stranger had made off with her ill-gotten prize, the other whale having sounded, and the chase been abandoned.

"Now, of all the disgustin' things that ever hap-

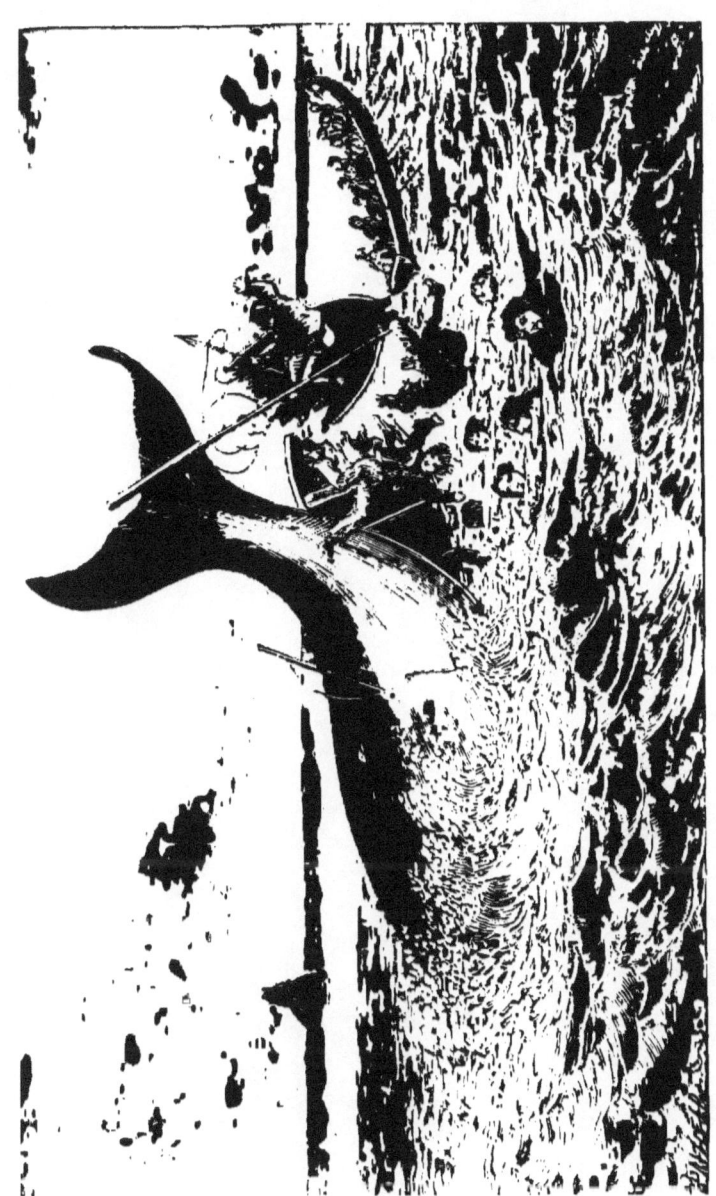

A DISPUTE SETTLED BY A WHALE.—Page 216.

pened to me, this is the worst," remarked Captain
Dunning, in a very sulky tone of voice, as he
descended to the cabin to change his garments,
Ailie having preceded him in order to lay out dry
clothes.

"Oh! my darling papa, what a fright I got,'
she exclaimed, running up and hugging him, wet
as he was, for the seventh time, despite his efforts
to keep her off. "I was looking through the spy-
glass at the time it happened, and when I saw you
all thrown into the air I cried—oh! I can't tell
you how I cried."

"You don't need to tell me, Ailie, my pet, for
your red, swelled-up eyes speak for themselves.
But go, you puss, and change your own frock.
You've made it as wet as my coat, nearly; besides,
I can't undress, you know, while you stand there."

Ailie said, "I'm so very, very thankful," and
then giving her father one concluding hug, which
completely saturated the frock, went to her own
cabin.

Meanwhile the crew of the captain's boat were
busy in the forecastle stripping off their wet garments, and relating their adventures to the men of
the other boats, who, until they reached the ship,
had been utterly ignorant of what had passed.

It is curious that Tim Rokens should open the
conversation with much the same sentiment, if not
exactly the same phrase, as that expressed by the
captain.

"Now, boys," said he, slapping his wet limbs,

"I'll tell ye wot it is, of all the aggrawations as has happened to me in my life, this is out o' sight the wust. To think o' losin' that there whale, the very biggest I ever saw——"

"Ah! Rokens, man," interrupted Glynn, as he pulled off his jacket, "the loss is greater to me than to you, for that was my *first* whale!"

"True, boy," replied the harpooner, in a tone of evidently genuine sympathy; "I feel for ye. I knows how I should ha' taken on if it had happened to me. But cheer up, lad; you know the old proverb, 'There's as good a fish in the sea as ever came out o't.' You'll be the death o' many sich yet, I'll bet my best iron."

"Sure, the wust of it all is, that we don't know who was the big thief as got that fish away with him," said Phil Briant, with a rueful countenance.

"Don't we, though!" cried Gurney, who had been in the mate's boat; "I axed one o' the men o' the stranger's boats—for we run up close along side durin' the chase—and he told me as how she was the Termagant of New York; so we can be down on 'em yet, if we live long enough."

"Humph!" observed Rokens; "and d'ye suppose he'd give ye the right name?"

"He'd no reason to do otherwise. He didn't know of the dispute between the other boats."

"There's truth in that," remarked Glynn, as he prepared to go on deck; "but it may be a year or more before we foregather.  No, I give up all claim to my first fish from this date."

"All hands ahoy !" shouted the mate ; "tumble up there !  Reef topsails !  Look alive !"

The men ran hastily on deck, completing their buttoning and belting as they went, and found that something very like a storm was brewing.  As yet the breeze was moderate, and the sea not very high, but the night was pitchy dark, and a hot oppressive atmosphere boded no improvement in the weather.

" Lay out there, some of you, and close reef the topsails," cried the mate, as the men ran to their several posts.

The ship was running at the time under a comparatively small amount of canvas; for, as their object was merely to cruise about in those seas in search of whales, and they had no particular course to steer, it was usual to run at night under easy sail, and sometimes to lay-to.  It was fortunate that such was the case on the present occasion ; for it happened that the storm which was about to burst on them came with appalling suddenness and fury.  The wind tore up the sea as if it had been a mass of white feathers, and scattered it high in air.  The mizen-topsail was blown to ribbons, and it seemed as if the other sails were about to share the same fate.  The ship flew from billow to billow, after recovering from the first rude shock, as if she were but a dark cloud on the sea, and the spray flew high over her masts, drenching the men on the topsail-yards while they laboured to reef the sails.

"We shall have to take down these t'gallant masts, Mr. Millons," said the captain, as he stood by the weather-bulwarks holding on to a belaying-pin to prevent his being washed away.

"Shall I give the order, sir?" inquired the first mate.

"You may," replied the captain.

Just as the mate turned to obey, a shriek was heard high above the whistling of the fierce wind.

"Did you hear that?" said the captain, anxiously.

"I did," replied the mate. "I fear—I trust—"

The remainder of the sentence was either suppressed, or the howling of the wind prevented its being heard.

Just then a flash of lightning lit up the scene, and a terrific crash of thunder seemed to rend the sky. The flash was momentary, but it served to reveal the men on the yards distinctly. They had succeeded in close-reefing the topsails, and were hurrying down the rigging. The mate came close to the captain's side and said, "Did you see, sir, the way them men on the mainyard were scramblin' down?"

The captain had not time to reply ere a shout, "Man overboard!" was heard faintly in the midst of the storm, and in another instant some of the men rushed aft with frantic haste, shouting that one of their number had been blown off the yard into the sea.

"Down your helm," roared the captain; "stand by to lower away the boats."

The usual prompt "Ay, ay, sir," was given, but before the men could reach their places a heavy sea struck the vessel amidships, poured several tons of water on the decks, and washed all the loose gear overboard.

"Let her away," cried the captain, quickly.

The steersman obeyed; the ship fell off, and again bounded on her mad course like a wild horse set free.

"It's of no use, sir," said the mate, as the captain leaped towards the wheel, which the other had already gained; "no boat could live in that sea for a moment. The poor fellow's gone by this time. He must be more than half a mile astern already."

"I know it," returned the captain, in a deep sad voice. "Get these masts down, Mr. Millons, and see that everything is made fast. Who is it, did you say?"

"The men can't tell, sir; one of 'em told me 'e thinks it was young Boswell. It was too dark to see 'is face, but 'is figure was that of a stout young fellow."

"A stout young fellow," muttered the captain, as the mate hurried forward. "Can it have been Glynn?" His heart sank within him at the thought, and he would have given worlds at that moment, had he possessed them, to have heard the voice of our hero, whom, almost unwittingly, he had begun to love with all the affection of a father. While he stood gazing up at the rigging, attempting to pierce the thick darkness, he felt his sleeve plucked, and, looking down, observed Ailie at his side.

"My child," he cried, grasping her by the arm convulsively, "*you* here! How came you to leave your cabin, dear? Go down, go down; you don't know the danger you run. Stay—I will help you. If one of those seas comes on board it would carry you overboard like a fleck of foam."

"I didn't know there was much danger, papa. Glynn told me there wasn't," she replied, as her father sprang with her to the companion-ladder.

"How! when! where! child? Did Glynn speak to you within the last ten minutes?"

"Yes; he looked down the hatch just as I was coming up, and told me not to be afraid, and said I must go below, and not think of coming on deck; but I heard a shriek, papa, and feared something had happened, so I came to ask what it was. I hope no one is hurt."

"My darling Ailie," replied the captain, in an agitated voice, "go down to your berth, and pray for us just now. There is not *much* danger; but in all times of danger, whether great or slight, we should pray to Our Father in Heaven, for we never know what a day or an hour may bring forth. I will speak to you about everything to-morrow; to-night I must be on deck."

He kissed her forehead, pushed her gently into the cabin, shut the door, and, coming on deck, fastened the companion-hatch firmly down.

In a short time the ship was prepared to face the worst. The topsails were close reefed; the top-gallant-masts sent down on deck; the spanker and jib were furled, and soon after the mainsail and foresail were also furled. The boats were taken in and secured on deck, and the ship went a little more easily through the raging sea; but as the violence of the gale increased, sail had to be further reduced, and at last everything was taken in except the main spencer and foretopmast staysail.

"I wouldn't mind this much," said the captain, as he and the first mate stood close to the binnacle, "if I only knew our exact position. But we've not had an observation for several days, and I don't feel sure of our whereabouts. There are some nasty coral reefs in these seas. Did you find out who the poor fellow is yet?"

"It's young Boswell, I fear. Mr. Markham is mustering the men just now, sir."

As he spoke, the second mate came aft and con-firmed their fears. The man who had thus been summoned in a moment, without warning, into the presence of his Maker, had been a quiet, modest youth, and a favourite with every one on board.

At any other time his death would have been
deeply felt; but in the midst of that terrible storm
the men had no time to think. Indeed, they could
not realize the fact that their shipmate was really
gone.

"Mr. Markham," said the captain, as the second
mate turned away, "send a hand into the chains
to heave the lead. I don't feel at all easy in my
mind, so near these shoals as we must be just now."

While the order was being obeyed, the storm
became fiercer and more furious. Bright gleams
of lightning flashed repeatedly across the sky,
lighting up the scene as if with brightest moonlight,
and revealing the horrid turmoil of the raging sea
in which the ship now laboured heavily. The
rapidity with which the thunder followed the
lightning showed how near to them was the
dangerous and subtle fluid; and the crashing,
bursting reports that shook the ship from stem to
stern gave the impression that mountains were
being dashed to atoms against each other in the air.

All the sails still exposed to the fury of the gale
were blown to shreds; the foretopmast and the
jib-boom were carried away along with them, and
the Red Eric was driven at last before the wind
under bare poles. The crew remained firm in the
midst of this awful scene; each man stood at his
post, holding on by any fixed object that chanced
to be within his reach, and held himself ready to
spring to obey every order. No voice could be

heard in the midst of the howling winds, the lash-
ing sea, and the rending sky.  Commands were
given by signs, as well as possible, during the
flashes of lightning ; but little or nothing remained
to be done.  Captain Dunning had done all that
a man thoroughly acquainted with his duties could
accomplish to put his ship in the best condition to
do battle with the storm, and he now felt that the
issue remained in the hands of Him who formed
the warring elements, and whose will alone could
check their angry strife.

During one of the vivid flashes of lightning the
captain observed Glynn Proctor standing near the
starboard gangway, and, waiting for the next flash,
he made a signal to him to come to the spot where
he stood.  Glynn understood it, and in a few
seconds was at his commander's side.

"Glynn, my boy," said the latter, "you wont
be wanted on deck for some time.  There's little
to be done now.  Go down and see what Ailie's
about, poor thing.  She'll need a little comfort.
Say I sent you.

Without other reply than a nod of the head,
Glynn sprang to the companion-hatch, followed by
the captain, who undid the fastenings to let him
down and refastened them immediately, for the sea
was washing over the stern continually.

Glynn found the child on her knees in the cabin
with her face buried in the cushions of one of the
sofas.  He sat down beside her and waited until

Q

she should have finished her prayer; but as she did not move for some time he laid his hand gently on her shoulder. She looked up with a happy smile on her face.

"Oh! Glynn, is that you? I'm so glad," she said, rising, and sitting down beside him.

"Your father sent me down to comfort you, my pet," said Glynn, taking her hand in his and drawing her towards him.

"I have got comfort already," replied the child; "I'm so very happy now."

"How so, Ailie? who has been with you?"

"God has been with me. You told me, Glynn, that there wasn't much danger, but I felt sure that there was. Oh! I never heard such terrible noises, and this dreadful tossing is worse than ever I felt it—a great deal. So I went down on my knees and prayed that God, for Christ's sake, would save us. I felt very frightened, Glynn. You can't think how my heart beat every time the thunder burst over us. But suddenly—I don't know how it was—the words I used to read at home so often with my dear aunts came into my mind; you know them, Glynn, ' Call upon me in the time of trouble, and I will deliver thee, and thou shalt glorify me.' I don't know where I read them. I forget the place in the Bible now; but when I thought of them I felt much less frightened. Do you think it was the Holy Spirit who put them into my mind? My aunts used to tell me that all my *good* thoughts

were given to me by the Holy Spirit. Then I
remembered the words of Jesus, 'I will never
leave thee nor forsake thee,' and I felt so happy
after that. It was just before you came down. I
*think* we shall not be lost. God would not make
me feel so happy if we were going to be lost, would
he ?"

"I think not, Ailie," replied Glynn, whose con-
science reproached him for his ignorance of the
passages in God's word referred to by his companion, and who felt that he was receiving rather
than administering comfort. "When I came down
I did not very well know how I should comfort
you, for this is certainly the most tremendous gale
I ever saw, but somehow I feel as if we were in less
danger now. I wish I knew more of the Bible,
Ailie. I'm ashamed to say I seldom look at it."

"Oh, that's a pity, isn't it, Glynn?" said Ailie,
with earnest concern expressed in her countenance,
for she regarded her companion's ignorance as a
great misfortune; it never occurred to her that it
was a sin. "But it's very easy to learn it," she
added, with an eager look. "If you come to me
here every day we can read it together. I would
like to have you to hear me say it off, and then
I would hear you."

Before he could reply the vessel received a tremendous shock which caused her to quiver from
stem to stern.

"She must have been struck by lightning,"

cried Glynn, starting up and hurrying towards the
door. Ailie's frightened look returned for a few
minutes, but she did not tremble as she had done
before.

Just as Glynn reached the top of the ladder the
hatch was opened and the captain thrust in his head.

"Glynn, my boy," said he, in a quick firm tone,
"we are ashore. Perhaps we shall go to pieces in
a few minutes. God knows. May He in his
mercy spare us. You cannot do much on deck.
Ailie must be looked after till I come down for
her. Glynn, *I depend upon you.*"

These words were uttered hurriedly, and the
hatch was shut immediately after. It is impossible
to describe accurately the conflicting feelings that
agitated the breast of the young sailor as he descended again to the cabin. He felt gratified at
the trust placed in him by the captain, and his love
for the little girl would at any time have made the
post of protector to her an agreeable one; but the
idea that the ship had struck the rocks, and that
his shipmates on deck were struggling perhaps for
their lives while he was sitting idly in the cabin,
was most trying and distressing to one of his ardent
and energetic temperament. He was not, however,
kept long in suspense.

Scarcely had he regained the cabin when the
ship again struck with terrific violence, and he
knew by the rending crash overhead that one or
more of the masts had gone over the side. The

ship at the same moment slewed round and was thrown on her beam-ends. So quickly did this occur that Glynn had barely time to seize Ailie in his arms and save her from being dashed against the bulkhead.

The vessel rose again on the next wave, and was hurled on the rocks with such violence that every one on board expected her to go to pieces immediately. At the same time the cabin windows were dashed in, and the cabin itself was flooded with water. Glynn was washed twice across the cabin and thrown violently against the ship's sides, but he succeeded in keeping a firm hold of his little charge and in protecting her from injury.

"Hallo, Glynn!" shouted the captain, as he opened the companion-hatch, "come on deck, quick! bring her with you!"

Glynn hurried up and placed the child in her father's arms.

The scene that presented itself to him on gaining the deck was indeed appalling. The first grey streak of dawn faintly lighted up the sky, just affording sufficient light to exhibit the complete wreck of everything on deck, and the black froth-capped tumult of the surrounding billows. The rocks on which they had struck could not be discerned in the gloom, but the white breakers ahead showed too clearly where they were. The three masts had gone over the side one after another, leaving only the stumps of each standing. Every-

thing above board—boats, binnacle, and part of the
bulwarks—had been washed away.  The crew were
clinging to the belaying-pins and to such parts of
the wreck as seemed likely to hold together longest.
It seemed to poor Ailie, as she clung to her father's
neck, that she had been transported to some far-
distant and dreadful scene, for scarcely a single
familiar object remained by which her ocean home,
the Red Eric, could be recognised.

But Ailie had neither desire nor opportunity to
remark on this tremendous change.  Every successive billow raised the doomed vessel, and let her
fall with heavy violence on the rocks.  Her stout
frame trembled under each shock as if she were
endued with life, and shrank affrighted from her
impending fate ; and it was as much as the captain
could do to maintain his hold of the weather bulwarks and of Ailie at the same time.  Indeed, he
could not have done it at all had not Glynn stood
by and assisted him to the best of his ability.

"It wont last long, lad," said the captain, as a
larger wave than usual lifted the shattered hull
and dashed it down on the rocks, washing the deck
from stern to stem, and for a few seconds burying
the whole crew under water.  "May the Almighty
have mercy on us ; no ship can stand this long."

"Perhaps the tide is falling," suggested Glynn,
in an encouraging voice, "and I think I see something like a shore ahead.  It will be daylight in
half an hour or less."

The captain shook his head. "There's little or no tide here to rise or fall, I fear. Before half an hour we shall——"

He did not finish the sentence, but looking at Ailie with a gaze of agony, he pressed her more closely to his breast.

"I think we shall be saved," whispered the child, twining her arms more closely round her father's neck, and laying her wet cheek against his.

Just then Tim Rokens crept aft, and said that he saw a low sandy island ahead, and a rocky point jutting out from it close to the bows of the ship. He suggested that a rope might be got ashore when it became a little lighter.

Phil Briant came aft to make the same suggestion, not knowing that Rokens had preceded him. In fact, the men had been consulting as to the possibility of accomplishing this object, but when they looked at the fearful breakers that boiled in white foam between the ship's bow and the rocky point, their hearts failed them, and no one was found to volunteer for the dangerous service.

"Is any one inclined to try it?" inquired the captain.

"There's niver a wan of us but 'ud try it, cap'en, *if you gives the order*," answered Briant.

The captain hesitated. He felt disinclined to order any man to expose himself to such imminent danger; yet the safety of the whole crew might depend on a rope being connected with the shore.

Before he could make up his mind, Glynn, who saw
what was passing in his mind, exclaimed—

"I'll do it, captain;" and instantly quitting his
position, hurried forward as fast as circumstances
would permit.

The task which Glynn had undertaken to perform turned out to be more dangerous and difficult
than at first he had anticipated. When he stood
at the lee bow, fastening a small cord round his
waist, and looking at the turmoil of water into
which he was about to plunge, his heart well-nigh
failed him, and he felt a sensation of regret that he
had undertaken what seemed now an impossibility.
He did not wonder that the men had one and all
shrunk from the attempt. But he had made up
his mind to do it. Moreover, he had *said* he would
do it, and feeling that he imperilled his life in a
good cause, he set his face as a flint to the accom-
plishment of his purpose.

Well was it for Glynn Proctor that day that in
early boyhood he had learned to swim, and had
become so expert in the water as to be able to beat
all his young companions !

He noticed, on looking narrowly at the foaming
surge through which he must pass in order to gain
the rocky point, that many of the submerged rocks
showed their tops above the flood, like black spots,
when each wave retired. To escape these seemed
impossible—to strike one of them he knew would
be almost certain death.

" Don't try it, boy," said several of the men, as
they saw Glynn hesitate when about to spring, and
turn an anxious gaze in all directions, " it's into
death ye'll jump, if ye do."

Glynn did not reply; indeed, he did not hear
the remark, for at that moment his whole attention
was rivetted on a ledge of submerged rock, which
ever and anon showed itself, like the edge of a
knife, extending between the ship and the point.
Along the edge of this the retiring waves broke in
such a manner as to form what appeared to be
dead water—tossed, indeed, and foam clad, but not
apparently in progressive motion. Glynn made up
his mind in an instant, and just as the first mate
came forward with an order from the captain that
he was on no account to make the rash attempt,
he sprang with his utmost force off the ship's side
and sank in the raging sea.

Words cannot describe the intense feeling of
suspense with which the men on the lee bow gazed
at the noble-hearted boy as he rose and buffeted
with the angry billows. Every man held his breath,
and those who had charge of the line stood nervously ready to haul him back at a moment's notice.

On first rising to the surface he beat the waves
as if bewildered, and while some of the men cried,
" He's struck a rock," others shouted to haul him
in; but in another second he got his eyes cleared
of spray, and seeing the ship's hull towering above
his head, be turned his back on it and made fa

the shore.  At first he went rapidly through the surge, for his arm was strong and his young heart was brave ; but a receding wave caught him and hurled him some distance out of his course—tossing him over and over as if he had been a cork. Again he recovered himself, and gaining the water beside the ledge, he made several powerful and rapid strokes, which carried him within a few yards of the point.

"He's safe," said Rokens, eagerly.

"No ; he's missed it !" cried the second mate, who, with Gurney and Dick Barnes, payed out the rope.

Glynn had indeed almost caught hold of the farthest out ledge of the point, when he was drawn back into the surge, and this time dashed against a rock, and partially stunned.  The men had already begun to haul in on the rope when he recovered, and making a last effort, gained the rocks, up which he clambered slowly.  When beyond the reach of the waves he fell down as if he had fainted.

This, however, was not the case ; he was merely exhausted, as well as confused, by the blows he had received on the rocks, and lay for a few seconds quite still in order to recover strength, during which period of inaction he thanked God earnestly for his deliverance, and prayed fervently that he might be made the means of saving his companions in danger.

After a minute or two he rose, unfastened the line from his waist, and began to haul it ashore. To the other end of the small line the men in the ship attached a thick cable, the end of which was soon pulled up, and made fast to a large rock.

Tim Rokens was now ordered to proceed to the shore by means of the rope in order to test it. After this a sort of swing was constructed, with a noose which was passed round the cable. To this a small line was fastened, and passed to the shore. On this swinging-seat Ailie was seated, and hauled to the rocks, Tim Rokens "shinning" along the cable at the same time to guard her from accident. Then the men began to land, and thus, one by one, the crew of the Red Eric reached the shore in safety; and when all had landed, Captain Dunning, standing in the midst of his men, lifted up his voice in thanksgiving to God for their deliverance.

But when daylight came the full extent of their forlorn situation was revealed. The ship was a complete wreck; the boats were all gone, and they found that the island on which they had been cast was only a few square yards in extent—a mere sandbank, utterly destitute of shrub or tree, and raised only a few feet above the level of the ocean.

# CHAPTER XVI.

### THE SANDBANK—THE WRECKED CREW MAKE THE BEST OF BAD CIRCUMSTANCES.

IT will scarcely surprise the reader to be told that, after the first emotions of thankfulness for deliverance from what had appeared to the shipwrecked mariners to be inevitable death, a feeling amounting almost to despair took possession of the whole party for a time.

The sandbank was so low that in stormy weather it was almost submerged. It was a solitary coral-reef in the midst of the boundless sea. Not a tree or bush grew upon it, and except at the point where the ship had struck, there was scarcely a rock large enough to afford shelter to a single man. Without provisions, without sufficient shelter, without the means of escape, and *almost* without the hope of deliverance, it seemed to them that nothing awaited them but the slow lingering pains and horrors of death by starvation.

As those facts forced themselves more and more powerfully home to the apprehension of the crew, while they cowered for shelter from the storm under the lee of the rocky point, they gave expression to their feelings in different ways. Some sat down in dogged silence to await their fate ; others fell on their knees and cried aloud to God for mercy ; while a few kept up their own spirits and

those of their companions by affecting a cheerful-
ness which, however, in some cases, was a little
forced. Ailie lay shivering in her father's arms,
for she was drenched with salt water and very cold.
Her eyes were closed, and she was very pale from
exposure and exhaustion, but her lips moved as if
in prayer.

Captain Dunning looked anxiously at Dr. Hopley, who crouched beside them, and gazed earnestly
in the child's face while he felt her pulse.

"It's almost too much for her, I fear," said the
captain, in a hesitating, husky voice.

The doctor did not answer for a minute or two,
then he said, as if muttering to himself rather than
replying to the captain's remark, "If we could
only get her into dry clothes, or had a fire, or even
a little brandy, but——" He did not finish the
sentence, and the captain's heart sank within him,
and his weatherbeaten face grew pale as he thought
of the possibility of losing his darling child.

Glynn had been watching the doctor with intense
eagerness, and with a terrible feeling of dread
fluttering about his heart. When he heard the last
remark he leaped up and cried—

"If brandy is all you want you shall soon have
't."

And running down to the edge of the water, he
plunged in and grasped the cable, intending to
clamber into the ship, which had by this time been
driven higher on the rocks, and did not suffer so

much from the violence of the breakers.   At the same instant Phil Briant sprang to his feet, rushed down after him, and before he had got a yard from the shore, seized him by the collar, and dragged him out of the sea high and dry on the land.

Glynn was so exasperated at this unceremonious, and at the moment unaccountable treatment, that he leaped up, and in the heat of the moment prepared to deal the Irishman a blow that would very probably have brought the experiences of the "ring" to his remembrance ; but Briant effectually checked him by putting both his own hands into his pockets, thrusting forward his face as if to invite the blow, and exclaiming—

"Och ! now, hit fair, Glynn, darlint ; put it right in betwane me two eyes !"

Glynn laughed hysterically, in spite of himself.

"What mean you by stopping me ?" he asked, somewhat sternly.

"Shure, I mane that I'll go for the grog meself. Ye've done more nor yer share o' the work this mornin', an' it's but fair to give a poor fellow a chance.   More betoken, ye mustn't think that nobody can't do nothin' but yerself.   It's Phil Briant that'll shin up a rope with any white man in the world, or out of it."

"You're right, Phil," said Rokens, who had come to separate the combatants.   "Go aboord, my lad, an' I'll engage to hold this here young alligator fast till ye come back."

"You don't need to hold me, Tim," retorted Glynn, with a smile; "but don't be long about it, Phil. You know where the brandy is kept—look alive."

Briant accomplished his mission successfully, and, despite the furious waves, brought the brandy on shore in safety. As he emerged like a caricature of old Neptune dripping from the sea, it was observed that he held a bundle in his powerful grasp. It was also strapped to his shoulders.

"Why, what have you got there?" inquired the doctor, as he staggered under the shelter of the rocks.

"Arrah! give a dhrop to the child, an' don't be wastin' yer breath," replied Briant, as he undid the bundle. "Sure I've brought a few trifles for her outside as well as her in." And he revealed to the glad father a bundle of warm habiliments which he had collected in Ailie's cabin, and kept dry by wrapping them in several layers of tarpaulin.

"God bless you, my man," said the captain, grasping the thoughtful Irishman by the hand. "Now, Ailie, my darling pet, look up, and swallow a drop o' this. Here's a capital rig out o' dry clothes too."

A few sips of brandy soon restored the circulation which had well-nigh been arrested, and when she had been clothed in the dry garments, Ailie felt comparatively comfortable, and expressed her thanks to Phil Briant with tears in her eyes.

A calm often succeeds a storm somewhat sud
denly, especially in southern latitudes. Soon after
daybreak the wind moderated, and before noon it
ceased entirely, though the sea kept breaking in
huge rolling billows on the sandbank for many
hours afterwards. The sun, too, came out hot and
brilliant, shedding a warm radiance over the little
sea-girt spot as well as over the hearts of the crew.

Human nature exhibits wonderful and sudden
changes. Men spring from the depths of despair
to the very summit of light-hearted hope, and very
frequently, too, without a very obvious cause to
account for the violent change. Before the day
after the storm was far advanced, every one on the
sandbank seemed to be as joyous as though there
was no danger of starvation whatever. There was,
however, sufficient to produce the change in the
altered aspect of affairs. For one thing, the warm
sun began to make them feel comfortable—and
really it is wonderful how ready men are to shut
their eyes to the actual state of existing things if
they can only enjoy a little present comfort. Then
the ship was driven so high on the rocks as to be
almost beyond the reach of the waves, and she had
not been dashed to pieces, as had at first been
deemed inevitable, so that the stores and provisions in her might be secured, and the party be
thus enabled to subsist on their ocean prison until
set free by some passing ship.

Under the happy influence of these improved

circumstances every one went about the work of
rendering their island home more comfortable, in
good, almost in gleeful spirits. Phil Briant indulged in jests which a few hours ago would have
been deemed profane, and Gurney actually volunteered the song of the "man wot got his nose
froze ;" but every one declined to listen to it, on the
plea that it reminded them too forcibly of the cold
of the early morning. Even the saturnine steward,
Tarquin, looked less ferocious than usual, and King
Bumble became so loquacious that he was ordered
more than once to hold his tongue and to " shut up."

The work they had to do was indeed of no light
nature. They had to travel to and fro between the
ship and the rocks on the rope-cable, a somewhat
laborious achievement, in order to bring ashore
such things as they absolutely required. A quantity of biscuit, tea, coffee, and sugar were landed
without receiving much damage, then a line was
fastened to a cask of salt-beef, and this, with a few
more provisions, were drawn ashore the first day,
and placed under the shelter of the largest rock
on the point. On the following day it was resolved that a raft should be constructed, and everything that could in any way prove useful be brought
to the sandbank and secured. For Captain Dunning well knew that anoth   storm might arise as
quickly as the former had done, and although the
ship at present lay in comparatively quiet water,
the huge billows that would be dashed against her

R

in such circumstances would be certain to break her up and scatter her cargo on the breast of the all-devouring sea.

In the midst of all this activity and bustle there sat one useless and silent, but exceedingly grave and uncommonly attentive spectator, namely, Jacko the monkey. That sly and sagacious individual, seeing that no one intended to look after him, had during the whole of the recent storm wisely looked after himself. He had ensconced himself in a snug and comparatively sheltered corner under the after-part of the weather bulwarks. But when he saw the men one by one leaving the ship, and proceeding to the shore by means of the rope, he began to evince an anxiety as to his own fate which had in it something absolutely human. Jacko was the last man, so to speak, to leave the Red Eric. Captain Dunning, resolving, with the true spirit of a brave commander, to reserve that honour to himself, had seen the last man, as he thought, out of the ship, and was two-thirds of the distance along the rope on his way to land, when Jim Scroggles, who was *always* either in or out of the way at the most inopportune moments, came rushing up from below, whither he had gone to secure a favourite brass finger-ring, and scrambled over the side.

It would be difficult to say whether Jim's head, or feet, or legs, or knees, or arms went over the side first—they all got over somehow, nobody knew how—and in the getting over his hat flew off and was lost for ever.

Seeing this, and feeling, no doubt, the momentous truth of that well-known adage—"Now or never," Master Jacko uttered a shriek, bounded from his position of fancied security, and seized Jim Scroggles firmly by the hair, resolved apparently to live or perish along with him. As to simply clambering along that cable to the shore, Jacko would have thought no more of it than of eating his dinner. Had he felt so disposed he could have walked along it, or hopped along it, or thrown somersaults along it. But to proceed along it while it was at one moment thirty feet above the sea, rigid as a bar of iron, and the next moment several feet under the mad turmoil of the raging billows—this it was that filled his little bosom with inexpressible horror, and induced him to cling with a tight embrace to the hair of the head of his bitterest enemy!

Having gained the shore, Jacko immediately took up his abode in the warmest spot on that desolate sandbank, which was the centre of the mass of cowering and shivering men who sought shelter under the lee of the rocks, where he was all but squeezed to death, but where he felt comparatively warm, nevertheless. When the sun came out he perched himself in a warm nook of the rock near to Ailie, and dried himself, after which, as we have already hinted, he superintended the discharging of the cargo and the arrangements made for a prolonged residence on the sandbank.

"Och ! but yer a queer cratur," remarked Briant, as he passed, chucking the monkey under the chin.

"Oo-oo-oo-ee-o !" replied Jacko.

"Very thrue, no doubt, but I haven't time to spake to ye jist yet, lad," replied Briant, with a laugh, as he ran down to the beach and seized a barrel which had just been hauled to the water's edge.

"What are you going to do with the wood, papa ?" asked Ailie.

The captain had seized an axe at the moment, and began vigorously to cut up a rough plank which had been driven ashore by the waves.

"I'm going to make a fire, my pet, to warm your cold toes."

" But my toes are not cold, papa ; you've no idea how comfortable I am."

Ailie did indeed look comfortable at that moment, for she was lying on a bed of dry sand, with a thick blanket spread over her.

"Well, then, it will do to warm Jacko's toes, if yours don't want it; and besides, we all want a cup of tea after our exertions.  The first step towards that end, you know, is to make a fire."

So saying, the captain piled up dry wood in front of the place where Ailie lay, and in a short time had a capital fire blazing, and a large tin kettle full of fresh water boiling thereon.

It may be as well to remark here, that the water had been brought in a small keg from the ship, for not a single drop of fresh water was found on the sandbank after the most careful search. Fortunately, however, the water-tanks of the Red Eric still contained a large supply.

During the course of that evening a sort of shed or tent was constructed out of canvas and a few boards placed against the rock. This formed a comparatively comfortable shelter, and one end of it was partitioned off for Ailie's special use. No one was permitted to pass the curtain that hung before the entrance to this little boudoir, except the captain, who claimed a right to do what he pleased, and Glynn, who was frequently invited to enter in order to assist its fair occupant in her multifarious arrangements, and Jacko, who could not be kept out by any means that had yet been hit upon, except by killing him ; but as Ailie objected to this, he was suffered to take up his abode there, and to do him justice, he behaved very well while domiciled in that place.

It is curious to note how speedily little children, and men too, sometimes, contrive to forget the unpleasant or the sad, or it may be the dangerous circumstances in which they may chance to be placed, while engaged in the minute details incident to their peculiar position. Ailie went about arranging her little nest under the rock with as much zeal and cheerful interest as if she were "playing at houses" in her own room at home. She decided that one corner was peculiarly suited for her bed, because there was a small rounded rock in it which looked like a pillow; so Glynn was directed to spread the tarpaulin and the blankets there Another corner exhibited a crevice in the rock, which seemed so suitable for a kennel to Jacko that the arrangement was agreed to on the spot. We say agreed to, because Ailie suggested everything to Glynn and Glynn always agreed to everything that Ailie suggested, and stood by with a hammer and nails and a few pieces of plank in his hands ready to fulfil her bidding, no matter what it should be. So Jacko was sent for to be introduced to his new abode, but Jacko was not to be found, for the very good reason that he had taken possession of the identical crevice some time before, and at that moment was enjoying a comfortable nap in its inmost recess. Then Ailie caused Glynn to put up a little shelf just over her head, which he did with considerable difficulty, because it turned out that nails could not easily be driven into the solid rock. After that a small cave at the foot of the apartment was cleaned out and Ailie's box placed there. All this, and sundry other pieces of work were executed by the young sailor and his little friend with an amount of cheerful pleasantry that showed they had, in the engrossing interest of their pursuit, totally forgotten the fact that they were cast away on a sandbank on which were neither food, nor water, nor wood, except what was to be found in the wrecked ship, and around which

for thousands of miles rolled the great billows of
the restless sea.

---

### . CHAPTER XVII.

LIFE ON THE SANDBANK — AILIE TAKES POSSESSION OF
    FAIRYLAND — GLYNN AND BUMBLE ASTONISH THE
    LITTLE FISHES.

IN order that the reader may form a just concep-
tion of the sandbank on which the crew of the
Red Eric had been wrecked, we shall describe it
somewhat carefully.

It lay in the Southern Ocean, a little to the west
of the longitude of the Cape of Good Hope, and some-
where between 2000 and 3000 miles to the south
of it. As has been already remarked, the bank at
its highest point was little more than a few feet
above the level of the ocean, the waves of which
in stormy weather almost, and the spray of which
altogether, swept over it. In length it was barely
fifty yards, and in breadth about forty. Being
part of a coral reef, the surface of it was composed
of the beautiful white sand that is formed from
coral by the dashing waves. At one end of the
bank—that on which the ship had struck—the reef
rose into a ridge of rock, which stood a few feet
higher than the level of the sand, and stretched
out into the sea about twenty yards, with its points
projecting here and there above water. On the
centre of the bank at its highest point one or two

very small blades of green substance were after-wards discovered. So few were they, however, and so delicate, that we feel justified in describing the spot as being utterly destitute of verdure. Ailie counted those green blades many a time after they were discovered. There were exactly thirty-five of them; twenty-six were, comparatively speaking, large; seven were of medium size, and two were extremely small—so small and thin that Ailie wondered they did not die of sheer delicacy of constitution on such a barren spot. The greater part of the surface of the bank was covered with the fine sand already referred to, but there were one or two spots which were covered with variously sized pebbles, and an immense number of beautiful small shells.

On such a small and barren spot one would think there was little or nothing to admire. But this was not the case. Those persons whose thoughts are seldom allowed to fix attentively on any subject, are apt to fall into the mistake of sup-posing that in this world there are a great many absolutely uninteresting things. Many things are, indeed, uninteresting to individuals, but there does not exist a single thing which has not a certain amount of interest to one or another cast of mind, and which will not afford food for contemplation, and matter fitted to call forth our admiration for its great and good Creator.

We know a valley so beautiful that it has been

for generations past, and will probably be for generations to come, the annual resort of hundreds of admiring travellers. The valley cannot be seen until you are almost in it. The country immediately around it is no way remarkable ; it is even tame. Many people would exclaim at first sight in reference to it, " How uninteresting." It requires a close view, a minute inspection, to discover the beauties that lie hidden there.

So was it with our sandbank. Ailie's first thoughts were, " Oh ! how dreary ; how desolate !" and in some respects she was right ; but she dwelt there long enough to discover things that charmed her eye and her imagination, and caused her sometimes to feel as if she had been transported to the realms of fairyland.

We do not say, observe, that the crew of the Red Eric were ever blessed with such dreams. Jim Scroggles, for instance, had no eye for the minute beauties or wonders of creation. Jim, according to his own assertion, could see about as far through a millstone as most men. He could apostrophize his eye, on certain occasions, and tell it—as though its own power of vision were an insufficient medium of information—that " that *wos* a stunnin' iceberg ;" or that " that *wos* a gale and a half, fit to tear the masts out o' the ship a'most." But for any less majestic object in nature, Jim Scroggles had nothing to say either to his eye, or his nose, or his shipmates.

As was Jim Scroggles, so were most of the other men. Hence they grumbled a good deal at their luckless condition. But upon the whole they were pretty cheerful—especially at meal-times—and considering their circumstances, they behaved very well.

Glynn Proctor was a notable exception to the prevailing rule of indifference to small things. By nature he was of a superior stamp of mind to his comrades ; besides, he had been better educated ; and more than all, he was at that time under the influence of Ailie Dunning. He admired what she admired ; he liked what she liked ; he looked with interest at the things which she examined. Had Ailie sat down beside the stock of an old anchor and looked attentively at it, Glynn would have sat down and stared at it too, in the firm belief that there was something there worth looking at ! Glynn laughed aloud sometimes at himself, to think how deeply interested he had become in the child, for up to that time he had rather avoided than courted the society of children ; and he used to say to Ailie that the sailors would begin to call her his little sweetheart, if he spent so much of his time with her ; to which Ailie would reply by asking what a sweetheart was ; whereat Glynn would laugh immoderately ; whereupon Ailie would tell him not to be stupid, but to come and play with her !

All the sailors, even including the taciturn Tarquin, had a tender feeling of regard for the little girl who shared their fortunes at that time, but with the exception of Glynn, none were capable of sympathizing with her in her pursuits. Tim Rokens, her father, and Dr. Hopley did to some extent, but these three had their minds too deeply filled with anxiety about their critical position to pay her much attention, beyond the kindest concern for her physical wants. King Bumble, too, we beg his pardon, showed considerable interest in her. The sable assistant of Nikel Sling shone conspicuous at this trying time, for his activity, good humour, and endurance, and in connexion with Phil Briant, Gurney, and Jacko, kept up the spirits of the ship-wrecked men wonderfully.

Close under the rocks, on the side farthest re-moved from the spot where the rude tent was pitched, there was a little bay or creek, not more than twenty yards in diameter, which Ailie appro-priated and called fairyland! It was an uncom-monly small spot, but it was exceedingly beautiful and interesting. The rocks, although small, were so broken and fantastically formed, that when Ailie crept close in amongst them, and so placed herself that the view of the sandbank was entirely shut out, and nothing was to be seen but little pools of crystal water and rocklets, with their margin of dazzling white sand, and the wreck of the ship in the distance, with the deep blue sea beyond, she quite forgot where she actually was, and began to wander in the most enchanting day-dreams. But when, as often happened, there came towering thick masses of snowy clouds, like mountain peaks and battlements in the bright blue sky, her delight was so great that she could find no words to express it.

At such times—sometimes with Glynn by her side, sometimes alone—she would sit in a sunny nook, or in a shady nook if she felt too warm, and invite innumerable hosts of fairies to come and conduct her through interminable tracts of pure-white cloud region, and order such unheard-of wild creatures (each usually wanting a tail, or a leg, or an ear) to come out of the dark caves, that had they been all collected in one garden for exhibition to the public, that zoological garden would have been deemed, out of sight, the greatest of all the wonders of the world !

When a little wearied with those aërial journeys she would return to "fairyland," and leaning over the brinks of the pools, peer down into their beautiful depths for hours at a time.

Ailie's property of fairyland had gardens, too, of the richest possible kind, full of flowers of the most lovely and brilliant hues. But the flowers were scentless, and, alas ! she could not pluck them, for those gardens were all under water ; they grew at the bottom of the sea ! Yes, reader, if the land was barren on that ocean islet, the pools there made up for it by presenting to view the most luxuriant marine vegetation. There were forests of branching coral of varied hues ; there were masses of fan-shaped sponges; there were groves of green and red sea-weeds; and beds of red, and white, and orange, and striped creatures that stuck to the rocks, besides little fish with bright-coloured backs that played there as if they really enjoyed living always under water—which is not easy for us, you know, to realize! And above all, the medium of water between Ailie and these things was so pure and pellucid when no breeze fanned the surface, that it was difficult to believe, unless you touched it, there was any water there at all.

While Ailie thus spent her time, or at least her leisure time, for she was by no means an idler in that busy little isle, the men were actively engaged each day in transporting provisions from the Red Eric to the sandbank, and in making them as secure as circumstances would admit of. For this purpose a raft had been constructed, and several trips a-day were made to and from the wreck, so that in the course of a few days a considerable stock of provision was accumulated on the bank. This was covered with tarpaulin, and heavy casks of salt junk were placed on the corners and edges to keep it down.

"I'll tell ye wot it is, messmates," remarked Gurney, one day, as they sat down round their wood fire to dine in front of their tent, "we're purvisioned for six months at least, an' if the weather only keeps fine I've no objection to remain wotiver."

"Maybe," said Briant, "ye'll have to remain that time whether ye object or not."

"By no means, Paddy," retorted Gurney; "I could swum off to sea and be drownded if I liked."

"No ye couldn't, avic," said Briant.

"Why not?" demanded Gurney.

"'Cause ye haven't the pluck," replied Phil.

"I'll pluck the nose off yer face," said Gurney, in affected anger.

"No ye wont," cried Phil, "'cause av ye do I'll spile the soup by heavin' it all over ye."

"Oh!" exclaimed Gurney, with a look of horror, "listen to him, messmates, he calls it '*soup*'—the nasty kettle o' dirty water! Well, well, it's lucky we hain't got nothin' better to compare it with."

"But, I say, lads," interposed Jim Scroggles, seriously, "wot'll we do if it comes on to blow a gale and blows away all our purvisions?"

"Ay, boys," cried Dick Barnes, "that ere's the question, as Hamlet remarked to his grandfather's ghost; wot *is* to come on us supposin' it comes on to blow sich a snorin' gale as 'll blow the whole sandbank away, carryin' us and our prog overboard along with it?"

"Wot's that there soup made of?" demanded Tim Rokens.

"Salt junk and peas," replied Nikel Sling.

"Ah! I thought there was somethin' else in it," said Tim, carelessly, "for it seems to perdooce oncommon bad jokes in them wot eats of it."

" Now, Tim, don't you go for to be sorcostic, but tell us a story."

" Me tell a story ?  No, no, lads ; there's Glynn Proctor, he's the boy for you.  Where is he ?"

" He's aboard the wreck just now.  The cap'n sent him for charts and quadrants, and suchlike cooriosities.  Come, Gurney, tell you one if Tim wont.  How wos it, now, that you so mistook yer trade as to come for to go to sea ?"

" I can't very well tell ye," answered Gurney, who, having finished dinner, had lit his pipe, and was now extended at full length on the sand, leaning on one arm.  " Ye see, lads, I've had more or less to do with the sea, I have, since ever I comed into this remarkable world—not that I ever, to my knowledge, knew one less coorous, for I never wos up in the stars ; no more, I 'spose, was ever any o' you.  I wos born at sea, d'ye see ?  I don't 'xactly know how I com'd for to be born there, but I wos told that I wos, and if them as told me spoke truth, I s'pose I wos.  I was washed overboard in gales three times before I comed for to know myself at all.  When I first came alive, so to speak, to my own certain knowledge, I wos a-sitting on the top of a hen-coop aboard an East Indiaman, roarin' like a mad bull as had lost his senses ; 'cause why ? the hens wos puttin' their heads through the bars o' the coops, and pickin' at the calves o' my legs as fierce as if they'd suddenly turned cannibals, and rather liked it.  From that time I began a life o'

misery. My life before that had bin pretty much
the same, it seems, but I didn't know it, so it didn't
matter. D'ye know, lads, when ye don't know a
thing it's all the same as if it didn't exist, an' so,
in coorse, it don't matter."

"Oh!" exclaimed the first mate, who came up
at the moment, "'ave hany o' you fellows got a
note-book in which we may record that horacular
and truly valuable hobserwation?"

No one happening to possess a note-book, Gurney
was allowed to proceed with his account of himself.

"Ships has bin my houses all along up to this
here date. I don't believe, lads, as ever I wos
above two months ashore at a time all the coorse
of my life, an' mostly not so long as that. The
smell o' tar and the taste o' salt water wos the fust
things I iver comed across—'xcept the Line, I
comed across that jist about the time I wos born,
so I'm told,—and the smell o' tar and taste o'
salt water's wot I've bin used to most o' my life,
and, moreover, wot I likes best. One old gen'leman as took a fancy to me w'en I wos a boy, said
to me, one fine day, w'en I chanced to be ashore
visitin' my mother—says he, 'My boy, would ye
like to gò with me and live in the country, and be
a gardner?' 'Wot,' says I, 'keep a garding, and
plant taters, and hoe flowers an' cabidges?' 'Yes,'
says he, 'at least, somethin' o' that sort.' 'No,
thankee,' says I; 'I b'long to the sea, I do; I
wouldn't leave that 'ere no more nor I would quit

my first love if I had one. I'm a sailor, I am, out
and out, through and through—true blue, and no
mistake, an' no one need go for to try to cause me
for to forsake my purfession, and live on shore like
a turnip'—that's wot I says to that old gen'leman.
Yes, lads, I've roamed the wide ocean, as the song
says, far an' near. I've bin tatooed by the New
Zealanders, and I've danced with the Hottentots,
and ate puppy dogs with the Chinese, and fished
whales in the North Seas, and run among the ice
near the South Pole, and fowt with pirates, and
done service on boord of men o' war and merchant-
men, and junks, and bumboats ; but I never,"
concluded Gurney, looking round with a sigh, " I
never came for to be located on a sandbank in the
middle of the ocean."

"No more did any on us," added Rokens.
" Moreover, if we're not picked up soon by a ship
o' some sort, we're not likely to be located here
long, for we can't live on salt junk for ever ; we
shall all die o' the scurvy."

There was just enough of possible and probable
truth in the last remark to induce a feeling of sadness among the men for a few minutes, but this
was quickly put to flight by the extraordinary
movements of Phil Briant. That worthy had left
the group round the fire, and had wandered out to
the extreme end of the rocky point, where he sat
down to indulge, possibly in sad, or mayhap hopeful reflections. He was observed to start suddenly

s

up, and gaze into the sea eagerly for a few seconds; then he cut a caper, slapped his thigh, and ran hastily towards the tent.

"What now? where away, Phil?" cried one of the men.

Briant answered not, but speedily reappeared at the opening of the tent door with a fishing-line and hook. Hastening to the point of rock, he opened a small species of shell-fish that he found there, wherewith he baited his hook, and then cast it into the sea. In a few minutes he felt a twitch, which caused him to return a remarkably vigorous twitch, as it were, in reply.

The fish and the sailor for some minutes acted somewhat the part of electricians in a telegraph office; when the fish twitched, Briant twitched; when the fish pulled and paused, Briant pulled and paused, and when the fish held on hard Briant pulled hard, and finally pulled him ashore, and a very nice plump rock-codling he was. There were plenty of them, so in a short time there was no lack of fresh fish, and Roken's fear that they would have to live on salt junk was not realized.

Fishing for rock-codlings now became one of the chief recreations of the men while not engaged in bringing various necessaries from the wreck. But for many days at first they found their hands fully occupied in making their new abode habitable, in enlarging and improving the tent, which soon by degrees came to merit the name of a hut, and in i..venting various ingenious contrivances for the improvement of their condition. It was not until a couple of weeks had passed that time began to hang heavy on their hands and fishing became a general amusement.

They all fished, except Jacko. Even Ailie tried it once or twice, but she did not like it and soon gave it up. As for Jacko, he contented himself with fishing with his hands, in a sly way, among the provision casks, at which occupation he was quite an adept ; and many a nice tit bit did he fish up and secrete in his private apartment for future use. Like many a human thief, Jacko was at least compelled to leave the greater part of his ill-gotten and hoarded gains behind him.

One day Glynn and Ailie sat by the margin of a deep pool in Fairyland, gazing down into its clear depths. The sun's rays penetrated to the very bottom, revealing a thousand beauties in form and colour that called forth from Ailie the most extravagant expressions of admiration. She wound up one of those eloquent bursts by saying—

"Oh ! Glynn, how very, *very* much I do wish I could go down there and play with the dear, exquisite, darling little fishes !"

"You'd surprise them, I suspect," said Glynn. "It's rather too deep a pool to play in unless you were a mermaid."

"How deep is it, Glynn ?"

"'Bout ten feet, I think."

"So much? It does not look like it. What a very pretty bit of coral I see over there, close to the white rock; do you see it? It is bright pink. Oh I would like *so* much to have it."

"Would you," cried Glynn, jumping up and throwing off his jacket; "then here goes for it."

So saying he clasped his hands above his head, and bending forward, plunged into the pool and went straight at the piece of pink coral, head foremost, like an arrow!

Glynn was lightly clad. His costume consisted simply of a pair of white canvas trousers and a blue striped shirt, with a silk kerchief round his neck, so that his movements in the water were little, if at all, impeded by his clothes. At the instant he plunged into the water King Bumble happened to approach, and while Ailie stood petrified with fear as she saw Glynn struggling violently at the bottom of the pool, her sable companion stood looking down with a grin from ear to ear that displayed every one of his bright teeth.

"Don't be 'fraid, Missie Ally," said the negro; "him's know wot him's doin', ho yis!"

Before Ailie could reply, Glynn was on the surface spluttering and brushing the hair from his forehead with one hand, while with the other he hugged to his breast the piece of pink coral.

"Here—it—ha!—is. My breath—ho—is a'most gone—Ailie—catch hold!" cried he, as he held out the coveted piece of rock to the child and scrambled out of the pool.

"Oh thank you, Glynn; but why did you go down so quick and stay so long? I got *such* a fright."

"You bin pay your 'spects to de fishes," said Bumble, with a grin.

"Yes I have, Bumble, and they say that if you stare at them any longer with your great goggle eyes they'll all go mad with horror and die right off. Have you caught any codlings, Bumble?"

"Yis me hab, an' me hab come for to make a preeposol to Missie Ally."

"A what, Bumble?"

"A preeposol—a digestion."

"I suppose you mean a suggestion, eh?"

"Yis, dat the berry ting."

"Well, out with it."

"Dis am it. Me ketch rock-coddles; well, me put 'em in bucket ob water an' bring 'em to you, Missie Ally, an' you put 'em into dat pool and tame 'em, an' hab great fun with 'em. Eeh! wot you tink?"

"Oh! it will be *so* nice. How good of you to think about it, Bumble; do get them as quick as you can."

Bumble looked grave and hesitated.

"Why, what's wrong?" inquired Glynn.

"Oh, noting. Me only tink me not take the trouble to put 'em into dat pool where de fishes speak so imperently ob me. Stop, me will go an' ask if dey sorry for wot de hab say."

So saying the negro uttered a shout, sprang

straight up into the air, doubled his head down and his heels up, and cleft the water like a knife. Glynn uttered a cry something between a yell and a laugh, and sprang after him, falling flat on the water and dashing the whole pool into foam, and there the two wallowed about like two porpoises, to the unbounded delight of Ailie, who stood on the brink laughing until the tears ran down her cheeks, and to the unutterable horror, no doubt, of the little fish.

The rock-codlings were soon caught and transferred to the pool, in which, after that, neither Glynn nor Bumble were suffered to dive or swim, and Ailie succeeded, by means of regularly feeding them, in making the little fish less afraid of her than they were at first.

But while Ailie and Glynn were thus amusing themselves and trying to make the time pass as pleasantly as possible, Captain Dunning was oppressed with the most anxious forebodings. They had now been several weeks on the sandbank. The weather had during that time been steadily fine and calm, and their provisions were still abundant, but he knew that this could not last. Moreover, he found on consulting his charts that he was far out of the usual course of ships, and that deliverance could only be expected in the shape of a chance vessel.

Oppressed with these thoughts, which, however, he carefully concealed from every one except Tim

Rokens and the doctor, the captain used to go on the point of rocks every day and sit there for hours, gazing out wistfully over the sea.

## CHAPTER XVIII.

MATTERS GROW WORSE AND WORSE—THE MUTINY—COM-MENCEMENT OF BOAT-BUILDING, AND THREATENING STORMS.

ONE afternoon, about three weeks after the Red Eric had been wrecked on the sandbank, Captain Dunning went out on the point of rocks, and took up his accustomed position there. Habit had now caused him to go to the point with as much regularity as a sentinel. But on the present occasion anxiety was more deeply marked on his countenance than usual, for dark, threatening clouds were seen accumulating on the horizon, an unnatural stillness prevailed in the hot atmosphere and on the glassy sea, and everything gave indication of an approaching storm.

While he sat on a low rock, with his elbows on his knees, and his chin resting in his hands, he felt a light touch on his shoulder, and looking round, found Ailie standing by his side. Catching her in his arms, he pressed her fervently to his heart, and for the first time spoke to her in discouraging tones.

"My own darling," said he, parting the hair from her forehead, and gazing at the child with an expression of the deepest sadness, " I fear we shall *never* quit this dreary spot."

Ailie looked timidly in her father's face, for his agitated manner, more than his words, alarmed her.

" Wont we leave it, dear papa," said she, "to go up yonder?" and she pointed to a gathering mass of clouds over head, which, although heavy with dark shadows, had still a few bright, sunny points of resemblance to the fairy realms in which she delighted to wander in her day-dreams.

The captain made no reply ; but, shutting his eyes, and drawing Ailie close to his side, he uttered a long and fervent prayer to God for deliverance, if He should see fit, or for grace to endure with Christian resignation and fortitude whatever He pleased to send upon them.

When he concluded, and again looked up, Dr. Hopley was standing beside them, with his head bowed upon his breast.

" I fear, doctor," said the captain, " that I have broken my resolution not to alarm my dear Ailie by word or look. Yet why should I conceal from her the danger of our position ? Her prayers for help ought to ascend, as well as ours, to Him who alone can deliver us from evil at any time, but who makes us to *feel*, as well as *know*, the fact at such times as these."

" But I'm not afraid, papa," said Ailie, quickly. " I'm never afraid when you are by me ; and I've known we were in danger all along, for I've heard

everybody talking about it often and often, and
I've *always* prayed for deliverance, and surely it
must come ; for has not Jesus said if we ask any
thing in His name, He will give it to us ?"

"True, darling ; but He means only such things
as will do us good."

"Of course, papa, if I asked for a bad thing,
I would not expect Him to give me that."

"Deliverance from death," said the doctor, "is
a good thing, yet we cannot be sure that God will
grant our prayer for that."

"There are worse things than death, doctor,"
replied the captain ; " it may be sometimes better
for men to die than to live. It seems to me that
we ought to use the words, ' if it please the Lord,'
more frequently than we do in prayer. Deliverance from sin needs no such ' if,' but deliverance
from death does."

At this point the conversation was interrupted
by Tim Rokens, who came up to the captain, and
said respectfully :—

"If ye please, sir, it 'ud be as well if ye wos to
speak to the men ; there's somethin' like mutiny
agoin' on, I fear."

"Mutiny ! why, what about ?"

"It's about the spirits. Some on 'em says as
how they wants to enjoy theirselves here as much
as they can, for they wont have much chance o'
doin' so ashore any more. It's my belief that
fellow Tarquin's at the bottom o't."

" There's not much spirits aboard the wreck to fight about," said the captain, somewhat bitterly, as they all rose, and hurried towards the hut. " I only brought a supply for medicine ; but it must not be touched, however little there is."

When the captain came up, he found the space in front of their rude dwelling a scene of contention and angry dispute that bade fair to end in a fight. Tarquin was standing before the first mate, with his knife drawn, and using violent language and gesticulations towards him, while the latter stood by the raft, grasping a handspike, with which he threatened to knock the steward down if he set foot on it. The men were grouped round them, some with looks that implied a desire to side with Tarquin, while others muttered, " Shame !"

" Shame !" cried Tarquin, looking fiercely round on his shipmates. " Who cried shame ? We're pretty sure all on us to be starved to death on this reef ; and it's my opinion, that since we haven't got to live long, we should try to enjoy ourselves as much as we can. There's not much spirits aboard, more's the pity ; but what there is I shall have. So again, I say, who cried ' Shame ?' "

" I did," said Glynn Proctor, stepping quickly forward ; " and I invite all who think with me to back me up."

" Here ye are, me boy," said Phil Briant, starting forward, and baring his brawny arms, as was his invariable custom in such circumstances. " It's meself as 'll stick by ye, lad, av the whole crew should go with that half-caste crokidile."

Gurney and Dick Barnes immediately sided with Glynn, also, but Jim Scroggles and Nickel Sling, and, to the surprise of every one, Markham, the second mate, sided with the steward. As the opposing parties glanced at each other, Glynn observed that, although his side was superior in numbers, some of the largest and most powerful men of the crew were among his opponents, and he felt that a conflict between such men must inevitably be serious. Matters had almost come to a crisis when Dr. Hopley and the captain approached the scene of action. The latter saw at a glance the state of affairs, and, stepping up to the steward, ordered him at once into the hut.

Tarquin seemed to waver for a moment under the stern gaze of his commander; but he suddenly swore a terrible oath, and said that he would not obey.

"You're no longer in command of us," he said, gruffly, "now that you have lost your ship. Every man may do what he pleases."

"May he?" replied the captain; "then it pleases me to do that!" and, launching out his clenched right hand with all his might, he hit the steward therewith right between the eyes.

Tarquin went down as if he had been shot, and lay stunned and at full length upon the sand.

"Now, my lads," cried the captain, turning

towards the men, " what he said just now is so far
right. Having lost my ship, I am no longer entitled to command you ; but my command does
not cease unless a majority of you choose that it
should. Tarquin has taken upon himself to decide
the question without asking your opinion, which
amounts to mutiny, and mutiny, under the circumstances in which we are placed, requires to be
promptly dealt with. I feel it right to say this,
because I am a man of peace, as you well know,
and do not approve of a too ready appeal to the
fists for the settlement of a dispute."

" Ah, then, more's the pity !" interrupted Briant,
"for ye use them oncommon well."

A suppressed laugh followed this remark.

"Silence, men, this is no time for jesting. One
of our shipmates has, not long since, been taken
suddenly from us ; it may be that we shall all of
us be called into the presence of our Maker before
many days pass over us. We have much to do
that will require to be done promptly and well,
if we would hope to be delivered at all, and the
question must be decided *now*, whether I am to
command you, or every one is to do what he
pleases.".

" I votes for Cap'en Duning," exclaimed Gurney.

"So does I," cried Jim Scroggles ; who being
somewhat weather-cockish in his nature, turned
always with wonderful facility to the winning side.

" Three cheers for the cap'en," cried Dick Barnes,
suiting the action to the word.

Almost every voice joined in the vociferous cheer with which this proposal was received.

"An' wan more for Miss Ailie," shouted Phil Briant.

Even Jacko lent his voice to the tremendous cheer that followed, for Briant in his energy chanced to tread on that creature's unfortunate tail, which always seemed to be in his own way as well as in that of every one else, and the shriek that he uttered rang high above the laughter into which the cheer degenerated, as some one cried, " Ah, Pat, trust you, my boy, for rememberin' the ladies !"

Order having been thus happily restored, and Captain Dunning having announced that the late attempt at mutiny should thenceforth be buried in total oblivion, a council was called, in order to consider seriously their present circumstances, and to devise, if possible, some means of escape.

" My lads," said the captain, when they were all assembled, " I've been ponderin' over matters ever since we were cast away on this bank, an' I've at last come to the conclusion that our only chance of gettin' away is to build a small boat and fit her out for a long voyage. I need not tell you that this chance is a poor one—well nigh a forlorn hope. Had it been better I would have spoken before now, and began the work sooner ; but I have lived from day to day in the hope of a ship heaving in sight. This is a vain hope. We are far out of the usual track of all ships here. None come this way, except such as may chance to be blown out of their course, as we were ; and even if one did come within sight, it's ten chances to one that we should fail to attract attention on such a low bank as this.

"I have had several reliable observations of late, and I find that we are upwards of two thousand miles from the nearest known land, which is the Cape of Good Hope. I propose, therefore, that we should strip off as much of the planking of the wreck as will suit our purpose, get the carpenter's chest landed, and commence work at once. Now, what say you ? If any one has a better plan to suggest, I'll be only too glad to adopt it, for such a voyage in so slim a craft as we can build here will be one necessarily replete with danger."

"I'll tell ye wot it is, cap'en," said Tim Rokens, rising up, taking off his cap, and clearing his throat, as if he were about to make a studied oration. "We've not none on us got no suggestions to make wotsomdiver. You've only got to give the word and we'll go to work ; an' the sooner you does so the better, for it's my b'lief we'll have a gale afore long that 'll pretty well stop work altogether as long as it lasts."

The indications in the sky gave such ample testimony to the justness of Rokens's observations that no more time was wasted in discussion. Dick Barnes, who acted the part of ship's-carpenter when not otherwise engaged, went out to the wreck on the raft, with a party of men under command of Mr. Millons, to fetch planking and the necessary material for the construction of a boat, while the remainder of the crew, under the captain's superintendence, prepared a place near Fairyland for laying the keel.

This spot was selected partly on account of the convenient formation of the shore for the launching of the boat when finished, and partly because that would be the lee side of the rocky point when the coming storm should burst. For the latter reason the hut was removed to Fairyland, and poor Ailie had the mortification in a few hours of seeing her little paradise converted into an unsightly wreck of confusion. Alas! how often this is the case in human affairs of greater moment; showing the folly of setting our hearts on the things of earth. It seems at first sight a hard passage, that, in the Word of God. "What?" the enthusiastic but thoughtless are ready to exclaim, "not love the world! the bright, beautiful world that was made by God to be enjoyed? Not love our fathers, mothers, brothers, sisters, wives? not give our warmest affections to all these?" Truly, ye hasty ones, if you would but earnestly consider it, you would find that God not only permits, but requires us to love all that is good and beautiful here, as much as we will, as much as we can; but we ought to love Himself *more*. If this be our happy condition, then our hearts are not " set on the world ;" on the

contrary, they are set free to love the world and all
that is loveable in it—of which there is very, very
much—more, probably, than the best of men sup
pose.    Else, wherefore does the Father love it and
care for it so tenderly ?

But Ailie had not set her heart on her posses-
sions on the sandbank.    She felt deep regret for
a time, it is true, and in feeling thus she indulged
a right and natural impulse, but that impulse did
not lead to the sin of murmuring.    Her sorrow soon
passed away, and she found herself as cheerful and
happy afterwards in preparing for her long, long
voyage as ever she had been in watching the
gambols of her fish, or in admiring the lovely hues
of the weeds and coral rocks in the limpid pools of
Fairyland.

It was a fortunate circumstance that Captain
Dunning set about the preparations for building the
boat that afternoon, for the storm burst upon them
sooner than had been expected, and long before
all the requisite stores and materials had been
rafted from the wreck.

The most important things, however, had been
procured—such as the carpenter's chest, a large
quantity of planking, oakum, and cordage, and
several pieces of sail-cloth, with the requisite thread
and needles for making boat sails.    Still, much
was wanting when the increasing violence of the
wind compelled them to leave off work.

Some of the men were now ordered to set about
securing such materials as had been collected,

while others busied themselves in fixing ropes to the hut and rolling huge masses of coral rock against its fragile walls to steady it.

"Av ye plaze, sir," said Briant to the captain, wiping his forehead as he approached with a lump of tarry canvas which he used in default of a better pocket-handkerchief, "av ye plaze, sir, wot 'll I do now ?"

"Do something useful, lad, whatever you do," said the captain, looking up from the hole which he was busily engaged in digging for the reception of a post to steady the hut. "There's lots of work ; you can please yourself as to choice."

"Then I comed fur to suggist that the purvisions and things a-top o' the sandbank isn't quite so safe as they might be."

"True, Briant ; I was just thinking of that as you came up. Go and see you make a tight job of it. Get Rokens to help you."

Briant hurried off, and calling his friend, walked with him to the top of the sandbank, leaning heavily against the gale, and staggering as they went. The blast now whistled so that they could scarcely hear each other talk.

"We'll be blowed right into the sea," shouted Tim, as the two reached the pile of casks and cases.

"Sure that's me own belaif entirely," roared his companion.

"Wot d'ye say to dig a hole and stick the things in it ?" yelled Rokens.

T

" We're not fit," screamed Phil.

" Let's try," shrieked the other.

To this Briant replied by falling on his knees on the lee side of the goods, and digging with his hands in the sand most furiously. Tim Rokens followed his example, and the two worked like a couple of sea-moles (if such creatures exist) until a hole capable of holding several casks was formed. Into this they stowed all the biscuit-casks and a few other articles, and covered them up with sand. The remainder they covered with tarpaulin, and threw sand and stones above it until the heap was almost buried out of sight. This accomplished, they staggered back to the hut as fast as they could.

Here they found everything snugly secured, and as the rocks effectually sheltered the spot from the gale, with the exception of an occasional eddying blast that drove the sand in their faces, they felt comparatively comfortable. Lighting their pipes they sat down among their comrades to await the termination of the storm.

# CHAPTER XIX.

## THE STORM.

A STORM in almost all circumstances is a grand and solemnizing sight, one that forces man to feel his own weakness and his Maker's might and majesty. But a storm at sea in southern latitudes, where the winds are let loose with a degree of violence that is seldom or never experienced in the temperate zones, is so terrific that no words can be found to convey an adequate idea of its appalling ferocity.

The storm that at this time burst upon the little sandbank on which the shipwrecked crew had found shelter, was one of the most furious, perhaps, that ever swept the seas. The wind shrieked as if it were endued with life, tore up the surface of the groaning deep into masses and shreds of foam, which it whirled aloft in mad fury, and then dissipated into a thin blinding mist that filled the whole atmosphere, so that one could scarcely see a couple of yards beyond the spot on which he stood The hurricane seemed to have reached its highest point soon after sunset that night, and a ray of light from the moon struggled ever and anon through the black hurtling clouds, as if to reveal to the cowering seamen the extreme peril of their situation. The great ocean was lashed into a wide sheet of foam, and the presence of the little isle in the midst of that swirling waste of water was indicated merely by a slight circle of foam that seemed whiter than the rest of the sea.

The men sat silently in their frail hut, listening to the howling blast without. A feeling of awe crept over the whole party, and the most careless and the lightest of heart among the crew of the Red Eric ceased to utter his passing jest, and became deeply solemnized as the roar of the breakers filled his ear, and reminded him that a thin ledge of rock alone preserved him from instant destruction.

" The wind has shifted a point," said the captain, who had just risen and opened a chink of the rude door of the hut in order to look out. " I see that the keel of the boat is all fast and the planking beside it. The coral rock shelters it just now ; but if the wind goes on shifting I fear it will stand a poor chance."

" We'd better go out and give it a hextra fasten-ing," suggested Mr. Millons.

" Not yet. There's no use of exposing any of the men to the risk of being blown away. The wind may keep steady, in which case I've no fear for it.",

" I dun know," said Rokens, who sat beside Ailie, close to the embers of their fire, with a glowing cinder from which he relighted his pipe for at least the twentieth time that night. " You never can tell wot's agoin' to turn up. I'll go out cap'en, if ye like, and see that all's fast."

" Perhaps you're right, Tim ; you may make a bolt across to it, and heave another rock or two on the planking if it seems to require it."

The seaman rose, and putting aside his pipe, threw off his coat, partly in order that he might present as small a surface to the wind as possible, and partly that he might have a dry garment to put on when he returned. As he opened the little door of the hut a rude gust of wind burst in, filling the apartment with spray, and scattering the em- bers of the fire.

" I feared as much," said the captain, as he and the men started up to gather together the pieces of glowing charcoal; "that shows the wind's shifted another point; if it goes round two points more it'll smash our boat to pieces. Look sharp, Tim."

" Lean well against the wind, me boy," cried Briant, in a warning voice.

Thus admonished, Rokens issued forth, and dashed across the open space that separated the hut from the low ledge of coral rock behind which the keel of the intended boat and its planking were sheltered. A very few minutes sufficed to show Tim that all was fast, and to enable him to place a few additional pieces of rock above the heap in order to keep it down. Then he prepared to dart back again to the hut, from the doorway of which his proceedings were watched by the captain and as many of the men as could crowd round it.

Just as the harpooneer sprang from the shelter of the rock the blast burst upon the bank with re-doubled fury, as if it actually were a sentient being, and wished to catch the sailor in its rude grasp and whirl him away. Rokens bent his stout frame against it with all his might, and stood his ground for a few seconds like a noble tree on some exposed mountain side that has weathered the gales of centuries. Then he staggered, threw his arms wildly in the air, and a moment after was swept from the spot and lost to view in the driving spray that flew over the island.

The thing was so instantaneous that the horrified onlookers could scarcely credit the evidence of their eyes, and they stood aghast for a moment or two ere their feelings found vent in a cry of alarm. Next instant Captain Dunning felt himself rudely pushed aside, and Briant leaped through the door-way, shouting, as he dashed out—

"If Tim Rokens goes, it's Phil Briant as 'll go along with him."

The enthusiastic Irishman was immediately lost to view, and Glynn Proctor was about to follow, when the captain seized him by the collar, dragged him back, and shut the door violently.

"Keep back, lads," he cried, "no one must leave the hut. If these two men cannot save themselves by means of their own strong muscles, no human power can save them."

Glynn, and indeed all of the men, felt this remark to be true, so they sat down round the fire, and looked in each other's faces with the expression of men who half believed they must be dreaming. Little was said during the next ten or fifteen minutes; indeed, it was difficult to make their voices heard, owing to the noise of the wind and dashing waves. The captain stood at the door, looking out from time to time with feelings of the deepest anxiety, each moment expecting to see the two sailors struggling back towards the hut; but they did not return. Soon the gale increased to such a degree that every one felt, although no one would acknowledge it even to himself, that there was now no hope of their comrades ever returning. The wind shifted another point; and now their lost shipmates were for a time forgotten in the anxieties of their own critical position, for their rocky ledge formed only a partial shelter, and every now and then the hut was shaken with a blast so terrible that it threatened to come down about their ears.

"Don't you think our house will fall, dear papa?" inquired Ailie, as a gust more furious than any that had hitherto passed swept round the rocks, and shook the hut as if it had been made of paste board.

"God knows, my darling; we are in His hands."

Ailie tried to comfort herself with the thought that her Heavenly Father was indeed the ruler of the storm, and could prevent it from doing them harm if He pleased ; but as gust after gust dashed against the frail building, and almost shook it down, while the loud rattling of the boards which composed it almost stunned her, an irresistible feeling of alarm crept over her, despite her utmost efforts to control herself.

The captain now ordered the men to go out and see that the fastenings to windward and the supports to leeward of the hut remained firm, and to add more of them if possible. He set the example by throwing off his coat and leading the way.

This duty was by no means so difficult or dangerous as that which had been previously performed by Rokens, for it must be remembered the hut as yet was only exposed to partial gusts of eddying wind, not to the full violence of the storm. It involved a thorough wetting, however, to all who went. In ten minutes the men re-entered, and put on their dry coats, but as no one knew how soon he might again be called upon to expose himself, none thought of changing his other garments.

" Now, Ailie, my pet," said Captain Dunning, sitting down beside his child on the sandy floor of the hut, " we've done all we can. If the wind remains as it is our house will stand."

"But have you not seen Rokens or Briant ?" inquired Ailie, with an anxious face, while the tears rolled over her cheeks.

The captain shook his head, but made no reply, and the men looked earnestly at each other, as if

each sought to gather a ray of hope from the countenance of his friend. While they sat thus, a
terrible blast shook the hut to its foundation.
Again and again it came with ever-increasing
violence, and then it burst on them with a continuous roar like prolonged thunder.

"Look out," cried the captain, instinctively clasping Ailie in his arms, while the men sprang to
their feet. The stout corner-posts bent over before
the immense pressure, and the second mate placed
his shoulder against one of those on the windward
side of the hut, while Dick Barnes and Nikel Sling
did the same to the other.

"It's all up with us," cried Tarquin, as part of
the roof blew off, and a deluge of water and spray
burst in upon them, extinguishing the fire and
leaving them in total darkness. At that moment
Ailie felt herself seized round the waist by a pair
of tiny arms, and putting down her hand, she felt
that Jacko was clinging to her with a tight but
trembling grasp.

Even in that hour of danger, the child experienced a sensation of pleasure at the mere
thought that there was one living creature there
which looked up to and clung to her for protection ;
and although she knew full well that if the stout
arm of her father which encircled her were removed,
her own strength, in their present circumstances,
could not have availed to protect herself, yet she
felt a gush of renewed strength and courage at her

heart when the poor little monkey put its trembling
arms around her.

"Lay your shoulders to the weather-wall, lads,"
cried the captain, as another rush of wind bore
down on the devoted hut.

The men obeyed, but their united strength
availed nothing against the mighty power that
raged without. The wind, as the captain had
feared, went round another point, and they were
now exposed to the unbroken force of the hurricane. For a few minutes the stout corner-posts
of the hut held up, then they began to rend and
crack.

"Bear down with the blast to the lee of the
rocks, lads," cried the captain; "it's your only
chance; don't try to face it."

Almost before the words left his lips the posts
snapped with a loud crash; the hut was actually
lifted off the ground by the wind, and swept completely away, while most of the men were thrown
violently to the ground by the wreck as it passed
over their heads. The captain fell like the rest,
but he retained his grasp of Ailie, and succeeded
in rising, and as the gale carried him away with
irresistible fury he bore firmly down to his right,
and gained the eddy caused by the rocks which
until now had sheltered the hut. He was safe;
but he did not feel secure until he had staggered
towards the most sheltered part, and placed his
child in a cleft of the rock.

Here he found Gurney and Tarquin before him, and soon after Glynn came staggering in, along with one or two others. In less than three minutes after the hut had been blown away, all the men were collected in the cleft, where they crouched down to avoid the pelting, pitiless spray that dashed over their heads.

It is difficult to conceive a more desperate position than that in which they were now placed, yet there and at that moment a thrill of joy passed through the hearts of most, if not all of them, for they heard a shout, which was recognised to be the voice of Tim Rokens. It came from the rocks a few yards to their right, and almost ere it had died away, Rokens himself staggered into the sheltering cleft of rock, accompanied by Phil Briant.

Some of the men who had faced the dangers to which they had been exposed with firm nerves and unblanched cheeks, now grew pale, and trembled violently, for they actually believed that the spirits of their lost shipmates had come to haunt them. But these superstitious fears were soon put to flight by the hearty voice of the harpooneer, who shook himself like a great Newfoundland dog as he came up, and exclaimed—

"Why, wot on airth has brought ye all here?"

"I think we may say, what has brought *you* here?" replied the captain, as he grasped them each by the hand, and shook them with as much energy as if he had not met with them for ten years past.

"It's aisy to tell that," said Briant, as he crouched down in the midst of the group; "Tim and me wos blow'd right across the bank, an' we should no doubt ha' bin blow'd right into the sea, but Tim went full split agin one o' the casks o' salt-junk, and I went slap agin *him*, and we lay for a moment all but dead. Then we crep' in the lee o' the cask, an' lay there till a lull came, when we clapped on all sail, an' made for the shelter o' the rocks, an' shure we got there niver a taste too soon, for it came on to blow the next minit, fit to blow the eyelids off yer face, it did."

"It's a fact,' added Rokens. "Moreover, we tried to git round to the hut, but as we wos twice nearly blowed away w'en we tried for to double the point, we 'greed to stay where we wos till the back o' the gale should be broke. But, now, let's hear wot's happened."

"The hut's gone," said Gurney, in reply. "Blowed clean over our heads to—I dun know where."

"Blowed away?" cried Rokens and Briant, in consternation.

"Not a stick left," replied the captain.

"An' the boat?" inquired Briant.

"It's gone, too, I fancy; but we can't be sure."

"Then it's all up, boys," observed Briant; "for nearly every morsel o' the prog that wos on the top o' the bank is washed away."

This piece of news fell like a thunderbolt on the men, and no one spoke for some minutes. At last the captain said—

"Well, lads, we must do the best we can. Thank God, we are still alive; so let us see if we can't make our present quarters more comfortable."

Setting his men the example, Captain Dunning began to collect the few boards and bits of canvas that chanced to have been left on that side of the rocky ledge when the hut was removed to the other side, and with these materials a very partial and insufficient shelter was put up. But the space thus inclosed was so small that they were all obliged to huddle together in a mass. Those farthest from the rock were not altogether protected from the spray that flew over their heads, while those nearest to it were crushed and incommoded by their companions.

Thus they passed that eventful night and all the following day, during which the storm raged with such fury that no one dared venture out to ascertain how much, if any, of their provisions and stores were left to them.

During the second night, a perceptible decrease in the violence of the gale took place, and before morning it ceased altogether. The sun rose in unclouded splendour, sending its bright and warm beams up into the clear blue sky and down upon the ocean, which glittered vividly as it still swelled and trembled with agitation. All was serene and calm in the sky, while below the only sound that

broke upon the ear was the deep and regular dash
of the great breakers that fell upon the shores of
the islet, and encircled it with a fringe of purest
white.

On issuing from their confined uneasy nest in
the cleft of the rock, part of the shipwrecked crew
hastened anxiously to the top of the bank to see
how much of their valuable store of food was left,
while others ran to the spot in Fairyland where
the keel of the new boat had been laid. The latter
party found to their joy that all was safe, everything having been well secured; but a terrible sight
met the eyes of the other men. Not a vestige of
all their store remained! The summit of the
sandbank was as smooth as on the day they
landed there. Casks, boxes, barrels—all were
gone; everything had been swept away into the
sea!

Almost instinctively the men turned their eyes
towards the reef on which the Red Eric had
grounded, each man feeling that in the wrecked
vessel all his hope now remained. It, too, was
gone! The spot on which it had lain was now
washed by the waves, and a few broken planks and
spars on the beach were all that remained to remind them of their ocean home!

The men looked at each other with deep
despondency expressed in their countenances.
They were haggard and worn from exposure,
anxiety, and want of rest; and as they stood

there in their wet, torn garments, they looked the very picture of despair.

"There's one chance for us yet, lads," exclaimed Tim Rokens, looking carefully round the spot on which they stood.

"What's that?" exclaimed several of the men, eagerly, catching at their comrade's words as drowning men are said to catch at straws.

"Briant an' me buried some o' the things, by good luck, when we were sent to make all snug here, an' I'm of opinion they'll be here yet, if we could only find the place. Let me see."

Rokens glanced round at the rocks beside which their hut had found shelter, and at the reef where the ship had been wrecked, in order to find the "bearin's o' the spot," as he expressed it. Then walking a few yards to one side, he struck his foot on the sand and said, "It should be hereabouts."

The blow of his heel returned a peculiar hollow sound, very unlike that produced by stamping on the mere sand.

"Shure ye've hit the very spot, ye have," cried Briant, falling on his knees beside the place, and scraping up the sand with both hands. "It sounds uncommon like a bread-cask. Here it is. Hurrah! boys, lind a hand, will ye. There now, heave away; but trate it tinderly! Shure it's the only friend we've got in the wide world."

"You're all wrong, Phil," cried Gurney, who almost at the same moment began to scrape

another hole close by.   " It's not our only one;
here's another friend o' the same family.   Bear a
hand, lads !"

" And here's another !" cried Ailie, with a little
scream of delight, as she observed the rim of a
small keg just peeping out above the sand.

" Well done, Ailie," cried Glynn, as he ran to
the spot and quickly dug up the keg in question,
which, however, proved to be full of nails, to Ailie's
great disappointment, for she expected it to have
turned out a keg of biscuits.

" How many casks did you bury ?" inquired the
captain.

" It's meself can't tell," replied Briant ; " d'ye
know, Tim ?"

" Three, I think ; but we was in sich a hurry
that I ain't sartin exactly."

" Well, then, boys, look here !" continued the
captain, drawing a pretty large circle on the sand,
" set to work like a band of moles an' dig up every
inch o' that till you come to the water."

" That's your sort," cried Rokens, plunging elbow
deep into the sand at once.

" Arrah ! then, here's at ye ; a fair field an' no
favor at any price," shouted Briant, baring his
arms, straddling his legs, and sending a shower of
sand behind him that almost overwhelmed Gurney,
before that stout little individual could get out of
he way.

The spirits of the men were farther rejoiced by

the coming up of the other party, bearing the good
news that the keel of the boat was safe, as well as
all her planking and the carpenter's tools, which
fortunately happened to have been secured in a
sheltered spot.  From the depths of despair they
were all suddenly raised to renewed and sanguine
hope, so that they wrought with the energy of
gold diggers, and soon their toil was rewarded by
the discovery of that which, in their circumstances,
they would not have exchanged for all the golden
nuggets that ever were or will be dug up from the
prolific mines of Australia, California, or British
Columbia—namely, three casks of biscuit, a small
keg of wine, a cask of fresh water, a roll of tobacco,
and a barrel of salt junk.

## CHAPTER XX.

PREPARATIONS FOR A LONG VOYAGE—BRIANT PROVES THAT
GHOSTS CAN DRINK—JACKO ASTONISHES HIS FRIENDS,
AND SADDENS HIS ADOPTED MOTHER.

"WOT *I* say is one thing ; wot *you* say is another
—so it is.  I dun know w'ich is right, or w'ich is
wrong—no more do you.  P'raps you is, p'raps I
is ; anywise we can't both on us be right or both
on us be wrong—that's a comfort, if it's nothin'
else.  Wot *you* say is—that it's morally imposs'ble
for a crew sich as us to travel over two thousand
miles of ocean on three casks o' biscuit and a barrel

o' salt junk. Wot *I* say is—that we can, an',
moreover, that morals has nothin' to do with it
wotsomediver. Now, wot then ?"

Tim Rokens paused and looked at Gurney, to
whom his remarks were addressed, as if he expected an answer. That rotund little seaman did
not, however, appear to be thoroughly prepared to
reply to "wot then," for he remained silent, but
looked at his comrade as though to say, " I'll be
happy to learn wisdom from your sagacious lips."

"Wot then ?" repeated Tim Rokens, assaulting
his knee with his clenched fist in a peculiarly emphatic manner ; " I'll tell ye wot then, as you may
be right and I may be right, an' nother on us can
be both right or wrong, I say as how that we don't
know nothin' about it."

Gurney looked as if he did not quite approve of
so summary a method of solving such a knotty
question, but observing from the expression of
Rokens' countenance that, though he had paused,
that philosopher had not yet concluded, he remained silent.

"An', furthermore," continued Tim, "it's my
opinion,—seein' that we're both on us in sich a state
o' cumblebofubulation, an' don't know nothin'—
we'd better go an' ax the cap'en, who does."

"You may save yourselves the trouble," observed
Glynn Proctor, who at that moment came up and
sat down on the rocks beside them, with a piece of
he salt junk that formed an element in the ques-

tion at issue, in his hand—" I've just heard the captain give his opinion on that subject, and he says that the boat can be got ready in a week or less, and that, with strict economy, the provisions we have will last us long enough to enable us to make the Cape, supposing we have good weather and fair winds. That's *his* opinion."

" I told ye so," said Tim Rokens.

" You did nothin' o' the sort," retorted Gurney.

" Well, if ye come fur to be oncommon strick in the use o' your lingo, I did *not* 'xactly tell ye so, but I *thought* so, w'ich is all the same."

" It ain't all the same," replied Gurney, whose temper seemed to have been a little soured by the prospects before him, " and you don't need to go for to be talkin' there like a great Solon as you are."

" Wot's a Solon ?" inquired Tim.

" Solon was a man as thought hisself a great feelosopher, but he worn't, he wor an ass."

" If I'm like Solon," retorted Rokens, " you're like a Solon-goose, w'ich is an animal as *don't* think itself an ass, 'cause it's too great a one to know it."

Having thus floored his adversary, the philosophic mariner turned to Glynn and said,—

" In course we can't expect to be on full allowance."

" Of course not, old boy ; the captain remarked, just as I left him, that we'd have to be content with short allowance—very short allowance indeed."

Gurney sighed deeply.

" How much ?" inquired Tim.

" About three ounces of biscuit, one ounce of salt junk, and a quarter of a pint of water per day."

Gurney groaned aloud.

" You, of all men," said Glynn, " have least reason to complain, Gurney, for you've got fat enough on your own proper person to last you a week at least !"

" Ay, a fortnight, or more," added Rokens ; " an even then ye'd scarcely be redooced to a decent size."

" Ah, but," pleaded Gurney, " you scarecrow creatures don't know how horrid sore the process o' comin' down is. An' one gets so cold, too. It's just like taking off yer clo's."

" Sarves ye right for puttin' on so many," said Rokens, as he rose to resume work, which he. and Gurney had left off three-quarters of an hour before, in order to enjoy a quiet, philosophical *téte-à-téte* during dinner.

"It's a bad business, that of the planking not being sufficient to deck or even half-deck the boat," observed Glynn, as they went together towards the place where the new boat was being built.

" It is," replied Rokens ; " but it's a good thing that we've got plenty of canvas to spare. It won't make an overly strong deck, to be sure ; but it's better than nothin'."

" A heavy sea would burst it in no time," re- marked Gurney.

"We must hope to escape heavy seas, then," said Glynn, as they parted, and went to their several occupations.

The boat that was now building with the most urgent despatch, had a keel of exactly 23 feet long, and her breadth, at the widest part, was seven feet. She was being as well and firmly put together as the materials at their command would admit of, and, as far as the work had yet proceeded, she bid fair to become an excellent boat, capable of containing the whole crew, and their small quantity of provisions. This last was diminishing so rapidly, that Captain Dunning resolved to put all hands at once on short allowance. Notwithstanding this, the men worked hard and hopefully; for, as each plank and nail was added to their little bark, they felt as if they were a step nearer home. The captain and the doctor, however, and one or two of the older men, could not banish from their minds the fact that the voyage they were about to undertake was of the most perilous nature, and one which, in any other than the hopeless circumstances in which they were placed at that time, would have been regarded as the most desperate of forlorn hopes.

For fourteen souls to be tossed about on the wide and stormy sea, during many weeks, it might be months, in a small open boat, crowded together and cramped, without sufficient covering, and on short allowance of food, was indeed a dreary prospect, even for the men—how much more so for the delicate child who shared their trials and sufferings? Captain Dunning's heart sank within him when he thought of it; but he knew how great an influence the conduct and bearing of a commander has, in such circumstances, on his men; so he strove to show a smiling, cheerful countenance, though oftentimes he carried a sad and anxious heart in his bosom. To the doctor and Tim Rokens alone did he reveal his inmost thoughts, because he knew that he could trust them, and felt that he needed their advice and sympathy.

The work progressed so rapidly, that in a few days more the boat approached completion, and preparations were being made in earnest for finally quitting the little isle on which they had found a home for so many days.

It was observed by the captain that as the work of boat-building drew to a close, Glynn Proctor continued to labour long after the others had retired to rest, wearied with the toils of the day—toils which they were not now so well able to bear as heretofore, on account of the slight want of vigour caused by being compelled to live on half allowance.

One evening, the captain went down to the building yard in Fairyland, and said to Glynn,—

" Hallo, my boy! at it yet? Why, what are you making? a dog-kennel, eh?"

" No; not exactly that," replied Glynn, laughing. " You'll hardly guess."

"I would say it was a house for Jacko, only it seems much too big."

"It's just possible that Jacko may have a share in it," said Glynn; "but it's not for him."

"Who, then?   Not for yourself, surely!"

"It's for Ailie," cried Glynn, gleefully.   "Don't you think it will be required?" he added, looking up, as if he half feared the captain would not permit his contrivance to be used.

"Well, I believe it will, my boy. I had intended to get some sort of covering for my dear Ailie put up in the stern sheets; but I did not think of absolutely making a box for her."

"Ah, you'll find it will be a capital thing at nights. I know she could never stand the exposure; and canvas don't keep out the rain well; so I thought of rigging up a large box, into which she can creep. I'll make air-holes in the roof that will let in air, but not water; and I'll caulk the seams with oakum, so as to keep it quite dry inside."

"Thank you, my boy, it's very kind of you to take so much thought for my poor child. Yet she deserves it, Glynn, and we can't be too careful of her."

The captain patted the youth on the shoulder, and, leaving him to continue his work, went to see Gurney, who had been ailing a little during the last few days. Brandy, in small quantities, had been prescribed by the doctor, and fortunately two bottles of that spirit had been saved from the wreck. Being their whole stock, Captain Dunning had stowed it carefully away in what he deemed a secret and secure place ; but it turned out that some member of the crew was not so strict in his principles of temperance as could be desired ; for, on going to the spot to procure the required medicine, it was found that one of the bottles was gone.

This discovery caused the captain much anxiety and sorrow, for, besides inflicting on them the loss of a most valuable medicine, it proved that there was a thief in their little society.

What was to be done ? To pass it over in silence would have shown weakness, which, especially in the circumstances in which they were at that time placed, might have led at last to open mutiny. To discover the thief was impossible. The captain's mind was soon made up. He summoned every one of the party before him, and, after stating the discovery he had made, he said :—

"Now lads, I'm not going to charge any of you with having done this thing, but I cannot let it pass without warning you that if I discover any of you being guilty of such practices in future, I'll have the man tied up and give him three dozen with a rope's end. You know I have never resorted, as many captains are in the habit of doing, to corporal punishment. I don't like it. I've sailed in command of ships for many years, and have never found it needful ; but now, more than ever, strict discipline must be maintained ; and I tell you, once for all, that I mean to maintain it *at any cost.*"

This speech was received in silence. All perceived the justice of it, yet some felt that, until the thief should be discovered, they themselves would lie under suspicion. A few there were, indeed, whose well-known and long-established characters raised them above suspicion, but there were others who knew that their character had not yet been established on so firm a basis, and they felt that until the matter should be cleared up, their honesty would be, mentally at least, called in question by their companions.

With the exception of the disposition to mutiny related in a previous chapter, this was the first cloud that had risen to interrupt the harmony of the shipwrecked sailors, and as they returned to their work, sundry suggestions and remarks were made in reference to the possibility of discovering the delinquent.

"I didn't think it wos poss'ble," said Rokens. "I thought as how there wasn't a man in the ship as could ha' done sich a low, mean thing as that."

"No more did I," said Dick Barnes.

"Wall, boys," observed Nikel Sling, emphatically, "I guess as how that I don't believe it yet."

"Arrah! D'ye think the bottle o' brandy stole hisself?" inquired Briant.

"I aint a-goin' fur to say that; but a ghost

might ha' done it, p'raps, a-purpose to get us into
a scrape."

There was a slight laugh at this, and from that
moment the other men suspected that Sling was
the culprit. The mere fact of his being the first to
charge the crime upon any one else—even a ghost
—caused them, in spite of themselves, to come to
this conclusion. They did not, however, by word
or look, show what was passing in their minds, for
the Yankee was a favourite with his comrades, and
each felt unwilling that his suspicion should prove
to be correct.

"I don't agree with you," said Tarquin, who
feared that suspicion might attach to himself, seeing that he had been the ringleader in the recent
mutiny ; "I don't believe that ghosts drink."

"Och ! that's all ye know !" cried Phil Briant.
"Av ye'd only lived a month or two in Owld
Ireland, ye'd have seen raison to change yer mind,
ye would. Sure I've seed a ghost the worse o'
liquor meself."

"Oh ! Phil, wot a stunner !" cried Gurney.

"It's as true as me name's Phil Briant—more's
the pity. Did I niver tell ye o' the Widdy Morgan,
as had a ghost come to see her frequently ?"

"No, never—let's hear it."

"Stop that noise with yer hammer, then, Tim
Rokens, jist for five minutes, and I'll tell it ye."

The men ceased work for a few minutes while
their comrade spoke as follows :—

"It's not a long story, boys, but it's long enough to prove that ghosts drink.

"Ye must know that, wance upon a time there wos a widdy as lived in a small town in the county o' Clare, in Owld Ireland, an' oh! but that was the place for drinkin' and fightin'. It wos there that I learned to use me flippers; and it wos there, too, that I learned to give up drinkin', for I comed for to see what a mighty dale o' harm it did to my poor countrymen. The sexton o' the place was the only man as niver wint near the grog-shop, and no wan iver seed him overtook with drink, but it was a quare thing, that no wan could rightly understand why he used to *smell* o' drink very bad sometimes. There wos a young widdy in that town, o' the name o' Morgan, as kep' a cow, an' owned a small cabin, an' a patch o' tater-ground about the size o' the starn sheets of our owld long-boat. She wos a great deal run after, wos this widdy—not that the young lads had an eye to the cow, or the cabin, or the tater-estate, be no manes—but she wos greatly admired, she wos. I admired her meself, and wint to see her pretty fraquent. Well, wan evenin' I wint to see her, an' says I, 'Mrs. Morgan, did ye iver hear the bit song called the Widdy Machree?' 'Sure I niver did,' says she. 'Would ye like to hear it, darlint?' says I. So she says she would, an' I gave it to her right off; an' when I'd done, says I, 'Now, Widdy Morgan, ochone! will ye take *me*?' But she shook her head, and looked melancholy.

'Ye aint agoin' to take spasms?' says I, for I got frightened at her looks. 'No,' says she; 'but there's a sacret about me; an' I like ye too well, Phil, to decaive ye; if ye only know'd the sacret, ye wouldn't have me at any price.'

"'Wouldn't I?' says I; 'try me, cushla, and see av I wont.'

"'Phil Briant,' says she, awful solemn like, 'I'm haunted.'

"'Haunted!' says I; 'av coorse ye are, bliss yer purty face; don't I know that ivery boy in the parish is after ye?'

"'It's not that I mane. It's a ghost as haunts me. It haunts me cabin, and me cow, and me tater-estate; an' it drinks.' .

"'Now, darlint,' says I, 'everybody knows yer aisy frightened about ghosts. I don't belave in one meself, an' I don't mind 'em a farden dip; but av all the ghosts in Ireland haunted ye, I'd niver give ye up.'

"'Will ye come an' see it this night?' says she.

"'Av coorse I will,' says I. An' that same night I wint to her cabin, and she let me in, and put a candle on the table, an' hid me behind a great clock, in a corner jist close by the cupboard, where the brandy bottle lived. Then she lay down on her bed with her clo's on, and pulled the coverlid over her, and pretended to go to slape. In less nor half an hour I hears a fut on the doorstep; then a tap at the door, which opened, it seemed to me, of

its own accord, and in walks the ghost, sure enough!
It was covered all over from head to fut in a white
sheet, and I seed by the way it walked that it wos
the worse of drink. I wos in a mortal fright, ye
may be sure, an' me knees shuk to that extint ye
might have heard them rattle. The ghost walks
straight up to the cupboard, takes out the brandy-
bottle, and fills out a whole tumbler quite full, and
drinks it off; it did, the baste, ivery dhrop. I
seed it with me two eyes, as sure as I'm a-standin'
here. It came into the house drunk, an' it wint
out drunker nor it came in."

"Is that all?" exclaimed several of Briant's
auditors.

"All! av coorse it is. Wot more would ye
have? Didn't I say that I'd tell ye a story as
would prove to ye that ghosts drink, more especially Irish ghosts. To be sure it turned out afterwards that the ghost was the sexton o' the parish
as took advantage o' the poor widdy's fears; but I
can tell ye, boys, that ghost niver came back
after the widdy became Mrs. Briant."

"Oh! then ye married the widder, did ye?"
said Jim Scroggles.

"I did; an' she's alive and hearty this day av
she's not——"

Briant was interrupted by a sudden roar of
laughter from the men, who at that moment caught
sight of Jacko, the small monkey, in a condition of
mind and body that, to say the least of it, did him

no credit. We are sorry to be compelled to state
that Jacko was evidently and undoubtedly tipsy.
Gurney said he was "as drunk as a fiddler."

We cannot take upon ourself to say whether he
was or was not as drunk as that. We are rather
inclined to think that fiddlers, as a class, are
maligned, and that they are no worse than their
neighbours in this respect, perhaps not so bad.
Certainly, if any fiddler really deserves the impu-
tation, it must be a violoncello player, because he
is, properly speaking, a *base*-fiddler.

Be this, however, as it may, Jacko was unmistakeably drunk—in a maudlin state of intoxication
—drunker, probably, than ever a monkey was before or since. He appeared, as he came slowly
staggering forward to the place where the men were
at work on the boat, to have just wakened out of
his first drunken sleep, for his eyes were blinking
like the orbs of an owl in the sunshine, and in his
walk he placed his right foot where his left should
have gone, and his left foot where his right should
have gone, occasionally making a little run forward to save himself from tumbling on his nose,
and then pulling suddenly up, and throwing up
his arms ,in order to avoid falling on his back.
Sometimes he halted altogether, and swayed to
and fro, gazing, meanwhile, pensively at the
ground, as if he were wondering why it had
taken to rolling and earthquaking in that preposterous manner ; or were thinking on the bald-

headed mother he had left behind him in the African wilderness. When the loud laugh of the men saluted his ears, Jacko looked up as quickly and steadily as he could, and grinned a ghastly smile—or something like it—as if to say, "What are you laughing at, villains?"

It is commonly observed that, among men, the ruling passion comes out strongly when they are under the influence of strong drink. So it is with monkeys. Jacko's ruling passion was thieving; but having, at that time, no particular inducement to steal, he indulged his next ruling passion—that of affection—by holding out both arms, and staggering towards Phil Briant to be taken up.

A renewed burst of laughter greeted this movement.

"It knows ye, Phil," cried Jim Scroggles.

"Ah! then, so it should, for it's meself as is good to it. Come to its uncle, then. O good luck to yer purty little yaller face. So it wos you stole the brandy, wos it? Musha! but ye might have know'd ye belonged to a timp'rance ship, so ye might."

Jacko spread his arms on Briant's broad chest; they were too short to go round his neck—laid his head thereon, and sighed. Perhaps he felt penitent on account of his wickedness; but it is more probable that he felt uneasy in body rather than in mind.

"I say, Briant," cried Gurney.

"That's me," answered the other.

"If you are Jacko's self-appointed uncle, and Miss Ailie is his adopted mother, wot relation is Miss Ailie to you?"

"You never does nothin' right, Gurney," interposed Nikel Sling; "you can't even preepound a pruposition. Here's how you oughter to ha' put it. If Phil Briant be Jacko's uncle, and Miss Ailie his adopted mother—all three bein' related in a sorter way by bein' shipmates, an' all on us together bein' closely connected in vartue of our bein' messmates—wot relation is Gurney to a donkey?"

"That's a puzzler," said Gurney, affecting to consider the question deeply.

"Here's a puzzler wot'll beat it, though," observed Tim Rokens; "suppose we all go on talkin' stuff till doomsday, w'en'll the boat be finished?"

"That's true," cried Dick Barnes, resuming work with redoubled energy; "take that young thief to his mother, Phil, and tell her to rope's-end him. I'm right glad to find, though, that he *is* the thief arter all, and not one o' us."

On examination being made, it was found that the broken and empty brandy bottle lay on the floor of the monkey's nest, and it was conjectured, from the position in which it was discovered, that that dissipated little creature, having broken off the neck in order to get at the brandy, had used the body of the bottle as a pillow whereon to lay its drunken little head. Luckily for its own sake, it had spilt the greater part of the liquid, with which everything in its private residence was saturated and perfumed.

On having ocular demonstration of the depravity of her pet, Ailie at first wept, then, on beholding its eccentric movements, she laughed in spite of herself. After that, she wept again, and spoke to it reproachfully, but failed to make the slightest impression on its hardened little heart. Then she put it to bed, and wrapped it up carefully in its sailcloth blanket.

With this piece of unmerited kindness Jacko seemed touched, for he said, "Oo-oo—oo-oo—ooee-ee !" once or twice in a peculiarly soft and peni-tential tone, after which he dropt into a calm, un-troubled slumber.

## CHAPTER XXI.

### THE BOAT FINISHED—FAREWELL TO FAIRYLAND—ONCE MORE AT SEA.

AT last the boat was finished. It had two masts and two lug-sails, and pulled eight oars. There was just sufficient room in it to enable the men to move about freely, but it required a little manage-ment to enable them to stow themselves away when they went to sleep, and had they possessed the proper quantity of provisions for their contemplated voyage, there is no doubt that they would have found themselves considerably cramped. The boat

x

was named the Maid of the Isle, in memory of the sand-bank on which she had been built, and, although in her general outline and details she was rather a clumsy craft, she was serviceable and strongly put together.

Had she been decked, or even half decked, the voyage which now began would not have been so desperate an undertaking; but having been only covered in part with a frail tarpaulin, she was not at all fitted to face the terrible storms that sometimes sweep the southern seas. Each man, as he gazed at her, felt that his chance of ultimate escape was very small indeed. Still, the men had now been so long contemplating the voyage and preparing for it, and they had become so accustomed to risk their lives upon the sea, that they set out upon this voyage at last in cheerful spirits, and even jested about the anticipated dangers and trials which they knew full well awaited them.

It was a lovely morning, that on which the wrecked crew of the whaler bade adieu to " Fairyland," as the islet had been named by Ailie—a name that was highly, though laughingly, approved of by the men. The ocean and sky presented that mysterious co-mingling of their gorgeous elements that irresistibly call forth the wonder and admiration of even the most unromantic and matter-of-fact men. It was one of Ailie's peculiarly beloved skies. You could not, without much consideration, have decided as to where was the exact line at which the glassy ocean met the clear sky, and it was almost impossible to tell, when gazing at the horizon, which were the real clouds and which the reflections.

The bright blue vault above was laden with clouds of the most gorgeous description, in which all the shades of pearly-grey and yellow were mingled and contrasted. They rose up, pile upon pile, in stupendous majesty, like the very battlements of Heaven, while their images, clear and distinct almost as themselves, rolled down and down into the watery depths, until the islet—the only well defined and solid object in the scene— appeared to float in their midst. The rising sun shot throughout the vast immensity of space, and its warm rays were interrupted and broken, and caught, and absorbed, and reflected in so many magical ways, that it was impossible to trace any of the outlines for more than a few seconds, ere the eye was lost in the confusion of bright lights and deep shadows that were mingled and mellowed together by the softer lights and shades of every degree of depth and tint into splendid harmony.

In the midst of this scene Captain Dunning stood, with Ailie by his side, and surrounded by his men, on the shores of the little island. Everything was now in readiness to set sail. The boat was laden, and in the water, and the men stood ready to leap in and push off.

" My lads," said the captain, earnestly, " we're about to quit this morsel of sand-bank on which it pleased the Almighty to cast our ship, and on which, thanks be to Him, we have found a pretty safe shelter for so long. I feel a sort o' regret almost at leavin' it now. But the time has come for us to begin our voyage towards the Cape, and I need scarcely repeat what you all know well enough—that our undertakin' is no child's play. We shall need all our bodily and our mental powers to carry us through. Our labour must be constant, and our food is not sufficient, so that we must go on shorter allowance from this day. I gave you half rations while ye were buildin' the boat, because we had to get her finished and launched as fast as we could, but now we can't afford to eat so much. I made a careful inspection of our provisions last night, and I find that by allowing every man four ounces a day, we can spin it out. We may fall in with islands, perhaps, but I know of none in these seas—there are none put down on the charts—and we may get hold of a fish now and then, but we must not count on these chances. Now it must be plain to all of you that our only chance of getting on well together in circumstances that will try our tempers, no doubt, and rouse our selfishness, is to resolve firmly before starting—each man for himself—that we will lay restraint on ourselves and try to help each other as much as we can."

There was a ready murmur of assent to this proposal ; then the captain continued :—" Now, lads,

one word more. Our best efforts, let us exert ourselves ever so much, cannot be crowned with success, unless, before setting out, we ask the special
favour and blessing of Him who, we are told in the
Bible, holds the waters of the ocean in the hollow
of His hand. If He helps us, we shall be saved;
if He does not help us, we shall perish. We will
therefore offer up a prayer now, in the name of our
blessed Redeemer, that we may be delivered from
every danger, and be brought at last in peace and
comfort to our homes."

Captain Dunning then clasped his hands together,
and while the men around him reverently bowed
their heads, he offered up a short and simple, but
earnest prayer to God.

From that day forward they continued the habit
of offering up prayer together once a day, and soon
afterwards the captain began the practice of reading a chapter aloud daily out of Ailie's Bible. The
result of this was that, not only were the more
violent spirits among them restrained, under frequent and sore privations and temptations, but all
the party were often much comforted and filled
with hope at times when they were by their sufferings well-nigh driven to despair.

"I'm sorry to leave Fairyland, papa," said Ailie,
sadly, as the men shoved the Maid of the Isle into
deep water and pulled out to sea.

"So am I, dear," replied the captain, sitting
down beside his daughter in the stern-sheets of the

boat, and taking the tiller; "I had no idea I could have come to like such a barren bit of sand so well."

There was a long pause after this remark. Every eye in the boat was turned with a sad expression on the bright-yellow sand-bank, as they rowed away, and the men dipped their oars lightly into the calm waters, as if they were loth to leave their late home.

Any spot of earth that has been for some time the theatre of heart-stirring events, such as rouse men's strong emotions, and on which happy and hopeful as well as wretched days have been spent, will so entwine itself with the affections of men that they will cling to it and love it, more or less powerfully, no matter how barren may be the spot or how dreary its general aspect. The sand-bank had been the cause, no doubt, of the wreck of the Red Eric, but it had also been the means, under God, of saving the crew and affording them shelter during many succeeding weeks—weeks of deep anxiety, but also of healthful, hopeful, energetic toil, in which, if there were many things to create annoyance or fear, there had also been not a few things to cause thankfulness, delight, and amusement.

Unknown to themselves, these rough sailors and the tender child had become attached to the spot, and it was only now that they were about to leave it for ever that they became aware of the fact. The circumscribed and limited range on which their thoughts and vision had been bent for the last few weeks, had rendered each individual as familiar with every inch of the bank as if he had dwelt there for years.

Ailie gazed at the low rocks that overhung the crystal pool in Fairyland, until the blinding tears filled her eyes, and she felt all the deep regret that is experienced by the little child when it is forcibly torn from an old and favourite toy—regret, that is not in the least degree mitigated by the fact that the said toy is but a sorry affair, a doll, perchance, with a smashed head, eyes thrust out, and nose flattened on its face or rubbed away altogether— it matters not; the long and happy hours and days spent in the companionship of that battered little mass of wood or wax rush on the infant memory like a dear delightful dream, and it weeps on separation as if its heart would break.

Each man in the boat's crew experienced more or less of the same feeling, and commented, according to his nature, either silently or audibly, on each familiar object as he gazed upon it for the last time.

"There's the spot where we built the hut wher we first landed, Ailie," said Glynn, who pulled the aft oar, "d'you see it?—just coming into view; look! There, it will be shut out again in a moment by the rock beside the coral-pool."

"I see it!" exclaimed Ailie, eagerly, as she brushed away the tears from her eyes.

"There's the rock, too, where we used to make

our fire," said the captain, pointing it out. "It doesn't look like itself from this point of view."

"Ah !" sighed Phil Briant, "an' it wos at the fut o' that, too, where we used to bile the kittle night an' mornin'. Sure it's many a swait bit and pipe I had beside ye."

"Is that a bit o' the wreck ?" inquired Tim Rokens, pointing to the low rocky point with the eagerness of a man who had made an unexpected discovery.

"No," replied Mr. Millons, shading his eyes with his hands, and gazing at the object in question, "it's himpossible. I searched every bit o' the bank for a plank before we came hoff, an' couldn't find a morsel as big as my 'and. W'at say you, doctor ?"

"I think with you," answered Dr. Hopley ; "but here's the telescope, which will soon settle the question."

While the doctor adjusted the glass, Rokens muttered that "He wos sure it wos a bit o' the wreck," and that "there wos a bit o' rock as nobody couldn't easy gitt a tother side of to look, and that that wos it, and the bit of wreck was there," and much to the same effect.

"So it is," exclaimed the doctor.

"Lay' on your oars, lads, a moment," said the captain, taking the glass and applying it to his eye.

The men obeyed gladly, for they experienced an unaccountable disinclination to row away from the island. Perhaps the feeling was caused in part by the idea that when they took their last look at it, it might possibly be their *last* sight of land.

" It's a  small piece of the foretopmast crosstrees," observed the captain, shutting up the telescope and resuming his seat.

" Shall we go back an' pick it up, sir ?" asked Dick Barnes, gravely, giving vent to the desires of his heart, without perceiving at the moment the absurdity of the question.

" Why, what would you do with it, Dick?" replied the captain, smiling.

"Sure ye couldn't ait it !" interposed Briant ; " but, afther all, there's no sayin'.  Maybe, Nikel Sling could make a tasty dish out of it stewed in oakum and tar."

" It wouldn't be purlite to take such a tit-bit from the mermaids," observed Gurney, as the oars were once more dipped reluctantly in the water.

The men smiled at the jest, for in the monotony of sea life every species of pleasantry, however poor, is swallowed with greater or less avidity ; but the smile did not last long.  They were in no jesting humour at that time, and no one replied to the passing joke.

Soon after this a soft gentle breeze sprang up. It came direct from Fairyland, as if the mermaids referred to by Gurney had been touched by the kindly feelings harboured in the sailors' bosoms towards their islet, and had wafted towards them a last farewell.  The oars were shipped immediately and the sails hoisted, and, to the satisfaction of all on board, the Maid of the Isle gave indications of being a swift sailer, for, although the puff of wind was scarcely sufficient to ruffle the glassy surface of the sea, she glided through the water under its influence a good deal faster than she had done with the oars.

"That's good!" remarked the captain, watching the ripples as they passed astern; "with fair winds, and not too much of 'em, we shall get on bravely; so cheer up, my lassie," he added, patting Ailie on the head, "and let us begin our voyage in good spirits, and with hopeful, trusting hearts."

"Look at Fairyland," said Ailie, clasping her father's hand, and pointing towards the horizon.

At the moment she spoke, an opening in the great white clouds let a ray of light fall on the sand-bank, which had now passed almost beyond the range of vision. The effect was to illumine its yellow shore, and cause it to shine out for a few seconds like a golden speck on the horizon. No one had ceased to gaze at it from the time the boat put forth; but this sudden change caused every one to start up, and fix their eyes on it with renewed interest and intensity. "Shall we ever see land again?" passed, in one form or another, through the minds of all. The clouds swept slowly on, the golden point melted away, and the shipwrecked mariners felt that their little boat was now all the world to them in the midst of that mighty world of waters.

## CHAPTER XXII.

REDUCED ALLOWANCE OF FOOD—JACKO TEACHES BRIANT
A USEFUL LESSON.

THE first few days of the voyage of the Maid of
the Isle were bright and favourable. The wind,
though light, was fair, and so steady, that the men
were only twice obliged to have recourse to their
oars. The boat behaved admirably. Once, during
these first days, the wind freshened into a pretty
stiff breeze, and a somewhat boisterous sea arose,
so that she was tested in another of her sailing
qualities, and was found to be an excellent sea-boat.
Very little water was shipped, and that little was
taken in rather through the awkwardness of King
Bumble, who steered, than through the fault of the
boat.

Captain Dunning had taken care that there
should be a large supply of tin and wooden scoops,
for baling out the water that might be shipped in
rough weather, as he foresaw that on the prompt-
ness with which this duty was performed, might
sometimes depend the safety of the boat and crew.

There was one thing that proved a matter of
much regret to the crew, and that was the want of
a fowling-piece, or fire-arm of any kind. Had they
possessed a gun, however old and bad, with ammu-
nition for it, they would have been certain, at some

period of their voyage, to shoot a few sea-birds, with which they expected to fall in on approaching the land, even although many days distant from it. But having nothing of the kind, their hope of adding to their slender stock of provisions was very small indeed. Fortunately, they had one or two fishing-lines, but in the deep water, over which for many days they had to sail, fishing was out of the question.

This matter of the provisions was a source of constant anxiety to Captain Dunning. He had calculated the amount of their stores to an ounce, and ascertained that at a certain rate of distribution they would barely serve for the voyage, and this without making any allowance for interruptions or detentions. He knew the exact distance to be passed over, namely, 2322 miles in a straight line, and he had ascertained the sailing and rowing powers of the boat and crew; thus he was enabled to arrive at a pretty correct idea of the probable duration of the voyage, supposing that all should go well  But in the event of strong contrary winds, arising, no fresh supplies of fish or fowl being obtained, or sickness breaking out among the men, he knew either that they must starve altogether, or that he must at once, before it was too late, still farther reduce the scanty allowance of food and drink to each man.

The captain sat at the helm one fine evening, about a week after their departure from Fairyland, brooding deeply over this subject. The boat was running before a light breeze, at the rate of about four or five knots, and the men, who had been obliged to row a good part of that day, were sitting or reclining on the thwarts, or leaning over the gunwale, watching the ripples as they glided by, and enjoying the rest from labour; for now that they had been for some time on reduced allowance of food, they felt less able for work than they used to be, and often began to look forward with intense longing to seasons of repose. Ailie was sitting near the entrance of her little sleeping apartment—which the men denominated a kennel —and master Jacko was seated on the top of it, scratching his sides and enjoying the sunshine.

"My lads," said the captain, breaking a silence which had lasted a considerable time, "I'm afraid I shall have to reduce our allowance still farther."

This remark was received by Gurney and Phil Briant with a suppressed groan—by the other men in silence.

"You see," continued the captain, "it wont do to count upon chances, which may or may not turn out to be poor. We can, by fixing our allowance per man at a lower rate, make quite certain of our food lasting us until we reach the Cape, even if we should experience a little detention; but if we go on at the present rate, we are equally certain that it will fail us just at the last."

" We're sartain to fall in with birds before we
near the land," murmured Gurney, with a rueful
expression of countenance.

" We are certain of nothing," replied the captain ; " but even suppose we were, how are we to
get hold of them ?"

"That's true," observed Briant, who solaced himself with his pipe in the absence of a sufficiency of
food.  " Sea-birds, no more nor land-birds, ain't
given to pluckin' and roastin' themselves, and flyin'
down people's throats ready cooked."

" Besides," resumed the captain, " the plan I
propose, although it will entail a little more present
self-denial, will, humanly speaking, ensure our
getting through the voyage with life in us, even at
the worst, and if we *are* so lucky as to catch fish
or procure birds in any way, why we shall fare
sumptuously."

Here Tim Rokens, to whom the men instinctively
looked up on all matters of perplexity, removed
his pipe from his lips, and said :—

" Wot Cap'en Dunnin' says is true.  If we take
his plan, why, we'll starve in a reg'lar way, little
by little, and p'raps spin out till we git to the
Cape ; w'ereas, if we take the other plan, we'll
keep a little fatter on the first part of the voyage,
mayhap, but we'll arrive at the end of it as dead
as mutton, every man on us."

This view of the question seemed so just to the
men, and so full of incontrovertible wisdom, that

it was received with something like a murmur of
applause.

" You're a true philosopher, Rokens. Now,
Doctor Hopley, I must beg you to give us your
opinion, as a medical man, on this knotty subject,"
said the captain, smiling. " Do you think that we
can continue to exist if our daily allowance is reduced one-fourth ?"

The doctor replied, " Let me see," and putting
his finger on his forehead, frowned portentously,
affecting to give the subject the most intense consideration. He happened to look at Jacko when
he frowned, and that pugnacious individual, happening at the same instant to look at the doctor,
and supposing that the frown was a distinct challenge to fight, first raised his eyebrows to the top
of his head in amazement, then pulled them down
over his flashing orbs in deep indignation, and displayed all his teeth, as well as an extent of gums
that was really frightful to behold !

" Oh ! Jacko, bad thing," said Ailie, in a re-
proachful tone, pulling the monkey towards her.

Taking no notice of these warlike indications,
the doctor, after a few minutes' thought, looked up
and said,—

" I have no doubt whatever that we can stand
it. Most of us are in pretty good condition still,
and have some fat to spare. Fat persons can
endure reduced allowance of food much better and
longer than those who are lean. There's Gurney,

now, for instance, he could afford to have his share even still further curtailed."

This remark was received with a grin of delighted approval by the men and with a groan by Gurney, who rubbed his stomach gently, as if that region were assailed with pains at the bare thought of such injustice.

"Troth, if that's true what ye say, doctor, I hope ye'll see it to be yer duty to give wot ye cut off Gurney's share to me," remarked Briant, "for it's nothing but a bag o' bones that I am this minute."

"Oh! oh! wot a wopper," cried Jim Scroggles, whose lean and lanky person seemed ill adapted to exist upon light fare.

"Well," observed the captain, "the doctor and I shall make a careful calculation and let you know the result by supper time, when the new system shall be commenced. What think you, Ailie, my pet, will you be able to stand it?"

"Oh yes, papa, I don't care how much you reduce my allowance."

"What! don't you feel hungry?"

"No, not a bit."

"Not ready for supper?"

"Not anxious for it, at any rate."

"Och! I wish I wos you," murmured Briant, with a deep sigh. "I think I could ait the foresail, av it wos only well biled with the laste possible taste o' pig's fat."

By suppei time the captain announced the future daily allowance, and served it out.

Each man received a piece of salt junk—that is, salt beef—weighing exactly one ounce ; also two ounces of broken biscuit ; a small piece of tobacco, and a quarter of a pint of water. Although the supply of the latter was small, there was every probability of a fresh supply being obtained when it chanced to rain, so that little anxiety was felt at first in regard to it ; but the other portions of each man's allowance were weighed with scrupulous exactness, in a pair of scales which were constructed by Tim Rokens out of a piece of wood—a leaden musket-ball doing service as a weight.

Ailie received an equal portion with the others, but Jacko was doomed to drag out his existence on a very minute quantity of biscuit and water. He utterly refused to eat salt junk, and would not have been permitted to use tobacco even had he been so inclined, which he was not.

Although they were thus reduced to a small allowance of food—a smaller quantity than was sufficient to sustain life for any lengthened period— no one in the slightest degree grudged Jacko his small portion. All the men entertained a friendly feeling to the little monkey, partly because it was Ailie's pet and partly because it afforded them great amusement at times by its odd antics.

As for Jacko himself, he seemed to thrive on short allowance, and never exhibited any unseemly haste or anxiety at meal times. It was observed, however, that he kept an uncommonly sharp eye on all that passed around him, as if he felt that his circumstances were at that time peculiar and worthy of being noted. In particular he knew to a nicety what happened to each atom of food, from the time of its distribution among the men to the moment of its disappearance within their hungry jaws, and if any poor fellow chanced to lay his morsel down and neglect it for the tenth part of an instant, it vanished like a shot, and immediately thereafter Jacko was observed to present an unusually serene and innocent aspect, and to become suddenly afflicted with a swelling in the pouch under his cheek.

One day the men received a lesson of carefulness, which they did not soon forget.

Breakfast had been served out, and Phil Briant was about to finish his last mouthful of biscuit— he had not had many mouthfuls to try his masticating powers, poor fellow—when he paused suddenly, and gazing at the cherished morsel addressed it thus—

"Shure it's a purty bit, ye are! Av there wos only wan or two more o' yer family here, it's meself as 'u'd like to be made beknown to them. I'll not ait ye yit. I'll look at ye for a little."

In pursuance of this luxurious plan, Briant laid the morsel of biscuit on the thwart of the boat before him, and taking out his pipe, began to fill it leisurely, keeping his eye all the time on the last bite. Just then Mr. Markham, who pulled the bow oar, called out :—

"I say, Briant, hand me my tobacco-pouch, it's beside you on the th'ort, close under the gun'le."

" Is it ?" said Briant, stretching out his hand to the place indicated, but keeping his eye fixed all the time on the piece of biscuit. "Ah, here it is ; ketch it."

For one instant Briant looked at the second mate in order to throw the pouch with precision. That instant was sufficient for the exercise of Jacko's dishonest propensities. The pouch was yet in its passage through the air when a tremendous roar from Tim Rokens apprized the unhappy Irishman of his misfortune. He did not require to be told to "look out !" although more than one voice gave him that piece of advice. An intuitive perception of irreparable loss flashed across his soul, and, with the speed of light, his eye was again on the thwart before him—but not on the morsel of biscuit. At that same instant Jacko sat down beside Ailie with his usual serene aspect and swelled cheek !

" Och, ye bottle imp !" yelled the bereaved one, " don't I know ye ?" and seizing a tin pannikin, in his wrath, he threw it at the small monkey's head with a force that would, had it been well-directed, have smashed that small head effectually.

Jacko made a quick and graceful nod, and the pannikin, just missing Ailie, went over the side into the sea, where it sank and was lost for ever, to the regret of all, for they could ill afford to lose it.

"Ye've got it, ye have, but ye shan't ait it," growled Briant through his teeth, as he sprang over the seat towards the monkey.

Jacko bounded like a piece of India-rubber on to Gurney's head ; next moment he was clinging to the edge of the mainsail, and the next he was comfortably seated on the top of the mast, where he proceeded calmly and leisurely to " ait " the biscuit in the face of its exasperated and rightful owner.

" Oh, Briant !" exclaimed Ailie, who was half-frightened, half-amused at the sudden convulsion caused by her favourite's bad conduct, " don't be vexed ; see, here is a little bit of my biscuit ; I don't want it—really I don't."

Briant, who stood aghast and overwhelmed by his loss and by the consummate impudence of the small monkey, felt rebuked by this offer. Bursting into a loud laugh, he said, as he resumed his seat and the filling of his pipe,—

" Sure, I'd rather ait me own hat, Miss Ailie, an' it's be no means a good wan—without sarce, too, not even a blot o' mustard—than take the morsel out o' yer purty mouth. I wos more nor half jokin', dear, an' I ax yer pardin for puttin' ye in sich a fright."

" Expensive jokin'," growled Tarquin, " if ye throw a pannikin overboard every time you take to it."

" Kape your tongue quiet," said Briant, redden-
ing, for he felt somewhat humbled at having given
way to his anger so easily, and was nettled at the
remark, coming as it did, in a sneering spirit, from
a man for whom he had no particular liking.

" Never mind, Briant," interposed the captain,
quickly, with a good-humoured laugh; " I feel for
you, lad. Had it been myself I fear I should have
been even more exasperated. I would not sell a
crumb of my portion just now for a guinea."

" Neither would I," added the doctor, " for a
thousand guineas."

"I'll tell ye wot it is, lads," remarked Tim
Rokens ; " I wish I only had a crumb to sell."

" Now, Rokens, don't be greedy," cried Gurney.

" Greedy !" echoed Tim.

" Aye, greedy ; has any o' you lads got a dick-
shunairy to lend him ? Come, Jim Scroggles, you
can tell him what it means—you've been to school,
I b'lieve, haint you ?"

Rokens shook his head gravely.

" No, lad, I'm not greedy, but I'm ready for
wittles. I wont go fur to deny that. Now, let
me ax ye a question. Wot—supposin' ye had the
chance—would ye give, at this good min'it, for a
biled leg o' mutton ?"

" With or without capers-sauce ?" inquired
Gurney.

" Wichever *you* please."

" Och ! we wouldn't need capers-sarse," inter-

posed Briant; " av we only had the mutton, I'd cut
enough o' capers meself to do for the sarce, I
would."

" It matters little what you'd give," cried Glynn,
" for we can't get it at any price just now. Don't
you think, captain, that we might have our breakfast to-night? It would save time in the morning,
you know."

There was a general laugh at this proposal, yet
there was a strong feeling in the minds of some
that if it were consistent with their rules to have
breakfast served out then and there, they would
gladly have consented to go without it next
morning.

Thus, with laugh, and jest, and good-natured
repartee, did these men bear the pangs of hunger
for many days. They were often silent during
long intervals, and sometimes they became talkative
and sprightly, but it was observed that, whether
they conversed earnestly or jestingly, their converse
ran, for the most part, on eating and drinking, and
in their uneasy slumbers, during the intervals between the hours of work and watching, they almost
invariably dreamed of food.

# CHAPTER XXIII.

### PROGRESS OF THE LONG VOYAGE—STORY-TELLING AND JOURNALIZING.

MANY weeks passed away, but the Maid of the Isle still held on her course over the boundles ocean.

Day after day came and went, the sun rose in the east morning after morning, ran its appointed course, and sank, night after night, on the western horizon, but little else occurred to vary the monotony of that long, long voyage. When the sun rose, its bright rays leapt from the bosom of the ocean ; when it set, the same bosom of the great deep received its descending beams. No land, no sail appeared to the anxious gazers in that little boat, which seemed to move across, yet never to reach the boundaries of that mighty circle of water and sky, in the midst of which they lay enchained, as if by some wicked enchanter's spell.

Breezes blew steadily at times and urged them swiftly on towards the circumference, but it fled as fast as they approached. Then it fell calm, and the weary men resumed their oars, and with heavy hearts and weakened arms tugged at the boat which seemed to have turned into a mass of lead. At such times a dead silence was maintained, for the work which once would have been to them

but child's-play, had now become severe and heavy
labour.    Still they did not murmur.    Even the
cross-grained Tarquin became subdued in spirit by
the influence of the calm endurance and good
humour of his comrades.    But the calms seldom
lasted long.    The winds, which happily continued
favourable, again ruffled the surface of the sea, and
sometimes blew so briskly as to oblige them to
take in a reef or two in their sails.    The oars
were gladly drawn in, and the spirits of the men
rose as the little boat bent over to the blast, lost
her leaden qualities, and danced upon the broad
backed billows like a cork.    There was no rain
during all this time ; little or no stormy weather
and but for their constant exposure to the hot sun
by day and the cold chills · by night, the time
might have been said to pass even pleasantly
despite the want of a sufficiency of food.    Thus
day after day and night after night flew by, and
week after week came and went, and still the
Maid of the Isle held on her course over the boundless ocean.

During all that time the one and a quarter ounces
of salt junk and biscuit and the eighth of a pint of
water ,were weighed and measured out to each
man, three times a day, with scrupulous care and
exactness, lest a drop or a crumb of the food that
was more precious than diamonds should be lost.
The men had all become accustomed to short
allowance now, and experienced no greater incon-

venience than a feeling of lassitude, which feeling increased daily, but by such imperceptible degrees that they were scarcely conscious of it, and were only occasionally made aware of the great reduction of their strength when they attempted to lift any article which, in the days of their full vigour, they could have tossed into the air, but which they could scarcely move now.   When, however, the fair breeze enabled them to glide along under sail, and they lay enjoying complete rest, they experienced no unwonted sensations of weakness; their spirits rose, as the spirits of sailors always will rise when the waves are rippling at the bow and a white track forming in the wake; and they spent the time—when not asleep—in cheerful conversation and in the spinning of long yarns.   They did not sing, however, as might have been expected— they were too weak for that—they called the feeling "lazy," some said they "couldn't be bothered" to sing.   No one seemed willing to admit that his strength was in reality abated.

In story-telling, the captain, the doctor, and Glynn shone conspicuous.   And when all was going smoothly and well, the anecdotes, histories, and romances related by these three were listened to with such intense interest and delight by the whole crew, that one would have thought they were enjoying a pleasure trip, and had no cause whatever for anxiety.   Gurney, too, and Briant, and Nikel Sling came out frequently in the

story-telling line, and were the means of causing
many and many an hour to pass quickly and
pleasantly by, which would otherwise have hung
heavily on the hands of all.

Ailie Dunning was an engrossed and delighted
listener at all times. She drank in every species
of story with an avidity that was quite amusing.
It seemed also to have been infectious, for even
Jacko used to sit hour after hour looking steadily
at each successive speaker, with a countenance so
full of bright intelligence, and grave surpassing
wisdom, as to lead one to the belief that he not
only understood all that was said, but turned it
over in his mind, and drew from it ideas and con-
clusions far more bright and philosophical than
could have been drawn therefrom by any human
being, however wise or ingenious.

He grinned, too, did Jacko, with an intensity
and frequency that induced the sailors at first to
call him a clever dog, in the belief that his perception of the ludicrous was very strong indeed;
but as his grins were observed to occur quite as
frequently at the pathetic and the grave as at the
comical parts of the stories, they changed their
minds, and said he was a "queer codger"—in
which remark they were undoubtedly safe, seeing
that it committed them to nothing very specific.

Captain Dunning's stories were, more properly
speaking, histories, and were very much relished,
for he possessed a natural power of relating what

he knew in an interesting manner and with a peculiarly pleasant tone of voice. Every one who has considered the subject at all must have observed what a powerful influence there lies in the mere manner and tone of a speaker. The captain's voice was so rich, so mellow, and capable of such varied modulation, that the men listened with pleasure to the words which rolled from ·his lips, as one would listen to a sweet song. He became so deeply interested, too, in the subject about which he happened to be speaking, that his auditors could not help becoming interested also. He had no powers of eloquence, neither was he gifted with an unusually bright fancy. But he was fluent in ·speech, and his words, though not chosen, were 'usually appropriate. The captain had no powers of invention whatever. He used to say, when asked to tell a story, that he " might as well try to play the fiddle with a handspike." But this was no misfortune, for he had read much, and his memory was good, and supplied him with an end- ·less flow of small-talk on almost every subject that usually falls under the observation of sea-captains, and on many subjects besides, about which most sea-captains, or land-captains, or any other captains whatsoever, are almost totally ignorant.

Captain Dunning could tell of adventures in the whale-fishery, gone through either by himself or by friends, that would have made your two eyes stare out of their two sockets until they looked like

saucers (to use a common but. not very correct
simile).    He could tell the exact latitude and
longitude of almost every important and prominent part of the globe, and give the distance,
pretty nearly, of any one place (on a large scale)
from any other place.    He could give the heights
of all the chief mountains in the world to within a
few feet, and could calculate, by merely looking at
its current and depth, how many cubic feet of
water any river delivered to the sea per minute.
Length, breadth, and thickness, height, depth, and
density, were subjects in which he revelled, and
with which he played as a juggler does with
golden balls ; and so great were his powers of
numerical calculation, that the sailors often declared
they believed he could work out any calculation
backwards without the use of logarithms !    He
was constantly instituting comparisons that were
by no means what the proverb terms " odious," but
which were often very astonishing, and in all his
stories so many curious and peculiar facts were introduced, that, as we have already said, they were
very much relished indeed.

Not less relished, however, were Glynn Proctor's
astounding and purely imaginative tales.    After
the men's minds had been chained intently on one
of the captain's semi-philosophical anecdotes, they
turned with infinite zest to one of Glynn's outrageous flights.    Glynn had not read much in his
short life, and his memory was nothing to boast of,

but his imagination was quite gigantic. He could invent almost anything ; and the curious part of it was, that he could do it out of nothing, if need be. He never took time to consider what he should say. When called on for a story he began at once, and it flowed from him like a flood of sparkling water from a fountain in fairy realms. Up in the clouds ; high in the blue ether ; down in the coral caves ; deep in the ocean waves ; out on the mountain heaths ; far in the rocky glens, or away in the wild woods green—it was all one to Glynn ; he leaped away in an instant, with a long train of adventurers at his heels—male and female, little and big, old and young, pretty and plain, grave and gay. And didn't they go through adventures that would have made the hair of mortals not only stand on end, but fly out by the roots altogether? Didn't he make them talk, as mortals never talked before ; and sing as mortals never dreamed of? And, oh ! didn't he just make them stew, and roast, and boil joints of savoury meat, and bake pies, and tarts, and puddings, such as Soyer in his wildest culinary dreams never imagined, and such as caused the mouths of the crew of the Maid of the Isle to water, until they were constrained, poor fellows, to tell him to " clap a stopper upon that," and hold his tongue, for they " couldn't stand it !"

Phil Briant and Gurney dealt in the purely comic line. They remarked—generally in an under tone—that they left poetry and prose to

Glynn and the captain ; and it was as well they
did, for their talents certainly did not lie in either of
these directions.    They came out strong after
meals, when the weather was fine, and formed a
species of light and agreeable interlude to the more
weighty efforts of the captain and the brilliant
sallies of Glynn.

Gurney dealt in *experiences* chiefly, and usually
endeavoured by asseveration and iteration to im-
press his hearers with the truth of facts said to
have been experienced by himself, which, if true,
would certainly have consigned him to a premature
grave long ago.    Briant, on the other hand, dealt
largely in ghost stories, which he did not vouch
for the truth of, but permitted his hearers to judge
of for themselves—a permission which they would
doubtless have taken for themselves at any rate.

But tales and stories occupied, after all, only a
small portion of the men's time during that long
voyage.    Often, very often, they were too much
exhausted to talk or even to listen, and when not
obliged to labour at the oars they tried to sleep';
but " Nature's sweet restorer" did not always come
at the first invitation, as was his wont in other days,
and too frequently they were obliged to resume
work unrefreshed.    Their hands became hard and
horny in the palms at last, like a man's heel, and
their backs and arms ached from constant work.

Ailie kept in good health, but she, too, began to
grow weak from want of proper nourishment.  She

slept better than the men, for the comfortable sleeping-box that Glynn had constructed for her sheltered her from the heat, wet, and cold, to which the former were constantly exposed. She amused herself, when not listening to stories or asleep, by playing with her favourite, and she spent a good deal of time in reading her Bible—sometimes to herself, at other times, in a low tone, to her father as he sat at the helm. And many a time did she see a meaning in passages which, in happier times, had passed meaningless before her eyes, and often did she find sweet comfort in words that she had read with comparative indifference in former days.

It is in the time of trial, trouble, and sorrow that the Bible proves to be a friend indeed. Happy the Christian who, when dark clouds overwhelm his soul, has a memory well stored with the comforting passages of the Word of God.

But Ailie had another occupation which filled up much of her leisure, and proved to be a source of deep and engrossing interest at the time. This was the keeping of a journal of the voyage. On the last trip made to the wreck of the Red Eric, just before the great storm that completed the destruction of that ship, the captain had brought away in his pocket a couple of note-books. One of these he kept to himself to jot down the chief incidents of the intended voyage; the other he gave to Ailie, along with a blacklead pencil. Being fond of trying to write, she amused herself for hours

together in jotting down her thoughts about the
various incidents of the voyage, great and small,
and being a very good drawer for her age, she
executed many fanciful and elaborate sketches,
among which were innumerable portraits of Jacko
and several caricatures of the men. This journal,
as it advanced, became a source of much interest
and amusement to every one in the boat ; and
when, in an hour of the utmost peril, it, along with
many other things, was lost, the men, after the
danger was past, felt the loss severely.

Thus they spent their time—now pleasantly, now
sadly—sometimes becoming cheerful and hopeful,
at other times sinking almost into a state of despair
as their little stock of food and water dwindled
down, while the Maid of the Isle still held on her
apparently endless course over the great wide sea.

## CHAPTER XXIV.

THE CALM AND THE STORM—A SERIOUS LOSS AND GREAT
GAIN — BIRD-CATCHING EXTRAORDINARY — SAVED AT
LAST.

ONE day a deep death-like calm settled down upon
the ocean. For some days before, the winds had
been light and uncertain, and the air had bee  :-
cessively warm. The captain cast uneasy glances
round him from time to time, and looked with a
sadder countenance than usual on the haggard faces

of the men as they laboured slowly and silently at the oars.

"I don't know what this will turn to, doctor," he said, in a low tone; "I don't like the look of it."

The doctor, who was perusing Ailie's journal at the moment, looked up and shook his head.

"It seems to me, captain, that whatever happens, matters cannot be made much worse."

"You are wrong, doctor," replied the captain, quietly; "we have still much to be thankful for."

"Did you not tell me a few minutes ago that the water was almost done?"

The doctor said this in a whisper, for the men had not yet been made aware of the fact.

"Yes, I did; but it is not *quite* done; that is matter for thankfulness."

"Oh, according to that principle," observed the doctor, somewhat testily, "you may say we have cause to be thankful for *everything*, bad as well as good."

"So we have! so we have! If everything good were taken from us, and nothing left us but our lives, we would have reason to be thankful for that —thankful that we were still above ground, still in the land of hope, with salvation to our immortal souls through Jesus Christ freely offered for our acceptance."

The doctor made no reply. He thought the captain a little weak in the matter of religion. If religion is false, his opinion of the captain no doubt

z

was right, but if true, surely the weakness lay all
the other way.

That morning the captain's voice in prayer was
more earnest, if possible, than usual, and he put
up a special petition for *water*, which was observed
by the men with feelings of great anxiety, and
responded to with a deep amen.　After morning
worship the scales were brought, and the captain
proceeded to weigh out the scanty meal, while the
men watched his every motion with an almost
wolfish glare, that told eloquently of the prolonged
sufferings they had endured.　Even poor Ailie's
gentle face now wore a sharp, anxious expression
when food was being served out, and she accepted
her small portion with a nervous haste that was
deeply painful and touching to witness.　She little
knew, poor child, that that portion of bread and
meat and water, small though it was, was larger
than that issued to the men, being increased by a
small quantity deducted from the captain's own
allowance and an equal amount from that of Glynn.
The latter had noticed the captain's habit of
regularly calling off the child's attention during the
distribution of each meal, for the purpose of thus
increasing her portion at the expense of his own,
and in a whispering conversation held soon after
he insisted that a little of his allowance should also
be transferred to her.　At first the captain firmly
refused, but Glynn said that if he did not accede
to his wish he would hand over the whole of his

portion in future to the monkey, let the result be what it might! As Glynn never threatened without a full and firm resolve to carry out his threats, the captain was compelled to give in.

When the water came to be served out that morning the captain paused, and looking round at the anxious eyes that were riveted upon him, said:—

"My lads, it has pleased the Almighty to lay His hands still heavier on us. May He who has said that He will not suffer men to be tempted above what they are able to bear, give us strength to stand it. Our water is almost done. We must be content with a quarter of our usual allowance."

This information was received in deep silence—perhaps it was the silence of despair, for the quantity hitherto served out had been barely sufficient to moisten their parched throats, and they *knew* that they could not exist long on the reduced allowance.

Jacko came with the rest as usual for his share, and held out his little hand for the tin cup in which his few drops of water were wont to be handed to him. The captain hesitated and looked at the men ; then he poured out a few drops of the precious liquid. For the first time a murmur of disapproval was heard.

"It's only a brute-beast; the monkey must die before *us*," said a voice which was so hollow and changed that it could scarcely be recognised as that of Tarquin, the steward.

No one else said a word. The captain did not even look up to see who had spoken. He felt the justice as well as the harshness of the remark, and poured the water back into the jar.

Jacko seemed puzzled at first, and held out his hand again ; then he looked round on the men with that expression of unutterable woe which is peculiar to some species of the monkey tribe. He seemed to feel that something serious was about to happen to him. Looking up in the sad face of his young mistress, he uttered a very gentle and plaintive " oo-oo-ee !"

Ailie burst into a passionate flood of tears, and in the impulse of the moment handed her own cup, which she had not tasted, to Jacko, who drained it in a twinkling—before the captain could snatch it from his hands.

Having emptied it, Jacko went forward, as he had been taught to do, and handed back the cup with quite a pleased expression of countenance— for he was easily satisfied, poor thing !

" You should not have done that, my darling," said the captain, as he gave Ailie another portion.

" Dear papa, I couldn't help it," sobbed the child ; " indeed I couldn't—and you need not give me any. I can do without it to-day."

" Can you ? But you shan't," exclaimed Glynn, with a degree of energy that would have made every one laugh in happier times.

" No, no, my own pet," replied the captain,

".you shan't want it. Here, you *must* drink it, come."

From that day Jacko received his allowance regularly as long as a drop of water was left, and no one again murmured against it. When it was finished he had to suffer with the rest.

The calm which had set in proved to be of longer duration than usual, and the sufferings of the crew of the little boat became extreme. On the third day after its commencement the last drop of water was served out. It amounted to a couple of teaspoonfuls per man each meal, of which there were three a day. During the continuance of the calm, the sun shone in an almost cloudless sky and beat down upon the heads of the men until it drove them nearly mad. They all looked like living skeletons, and their eyes glared from their sunken sockets with a dry fiery lustre that was absolutely terrible to behold. Had each one in that boat possessed millions of gold he would have given all, gladly, for one drop of fresh water ; but, alas ! nothing could purchase water there. Ailie thought upon the man who, in the Bible, is described as looking up to heaven from the depths of hell and crying for one drop of water to cool his tongue, and she fancied that she could now realize his agony. The captain looked up into the hot sky, but no blessed cloud appeared there to raise the shadow of a hope. He looked down at the sea, and it seemed to mock him with its clear blue depths, which looked

so sweet and pleasant.  He realized the full signi-
ficance of that couplet in Coleridge's " Ancient
Mariner :"—

> " Water, water everywhere,
> But not a drop to drink ;"

and drawing Ailie to his breast, he laid his cheek
upon hers and groaned aloud.

" We shall soon be taken away, dear papa," she
said—and she tried to weep, but the tears that
came unbidden and so easily at other times to her
bright blue eyes refused to flow now.

The men had one by one ceased to ply their
useless oars, and the captain did not take notice of
it, for he felt that unless God sent relief in some almost miraculous way, their continuing to row would
be of no avail.  It would only increase their agony
without advancing them more than a few miles on
the long, long voyage that he knew still lay before
them.

" O God, grant us a breeze !" cried Mr. Millons,
in a deep, tremulous tone, breaking a silence that
had continued for some hours.

" Messmates," said Tim Rokens, who for some
time had leaned with both elbows on his oar and
his face buried in his hands, " wot d'ye say to a
bath.  I do believe it 'ud do us good."

" P'raps it would," replied King Bumble ; but he
did not move, and the other men made no reply,
while Rokens again sank forward.

Gurney and Tarquin had tried to relieve their

thirst the day before by drinking sea-water, but their inflamed and swollen throats and lips now showed that the relief sought had not been obtained.

"It's time for supper," said the captain, raising his head suddenly, and laying Ailie down, for she had fallen into a lethargic slumber; "fetch me the bread and meat can."

Dick Barnes obeyed reluctantly, and the usual small allowance of salt junk was weighed out, but there were no eager glances now. Most of the crew refused to touch food—one or two tried to eat a morsel of biscuit without success.

"I'll try a swim," cried Glynn, suddenly starting up with the intention of leaping overboard. But his strength was more exhausted than he had fancied, for he only fell against the side of the boat. It was as well that he failed. Had he succeeded in getting into the water he could not have clambered in again, and it is doubtful whether his comrades had sufficient strength left to have dragged him in.

"Try it this way, lad," said Tim Rokens, taking up a bucket, and dipping it over the side. "P'raps it'll do as well."

He raised the bucket with some difficulty and poured its contents over Glynn's head.

"Thank God!" said Glynn, with a deep, long-drawn sigh. "Do it again, Tim, do it again. That's it—again, again! No, stop; forgive my

?elfishness; here, give me the bucket, I'll do it to you now."

Tim Rokens was quickly drenched from head to foot, and felt great and instantaneous relief. In a few minutes every one in the boat, Jacko included, was subjected to this species of cold bath, and their spirits rose at once. Some of them even began to eat their food, and Briant actually attempted to perpetrate a joke, which Gurney seconded promptly, but they failed to make one, even a bad one, between them.

Although the cold bathing seemed good for them at first, it soon proved to be hurtful. Sitting and lying constantly night and day in saturated clothes had the effect of rendering their skins painfully sensitive, and a feverish feeling was often alternated with cold shivering fits, so they were fain to give it up. Still they had found some slight relief, and they bore their sufferings with calm resignation—a state of mind which was fostered, if not induced, by the blessed words of comfort and hope which the captain read to them from the Bible as frequently as his strength would permit, and to which they listened with intense, all-absorbing interest.

It is ever thus with men. When death approaches, in almost all instances, we are ready— ay, anxious—to listen with the deepest interest to God's message of salvation through His Son, and to welcome and long for the influences of the Holy

Spirit. Oh! how happy should we be, in life and in death, did we only give heartfelt interest to our souls' affairs *before* the days of sorrow and death ⌐\ ` arrive.

On the fifth morning after the water had been exhausted the sun arose in the midst of dark clouds. The men could scarcely believe their eyes. They shouted, and, in their weakness, laughed for joy.

The blessing was not long delayed. Thick vapours veiled the red sun soon after it emerged from the sea, then a few drops of rain fell. Blessed drops! How the men caught at them! How they spread out oiled cloths and tarpaulins and garments to gather them! How they grudged to see them falling around the boat into the sea, and being lost to them for ever. But the blessing was soon sent liberally. The heavens above grew black, and the rain came down in thick heavy showers. The tarpaulins were quickly filled, and the men lay with their lips to the sweet pools, drinking in new life, and dipping their heads and hands in the cool liquid when they could drink no more. Their thirst was slaked at last, and they were happy. All their past sufferings were forgotten in that great hour of relief, and they looked, and laughed, and spoke to each other like men who were saved from death. As they stripped off their garments and washed the encrusted salt from their shrunken limbs, all of them doubtless felt, and some of them

audibly expressed, gratitude to the " Giver of every
good and perfect gift."

So glad were they, and so absorbed in their occupation, that they thought not of and cared not
for the fact that a great storm was about to break
upon them. It came upon them almost before
they were aware, and before the sails could be taken
in the boat was almost upset.

" Stand by to lower the sails !" shouted the captain, who was the first to see their danger.

The old familiar command issued with something of the old familiar voice and energy caused
every one to leap to his post, if not with the agility
of former times, at least with all the good-will.

" Let go !"

The halyards were loosed, and the sails came
tumbling down ; at the same moment the squall
burst on them. The Maid of the Isle bent over so
quickly that every one expected she would upset ;
the blue water curled in over the edge of the gunwale, and the foam burst from her bows at the
rude shock. Then she hissed through the water
as she answered the helm, righted quickly, and
went tearing away before the wind at a speed that
she had not known for many days. It was a narrow escape. The boat was nearly filled with water,
and, worst of all, the provision can, along with
Ailie's sleeping box, were washed overboard and lost.

It was of no use attempting to recover them.
All the energies of the crew were required to bale

out the water and keep the boat afloat, and during the whole storm some of them were constantly employed in baling. For three days it blew a perfect hurricane, and during all that time the men had nothing whatever to eat; but they did not suffer so much as might be supposed. The gnawing pangs of hunger do not usually last beyond a few days when men are starving. After that they merely feel ever-increasing weakness. During the fall of the rain they had taken care to fill their jars, so that they had now a good supply of water.

After the first burst of the squall had passed, the tarpaulins were spread over the boat, and under one of these, near the stern, Ailie was placed, and was comparatively sheltered and comfortable. Besides forming a shelter for the men while they slept, these tarpaulins threw off the waves that frequently broke over the boat, and more than once bid fair to sink her altogether. The sea rose in enormous billows, and the gale was so violent that only the smallest corner of the foresail could be raised—even that was almost sufficient to tear away the mast.

At length the gale blew itself out, and gradually decreased to a moderate breeze, before which the sails were shaken out, and on the fourth morning after it broke they found themselves sweeping quickly over the waves on their homeward way, but without a morsel of food, and thoroughly exhausted in body and in mind.

On that morning, however, they passed a piece of floating seaweed, a sure indication of their approach to land. Captain Dunning pointed it out to Ailie and the crew with a cheering remark that they would probably soon get to the end of their voyage ; but he did not feel much hope ; for, without food, they could not exist above a few days more at the furthest—perhaps not so long. That same evening, several small sea-birds came towards the boat, and flew inquiringly round it, as if they wondered what it could be doing there, so far away from the haunts of men. These birds were evidently unaccustomed to man, for they exhibited little fear. They came so near to the boat that one of them was at length caught. It was the negro who succeeded in knocking it on the head with a boathook as it flew past.

Great was the praise bestowed on King Bumble for this meritorious deed, and loud were the praises bestowed on the bird itself, which was carefully divided into equal portions (and a small portion for Jacko), and eaten raw. Not a morsel of it was lost —claws, beak, blood, bones, and feathers—all were eaten up. In order to prevent dispute or jealousy, the captain made Ailie turn her back on the bird when thus divided, and pointing to the different portions, he said :—" Who shall have this ?" Whoever was named by Ailie had to be content with what thus fell to his share.

"Ah, but ye wos always an onlucky dog !"

exclaimed Briant, to whom fell the head and claws.

"Ye've no reason to grumble," replied Gurney; "ye've got all the brains to yerself, and no one needs them more."

The catching of this bird was the saving of the crew, and it afforded them a good deal of mirth in the dividing of it. The heart and a small part of the breast fell to Ailie—which every one remarked was singularly appropriate; part of a leg and the tail fell to King Bumble; and the lungs and stomach became the property of Jim Scroggles, whereupon Briant remarked that he would "think as much almost o' *that* stomach as he had iver done of his own!" But there was much of sadness mingled with their mirth, for they felt that the repast was a peculiarly light one, and they had scarcely strength left to laugh or jest.

Next morning they knocked down another bird, and in the evening they got two more. The day after that they captured an albatross, which furnished them at last with an ample supply of fresh food.

It was Mr. Markham, the second mate, who first saw the great bird looming in the distance, as it sailed over the sea towards them.

"Let's try to fish for him," said the doctor. "I've heard of sea-birds being caught in that way before now."

"Fish for it!" exclaimed Ailie in surprise.

"Ay, with hook and line, Ailie."

"I've seen it done often," said the captain. "Hand me the line, Bumble, and a bit o' that bird we got yesterday. Now for it."

By the time the hook was baited, the albatross had approached near to the boat, and hovered round it with that curiosity which seems to be a characteristic feature of all sea-birds. It was an enormous creature; but Ailie, when she saw it in the air, could not have believed it possible that it was so large as it was afterwards found to be on being measured.

"Here, Glynn, catch hold of the line," said the captain, as he threw the hook overboard, and allowed it to trail astern; "you are the strongest man amongst us now, I think; starvation don't seem to tell so much on your young flesh and bones as on ours!"

"No; it seems to agree with his constitution," remarked Gurney.

"It's me that wouldn't give much for his flesh," observed Briant; "but his skin and bones would fetch a good price in the leather and rag market."

While his messmates were thus freely remarking on his personal appearance—which, to say truth, was dreadfully haggard, Glynn was holding the end of the line, and watching the motions of the albatross with intense interest.

"He wont take it," observed the captain.

"Me tink him will," said Bumble.

" No go," remarked Nikel Sling, sadly.

" That was near," said the first mate, eagerly, as the bird made a bold swoop down towards the bait, which was skipping over the surface of the water.

" No, he's off," cried Mr. Markham in despair.

" Cotched ! or I'm a Dutchman !" shouted Gurney.

" No !" cried Jim Scroggles.

" Yes !" screamed Ailie.

" Hurrah !" shouted Tim Rokens and Tarquin in a breath.

Dick Barnes, and the doctor, and the captain, and, in short, everybody, echoed the last sentiment, and repeated it again and again with delight as they saw the gigantic bird once again swoop down upon the bait and seize it.

Glynn gave a jerk, the hook caught in its tongue, and the albatross began to tug, and swoop, and whirl madly in its efforts to escape.

Now, to talk of any ordinary bird swooping, and fluttering, and tugging, does not sound very tremendous ; but, reader, had you witnessed the manner in which that enormous albatross conducted itself, you wouldn't have stared with amazement—oh, no ! You wouldn't have gone home with your mouth as wide open as your eyes, and have given a gasping account of what you had seen—by no means ! You wouldn't have talked of feathered steam-engines, or of fabled rocs, or of winged elephants in the air—certainly not !

Glynn's arms jerked as if he were holding on to the sheet of a shifting mainsail of a seventy-four.

"Bear a hand," he cried, "else I'll be torn to bits."

Several hands grasped the line in a moment.

"My! wot a wopper," exclaimed Tim Rokens.

"Och! don't he pull? Wot a fortin he'd make av he'd only set hisself up as a tug-boat in the Thames!"

"If we only had him at the oar for a week," added Gurney.

"Hoich! doctor, have ye strength to set dis-jointed limbs?"

"Have a care, lads," cried the captain, in some anxiety; "give him more play, the line wont stand it. Time enough to jest after we've got him."

The bird was now swooping, and waving, and beating its great wings so close to the boat that they began to entertain some apprehension lest any of the crew should be disabled by a stroke from them before the bird could be secured. Glynn, therefore, left the management of the line to others, and, taking up an oar, tried to strike it. But he failed in several attempts.

"Wait till we haul him nearer, boy," said the captain. "Now, then!"

Glynn struck again, and succeeded in hitting it a slight blow. At the same instant the albatross swept over the boat, and almost knocked the doctor overboard. As it brushed past, King Bumble, who

CAPTURE OF AN ALBATROSS.—Page 352

was gifted with the agility of a monkey, leaped up, caught it round the neck, and the next moment the two were rolling together in the bottom of the boat.

The creature was soon strangled, and a mighty cheer greeted this momentous victory.

We are not aware that albatross flesh is generally considered very desirable food, but we are certain that starving men are particularly glad to get it, and that the supply now obtained by the wrecked mariners was the means of preserving their lives until they reached the land, which they did ten days afterwards, having thus accomplished a voyage of above two thousand miles over the ocean in an open boat in the course of eight weeks, and on an amount of food that was barely sufficient for one or two weeks' ordinary consumption.

Great commiseration was expressed for them by the people at the Cape, who vied with each other in providing for their wants, and in showing them kindness.

Ailie and her father were carried off bodily by a stout old merchant, with a broad, kind face, and a hearty, boisterous manner, and lodged in his elegant villa during their stay in that quarter of the world, which was protracted some time in order that they might recruit the wasted strength of the party ere they commenced their voyage home in a vessel belonging to the same stout, broad-faced, and vociferous merchant.

A A

Meanwhile, several other ships departed for America, and by one of these Captain Dunning wrote to his sisters Martha and Jane. The captain never wrote to Martha or to Jane separately—he always wrote to them conjointly as "Martha Jane Dunning."

The captain was a peculiar letter-writer. Those who may feel curious to know more about this matter, are referred for further information to the next chapter.

## CHAPTER XXV.

HOME, SWEET HOME!—THE CAPTAIN TAKES HIS SISTERS BY SURPRISE—A MYSTERIOUS STRANGER.

IT is a fact which we cannot deny, however much we may feel disposed to marvel at it, that laughter and weeping, at one and the same time, are compatible. The most resolute sceptic on this point would have been convinced of the truth of it had he been introduced into the Misses Martha and Jane Dunning's parlour on the beautiful summer morning in which the remarkable events we are about to relate occurred.

On the morning in question, a letter-carrier walked up to the cottage with the yellow painted face, and with the green door, so like a nose in the middle; and the window on each side thereof, so like its eyes; and the green Venetian blinds, that served so admirably for eyelids, attached thereto—

all of which stood, and beamed, and luxuriated, and vegetated, and grew old in the centre of the town on the eastern sea-board of America, whose name (for strictly private reasons) we have firmly declined, and do still positively refuse to communicate.

Having walked up to the cottage, the letter-carrier hit it a severe smash on its green nose, as good Captain Dunning had done many, many months before. The result now, as then, was the opening thereof by a servant-girl—*the* servant-girl of old. The letter-carrier was a taciturn man; he said nothing, but handed in the letter, and went his way. The servant-girl was a morose damsel; she said nothing, but took the letter, shut the door, and laid it (the letter, not the door) on the breakfast-table, and went her way—which way was the way of all flesh, fish, and fowl—namely, the kitchen, where breakfast was being prepared.

Soon after the arrival of the letter Miss Jane Dunning—having put on an immaculately clean white collar and a spotlessly beautiful white cap with pink ribbons, which looked, if possible, taller than usual—descended to the breakfast-parlour. Her eye instantly fell on the letter, and she exclaimed—

"Oh !" at the full pitch of her voice. Indeed, did not respect for the good lady forbid, we would say that she *yelled* "Oh !"

Instantly, as if by magic, a faint "oh !" came

downstairs like an echo, from the region of Miss
Martha Dunning's bedroom, and was followed up
by a "What is it?" so loud that the most unimagi-
native person could not have failed to perceive that
the elder sister had opened her door and put her
head over the banisters.

"What is it?" repeated Miss Martha.

"A letter!" answered Miss Jane.

"Who from?" (in eager surprise, from above.)

"Brother George!" (in eager delight, from below.)

Miss Jane had not come to this knowledge because of having read the letter, for it still lay on
the table unopened, but because she could not read
it at all! One of Captain Dunning's peculiarities
was that he wrote an execrably bad and illegible
hand. His English was good, his spelling pretty
fair, considering the absurd nature of the ortho-
graphy of his native tongue, and his sense was excellent, but the whole was usually shrouded in hiero-
glyphical mystery. Miss Jane could only read the
opening "My dearest Sisters," and the concluding
"George Dunning," nothing more. But Miss
Martha could, by the exercise of some rare power,
spell out her brother's hand, though not without
much difficulty.

"I'm coming," shouted Miss Martha.

"Be quick!" screamed Miss Jane.

In a few seconds Miss Martha entered the room
with her cap and collar, though faultlessly clean
and stiff, put on very much awry.

" Give it me !   Where is it ?"

Miss Jane pointed to the letter, still remaining
transfixed to the spot where her eye had first met
it, as if it were some dangerous animal which would
bite if she touched it.

Miss Martha snatched it up, tore it open, and
flopped down on the sofa.   Miss Jane snatched up
an imaginary letter, tore it open (in imagination),
and flopping down beside her sister, looked over
her shoulder, apparently to make believe to herself
that she read it along with her.   Thus they read
and commented on the captain's letter in concert.

" ' Table Bay' — dear me ! what a funny bay
that must be—' My dearest Sisters'—the darling
fellow, he always begins that way, don't he, Jane
dear ?"—" Bless him ! he does, Martha dear."—
" ' We've been—all'—I can't make this word out,
can you, dear?"—" No, love."—" ' We've been all—
worked !' no, it can't be that.   Stay, ' We've been
all *wrecked !*' "

Here Martha laid down the letter with a look of
horror, and Jane, with a face of ashy paleness, exclaimed, " Then they're lost !"

" But no," cried Martha, " George could not
have written to us from Tablecloth Bay had he
been lost."

" Neither he could !" exclaimed Jane, eagerly.

Under the influence of the revulsion of feeling
this caused, Martha burst into tears and Jane into
laughter.   Immediately after, Jane wept and

Martha laughed ; then they both laughed and cried together, after which they felt for their pocket-handkerchiefs, and discovered that in their haste they had forgotten them ; so they had to call the servant-girl and send her upstairs for them ; and when the handkerchiefs were brought, they had to be unfolded before the sisters could dry their eyes. When they had done so, and were somewhat composed, they went on with the reading of the letter :—

"'We've been all wrecked'—Dreadful !—'and the poor Red Angel'—Oh ! it can't be that, Martha dear !"—"Indeed, it looks very like it, Jane darling. Oh ! I see ; it's Eric"—'and the poor Red Eric has been patched,' or—'pitched on a rock and smashed to sticks and stivers'—Dear me ! what can that be? I know what 'sticks' are, but I can't imagine what 'stivers' mean. Can you, Jane ?"—"Haven't the remotest idea ; perhaps Johnson, or Walker, or Webster may—yes, Webster is sure to."—"Oh! never mind just now, dear Jane, we can look it up afterwards —'stivers—sticks and stivers' — something very dreadful, I fear.—'But we're all safe and well now'—I'm so thankful !—'and we've been stumped'—No—'starved nearly to death, too. My poor Ailie was thinner than ever I saw her before' —This is horrible, dear Jane."—"Dreadful, darling Martha."—"'But she's milk and butter'—It can't be that—'milk and'—oh !—'much better now.'"

At this point Martha laid down the letter, and the two sisters wept for a few seconds in silence.

"Darling Ailie !" said Martha, drying her eyes, " how thin she must have been !"

" Ah ! yes, and no one to take in her frocks."

" 'We'll be home in less than no time,' " continued Martha, reading, " 'so you may get ready for us. Glynn will have tremendous long yarns to spin to you when we come back, and so will Ailie. She has seen a Lotofun since we left you'—Bless me ! what *can* that be, Jane ?"—" Very likely some terrible sea monster, Martha ; how thankful we ought to be that it did not eat her !—' seen a Lotofun'—strange !—' a Lot—o' '—Oh !—*lot o' fun !*'—that's it ! how stupid of me !—' and my dear pet has been such an ass'—Eh ! for shame, brother. Don't you think, dear Martha, that there's some more of that word on the next line ?" " So there is, I'm *so* stupid—'istance'—It's not rightly divided, though—' as-sistance and a comfort to me.' I knew it couldn't be ass." " So did I. Ailie an ass ! precious child !—' Now, good-bye t'ye, my dear lassies,

  " 'Ever your affectionate brother,
   " (Dear fellow !)
    " 'GEORGE DUNNING.' "

Now it chanced that the ship which conveyed the above letter across the Atlantic was a slow sailer and was much delayed by contrary winds

And it also chanced—for odd coincidences do happen occasionally in human affairs—that the vessel in which Captain Dunning with Ailie and his crew embarked some weeks later was a fast sailing ship, and was blown across the sea with strong favouring gales. Hence it fell out that the first vessel entered port on Sunday night, and the second cast anchor in the same port on Monday morning.

The green painted door, therefore, of the yellow-faced cottage had scarcely recovered from the assault of the letter-carrier, when it was again struck violently by the impatient Captain Dunning.

Miss Martha, who had just concluded and re-folded the letter, screamed " Oh !" and leaped up.

Miss Jane did the same, with this difference, that she leaped up before screaming " Oh !" instead of after doing so. Then both ladies, hearing voices outside, rushed towards the door of the parlour with the intention of flying to their room and there carefully arranging their tall white caps and clean white collars, and keeping the early visitor, whoever he or she might be, waiting fully a quarter of an hour or twenty minutes, before they should descend, stiffly, starchly, and ceremoniously, to receive him—or her.

These intentions were frustrated by the servant-girl, who opened the green-painted door and let in the captain, who rushed into the parlour and rudely kissed his speechless sisters.

" Can it be ?" gasped Martha.

Jane had meant to gasp "Impossible!" but seeing Ailie at that moment bound into Martha's arms, she changed her intention, uttered a loud scream instead, and fell down flat upon the floor under the impression that she had fainted. Finding, however, that this was not the case, she got up again quickly—ignorant of the fact that the tall cap had come off altogether in the fall—and stood before her sister weeping, and laughing, and wringing her hands, and waiting for her turn.

But it did not seem likely to come soon, for Martha continued to hug Ailie, whom she had raised entirely from the ground, with passionate fervour. Seeing this, and feeling that to wait was impossible, Jane darted forward, threw her arms round Ailie—including Martha, as an unavoidable consequence—and pressed the child's back to her throbbing bosom.

Between the two, poor Ailie was nearly suffocated. Indeed, she was compelled to scream, not because she wished to, but because Martha and Jane squeezed a scream out of her. The scream acted on the former as a reproof. She resigned Ailie to Jane, flung herself recklessly on the sofa, and kicked.

Meanwhile, Captain Dunning stood looking on, rubbing his hands, slapping his thighs, and blowing his nose. The servant-girl also stood looking on doing nothing—her face was a perfect blaze of amazement.

"Girl," said the captain, turning suddenly towards her, "is breakfast ready?"

"Yes!" gasped the girl.

"Then fetch it."

The girl did not move.

"D'ye hear?" cried the captain.

"Ye—es,"

"Then look alive."

The captain followed this up with a roar and such an indescribably ferocious demonstration, that the girl fled in terror to the culinary regions, where she found the cat breakfasting on a pat of butter. The girl yelled, and flung first a saucepan, and after that the lid of a tea-pot, at the thief. She failed, of course, in this effort to commit murder, and the cat vanished.

Breakfast was brought, but, excepting in the captain's case, breakfast was not eaten. What between questioning, and crying, and hysterical laughing, and replying, and gasping, explaining, misunderstanding, exclaiming, and choking, the other members of the party that breakfasted that, morning in the yellow cottage with the much-abused green door, did little else than upset tea-cups and cream-pots, and sputter eggs about, and otherwise make a mess of the once immaculate table-cloth.

"Oh, Aunt Martha!" exclaimed Ailie, in the midst of a short pause in the storm, "I'm *so* very, very, *very* glad to be home!"

The child said this with intense fervour. No one but he who has been long, long away from the home of his childhood, and has come back after having despaired of ever seeing it again, can imagine with what deep fervour she said it, and then burst into tears.

Aunt Jane at that moment was venturing to swallow her first mouthful of tea, so she gulped and choked, and Aunt Martha spent the next five minutes in violently beating the poor creature's back, as if she deemed choking a serious offence which merited severe punishment. As for the captain, that unfeeling monster went on grinning from ear to ear, and eating a heavy breakfast, as if nothing had happened. But a close observer might have noticed a curious process going on at the starboard side of his weather-beaten nose.

In one of his many desperate encounters with whales, Captain Dunning had had the end of a harpoon thrust accidentally into the prominent member of his face just above the bridge. A permanent little hole was the result, and on the morning of which we write, a drop of water got into that hole continually, and when it rolled out—which it did about once every two minutes—and fell into the captain's tea-cup, it was speedily replaced by another drop, which trickled into the depths of that small cavern on the starboard side of the captain's nose. We don't pretend to account for that curious phenomenon. We merely record the fact.

While the breakfast party were yet in this April mood, a knock was heard at the outer door.

"Visitors!" said Aunt Martha, with a look that would have led a stranger to suppose she held visitors in much the same estimation as tax-gatherers.

"How awkward!" exclaimed Aunt Jane.

"Send 'em away, girl," cried the captain. "We're all engaged. Can't see any one to-day."

In a moment the servant-girl returned.

"He says he *must* see you."

"See who?" cried the captain.

"See *you*, sir."

"Must he; then he shan't. Tell him that."

"Please, sir, he says he wont go away."

"Wont he?"

As he said this the captain set his teeth, clenched his fists, and darted out of the room.

"Oh! George! Stop him! do stop him. He's *so* violent! He'll do something dreadful!" said Aunt Martha.

"Will no one call out murder?" groaned Aunt Jane, with a shudder.

As no one, however, ventured to check Captain Dunning, he reached the door and confronted a rough big burly sailor, who stood outside with a free-and-easy expression of countenance, and his hands in his trowsers pockets.

"Why don't you go away when you're told, eh?" shouted the captain.

" 'Cause I wont," answered the man, coolly.

The captain stepped close up, but the sailor stood his ground and grinned.

"Now, my lad, if you don't up anchor and make sail right away, I'll knock in your daylights."

"No, you wont do nothin' o' the kind, old gen'lem'n ; but you'll double-reef your temper, and listen to wot I've got to say ; for its very partikler, an' wont keep long without spilin'."

"What have you got to say, then ?" said the captain, becoming interested, but still feeling nettled at the interruption.

" Can't tell you here."

" Why not ?"

" Never mind ; but put on your sky-scraper, and come down with me to the grog-shop wot I frequents, and I'll tell ye."

"I'll do nothing of the sort; be off," cried the captain, preparing to slam the door.

"Oh ! it's all the same to me, in coorse, but I rather think if ye know'd that it's 'bout the Termagant, and that 'ere whale wot—but it don't matter. Good mornin'."

" Stay," cried the captain, as the last words fell on his ears.

" Vell."

" Have you really anything to say to me about that ship ?"

" In coorse I has."

" Wont you come in and say it here ?"

"Not by no means.   You must come down to the grog-shop with *me*."

"Well, I'll go."

So saying the captain ran back to the parlour; said, in hurried tones, that he had to go out on matters of importance, but would be back to dine at five, and putting on his hat, left the cottage in company with the strange sailor.

---

## CHAPTER XXVI.

### CAPTAIN DUNNING ASTONISHES THE STRANGER—SURPRISING NEWS, AND DESPERATE RESOLVES.

STILL keeping his hands in his pockets and the free-and-easy expression on his countenance, the sailor swaggered through the streets of the town, with Captain Dunning at his side, until he arrived at a very dirty little street, near the harbour, the chief characteristics of which were noise, compound smells, and little shops with sea-stores hung out in front.   At the farther end of this street the sailor paused before a small public-house.

"Here we are," said he; "this is the place w'ere I puts up w'en I'm ashore—w'ich ain't often—that's a fact.   After you, sir."

The captain hesitated.

"You ain't afraid, air you?" asked the sailor, in an incredulous tone.

"No I'm not, my man ; but I have an objection to enter a public-house, unless I cannot help it. Have you had a glass this morning ?"

The sailor looked puzzled, as if he did not see very clearly what the question had to do with the captain's difficulty.

"Well, for the matter o' that, I've had three glasses this mornin'."

"Then I suppose you have no objection to try a glass of my favourite tipple, have you ?"

The man smiled, and wiping his mouth with the cuff of his jacket, as if he expected the captain was, then and there, about to hand him a glass of the tipple referred to, said :—

"No objection, wotsomediver."

"Then follow me; I'll take you to the place where *I* put up sometimes when I'm ashore. It's not far off."

Five minutes sufficed to transport them from the dirty little street near the harbour to the back parlour of the identical coffee-house in which the captain was first introduced to the reader. Here, having whispered something to the waiter, he proceeded to question his companion on the mysterious business for which he had brought him there.

"Couldn't we have the tipple first ?" suggested the sailor.

"It will be here directly. Have you breakfasted ?"

"'Xceptin' the three glasses I told ye of—no."

"Well, now, what have you to tell me about the Termagant ? You have already said that you are one of her crew, and that you were in the boat that day when we had a row about the whale. What more can you tell me ?"

The sailor sat down on a chair, stretched out his legs quite straight, and very wide apart, and thrust his hands, if possible, deeper into his pockets than they even were thrust before—so deep, in fact, as to suggest the idea that there were no pockets there at all—merely holes. Then he looked at Captain Dunning with a peculiarly sly expression of countenance and winked.

"Well, that's not much. Anything more ?" inquired the captain.

"Ho, yes ; lots more. The Termagant's in this yere port—at—this—yere—moment !"

The latter part of this was said in a hoarse, emphatic whisper, and the man raising up both legs to a horizontal position, let them fall so that his heels came with a crash upon the wooden floor.

"Is she ?" cried the captain, with lively interest ; "and her captain ?"

"He's—yere—too !"

Captain Dunning took one or two hasty strides across the floor, as if he were pacing his own quarterdeck—then stopped suddenly and said :—

"Can you get hold of any more of that boat's crew ?"

"I can do nothin' more wotiver, nor say nothin'

more wotsomediver, till I've tasted that 'ere tipple o' yourn."

The captain rang the bell, and the waiter entered with ham and eggs, buttered toast, and hot coffee for two.

The sailor opened his eyes to their utmost possible width, and made an effort to thrust his hands still deeper into his unfathomable trowsers pockets; then he sat bolt upright, and gathering his legs as close under his chair as possible, clasped his knees with his hands, hugged himself, and grinned from ear to ear. After sitting a second or two in that position, he jumped up, and going forward to the table, took up the plate of ham and eggs, as if to make sure that it was a reality, and smelt it.

"Is *this* your favourite tipple ?" he said, on being quite satisfied of the reality of what he saw.

"Coffee is my favourite drink," replied the captain, laughing. "I never take anything stronger."

"Ho ! you're a to-teetler ?"

"I am. Now, my man, as you have not yet had breakfast, and as you interrupted me in the middle of mine, suppose we sit down and discuss the matter of the whale over this."

"Well, this is the rummiest way of offerin' to give a fellow a glass as I ever did come across since I was a tadpole, as sure as my name's Dick Jones," remarked the sailor, sitting down opposite the captain, and turning up the cuffs of his coat.

Having filled his mouth to its utmost possible extent, the astonished seaman proceeded, at one and the same time, to masticate and to relate all that he knew in regard to the Termagant.

He said that not only was that vessel in port at that time, but that the same men were still aboard; that the captain—Dixon by name—was still in command, and that the whale which had been seized from the crew of the Red Eric had been sold along with the rest of the cargo. He related, moreover, how that he and his comrades had been very ill-treated by Captain Dixon during the voyage, and that he (Captain D.) was, in the opinion of himself and his shipmates, the greatest blackguard afloat, and had made them so miserable by his brutality and tyranny, that they all hoped they might never meet with his like again—not to mention the hopes and wishes of a very unfeeling nature which they one and all expressed in regard to that captain's future career. Besides all this, he stated that he (Dick Jones) had recognised Captain Dunning when he landed that morning, and had followed him to the cottage with the yellow face and the green door; after which he had taken a turn of half an hour or so up and down the street to think what he ought to do, and had at last resolved to tell all that he knew, and offer to stand witness against his captain, which he was then and there prepared to do, at that time or at any future period, wherever he (Captain Dunning) liked, and whenever he pleased, and that there was an end of the whole matter, and that was a fact.

Having unburdened his mind, and eaten all the ham, and eggs, and toast, and drunk all the coffee, and asked for more and got it, Dick Jones proceeded to make himself supremely happy by filling his pipe and lighting it.

"I'll take him to law," said Captain Dunning, firmly, smiting the table with his fist.

"I know'd a feller," said Jones, "wot always said, w'en he heard a feller say that, ' You'll come for to wish that ye hadn't ;' but I think ye're right, cap'en ; for it's a clear case, clear as daylight ; an' we'll all swear to a'most anything as'll go fur to prove it."

"But are you sure your messmates are as willing as you are to witness against their captain ?"

"Sure ? In coorse I is—sartin' sure. Didn't he larup two on 'em with a rope's-end once till they wos fit to bust, and all for nothin' but skylarkin' ? They'll all go in the same boat with me, 'cept p'raps the cook, who is named Baldwin. He's a cross-grained critter, an'll stan' by the cap'en through thick an' thin, an' so will the carpenter—Box they calls him—he's dead agin' us ; but that's all."

"Then I'll do it at once," cried Captain Dunning, rising and putting on his hat firmly, as a man does when he has made a great resolve, which he more than half suspects will get him into a world of difficulties and trouble.

"I s'pose I may set here till ye come back?" inquired Dick Jones, who now wore a dim mysterious aspect, in consequence of the cloud of smoke in which he had enveloped himself.

"You may sit there till they turn you out; but come and take breakfast with me at the same hour to-morrow, will ye?"

"Wont I?"

"Then good day."

So saying, the captain left the coffee-house, and hurried to his sisters' cottage, where he rightly conjectured he should find Glynn Proctor. Without telling his sisters the result of the interview with the "rude seaman," he took Glynn's arm, and sallied forth in search of Tim Rokens and Mr. Millons, both of whom they discovered enjoying their pipes, after a hearty breakfast, in a small, unpretending, but excellent and comfortable "sailors' home," in the dirty little street before referred to.

The greater part of the crew of the late Red Eric (now "sticks and stivers") were found in the same place, engaged in much the same occupation, and to these, in solemn conclave assembled, Captain Dunning announced his intention of opening a law-suit against the captain of the Termagant for the unlawful appropriation of the whale harpooned by Glynn. The men highly approved of what they called a "shore-going scrimmage," and advised the captain to go and have the captain and crew of the Termagant "put in limbo right off."

Thus advised and encouraged, Captain Dunning went to a lawyer, who, after hearing the case, stated it as his opinion that it was a good one, and forthwith set about taking the needful preliminary steps to commencing the action.

Thereafter Captain Dunning walked rapidly home, wiping his hot brow as he went, and entering the parlour of the cottage—the yellow-faced cottage—flung himself on the sofa with a reckless air, and said, " I've done it !"

" Horror !" cried Aunt Martha.

" Misery !" gasped Aunt Jane, who happened to be fondling Ailie at the time of her brother's entrance.

" Is he dead ?"

" *Quite* dead ?" added Martha.

" Is *who* dead ?" inquired the captain, in surprise.

" The man—the rude sailor !"

" Dead ! No."

" You said just now that you had done it."

" So I have. I've done the deed. I've gone to law."

Had the captain said that he had gone to "sticks and stivers," his sisters could not have been more startled and horrified. They dreaded the law, and hated it with a great and intense hatred, and not without reason ; for their father had been ruined in a law-suit, and his father had broken the law, in some political manner they could never clearly understand, and had been condemned by the law of perpetual banishment.

"Will it do you much harm, dear papa?" inquired Ailie, in great concern.

"Harm? Of course not. I hope it'll do me, and you too, a great deal of good."

"I'm *so* glad to hear that; for I've heard people say that when you once go into it you never get out of it again."

"So have I," said Aunt Martha, with a deep sigh.

"And so have I," added Aunt Jane, with a deeper sigh; "and I believe it's true."

"It's false!" cried the captain, laughing, "and you are all silly geese; the law is——"

"A bright and glorious institution! A desirable investment for the talents of able men! A machine for justice usually — injustice occasionally — and, like all other good things, often misused, abused, and spoken against!" said Glynn Proctor, at that moment entering the room, and throwing his hat on one chair and himself on another. "I've had enough of the sea, captain, and have come to resign my situation and beg for dinner."

"You shall have it immediately, dear Glynn," said Martha, whose heart warmed at the sight of me who had been so kind to her little niece.

"Nay, I'm in no hurry," said Glynn, quickly; ' I did but jest, dear madam, as Shakspeare has it. Perhaps it was Milton who said it; one can't be sure: but whenever a truly grand remark escapes you, you're safe to clap it down to Shakspeare."

At this point the servant-girl announced dinner. At the same instant a heavy foot was heard in the passage, and Tim Rokens announced himself, saying that he had just seen the captain's lawyer, and had been sent to say that he wished to see Captain Dunning in the course of the evening."

"Then let him go on wishing till I'm ready to go to him. Meanwhile do you come and dine with us, Rokens, my lad."

Rokens looked awkward, and shuffled a little with his feet, and shook his head.

"Why, what's the matter, man?"

Rokens looked as if he wished to speak, but hesitated.

"If ye please, cap'en, I'd raither not, axin' the ladies' parding. I'd like a word with you in the passage."

"By all means," replied the captain, going out of the room with the sailor. "Now, what's wrong?"

"My flippers, cap'en," said Rokens, thrusting out his hard, thick, enormous hands, which were stained all over with sundry streaks of tar, and were very red as well as extremely clumsy to look at—"I've bin an' washed 'em with hot water and rubbed 'em with grease till I a'most took the skin off, but they wont come clean, and I'm not fit to sit down with ladies."

To this speech the captain replied by seizing
Tim Rokens by the collar and dragging him fairly
into the parlour.

" Here's a man," cried the captain, enthusias-
tically, presenting him to Martha, " who's sailed
with me for nigh thirty years, and is the best harpooneer I ever had, and has stuck to me through
thick and thin, in fair weather and foul, in heat
and cold, and was kinder to Ailie during the last
voyage than all the other men put together, ex-
ceptin' Glynn, and who tells me his hands are
covered with tar, and that he can't wash 'em clean
nohow, and isn't fit to dine with ladies; so you
will oblige me, Martha, by ordering him to leave
the house."

" I will, brother, with pleasure. I order you,
Mr. Rokens, to leave this house *at your peril!*
And I invite you to partake of our dinner, which is
now on the table in the next room."

Saying this, Aunt Martha grasped one of the
great tar-stained " flippers" in both of her own
delicate hands, and shook it with a degree of vigour
that Tim Rokens afterwards said he could not have
believed possible had he not felt it.

Seeing this, Aunt Jane turned aside and blew
her nose violently. Tim Rokens attempted to
make a bow, failed, and grinned. The captain
cried—" Now, then, heave ahead !" Glynn, in the
exuberance of his spirits, uttered a miniature cheer.
Ailie gave vent to a laugh, that sounded as sweet

as a good song; and the whole party adjourned to the dining-room, where the servant-girl was found in the sulks because dinner was getting rapidly cold, and the cat was found

> " Prowling round the festal board
> On thievish deeds intent." *

---

## CHAPTER XXVII.

### THE LAW-SUIT—THE BATTLE, AND THE VICTORY.

THE great case of Dunning *versus* Dixon came on at last.

On that day Captain Dunning was in a fever; Glynn Proctor was in a fever; Tim Rokens was in a fever; the Misses Dunning were in two separate fevers—everybody, in fact, on the Dunning side of the case was in a fever of nervous anxiety and mental confusion. As witnesses in the case, they had been precognosced to such an extent by the lawyers that their intellects were almost overturned. On being told that he was to be precognosced, Tim Rokens said stoutly—" He'd like to see the man as 'ud do it;" under the impression that that was the legal term for being kicked, or otherwise mal-treated; and on being informed that the word sig-nified merely an examination as to the extent of his knowledge of the facts of the case, he said,

* See Milton's " Paradise Regained," latest edition.

quietly, "Fire away!" Before they had done
firing away, the gallant harpooneer was so confused
that he began to regard the whole case as already
hopeless.

The other men were much in the same condition; but in a private meeting held among themselves the day before the trial, Rokens made the following speech, which comforted them not a little:—

"Messmates and shipmates," said Tim, "I'll tell
ye wot it is. I'm no lawyer—that's a fact—but
I'm a man; an' wot's a man?—it ain't a bundle o'
flesh an' bones on two legs, with a turnip a top o't,
is it?"

"Be no manes," murmured Briant, with an
approving nod.

"Cer'nly not," remarked Dick Barnes. "I
second that motion."

"Good," continued Rokens. "Then, bein' a
man, I've got brains enough to see that, if we don't
want to contredick one another, we must stick to
the truth."

"You don't suppose I'd go fur to tell lies, do
you?" said Tarquin, quickly.

"In coorse not. But what I mean to say is,
that we must stick to what we *knows* to be the
truth, and not be goin' for to guess at it, or *think*
that we knows it, and then swear to it as if we wos
certain sure.'

"Here! here!" from the assembled company.

"In fact," observed Glynn, "let what we say be

absolutely true, and say just as little as we can.
That's how to manage a good case."

"An', be all manes," added Briant, "don't let
any of ye try for to improve matters be volunteerin'
yer opinion. Volunteerin' opinions is stuff. Volunteerin' is altogether a bad look-out. I know'd a
feller, I did—a strappin' young feller he was, too,
more betoken—as volunteered himself to death, he
did. To be sure, his wos a case o' volunteerin'
into the Louth Militia, and he wos shot, he was, in
a pop'lar riot, as the noosepapers said—a scrimmage I calls it—so don't let any o' us be goin' for
to volunteer opinions w'en nobody axes 'em—no,
nor wants 'em."

Briant looked so pointedly at Gurney while de-
livering this advice that that obese individual felt
constrained to look indignant and inquire whether
"them ere imperent remarks wos meant for him."
To which Briant replied that "they wos meant for
him, as well as for ivery man then present."
Whereupon Gurney started up and shook his fist
across the table at Briant, and Briant made a face
at Gurney, at which the assembled company of
mariners laughed, and immediately thereafter the
meeting was broken up.

Next day the trial came on, and as the case was
expected to be more than usually interesting, the
house was filled to overflowing long before the
hour.

The trial lasted all that day, and all the next,

and a great part of the third, but we do not purpose going into it in detail. The way in which
Mr. Rasp (Captain Dunning's counsel) and Mr.
Tooth (Captain Dixon's counsel) badgered, brow-
beat, and utterly bamboozled the witnesses on
both sides, and totally puzzled the jury, can only
be understood by those who have frequented courts
of law, but could not be fully or adequately described in less than six hundred pages.

In the course of the trial the resolutions come
to by the crew of the Red Eric, that they would
tell *nothing* but the truth, and carefully refrain
from touching on what they were not quite sure
of, proved to be of the greatest advantage to the
pursuer's case. We feel constrained here to turn
aside for one moment to advise the general adop-
tion of that course of conduct in all the serious
affairs of life.

The evidence of Tim Rokens was clear and to
the point. The whale had been first struck by
Glynn with a harpoon, to which a drog was attached : it had been followed up by the crew of
the Red Eric and also by the crew of the
Termagant. The boats of the latter overtook the
fish first, fixed a harpoon in it, and lanced it
mortally. The drog and harpoon of the Red Eric
were still attached to the whale when this was done,
so that, according to the laws of the fishery, the
crew of the Termagant had no right to touch the
whale—it was a " fast " fish. If the drog had become detached the fish would have been free, and

both crews would have been entitled to chase and capture it if they were able. Angry words and threats had passed between the crews of the opposing boats, but the whale put a stop to that by smashing the boat of the Red Eric with its tail, whereupon the boat of the Termagant made off with the fish (which died almost immediately after), and left the crew of the boat belonging to the Red Eric struggling in the water.

Such was the substance of the evidence of the harpooneer, and neither cross-examination nor re-cross-examination by Mr. Tooth, the counsel for the defendant, could induce Tim Rokens to modify, alter, omit, or contradict one iota of what he had said.

It must not be supposed, however, that all of the men gave their evidence so clearly or so well. The captain did, though he was somewhat nervous, and the doctor did, and Glynn did. But that of Nikel Sling was unsatisfactory, in consequence of his being unable to repress his natural tendency to exaggeration. Tarquin also did harm ; for, in his spite against the crew of the Termagant, he made statements which were not true, and his credit as a witness was therefore totally destroyed.

Last of all came Jim Scroggles, who, after being solemnly sworn, deposed that he was between thirty-five and thirty-six years of age, on hearing which Gurney said "Oh !" with peculiar emphasis, and the people laughed, and the judge cried "silence," and the examination went on. After

some time Mr. Tooth rose to cross-question Jim
Scroggles, who happened to be a nervous man in
public, and was gradually getting confused and
angry.

"Now, my man, please to be particular in your
replies," said Mr. Tooth, pushing up his spectacles
on his forehead, thrusting his hands into his trowsers
pockets, and staring very hard at Jim. "You said
that you pulled the second oar from the bow on
the day in which the whale was killed."

"Yes."

"Are you quite sure of that? Was it not the
*third* oar, now?"

"Vell, p'raps——"

"Yes or no," interrupted Mr. Tooth.

"It's so long since——"

"Yes or no," repeated Mr. Tooth.

"Yes," roared Scroggles, forgetting at the moment, in his confusion and indignation at not being
allowed to speak, in what manner the question had
been put.

"Yes," echoed Mr. Tooth, addressing the judge,
but looking at the jury. "You will observe, gentlemen. Would your lordship be so good as to note
that? This witness, on that very particular occasion, when every point in the circumstances must
naturally have been impressed deeply on the me-
mories of all present, appears to have been so confused as not to know which oar of the boat he
pulled. So, my man (turning to the witness) it

appears evident that either you are now misstating the facts of the case or were then incapable of judging of them."

Jim Scroggles felt inclined to leap out of the witness-box, and knock the teeth of Mr. Tooth down his throat ! But he repressed the inclination, and that gentleman went on to say,—

"When the boat of the Red Eric came up to the whale was the drog still attached to it ?"

"In coorse it was. Didn't ye hear me say that three or——"

"Be so good as to answer my questions simply, and do not make unnecessary remarks, sir. Was the drog attached when the boat came up ? Yes or no."

"Yes."

"How do you know ?"

"'Cause I seed it."

"You are quite sure that you saw it ?"

"In coorse !—leastwise, Tim Rokens seed it, and all the men in the boat seed it, and said so to me afterwards—w'ich is the same thing, though I can't 'xactly say I seed it myself, 'cause I was looking hard at the men in the enemy's boat, and considerin' which on 'em I should give a dab in the nose to first w'en we come alongside of 'em."

"Oh ! then you did *not* see the drog attached to the whale?" said Mr. Tooth, with a glance at the jury ; "and you were so taken up with the anticipated fight, I suppose, that you scarcely gave your attention to the whale at all! Were the other men in your boat in a similarly unobservant condition?"

"Eh?" exclaimed Scroggles.

"Were the other men as eager for the fight as you were?"

"I s'pose they wos; you'd better ax 'em. *I* dun know."

"No, I don't suppose you do, considering the state of mind you appear to have been in at the time. Do you know which part of the whale struck your boat? Was it the head?"

"No; it was the tail."

"Are you quite sure of that?"

"Ho, yes, quite sartin, for I've got a knot on my head this day where the tip of its flukes came down on me."

"You're quite sure of that? Might it not have been the part of the fish near the tail, now, that struck you, or the fin just under the tail?"

"No; I'm quite sartin sure it warn't *that*."

"How are you so sure it wasn't that?"

"Because whales hain't got no fins just under their tails!" replied Scroggles, with a broad grin.

There was another loud laugh at this, and Mr. Tooth looked a little put out, and the judge cried silence again, and threatened to clear the court.

After a few more questions Jim Scroggles was permitted to retire, which he did oppressed with a feeling that his evidence had done the case little good, if not some harm, yet rather elated than otherwise at the success of his last hit.

That evening Captain Dunning supped with Ailie and his sisters in low spirits. Glynn and the doctor and Tim Rokens and the two mates, Millons and Markham, supped with him, also in low spirits ; and King Bumble acted the part of waiter, for that sable monarch had expressed an earnest desire to become Captain Dunning's servant, and the captain had agreed to " take him on," at least for a time. King Bumble was also in low spirits ; and, as a natural consequence, so were Aunts Martha and Jane and little Ailie. It seemed utterly incomprehensible to the males of the party, how so good a case as this should come to wear such an unpromising aspect.

" The fact is," said the captain, at the conclusion of a prolonged discussion, " I don't believe we'll gain it."

" Neither do I," said the doctor, helping himself to a large quantity of salad, as if that were the only comfort now left to him, and he meant to make the most of it before giving way to total despair.

" I knew it," observed Aunt Martha, firmly. " I always said the law was a wicked institution."

" It's a great shame !" said Aunt Jane, indignantly ; " but what could we expect ? It treats every one ill."

"Wont it treat Captain Dixon well, if he wins, aunt?" inquired Ailie.

"Dear child, what can you possibly know about law?" said Aunt Martha.

"Would you like a little more tart?" asked Aunt Jane.

"Bravo! Ailie," cried Glynn, "that's a fair question. I back it up."

"How much do you claim for damages, George?" inquired Aunt Martha, changing the subject.

(Question!) whispered Glynn.

"Two thousand pounds," answered the captain.

"What!" exclaimed the aunts, in a simultaneous burst of amazement. "All for *one* fish?"

"Ay, it was a big one, you see, and Dick Jones, one of the men of the Termagant, told me it was sold for that. It's a profitable fishing, when one doesn't lose one's ship. What do you say to go with me and Ailie on our next trip, sisters. You might use up all your silk and worsted thread and crooked pins."

"What nonsense you talk, George; but I suppose you really do use pretty large hooks and lines when you fish for whales?"

Aunt Martha addressed the latter part of her remark to Tim Rokens, who seemed immensely tickled by the captain's pleasantry.

"Hooks and lines! ma'am," cried Rokens, regarding his hostess with a look of puzzled surprise.

"To be sure we do," interrupted Glynn; "we use anchors baited with live crocodiles—sometimes elephants, when we can't get crocodiles. But hippopotamuses do best."

"Oh! Glynn!" cried Ailie, laughing, "how can you?"

"It all depends on the drog," remarked the doctor. "I'm surprised to find how few of the men can state with absolute certainty that they saw the drog attached to the whale when the boat came up to it. It all hinges upon that."

"Yes," observed Mr. Millons, "the 'ole case 'inges on that, because that proves it was a fast fish."

"Dear me, Mr. Millons," said Aunt Martha, smiling, "I have heard of fast young men, but I never heard of a fast fish before."

"Didn't you, ma'am?" exclaimed the first mate, looking up in surprise, for that matter-of-fact seaman seldom recognised a joke at first sight.

Aunt Martha, who very rarely ventured on the perpetration of a joke, blushed, and turning somewhat hastily to Mr. Markham, asked if he would take "another cup of tea." Seeing that there was no tea on the table, she substituted "another slice of ham," and laughed. Thereupon the whole company laughed, and from that moment their spirits began to rise. They began to discuss the more favourable points of the evidence led that day, and wher they retired at a late hour to rest, their hopes had again become sanguine.

Next morning the examination of the witnesses for the defendant came on. There were more of them than Dick Jones had expected ; for the crew of the Termagant happened to be partly made up of very bad men, who were easily bribed by their captain to give their evidence in his favour. But it soon became evident that they had not previously determined, as Captain Dunning's men had done, to stick to the simple truth. They not only contradicted each other, but each contradicted himself more than once ; and it amazed them all, more than they could tell, to find how easily Mr. Rasp turned their thoughts outside in, and caused them to prove conclusively that they were telling falsehoods.

After the case had been summed up by the judge, the jury retired to consult, but they only remained five minutes away, and then came back with a verdict in favour of the pursuers.

"Who's the 'pursooers?'" inquired Gurney, when this was announced to him by Nikel Sling. "Ain't we all pursooers?" Wosn't we all pursooing the whale together?"

"Oh,' you grampus!" cried Nikel, laughing. "Don't ye know that *we* is the purshooers, 'cause why ? We're purshooin' the cap'en and crew of the Termagant at law, and means to purshoo 'em too, I guess, till they stumps up for that air whale.

And they is the defendants, 'cause they're s'posed to defend themselves to the last gasp ; but it ain't o' no manner o' use."

Nikel Sling was right. Captain Dixon *was* pursued until he paid back the value of his ill-gotten whale, and was forcibly reminded by this episode in his career, "that honesty is the best policy" after all. Thus Captain Dunning found himself suddenly put in possession of a sum of two thousand pounds.

## CHAPTER XXVIII.

### THE CONCLUSION.

THE trouble, and worry, and annoyance that that sum of 2000*l.* gave to Captain Dunning is past all belief. That worthy man, knowing that Glynn Proctor had scarcely a penny in the world, not even his "kit" (as sailors name their sea-chests), which had been lost in the wreck of the Red Eric, and that the boy was about to be cast upon the world again an almost friendless wanderer—know-ing all this, we say, Captain Dunning insisted that as Glynn had been the first to strike the whale, and as no one else had had anything to do with its capture, he (Glynn) was justly entitled to the money.

Glynn firmly declined to admit the justice of this view of the case ; he had been paid his wages ; that was all he had any right to claim ;

so he positively refused to take the money. But the captain was more than his match. He insisted so powerfully, and argued so logically, that Glynn at last consented, on condition that 500*l.* of it should be distributed among his shipmates. This compromise was agreed to, and thus Glynn came into possession of what appeared in his eyes a fortune of 1500*l.*

"Now, what am I to do with it? that is the question."

Glynn propounded this knotty question one evening, about three weeks after the trial, to his friends of the yellow cottage with the green-painted door.

"Put it in the bank," suggested Aunt Martha.

"Yes, and live on the interest," added Aunt Jane.

"Or invest in the whale fishery," said Captain Dunning, emitting a voluminous cloud of tobacco smoke, as if to suggest the idea that the investment would probably end in something similar to that. (The captain was a peculiarly favoured individual; he was privileged to smoke in the Misses Dunning's parlour.)

"Oh! I'll tell you what to do, Glynn," cried Ailie, clapping her hands; "it would be *so* nice. Buy a cottage with it—a nice, pretty, white-painted cottage, beside a wood, with a little river in front of it, and a small lake with a boat on it not far off, and a far, far view from the windows of fields and

villages, and churches, and cattle, and sheep
and——"

"Hurrah! Ailie, go it, my lass!" interrupted
Glynn; "and horses, and ponies, and carts, and
cats, and blackbirds, and cocks and hens, and
ploughmen, and milkmaids, and beggars, all in the
foreground; and coaches, and railroads, and steam-
boats, and palaces, and canals, in the middle distance; with a glorious background of the mighty
sea glittering for ever under the blazing beams of
a perpetually setting sun, mingled with the pale
rays of an eternally rising moon, and laden with
small craft, and whale-ships, and seaweed, and fish,
and bumboats, and men-of-war!"

"Oh, how nice!" cried Ailie, screaming with
delight.

"Go ahead, lad, never give in!" said the
captain, whose pipe during this glowing description had been keeping up what seemed like a
miniature sea-fight. "You've forgot the main
point."

"What's that?" inquired Glynn.

"Why, a palace for Jacko close beside it, with a
portrait of Jacko over the drawing-room fireplace,
and a marble bust of Jacko in the four corners of
every room."

"So I did; I forgot that," replied Glynn.

"Dear Jacko!" said Ailie, laughing heartily,
and holding out her hand.

The monkey, which had become domesticated

in the house, leaped nimbly upon her knee, and looked up in her face.

"Oh! Ailie dear, do put it down," cried Aunt Jane, shuddering.

"How can you?" said Aunt Martha; "dirty beast!"

Of course Aunt Martha applied the latter part of her remark to the monkey, not to the child.

"I'll never be able to bear it," remarked Aunt Jane.

"And it will never come to agree with the cat," observed Aunt Martha.

Ailie patted her favourite on the cheek and told it to go away, adding, that it was a dear pet— whereupon that small monkey retired modestly to a corner near the sideboard. It chanced to be the corner nearest to the sugar-basin which had been left out by accident; but Jacko didn't know that of course—at least, if he did, he did not say so. It is probable, however, that he found it out in course of time; for an hour or two afterwards the distinct marks of ten very minute fingers were visible therein, a discovery which Aunt Martha made with a scream, and Aunt Jane announced with a shriek—which caused Jacko to retire precipitately.

"But really," said Glynn, "jesting apart, I must take to something on shore, for although I like the sea very well, I find that I like the land better."

"Well, since you wish to be in earnest about it,"

said Captain Dunning, "I'll tell you what has been passing in my mind of late. I'm getting to be an oldish young man now, you see, and am rather tired of the sea myself, so I also think of giving it up. I have now laid by about five thousand pounds, and with this I think of purchasing a farm. I learnt something of farming before I took to the sea, so that I'm not quite so green on such matters as you might suppose, though I confess I'm rather rusty and behind the age ; but that wont much matter in a fine country like this, and I can get a good steward to take command and steer the ship until I have brushed up a bit in shore-goin' navigation. There is a farm which is just the very thing for me not more than twenty miles from this town, with a cottage on it and a view *somewhat* like the one you and Ailie described a few minutes ago, though not *quite* so grand. But there's one great and in-superable objection to my taking it."

"What is that?" inquired Aunt Martha, who, with her sister, expressed in their looks unbounded surprise at the words of their brother, whom they regarded as so thoroughly and indissolubly con-nected with the sea that they would probably have been less surprised had he announced it to be his intention to become a fish and thenceforward dwell in a coral-cave.

" I have not enough of money wherewith to buy and stock it."

" *What* a pity!" said Ailie, whose hopes had been

rising with extraordinary rapidity, and were thus quenched at once.

Glynn leaped up and smote his thigh with his right hand, and exclaimed in a triumphant manner —"That's the very ticket!"

"What's the very ticket?" inquired the captain.

"I'll lend you *my* money," said Glynn.

"Ay, boy, that's just the point I was comin' to. A thousand pounds will do. Now, if you lend me that sum, I'm willin' to take you into partnership, and we'll buy the place and farm it together. I think we'll pull well in the same boat, for I think you like me well enough, and I'm sure I like you, and I know Ailie don't object to either of us; and after I'm gone, Glynn, you can work the farm for Ailie and give her her share. What say you?"

"Done," exclaimed Glynn, springing up and seizing the captain's hand. "I'll be your son and you'll be my father, and Ailie will be my sister— and *wont* we be jolly, just?"

Ailie laughed, and so did the two aunts, but the captain made no reply. He merely smoked with a violence that was quite appalling, and nodding his head, winked at Glynn, as if to say—"That's it, exactly!"

The compact thus half jestingly entered into was afterwards thoroughly ratified and carried into effect. The cottage was named the Red Eric, and the property was named the Whale Brae, after an ancestral estate which, it was supposed, had, at

THE COTTAGE WAS NAMED THE RED ERIC.—Page 394.

ome remote period, belonged to the Dunning
amily in Scotland. The title was not inappropriate,
or it occupied the side of a rising ground, which,
.s a feature in the landscape, looked very like a
vhale, "only," as Glynn said, "not quite so big,"
vhich was an outrageous falsehood, for it was a
great deal bigger! A small wooden palace was
)uilt for Jacko, and many a portrait was taken of
nim by Glynn, in charcoal, on many an outhouse
wall, to the immense delight of Ailie. As to
naving busts of him placed in the corners of every
room, Glynn remarked that that was quite unnecessary, for Jacko *almost* "bu'st" himself in every
possible way, at every conceivable time, in every
imaginable place, whenever he could conveniently
collect enough of food to do so—which was not
often, for Jacko, though small, was of an elastic as
well as an amiable disposition.

Tim Rokens stuck to his old commander to the
last. He said he had sailed with him the better
part of his life, in the same ships, had weathered
the same storms, and chased the same fish, and
now that the captain had made up his mind to lay
up in port, he meant to cast anchor beside him.
So the bold harpooneer became a species of over-
seer and jack-of-all-trades on the property. Phil
Briant set up as a carpenter in the village close by,
took to himself a wife (his first wife having died),
and became Tim Rokens' boon companion and
'bosom friend. As for the rest of the crew of the

Red Eric, they went their several ways, got into separate ships, and were never again re-assembled together; but nearly all of them came, at separate times, in the course of years, to visit their old captain and shipmates in the Red Eric at Whale Brae.

In course of time Ailie grew up into such a sweet, pretty, modest, loveable woman, that the very sight of her did one's heart good. Love was the ruling power in Ailie's heart—love to her God and Saviour and to all His creatures. She was not perfect. Who is? She had faults, plenty of them. Who has not? But her loving nature covered up everything with a golden veil so beautiful, that no one saw her faults, or, if they did, would not believe them to be faults at all.

Glynn, also, grew up and became a *man*. Observe, reader, we don't mean to say that he became a thing with long legs, and broad shoulders, and whiskers. Glynn became a real man; an out-and-out man; a being who realized the fact that he had been made and born into the world for the purpose of doing that world good, and leaving it better than he found it. He did not think that to strut, and smoke cigars, and talk loud or big, and commence most of his sentences with, " Aw ! 'pon my soul !" was the summit of true greatness. Neither did he, flying in disgust to the opposite extreme, speak like a misanthrope, and look like a bear, or dress like a savage. He came to know the ruth of the proverb, that "there is a time for all hings," and following up the idea suggested by hose words, he came to perceive that there is a lace for all things—that place being the human eart, when in a true and healthy condition in all :s parts, out of which, in their proper time, some of hose "all things" ought to be ever ready to flow. Ience Glynn could weep with the sorrowful and augh with the gay. He could wear a red or a blue lannel shirt, and pull an oar (ay, the best oar,) at , rowing-match, or he could read the Bible and >ray with a bedridden old woman. Had Glynn ?roctor been a naval commander, he might have unk, destroyed, or captured fleets. Had he >een a soldier, he might have stormed and taken :ities; being neither, he was a greater man than :ither, for he could "*rule his own spirit.*" If you ire tempted, dear reader, to think that an easy natter, just try it. Make the effort. The first ime you chance to be in a towering rage (which I :rust, however, may never be), try to keep your :ongue silent, and, most difficult of all, try at that noment to pray, and see whether your opinion as .o your power over your own spirit be not changed.

Such were Glynn and Ailie. "So they married, >f course," you remark. Well, reader, and why 1ot? Nothing could be more natural. Glynn 'elt, and said, too, that nothing was nearer his 1eart. And Ailie admitted—after being told by Glynn that she must be his wife, for he wanted to have her, and was determined to have her whether she would or not—that her heart was in similar proximity to the idea of marriage. Captain Dunning did not object—it would have been odd if he had objected to the fulfilment of his chief earthly desire. Tim Rokens did not groan when he heard of the proposal—by no means ; on the contrary, he roared, and laughed, and shouted with delight, and went straight off to tell Phil Briant, who roared a duet with him, and they both agreed that it " wos the most gloriously nat'ral thing they ever did know since they wos launched upon the sea of time !"

So Glynn Proctor and Ailie Dunning were married, and lived long, and happily, and usefully at Whale Brae. Captain Dunning lived with them until he was so old, that Ailie's eldest daughter (also named Ailie) had to lead him from his bed-room each morning to breakfast, and light his pipe for him when he had finished. And Ailie the second performed her duties well, and made the old man happy—happier than he could find words to express— for Ailie the second was like her mother in all things, and greater praise than that could not possibly be awarded to her.

The affairs of the cottage with the yellow face and the green door were kept in good order for many years by one of Ailie the second's little sisters—Martha by name ; and there was much traffic and intercourse between that ancient build-

ıg and the Red Eric, as long as the two aunts
ved, which was a very long time indeed. Its
reen door was, during that time, almost battered
ff its hinges by successive juvenile members of the
'roctor family. And truly deep and heartfelt was
ıe mourning at Whale Brae when the amiable
sters were taken away at last

As for Tim Rokens—that ancient mariner be-
ame the idol of the young Proctors, as they
uccessively came to be old enough to know his
vorth. The number of ships and boats he made
ɔr the boys among them was absolutely fabulous.
Equal, perhaps, to about a twentieth part of the
ıumber of pipes of tobacco ne smoked during his
esidence there, and about double the number of
tories told to them by Phil Briant during the
ame period.

King Bumble lived with the family until his
voolly head became as white as his face was
black; and Jacko—poor little Jacko—lived so
ong, that he became big, but he did not become
ess amiable, or less addicted to thieving. He turned
grey at last, and became as blind as a bat, and
inally crawled about the house, enfeebled by old
ıge, and wrapped in a flannel dressing-gown.

Sorrows and joys are the lot of all; they chase
each other across the sky of human life like cloud
ınd sunshine on an April day. Captain Dunning
ınd his descendants were not exempt from the
'pains, and toils, and griefs of life, but they me'

them in the right spirit, and diffused so sweet an influence around their dwelling that the neighbours used to say—and say truly—of the family at the Red Eric, that they were always good-humoured and happy—as happy as the day was long.

THE END.

Edinburgh University Press:

F. AND A. CONSTABLE, PRINTERS TO HER MAJESTY.

www.ingramcontent.com/pod-product-compliance
Lightning Source LLC
Chambersburg PA
CBHW021340110726
47900CB00005B/1546